THE

SAZERAC LYING CLUB.

A NEVADA BOOK,

BY

FRED. H. HART,

EDITOR OF THE AUSTIN "REVEILLE," STATE OF NEVADA.

"Staging aint what it used to be."

FIFTH EDITION.

SAN FRANCISCO:
Published by
SAMUEL CARSON,
120 Sutter Street.

BOSTON:
LEE & SHEPARD.

NEW YORK:
C. T. DILLINGHAM.

BACON & COMPANY
SAN FRANCISCO

Some books are lies frae end to end,
And some great lies were never penn'd.
E'en ministers, they ha'e been kenn'd
In holy rapture,
A rousing whid, at times, to vend,
And nail't wi' Scripture.

BURNS.

DEDICATION.

To each and every person who may purchase it, and pay cash for it, this volume is respectfully dedicated, by

THE AUTHOR.

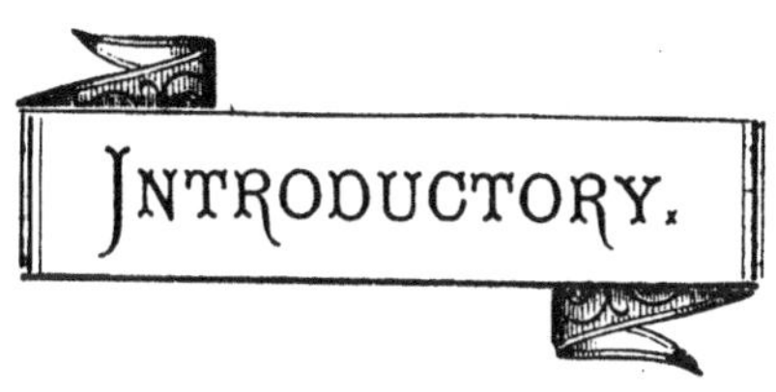

LYE ING, LIKE other arts and sciences, keeps pace with our education, refinement, and culture, and is fast becoming familiarized to the American people. Though I have classed it with the arts and sciences, and although there *is* something artistic in the construction of a good lie, and notwithstanding that a good, square, solid lie is a scientific triumph, still, I am of the opinion that lying should more properly be considered as an accomplishment. A "gentlemanly accomplishment," it was once designated by a Nevada newspaper. And yet, I have seen men who possessed the accomplishment in the highest degree of perfection, and still were not gentlemen. That, however, does not prove or premise that gentlemen cannot lie.

In the days of the Father of his Country—if we are to believe a little story about an adventure he is said to have had in connection with a cherry tree, and which story is still extant—lying was looked upon as wrong. But that was before the time of the steam-engine, the electric telegraph, daily newspapers, stocks and stock-brokers, and other modern improvements. To-day, to lie, and lie well, is meritorious, and besides, there's money in it, which of itself is sufficient to make it commendable. I am personally acquainted with some of the most prominent citizens of the Pacific Coast, who have made colossal fortunes simply by lying, or—to speak with gloved words—by doctoring the truth about stocks and mines; and those men are respected and looked up to, courted and flattered, called smart, and good business men, when the unadorned English of it is that they are only good liars, and have made their lying pay.

It is hardly worth while to say anything about political liars, because every one knows that lying is part of a politician's trade, and will continue to be, in spite of the Scriptures, earthquakes, and Civil Service Reform, as long as politicians are human. There may be politicians who cannot lie by word of mouth, but they *lie* in the silent tomb. In other words, the race of truthful politicians is extinct; or if there are still living men who will not or cannot lie to get office, it is because they are not office-seekers.

This purports to be a book on lies and lying, but it does not treat of the lies of politicians, stock-brokers, newspaper men, authors, and others, who lie for money; neither does it touch on the untruths of scandal, mischief, or malice, but only on those lies which amuse, instruct and elevate, without harm. It is a record of lies told in a club known as the Sazerac Lying Club, whose objects, as its name implies, are lying. A chapter is devoted to the rise, progress, and history of this club, interspersed with these lies. The book contains a number of sketches of odd characters in Nevada, and local narratives of life in Austin, written by the Author, and published from time to time in the columns of the AUSTIN REVEILLE, of which paper the writer has for several years been editor, and which have been clipped from the files of that journal, and made to do service in padding out this book to a sellable size.

The book has been compiled and prepared in the intervals of daily editorial labor, and no claim of literary merit is made for it. The majority of the clipped sketches have been widely copied by the press, which circumstance has had weight in causing him to believe that they possess some little merit in a humorous sense; but of that, as well as the other material herein contained, which has never before appeared in print, the reader must be the judge. This is not a "no cure no pay" book, and booksellers are instructed, under no circumstances, to return money to persons who pronounce it a fraud. If his wishes in this matter are strictly carried into effect, the bookseller will at once proceed to bounce the dissatisfied customer, and reason with him to the fullest extent of his muscular ability. All of which is respectfully submitted by

THE AUTHOR.

THE CLUB IN SESSION.

Part I.

Origin of the Sazerac Lying Club.

In the year 1873, I was employed in an editorial capacity on a small daily paper, the "REESE RIVER REVEILLE," published in the town of Austin, State of Nevada. This was a sort of general utility position, comprising all the branches of interior journalism, from writing an advertisement about a lost dog up to heavy dissertations on leading topics. But the main object was to get items of local news.

Austin is a small, interior mining town, ninety miles, by a rough road, from the Central Pacific Railroad, having its communication with the outer world carried on by means of mud-wagons, called by courtesy stages; and, it can readily be conceived, a quiet place, in which anything of a startling nature in the line of news seldom transpires.

There was no difficulty about the leaders or other editorial matter; a pair of sharp shears, a raid on the exchanges, and texts from the telegraphic news daily supplied to the paper, would readily furnish them; but to make up respectable local columns was a constant strain on the mental capacity and legs of the writer, and he had almost said, "on the imagination," but a strict moral training in early life, etc., caused him to confine himself strictly to facts.

The First President.

Situated on the main street of the town is a drinking saloon, bearing the sign of "The Sazerac," after the famous brand of brandy of that name. This saloon was the resort of a number of choice spirits other than those kept behind the bar—old forty-niners and California pioneers for the most part—who during the long winter evenings sat around the stove, smoked their pipes, fired tobacco juice at a mark on the stovepipe, and swapped lies and other reminiscences. I had long had my eye on the place as one liable at any time to pan out the text for a local, and would drop in there nearly every evening and listen to the conversation, in the hope of picking up from it the hoped-for item; but the stories were generally so outrageously devoid of all semblance of truth or appearance of probability that, as a consistent journalist, whose mission and duty it was to present the public with cold, bald-faced facts, I was unable to reconcile my conscience to the "writing up" and publication of the yarns. On one of these visits I found the old crowd in the saloon, sitting around the stove as usual, but the orator of the evening was a new man—one well known in the town, although this was his first appearance at the re-unions.

He was sitting in front of the fire, in an arm-chair tilted back, and the heels of his boots resting on the top of the stove, his feet shutting entirely from view two-thirds of the company. One of the most remarkable things about this man, next to his legs of course, was his feet. They were fearfully and wonderfully made, and their owner had repeatedly refused liberal offers for their use as battery stamps in a quartz mill; but had on one occasion consented for a valuable consideration to stand during a fire on the top of three cases of dry goods to protect them from damage by water. Of his legs I will speak hereafter.

Mr. George Washington Fibley, which is not his true name, but by which I designate him, through dread of the law of libel, was telling the assemblage a yarn about a pile of silver bars he had seen in one of the Pacific Mexican ports. It appears that before my entrance the discussion was concerning silver bullion, and Mr. Fibley—to use the language of one of the gentlemen present—was "jest raisin' the rest of 'em out of their boots." His story was evidently an outrageous exaggeration—there could be no doubt of that; for all the silver ever produced by the famed bonanzas of the Comstock, if heaped up, would not make a pile seven miles long, forty feet high, and thirteen feet wide, and it was in the neighborhood of these figures that Mr. Fibley placed the dimensions of the stack of silver he was describing. The story did not impress me at the time as being worthy of publication as a local item; and I went out of the saloon, thinking what a magnificent liar this man was, how he had mistaken his vocation,and what a splendid journalist that elastic and towering imagination might make of him.

The next day was fearfully stormy—such a storm of snow and wind as is only seen in the mountains—and "local" was as scarce as honest savings bank presidents. I was almost in despair about filling the local columns, and mechanically went to the door, opened it, and looked out into the storm for inspiration. The street was deserted, all was bleak and blank, and I was on the point of going back into my sanctum to meditate on the most painless method of death by suicide, when the narrator of the preceding evening crossed the street.

Just then the office devil howled "copy!"

I seized pencil and paper, and the following was the result:

"ELECTED PRESIDENT.—The Sazerac Lying Club was organized last night, our esteemed, prominent, and respected fellow-citizen, Mr. George Washington Fibley, being unanimously chosen president of the organization. There was no opposing candidate; his claims and entire fitness for the honorable position being conceded by common consent of the Club."

The above appeared in the paper that evening, and created considerable amusement, not only among the Sazerac frequenters, but for all those who knew the subject of the item.

There was trouble next day. Mr. Fibley read the paragraph about his elevation to the Presidency of the Club, and was exceedingly wroth; and in the course of the afternoon he rushed into the sanctum to demand an apology, or a retraction, or some similar foolishness. Happening to look through a window, I could see him coming. He had ridiculously long legs, and walked with a cane and an extraordinarily long stride, which increased when he was angry in proportion as his indignation grew; and when he was real, downright mad, as on this occasion, they seemed to stretch the width of an average street at every step. At such a time he appeared to be nothing but legs and head—as if an effort had been made to split his body in two, and had failed through the cutting instrument striking an obstruction at his chin. He was mad this time, sure enough; I could tell it by his walk; and as he entered the office door there was blood in his eye and rage in his face. In his right hand he held a roll of manuscript of nearly the diameter of a stove-drum, and his cane was raised threateningly on high. My eyes were fixed principally on the cane; but as he strode into the door-way he thrust the manuscript at me, and exclaimed:

"He who steals my purse, steals trash."

"He who steals my purse, steals trash!"

"Stop! stop! Mr. Fibley," I interrupted, thankful that hostilities had opened in so mild a form. "Never mind your purse, nor your good name, nor that communication in your hand. It was all a mistake. I will apologize."

"See that you do, sir, and amply, or by Jehosaphat—" and then he tucked his roll of paper under his arm, and without another word walked out, but looking back as he closed the door, and giving his legs, body, and paper a threatening shake more emphatic than speech.

I had promised to apologize. Writing an apology is not a pleasant task for an editor. His soul revolts at it. When one has said that the minister ran away with the deacon's wife, and it turns out that it was not the deacon's wife, but the deacon's wife's mother who accompanied the minister in his flight, it is rough to be compelled to apologize to the old lady on her return—not that ministers ever run away with deacons' wives' mothers, but just to suppose a case, for the sake of illustration. When you have written up a public ball, and said that "Mrs. Smithers, wife of our respected fellow-citizen, Hon. Thomas Jefferson Smithers, who did himself and the county so much credit in the Legislature eleven years ago, was charmingly dressed in green tarletan, and had her hair in curls," when the fact of the case is that she looked like the last rose of summer, and was dressed in a yellow silk, and had her hair done up in a wad on top of her head, it is mortifying to the editorial heart to have to take back the green tarletan and curls in the next issue of the paper. These, however, are but chips of the cross a country editor has to bear.

But I had said that I would atone in the REVEILLE for the slight cast upon Mr. Fibley's fair fame, and it had to be done. I did it, and the retraction, *verbatim et literatim*, read as follows:

"APOLOGETIC.—An apology is due from the REVEILLE to Mr. George Washington Fibley. We said in yesterday's issue that he was elected President of the Sazerac Lying Club. This was an error; he was defeated."

Mr. Fibley was satisfied, his ruffled feelings modified, and from that time forward we were the best of friends.

Part II.

"UNCLE JOHN."

"Uncle John" Gibbons is a stage-driver, and a perfect type of his class. He belongs to an order of men rapidly passing away, and who now number but few. Uncle John drove stage in "York State" when he was a boy—a great many years ago, and before that State was gridironed by railroads; and he has driven stage, as a natural profession, ever since. He immigrated to California in its early and golden days, a young man,

but a first-class stage-driver. In those times he drove for the California Stage Company, the great monopoly which then controlled the land travel of California as completely as the Central Pacific Railroad Company does now. When the Washoe silver mining excitement broke out, and the Pioneer line of stages from Sacramento to Virginia City was put on, Uncle John was the first driver on one of the mountain routes, driving six horses and a Concord passenger coach across the Sierra Nevada.

"Staging was staging in those days," and such staging is known no more on the Pacific Coast. A broad grade over the steep and precipitous mountains—a marvel of engineering skill—from whence the traveler looked dizzily down thousands of feet into the little valleys set in the heart of the Sierras, or gazed at the bottom of some dark, deep cañon, with a foaming torrent, roaring, flashing, rushing on its course, the coach, meanwhile, rattling along the grade at the highest speed of six big American horses, the wheels at times appearing to the passengers as if running on the very verge of destruction, and as if but a fraction of an inch nearer and the edge would crumble away beneath the weight and hurl the coach and its load of humanity crashing into the depths below. Freighting, in those days, was done by means of wagons, popularly known as "prairie schooners." These consisted of one immense forward wagon with towering sides, followed by from two to four "back-actions," or other smaller vehicles—if they can be so called—attached like cars to a steam-engine. The locomotives of these trains were teams of from twelve to twenty mules, every mule's harness being provided with an iron bow set over the animal's shoulders, on which was fastened a chime of sweet-toned bells. The road was at all times crowded with these teams, and passing them was one of the greatest dangers encountered by the mail-stage. The teamsters were as accommodating as it was in their power to be, and even those members of the fraternity who were not naturally of an obliging disposition were always willing to do their utmost to let the stage pass, being influenced by a popular superstition that "everything must make way for the mail," under severest penalties of the law. The coaches ran day and night, with changes every eight or ten miles, the harnessing and unharnessing being done with an astonishing celerity, so that the stage might run on time and the all-important United States Mail suffer no delay. Notwithstanding the dangers which beset the stage, but few accidents occurred on the Pioneer Line during its existence; though many a timid traveler has been frightened out of a year's growth by the crack of the driver's whip as he sent his team spinning, at what seemed a reckless, break-neck pace, down some steep grade, while to the passenger peering over the side next to the brink, it looked as if the wheels were running in dangerous proximity to nothingness.

When Uncle John had one of these passengers riding on the box with him, and the timid one clutched nervously at the railing of the seat, or otherwise displayed signs of fear, he would reassure him by saying:

"Don't be scar't; the Pioneer Company's rich and responsible, and if you git killed they'll pay you all you're worth, without buckin' or sweatin' a ha'r"; and he would crack his whip with an emphasis that sounded doubly loud in the clear, still air.

A more kind-hearted set of men than these stage-drivers never lived. Ready at any minute, on a freezing night, to surrender wraps sorely needed by themselves to any woman who complained of cold—fatherly, polite, and carefully attentive to ladies in their charge (though sometimes gruff and coarse to male passengers who had not experience or policy enough to get on their blind side)—watchful of the lives entrusted to their skill and steady nerve—apparently reckless, but in reality vigilant with hand, ear, and eye—they composed a class as distinct in itself from other men as the Caucasian is from the Mongolian. Hundreds of stories are extant of their wit, their bravery, their skill, and their kindness—but this book purports to be a chronicle of the Sazerac Lying Club, and must not be diverted from its object to the relation of stage-drivers' yarns, however interesting. It has a higher mission and a nobler purpose.

The building of the Pacific Railroad drove the Pioneer Stage Line out of existence, and as the railroad and its concomitant civilization advanced, Uncle John receded. He first went on the "Overland," the stage route across the continent; but the railroad, in its eastern course, running parallel with its line of travel, varying from twenty to one hundred miles north, kept pushing Uncle John further and further from its track, and when at last the final spike was driven in Utah, and the Overland Mail was no more, Uncle John betook himself to the mountains, where stages were still the only mode of travel, and where there was little likelihood of the innovating railroad penetrating during the rest of the old stage-driver's lifetime.

For several years past, Uncle John has "drove stage" from Austin to Belmont, a mining camp some ninety miles to the southward. Every day of his life—except when laid up with the rheumatism, which periodically attacks him—Uncle John is on the box, starting at daylight in summer and completing his task in the evening; but in winter, frequently not reaching his destination till midnight, or even daylight next morning. In summer, over the hot alkali deserts and parched mountain ranges; in winter, through cold and ice and snow and wind such as constitute the almost arctic severity of that season in the mountains, Uncle John is ever at his post, calmly fulfilling the destiny which made him a stage-driver, and which will keep him one till Death puts on the brakes and he "pulls up" at the "Home Station" at the end of his life's "route." He never leaves his box, except when rheumatism knocks him. Then he wraps his feet in barley sacks, gets him a cane, pulls his broad-brimmed hat down over his eyes, takes his place at the stove, and joins the Sazerac Lying Club.

The most widely circulated lie ever told in the Club was related by Uncle John, and was one of the first Sazerac lies ever recorded in print. It appeared in the Reveille as follows:

Uncle John and the Sage-Hens.

When it came his turn at the regular called session of the Sazerac Lying Club last night, Uncle John Gibbons stated the circumstances that caused the detention of the Belmont and Austin stage the other day. He said that while crossing Smoky Valley, a short distance this side of the salt-marsh, he observed what he at first supposed to be a heavy bank of dark clouds descended on the valley. [A phenomenon by no means unusual in this section, and termed by the Shoshone Indians "Pogonip."] As the stage approached nearer to the object, however, he became convinced that the mass was composed of living creatures. From here we will tell the story in his own words:

"The team was gittin' kind of scary, but I held 'em level, and as I kept gittin' nearer I saw the thing warn't nothin' but a flock of sage-hen; so I jest threw the silk at the leaders, and yelled fire and brimstone to the wheelers, calk'latin' to slash the team squar' through the flock without any trouble. But, boys, thar' was more sage-hen obstructin' of that road than I had reckoned on; and when them thar leaders struck into them thar sage-hen they was throwed back on their ha'nches jest as if they had butted clean up ag'in a stun' wall. As far's you could see there warn't nothin' but sage-hen; you could about see the top of the pile of 'em; but there was no more estimatin' how thick it was through than estimatin' how old a hoss is by twistin' its tail. Thar I was banked up by a lot of insignificant sage-hen, and the United States mail detained in the big road by feathers—as you might remark. Wal, to make a long story short, I unhitched one of the wheelers and straddled him and rode back to the station for help.

"Thar was a feller from town doin' some prospectin' on one of the hills near the station, and when I got to the house this here prospector was sittin' by the fire, hevin' come down to borrow some matches. I stated the situation in a hurry, and the hostler and the cook they saddled up some of the stage stock and got a couple of axes, intendin' to go back with me and chop a road through the sage-hen. But this here prospector he spoke up and says he:

"'See here, boys,' says he, 'don't you think we could blast 'em out quicker'n we could chop through em?'

"And the hostler and the cook spoke up and said they thought so, too.

"And then this here prospector he went up on the hill and got his drills and his sledges and a lot of giant-powder cartridges and some fuse, and the rest of the blastin' apparatus, and then the whole raft of us started back for the place where the stage was; and when we got thar—well I wish I may be runned over by a two-horse jerk-water if there was a sage-hen in sight as far's a man could see with a spy-glass.

"I hope you fellers is contented now you know what kept the stage late the other night."

The above lie was copied first in one paper and then in another, till it finally crossed the Atlantic and reached Germany, and a German paper getting hold of it put it into the language of its readers in print. The name of this paper was the *Carlsrhuer Zeitung*, and it set forth the case as follows:

In Austin, Nevada, Nordamerika, besteht ein Verein, dessen Zweck es ist, gegenseitig Lügen auszutauschen. Derselbe steht unter Regierungs-Schutz und das Vereins-Mitglied, welches die beste und unvernünftigste Lüge zu erzählen vermag, wird mit einem goldenen Medaillon im Werthe von 50,000 Thalern beschenkt.

Die Geschenke werden jährlich von einer Commission, ernannt vom Statthalter zu Boston, welche ihre immerwährende Sitzung in der Bundeshauptstadt New-York abhält, gemacht.

Die Lüge, welche d. J. das Prämium erhielt, wurde von Allerwelts-Vetter, Herrn John Gibbons, erzählt. Er sagte, während er unlängst mit der Postchaise das Räucherthal kreuzte, flogen eine Heerde Gänse auf, so zahlreich, daß sie den Weg blockirten und sogar das Tageslicht verdunkelten; um nun die Blockade zu heben und der königlichen Post wieder fortzuhelfen, war es nothwendig, für ein Heer Sapeur und Bergleute nach den Regierungs-Barracken zu telegraphiren, welche einen Tunnel durch die Masse Gänse brachen, und der Postwagen fuhr seines Weges fort.

In due course of time a German resident of Austin received from a relative in Fatherland a copy of the paper containing the above curious and truthful story, and showing me the marked paragraph, explained its purport. To verify his translation I took it to a German friend, and him requested to render it into English, which he did, and as a result handed me the following:

"In Austin, Nevada, America, there is a society whose objects are competitive lying. It is under Government patronage, and the member of the Association who tells the best and most unreasonable lie is awarded a gold medal worth fifty thousand thalers. The awards are made annually by a commission appointed by the Governor of Boston, and which is in perpetual session at the seat of National Government in New York. The lie which took the premium this year was told by Uncle John Gibbonich. He said that while riding post across the Valley of the Smoke, there arose from the earth a flock of geese so numberless that they blocked the road and shut out the light of day. And in order that the blockade might be raised, and the royal mails pass on their way, it was deemed useful to telegraph for a corps of sappers and miners from the Government barracks, who mined a tunnel through the mass of geese, and the post proceeded on its way."

NOTE—The sage-hen, so-called, is a bird of the grouse family, inhabiting Nevada, and feeds on the sage-brush which, in the main, constitutes the vegetation of the "Silver State." From this circumstance it derives its name.

The bird is unknown in Germany, of course, but in order to reach the comprehension of his readers, the editor of the *Zeitung* converted it into geese.

An April Fool Joke.

How Uncle John once got even on a man who had April-fooled him a year before was thus recorded in the REVEILLE at the time:

A HOT COIN.—In the Sazerac Saloon, this morning, Uncle John Gibbons could have been seen heating a four-bit piece in the drum of the stove. He watched the coin carefully, now and then turning it over to make sure that it would get warmed through. While that half-dollar lay baking in the stove-drum, a distinguished member of the Sazerac Lying Club was hastening to the saloon for his morning cocktail, never dreaming of guile or the first of April. As he entered the door the coin was about cooked, and Uncle John took it up carefully in his hand, which was protected with a heavy buckskin driving glove. Then he called to the brother member who was in search of his matutinal refreshment, and taking him aside, whispered confidentially in his ear:

"See here, George, I'm most dead for a drink, but I can't ask up this crowd of beats, 'cause I've only got four bits. You take this four bits and treat me."

Ever willing to accommodate, George closed down his hand on the piece; but he did not keep it down. In about the seventeenth part of a second from the time he grasped it, that half-dollar went crashing through the glass in the front door, and George was snapping his fingers and hopping around as though he had just got up from sleeping with a tarantula. Ever and anon he stopped jumping, and looking at the *fac simile* of the American eagle which was branded on the palm of his hand, raised it towards high heaven, and solemnly vowed that he would get even on the man that "fixed" that half-dollar for him, if he had to live seven thousand years to do it.

Wanted it on the Surface.

At one of the meetings of the Club a member stated that it was a well-known fact that a ghost appeared nightly in one of the levels of the North Star Mine, and that all the men working on that level had seen his ghostship. Uncle John Gibbons was present, and expressed his doubts about it—in fact he didn't believe in ghosts at all. "Well," said the speaker, "the ghost is there, and if you'll go down I'll show him to you any night." Now Uncle John knows all about horses, and harness, and buckboards, and Concord wagons, and such traps, but he never was in a mine in all his life, and would as soon enter the mouth of hell as the mouth of a shaft, and he fairly shuddered at the thought of going underground to interview a departed spirit. "I'm afeared of mines," he said, "and don't want to drop down none o' them thar' straight holes; but I tell you what I'll do: You trot your ghost out into the big road, and I'll harness him up, and drive him tandem all day with Brown Bill and Dick. I aint afeard of anything with a bit in its mouth."

Failed to Hatch.

A trick that was once played on Uncle John is worthy of record: He had a favorite hen at the stage barn, which showed a disposition to set. So he placed her on fifty-three eggs, and after five weeks of anticipation, concluded it was time for some results, as she was worn down to a shadow, and ne'er a cheep of a chicken had been heard in that barn. So, to save her life, he removed her from the nest. An examination of the eggs revealed the fact that every mother's son of them was boiled as hard as the hinges of perdition. It was a mooted question whether the Club rung in the boiled eggs on the old stage-driver, or whether he set the hen on them himself, in the hope of raising boiled chickens. The members asserted the latter; but Uncle John said it was a base aspersion on an honest man's character.

Part III.

"OLD DAD."

"He was always called 'Old Dad,'" said an intimate of his one day, "I knowed him in Californy in 'fifty,' when he was young and spry as a chicken, and as likely a lookin' cuss as you could see in the mountings, and they called him 'Old Dad' then."

"Dad" is a perfect type of the California pioneer. He immigrated to California from his native State—Virginia—with the first rush of gold-seekers to the then new El Dorado. Like the majority of the Californians of his time, he was rich and poor by turns; and now that the "flush days" are gone, never to return, he is, like nearly all the pioneers, rich only in reminiscences. "Dad" came to Austin in what was called the "Reese River excitement of sixty-three"—the first discovery of the mines of Reese River district, which were then supposed to be fabulously rich and marvelously extensive, capable of affording employment and fortunes to a large population. As with all new mining camps, its resources were overrated, and in the natural course of things the district found its level; and though not the "second Comstock"—which all mining districts are, in the excitement of their discovery, supposed to be—it is yet one of the most staple and prosperous on the Pacific coast. "Dad" points proudly to his record as a pioneer, claiming that he enjoys that distinction in a double sense.

"A California pioneer and a Reese River pioneer; it's such men as me that opens a country to civilization, and paves the way for them tender feet to come in from the States on the railroads and make all the money, while us pioneers—who stood the brunt, and bore the hardships, and lived on slapjacks and sage-brush straight—we, why we get the soup that the eggs was boiled in."

When "Dad" arrived in California, "the plains across," he took up his residence in Nevada County, in that State. There, to use his own words, he engaged in mining and speculating, under which head may properly be classed the financial operation herewith detailed:

Buying a Clown.

"Old Dad" related his "experience" in the circus business in the Sazerac Lying Club one night:

It was in the early days of Nevada County, California. Money was more plentiful than mosquitoes on the San Joaquin; gambling was as common as praying at camp-meeting, and whisky as free as water. But the boys pined for a little excitement, and "Dad," who in those days was a moneyed prince, concluded to give it to them, and at the same time make a nice little clean-up for himself. "Dad" had a partner, and to him he communicated his plan, which was to build an amphitheater a short distance out of town, send a hunter into the mountains to trap a bear, (bears were numerous in the Sierras) procure a bull, and have a regular old-fashioned bull-and-bear fight on the Mexican plan, and charge two dollars a head admission to view it. The partner fell in with the project; the amphitheater was built, the animals procured, and a day set for the fight, the announcement of the "entertainment" throwing three counties into the wildest excitement.

It appeared that in order to have the show go off in strict accordance with Mexican custom and rule, it was necessary to have a colored man to act the part of clown. The American colored men knew nothing about bull-fighting, and it was found impossible to persuade one of them to act the part, and the projectors of the show were in despair. They had bears, bulls, and Mexican bull-fighters, but no clown. Finally they found a Central American negro who understood the business, but he was known as such a tricky customer that it was not considered safe to employ him and pay him any money to bind the bargain, for fear he would run off without fulfilling his contract. As this was in the days of negro slavery, the showmen determined to buy the negro, and own him out and out. He had no master, and belonged to no man but himself, so it was determined to purchase him of himself. In pursuance of a bargain which was struck up, the negro was taken before a lawyer, by whom a bill of sale was drawn up, in which the Central American sold himself to the show proprietors for the sum of $500. He could neither read nor write, but affixed his mark to the document, and the sale was consummated. On the day of the fight a procession was formed, headed by the negro, tricked out in red flannel drawers and a spangled shirt, a brass band, and the Mexican bull experts, which marched to the amphitheater in the outskirts of the town, followed by a concourse of three thousand men. To make a long story short, the bull-and-bear fight was a failure. The bull, maddened at the sight of the clown's red flannel drawers, made a lunge at the unfortunate colored individual, and tossed him over its head, spoiling him for service as a clown for many a long day; to save the negro's life the Mexicans were forced to kill the bull, and the door-keeper ran away with the gate-money, amounting to some $6,000. As the bull had rendered the negro useless to them, the showman made him a present of himself back to himself; and there was not another bull-and-bear fight in Nevada County for three weeks.

A Sly Fox.

The following creation of "Dad's" fertile imagination was recorded in the columns of the REVEILLE as it here appears, and had the distinguished honor of being copied in one of the New York illustrated weeklies, and of being illustrated by "our artist on the spot."

At the Sazerac Lying Club *séance* last night the gentleman from Virginia related the following:

"Back in the Shenandoah Valley, very many years ago, when the narrator was a young man, fox-hunting was one of the most popular sports, in which he frequently took part. There was one old fox which for a period of several years had continually evaded the fleetest and keenest-scented hounds, the scent invariably being lost in the vicinity of a house situated in the woods, and far removed from any habitation, and which was used as a storehouse for pelts. At last, one day, the dogs started the old fox, and away he went in the direction of the house, with a pack of young hounds in full cry after him, but on nearing the house he disappeared, leaving the hounds and hunters nonplussed, as usual. While the hunters were gathered in and about the house, discussing the frequent mysterious disappearances of the fox, an old veteran hound came limping up, and entering the door, set up a vigorous barking, and tried to jump up on the wall. His singular actions attracted the attention of the hunters, and, an examination being made, the old fox was found suspended by his tail to a nail in the wall, keeping perfectly still and looking, unless closely observed, like the pelts with which the walls were hung. This plainly showed that the old fox, when too closely pressed, had taken refuge in the house, and hung himself up on the nail by his tail, which was the reason for the dogs always losing the scent at that particular place."

A Stout Man.

The subject of debate at the regular session of the Club was strong men. Old Dad took the floor, and told about the strongest man, of his inches, he had ever seen. They were mining over in Marshall Cañon. The shaft was 210 feet deep, and they hoisted the dirt in a car as large as is used in a steam hoisting-works, but there was only a windlass at the top of the shaft to hoist the car with. The windlass-man was a little bit of a fellow—only weighed ninety-one pounds—but it was noticed that he never weakened, and always hoisted the loaded car to the surface without an apparent overtaxing of his strength. One day the boys in the bottom put up a job on him. They loaded the car with wet clay, and batted it down hard, and piled it up in a mound over the top of the car. Then the men —four of them—got on the car, and sung out to the windlass-man to hoist. "She commenced mountin' that shaft just as easy as if a ninety-horse-power engine was a hoistin' her out, and every bit of the machinery greased within an inch of its life." "When we got to the surface," said Dad, "we was as ashamed as a dog caught suckin' eggs. Thar was that little fellow, as cool like and as ca'm as one of them icebergs, never sweatin' a ha'r nor puffin' a puff, and a-turnin' the windlass-crank with one hand; and as the boys stepped off the car he said, kinder quiet like: 'Boys, can't yer put a load on the car some time? I've got the dyspepsy, and the doctor told me I must take exercise.'"

The topics discussed in the Club are always seasonable; no stale, flat, and unprofitable themes contract the powers or impair the usefulness of the organization. At the same meeting, as soon as Old Dad had finished his Samsonian story the subject of climate was introduced. The snow and mud and winds, and the general uncertainties of the climate of this region, were duly cursed and commented on; and the special lie of the evening being announced as in order, the member known as "The Traveler" rose and said:

"Talk about climate! Give me a tropical climate—a region of perpetual sunshine! The West Injys is the country for me; I've bin thar. Why, Mr. President and gentlemen of the Club, in them islands Natur has so arranged things that a feller don't have to do a stroke of work to get a livin'; the necessaries of life just drop down inter his mouth, as it were, like the manner onter the children of Isrell on the forty-mile desert, and the only man what ever starved to death thar was a feller who was too dog-goned lazy to open his mouth for the nourishment to enter. Thar's the bread-fruit; it grows spontan'ous like, as they call it, all ready baked as brown as a meersham pipe and hot and smokin' and light as a feather, and all a man has to do is to lay down on his back under one of the trees and let the food drop inter his mouth. But then the bread-fruit aint nowhar along of the sago. Sago's the truck—it's meat and drink and clothin' and shelter. All a man of family has to do is to take his folks and camp under one of them sago trees, and I'll tell yer, Mr. President and gentlemen, how he's fixed: The branches of the trees grows like the rafters of a house, and the little leaves weave inter each other jest like shingles, and the big leaves drop down from the end of the branches and make walls. Thar's his house; and the ceilin' is jest kivered with sago, which drops down reg'lar every mornin' of its own accord inter a dish on the dinin'-

room table. It rains every night, and the water actin' on the sago makes a liquid that just knocks the spots clean off'n the best kinder coffee, and the sun cooks it up on the roof and it drops down off'n the leaves inter nice China cups made out'n cocoanut shells, and the little nigger boys, that air delighted to be yer servants for the honor of the thing, bring the cups in and set 'em on a marble-top table alongside of yer gold-mounted hammock set with di'monds and other precious stones. Sago, Mr. President and gentlemen of the Club, sago——"

"Sago off on your ear with that yarn," interrupted a stranger, who had entered at this point in the narrative, and was taking whisky-straight at the bar.

As by a common impulse, the Club rose to its feet to resent this outrageous interruption; but observing that the stranger had two whistler six-shooters in his belt and the handle of a fourteen-inch bowie-knife sticking out of his left boot, they sat down again. And the President's voice was tremulous with emotion as he declared the Club adjourned, and remarked, in response to the stranger's invitation to "jine" him, that he would take the least bit of sour in his'n.

Passover.

On one occasion, a Hebrew fellow-citizen presented a member of the Sazerac Lying Club with a cake of unleavened, or Passover bread. This being exhibited at the next meeting of the Club, led to a discussion on the origin and uses of the Jewish holiday of Passover. Uncle John asserted that the holiday was kept by the Jews in commemoration of the deliverance of Moses from the bulrushes, and his being "passed over" to Pharaoh's daughter; but the "Theological Member" told him to "shut up" talking of something he knew nothing about; and if the President would maintain order and enforce the rules, he would tell them what Passover bread was for. Mr. Fibley said he would, and the "Theological Member" turned himself loose in a narrative, of which the following is the substance, as nearly as I am able to reproduce it from memory:

"When Pharaoh was Khedive of Egypt he was building government buildings by contract, and the Israelites were working for him making brick by the day. Like all government contractors, he neither furnished a good article nor treated his employees with justice.

"The Israelites struck for higher wages and eight hours a day, and organized a trade union and elected a man named Moses as President. Moses was in the clothing business; and because he didn't know anything about labor the Israelites thought he would make a good presiding officer of a labor organization.

"When the Israelites struck, old Pharaoh hired a new set of hands, and they (the Israelites) concluded to go on a prospecting trip into Canaan

District, where there was represented to be a big milk and honey ledge. Owing to the snow blockade on the Suez Canal the market was bare of yeast powders, and the mill that made the self-rising flour had shut down; and as the Israelites were afraid the claims would all be located if they didn't get there quick, they started off with a few sacks of flour and mixed their bread in the flour sack and baked it on a hot rock.

"After they had crossed the creek Pharaoh missed some picks and shovels, and thinking the Israelites had stolen them, he swore out a search-warrant and sent a sheriff's posse after them. The sheriff's party missed the ford and were drowned, and to this day the Israelites eat unleavened bread in commemoration of the event."

The Club boasts, not only a Theological, but a Medical Member, and as soon as the former had finished, the latter arose and delivered himself of the following, which, whether it be original or not, is worthy of preservation:

"Once when I was a practicin' over in Syerra County, Californy, a feller got caved on by a bank and got his skull fractured clean out of shape. They picked him up and brung him to me, and I made a diagnosis of his case, and found that his brain, which was exposed, was full of dirt and bits of rock. There wasn't nothin' to do but to take it out and clean it; the idear of a man goin' around with the action of his brain bein' interfered with by three or four pounds of clay and gravel was clear out of the question, and I set too much store by my medical reputation to consent to any such doin's. I took out the brain and put it in a tin pan, and while I was washin' of it the patient seed a feller across the street what he had some bizness with, and went over to have a talk with him. He forgot to come back after his brains, and I didn't see him ag'in for two months, when one day, bein' in the jinin' county, I seed him. I hailed him and told him them thar brains was up at my office, and if he wanted 'em he better come and git 'em.

"'Don't want 'em,' said he.

"'Why not?' said I.

"'Wal, you see,' said he, 'I'm runnin' for office now and I don't need 'em; got no use in the world for 'em; fact is, they'd be an incumbrance, under the circumstances.'"

This lie met with the hearty approbation of the Club, the President especially manifesting his approval by ordering another whisky-straight, and drinking it off at a gulp, with a "Here's to you," as he looked across at the Medical Member. There was a general replenishing of tobacco quids, and as Mr. Fibley declared a recess of five minutes, the members, not to waste time, started an informal discussion on the hardships and privations many of them had undergone in the pioneer days of California, Old Dad more particularly thrilling the assembly by recounting his adventures by flood and field.

The last one to speak was the Fighting Member. Referring to a story told by his distinguished colleague, he recounted the following:

Rough Experience.

"Oh, that aint nothin' to the time I was with Kit Carson." "You with Kit Carson!" exclaimed several members. "Yes, me and Kit crossed the plains in forty-seven. We was camped up in the Sierra Nevadys, and one mornin' we thought we'd go out and hunt some meat for breakfast. We found b'ar signs, and had just got on the track of the varmint, when there come up one of them hell-roarin' big snow-storms like they have in them mountings, when it snows a foot a minnit. It covered up our camp and we couldn't find our grub, and was four days without a thing to eat, and we'd have starved to death only for my going to a farm-house close by and stealing some chickens. I tell you, I was so thirsty that my feet cracked open, and besides, I suffered awful from cold through falling into a lake, tryin' to reach for some water-lilies. We was most famished for water, and had to chew bullets to get a little moisture in our mouths. We saw considerable game, but our ammunition got wet, and besides, I liked to burned my hand off trying to light a fire with some powder so's to cook a mountain sheep that I shot with my six-shooter. I don't even believe the Donner party had a worse time than we did, and I've seen some pretty tough times myself. Why, when I first came to Californy, around the Horn in fifty-two, we struck a storm comin' up the Chagres River, on the isthmus, just this side of Panamar—.' Just here the President's gavel fell, and he said that much as he disliked to do so, he felt that the welfare of the Club demanded that he must enforce the rule requiring that members should not contradict themselves. "Does anybody here present doubt what I've been tellin'?" said the Fighting Member, reaching for the back part of his waistband. "Not a doubt," responded the Club unanimously. And then the meeting was declared adjourned.

Part IV.

"STUB."

Of the many odd characters in Austin, one of the most peculiar is Stub. Like Uncle John Gibbons, Stub is a stage-driver; but there is caste even among stage-drivers, and Stub's caste is to Uncle John's as a "buck-board" is to a Concord coach. Uncle John is a four, six, eight, or any number horse that can be hitched up driver. Stub's ambition never soared higher than "buck-boards" and "jerkies." Stub runs an "express" between Austin and Ione, the latter being a mining camp, about fifty-five miles distant from the former. He makes one round trip a week, carrying the mail and driving a two-horse "buck-board." A buck-board is a contrivance consisting of a narrow spring floor set on two axles, usually with a seat in the center for the driver; but in some cases, where passengers are carried, it has two seats, one forward and one aft. Buck-boards are used principally for carrying the mails over deserts, and are in common use for that purpose in Arizona. On account of their lightness, they can, with the aid of a good team, be made to get over a great deal of ground in a very short time; but they are the meanest things to ride on that ever were invented, and the man who is so unfortunate as to be compelled to take a few hours' journey on one, finds himself at the end of it with every joint in his body dislocated.

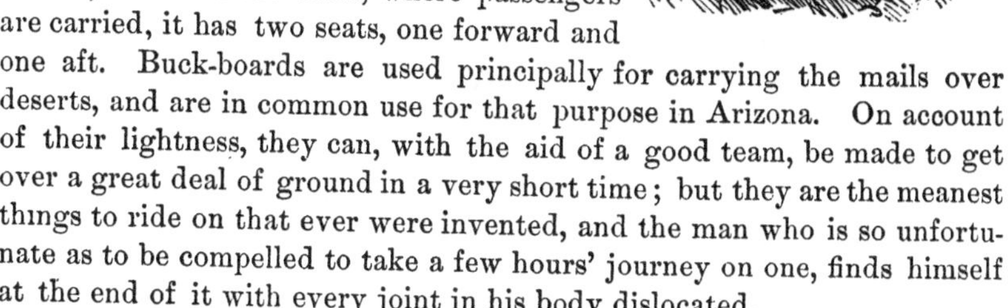

"Staging aint what it used to be," and buck-boards have taken the place of coaches on nearly every stage-route in interior Nevada, the population being so small that the travel is too light to afford coaches and four or six-horse stock.

"Staging aint what it used to be."

Stub's route lies for the most part through Reese River Valley, in which are situated a number of ranches or farms. The valley is a bleak, barren-looking stretch of country, covered for the most part with sage-brush; but the soil is capable, by irrigation, of producing cereals in abundance and the finest potatoes in the world. The hills surrounding it are covered with the nutritious bunch-grass, and afford a range for large numbers of cattle, while in the valley itself there grows in places a plant called white sage, which, after it is touched by the frost in the autumn, is a very sweet and nourishing food for cattle. Such a thing as housing or feeding stock is all but unknown in Eastern and Central Nevada. The section abounds in cattle-ranges, as they are called, and thousands of neat stock are constantly running over them, getting fat in summer, and "rustling" for a living, or dying from cold and exposure in the winter. This cattle interest and the patches of irrigated land are what make the ranches in the valley. The irrigation is obtained by systems of ditches from Reese River, a narrow stream which rises in the mountains at the head of the valley, and is fed by springs and snows, and, traversing its entire length, empties into the Humboldt, near Battle Mountain, on the Central Pacific Railroad. It abounds in trout, and in the trouting season is largely resorted to by anglers from Austin. To the trouting of Reese River I owe my first acquaintance with Stub. The people who go there to fish generally make up large parties, with a full camping outfit, and provisions enough to last a month. Their advent on the river is hailed with delight by the Indians, crows, and coyotes; for camp-life in the reality don't begin to be as good a thing as it was in the anticipation, and the campers almost invariably start home sooner than was intended, leaving the banks of the river lined with half-consumed cans of fruits, preserved meats, and other edibles. Some of the surplus edibles is usually expended in hiring Indians to catch fish, so that the party may return home and exhibit good baskets; but, as a rule, the guileless native demands coin for his services, knowing that, in the natural course of events, the remnants will fall to his lot, with none to dispute his right but the beasts and birds of prey.

But I am digressing from Stub.

One summer, having a week's vacation from my editorial labors, I concluded to spend it in a fishing trip to Reese River, and to go to that stream in a crowd by myself, and put up at one of the ranches in the valley. In pursuance of this plan, I requested Stub to interview some of the ranchers, and obtain for me accommodations. Executing commissions is Stub's strong suit. Every time he drives out of Austin his mind is charged with numerous messages for the ranchers, or for people at Ione and Ellsworth, and his express loaded down with small packages for delivery. The women at the ranches depend on Stub for their needles and thread and worsted, and fruit and candy for the childen, and a thousand and one other articles which they have no way of getting except through Stub. The men commission him to bring them tobacco and newspapers; to get mowing-machine knives sharpened, saddles mended, and impose on him a multiplicity of errands that would confuse any other person. At every house along his route, some man, woman, or child runs out, and with a hail, says: "Stub, bring me some fine cut"; or, "Stub, I want a piece of muslin"; or, "Stub, go and see Jones and get my saddle"; or, "Stub, call on Smith and tell him I'll drive them cattle in next week"; or, "Stub, go and see the doctor, and tell him baby aint no better, and he better send some more of that mixture." All these errands and commissions are remembered and faithfully performed, for Stub is faultless in attending to such duties. On his return trip, Stub informed me that he had secured the needful accommodation, and, naming the place, said: "They'll take you in and treat you on the squar', and the fishin's as good thar as any place on the stream, except you go clear to the head."

The next trip of Stub's Express, outward-bound, found me a passenger on the buck-board. There were two other passengers besides myself—one male, and a garrulous old lady, who smoked a clay pipe, and drank whisky from a bottle with as much gusto as any member of the Club. She was an old acquaintance of Stub's, and, like him, a pioneer of Eastern Nevada; and the two knew, or knew of, every man, woman, and child in Austin, Belmont, Ione, Ellsworth, and Reese River Valley; and the way they discussed their friends, and handled and soiled and destroyed characters, and smoked pipes and drank whisky, sent the jack-rabbits scampering in affright to their holes.

One of Stub's peculiarities is that he laughs. He laughs at everything that is said to him—a loud, long laugh that sounds more like the neigh of a horse than anything else. Stub is deaf as a post, and laughs so as to show that he is appreciative. It makes no difference whether it is a joke or a catastrophe, Stub laughs as heartily at one as at the other. Tell him a joke about a man's mother-in-law getting killed, and he will laugh; or relate to him a frightful mining accident that has just occurred, and he laughs just the same. The old woman would tell how so-and-so up at Austin was no better than she should be, and Stub laughed; or that Gardly, the dry-goods man at Belmont, was on the verge of bankruptcy, and Stub laughed; or that Tim Green's wife, up at Ione, was at the point of death, and her with half a dozen children who would be motherless, and Stub laughed with just the same peculiar horse-laugh that he would bestow on the funniest joke.

Further particulars of this fishing trip can be best detailed by extracts from an account of it written up for the REVEILLE on my return, and which I present herewith:

Stub's Express.

Stub's Express is one of the institutions of this section. Perhaps everybody in town don't know Stub, but everybody in Reese River Valley does. Stub's Express consists of a two-seated buck-board wagon and Stub. We embarked in the buck-board in front of Dinsmore's store, the other freight consisting of a feather bed, a mowing-machine, a roll of leather, three butter barrels, a threshing machine, a paper of needles, a case of coal oil, an old woman, a plough, a small quartz-mill, another passenger, and Stub. The team consisted of two stout little ponies, which seemed to be acquainted with Stub, and when he would throw the whip and say, "Git up, you consarned critters," they knew that Stub meant business.

A journey up Reese River Valley is not one of the most eventful affairs in life. The landscape in general is of that barren and uninteresting nature which characterizes the greater portion of Nevada. It consists of a great expanse of sage-brush and grease-wood, with an occasional ranch at long intervals, on which the waving grain and small cultivated patches relieve the monotonous barrenness, and remind the traveler that he is still in an inhabited country.

After leaving Silver Age Ranch, the journey over the dusty road, with nothing to direct the attention from the dry plains and hills, became very monotonous.

Almost the first question asked was: "Shall we get anything to eat on the road?" "Certainly," said Stub, "git dinner at noon"; and then, *sotto voce*, which I did not hear, "if you've brought it with you—not otherwise." When noon came, we looked in vain for a resting place, and loud were the lamentations of the old lady at finding herself deprived of the usual meal. As if to sharpen our appetites, Stub, without any provocation, told us the following yarn:

"Once when I was up in Montanny, me and four other fellers struck some pritty fair diggin's up in a gulch in the mountings, about 220 miles from anywhar. We didn't have much grub and couldn't afford to leave the diggin's to go after some, 'cause the water was gittin' low and we wanted to put in every minnit on the claim, so's to take out all the dust we could afore snow flew, and winter was a-comin' on pritty close. Thar was any quantity of game in the country, but we didn't hev' a dog-goned thing to shoot it with, and many and many a mornin' hev' I laid in my blankets as hungry as a she-wolf, and seen millions of grouse a-flyin' over my head, and the deer and antelope was so thick they used to tramp over us as we lay in our blankets. Down below our camp, at the foot of the gulch, was a little spring whar a drove of deer used to come for water at night, and seein' this, we fixed up a job to git fresh meat. Durin' the day-time we built a fence round the place, leavin' the bars down whar the deer used to come in for water, and that night we laid in the brush clus' by, and when the deer came in, we just put up the bars and we had 'em kerrelled. After that, whenever we wanted any fresh meat, we'd jest go inter the kerrell and lass a doe or a fawn and butcher it, and we was fixed for meat for several days to come; had deer-meat to sell, in fact."

The rest of that dreary ride is impressed on my memory by the recollection of the pangs of hunger endured; and when late that night the buck-board stopped at its destination, and I attacked my first meal since daylight, I was thoroughly satisfied that Stub had qualifications for the Sazerac Lying Club other than his Montana adventure.

After a hearty supper of homely and wholesome fare, to which my long fast enabled me to do full justice, an hour was pleasantly spent in discussing agricultural topics. This subject struck me where I lived, and we learnedly exchanged notes about the proper time to pull hay, the best mode of cutting potatoes, and the latest improvements in digging barley. The family was much impressed with my farming lore, and the lady of the house suggested that I should be a splendid hand to feed the pigs and chickens. Merit always commands recognition.

A Neglected Education.

The owner of the ranch was a Missourian; his wife was also a Missourian, and several male relatives and all the hands about the place were Missourians. They had all immigrated from Missouri to California at an early day, and their customs and manners were of the backwoods. The day after my arrival the entire family and the hired hands became absorbed in the engaging operation of killing and dressing a hog, and it seemed to be expected that, as a matter of politeness, I should at least be a spectator of the proceedings. The circumstance of the hog's customary death possesses in itself no significance, and its relation is really not absolutely necessary to insure the success of this book; but it will serve as an introduction to an occurrence which at the time, and since, impressed me as being very ludicrous.

When supper time came, a large party of us were seated around the table—the rancher, his wife, the male relatives, the farm hands, a number of lads and lasses, and myself. Every member of the company, with the exception of myself, was Missourian either by birth or parentage, and consequently they were wise in many things of which I was in dense ignorance; and perhaps *vice versa*. One of the things which they all could do, and I could not, was hog-killing. The principal dish on the table was pork—the meat of the unfortunate slaughtered that evening; and the conversation, by a natural fitness, turned on the best method of dispatching and dressing the animal. I remained silent, taking no part in the conversation, for fear of committing myself and exposing my ignorance. During the discussion, which had taken on a lively turn, the rancher's wife, who presided at the head of the table, "tendin' to the tea," spoke up, and said:

"I've heern tell that thar be people as can't kill a hog."

This seemed to be a direct shot at me, and I could feel myself blush, *actually blush*, in the consciousness of my neglected education. It seemed as if the eyes of the entire company were centered upon me, and that there was nothing for it but a full, free, and frank confession. Casting my eyes downward and looking squarely on the piece of pork on my plate, almost expecting that it, too, would be startled at my ignorance, I faltered out:

"Mrs. Brown, I—I—don't know how to kill a hog."

"Lor' sakes!" exclaimed the old lady, and her hand dropped as if nerveless from the handle of the tea-pot. Then she raised both her fat arms on high—and I have never seen on another human countenance such a vivid expression of mingled pity and contempt as was depicted on hers—and while an awful and impressive silence reigned around the table, she sighed deeply, and said:

"Lor' sakes! what *was* your folks a-thinkin' of when they raised you? Why, thar aint a gal on this ranch as can't kill and dress a hog!"

The only reply I could command at the time was, that I was born an orphan, and had not had the advantages of a Missourian education.

"Wal, you air to be pitied, sure enough," said the mouth-piece of the family; and I fancied that during the rest of the evening she gazed at me continuously with a motherly expression of commiseration. I turned the conversation on the best method of sowing straw and sundry other agricultural topics, in which, I hope, I showed myself to be more at home than on the hog question.

A Dead-Letter Office.

On the return trip of Stub's Express I was the only passenger, and Stub entertained me with various reminiscences of the early days of the section and in "pointing out the country." In the hills in sight from the valley there had been at an earlier date several mining excitements—that is, supposed important discoveries of mines—which, being heralded from camp to camp and from town to town, had brought about an excitement and a rush to the new diggings. These "stampedes" had resulted in the hurried building of towns, the establishment of mail routes, and all the various preparations for the founding of mining cities, many of which, like mushrooms, come up in a night and go down to oblivion in an equal space of time. Such had been the fate of the camps in the range of mountains bordering Reese River Valley, and at the time of which I write they were all deserted by human beings, and the houses which had made them towns had been hauled away to build up other new camps. Passing a certain mountain peak, Stub pointed his finger at it, and said:

"Over yonder thar is the old Washington Deestrick. It was a lively camp in its time. They had croppin's that was mighty rich with silver, but the ledges didn't pan out wuth a cuss. They built a town thar, and was goin' to have a city hall, and a couple of dance-houses, and seven or eight quartz-mills, and a daily mail and express, and mebbe they even figgered on a church and a school-house, but the mines petered out kind of suddin like. I was in thar one day, and the boys was playin' poker at four bits ante and shove the buck, and whisky was a flowin' like this here Reese River—and that very next mornin' the camp went down like a stun in a pond, and you could buy the best corner lot in the place for about two dollars in money. They did git a post-office established thar, and it's on this here mail-route yet, but I don't run over thar, though the contract calls for it. The postmaster was the last man to leave the place; he got twelve dollars a year and he wanted to stick to a Guv'ment situation, but he got killed one day by a tree fallin' down a-top of him. Some herders goin' through thar found him a-lyin' dead on the ground. Thar was pritty nigh all of him thar, cause the tree kivered the body so the coyotes couldn't git at all of him. They buried him with his clothes on. The key of the post-office was in his breeches pocket, and when they buried him they buried the whole postoffice, and it's a dead-letter office now."

Stub as a Fiddler.

Stub's forte—that is, his chief delight—is in playing the fiddle. He only knows two tunes, but he subjects them to all the variations that catgut and horsehair can extract from them. Give Stub his fiddle and a company of young folks at a ranch on the river, and let them get up a dance, with Stub to furnish the music and call the figures, and he is in his element of glory. If Stub happens to be in town when there is a public ball, and is allowed to call the figures for a quadrille, he is in the seventh heaven of delight. On such occasions Stub "dresses up." Usually, he presents a shabby appearance, and carries the odor acquired from sleeping with his horses. But when there is any dancing going on, he is transformed into absolute gorgeousness. The pride of his heart is a velvet vest of many colors, made by a tailor to Stub's special order, and after a model of his own designing. Stub is proud of this garment, but the particular part of it which he thinks should challenge the admiration of all beholders is a narrow strap which buttons on each side of the collar, and on which is pinned a golden horse. Arrayed in this vest, a linen duster, a pair of pants turned up at the bottoms, carpet slippers and clean white socks, and on his head a curly chestnut wig, Stub is a sight to behold, and just about that time would not change places with the Czar of all the Russias. He seldom joins in the dance; but there was an occasion when he ventured on the floor, and while trying to execute some very artistic and elaborate pigeon-wing, came to grief. His wig came off, and there was exposed to the vulgar gaze a head as bare of hair and as shiny as a billiard ball. Stub didn't laugh for full five minutes.

Stub's Birthday.

Once upon a time Stub had a birthday. As the day approached, he concluded to celebrate it by a dance that should astonish the natives. In pursuance of this plan he prepared an advertisement for insertion in the REVEILLE, and brought it to the office for publication, saying he had "writ it all out of his own head." The advertisement was as follows:

HURRAH FOR STUB'S DANCE!

STUB WILL HAVE A GRAND BALL at International Hotel of Austin, Nevada, on the night of his Birthday, which will be on the

26th of May, 1876.

Stub gives a general invitation to all the Ladies and Gents of Austin, and also throughout the whole country, for all hands to come.

Ball Room Directors:

For President, —— ——.
Officer of the Hall, —— ——.
Floor Directors, —— ——, —— ——, —— ——.
Floor Managers, —— ——, —— ——, —— ——.
For Inspector, —— ——.
For Door Tender, —— ——.

Special invitation for all the ladies is given by Stub to be on hand. Good Music in attendance.

ap26-td STUB, Proprietor.

The places in the above which are marked thus, —, were in the advertisement as it appeared in the paper filled with the names of the principal business men of the town. Strange to say, they were not at all flattered by the honor done them; and on the following day several of them called on the editor with clubs, and remonstrated with him.

The dance came off according to announcement, and was a comical affair. Stub was so anxious to secure a large attendance that he had given nearly every man in town a complimentary ticket. He had gone to an expense of a couple of hundred dollars for hall-rent, music, printing and advertising, etc., and there was not to exceed ten dollars taken in at the door, although the attendance was very large. The ball was, financially, a failure; but socially, from Stub's standpoint, it was a grand success. To give an idea of Stub's style, I reproduce an item published in the REVEILLE about this time:

STUB AS A CALLER.—Stub has had a great deal of experience as a caller of the figures in quadrilles, and most of them are original and peculiar to himself. Stub will call at the grand ball to be given by himself at International Hall on the 26th instant, and those who attend may expect to have their ears regaled with some novel directions. The story is told, that, some time ago, at a dance at Ione, there was a young lady on the floor who wore a red calico dress with a brown stripe down the back, and Stub, who was calling the figures, yelled out: "Balance to that line-back heifer!" If there is one thing more than another that Stub is noted for, it is the exquisite refinement of his language.

At his birthday dance Stub fully sustained his reputation as a unique and original master of unpolluted English.

Stub's Name.

How Stub came to be dubbed "Stub" is a matter that is shrouded in impenetrable mystery. His real name is Charles Burns, but he has been called Stub for so long a time that he would not answer to Charles Burns if that name was shouted in his ear through a speaking-trumpet or a telephone. He is very reticent about the acquisition of his non-baptismal name, and refuses to be interviewed on the subject. It is related of him that he once went all through the town of Ione looking for himself. Letters for Ione and other places on his route are frequently handed into the office of his express, (which is in one of the principal stores) for personal delivery by the driver. These are put into a way-sack, and at each ranch or stopping-place Stub sorts them over, and picks out and delivers such as may be destined for that particular place. On one occasion there was a letter in the sack directed to "Charles Burns, Ione," and it is asserted that Stub went to every saloon and every residence and boarding house in the town, and inquired of the inmates if they knew a "feller" named Charles Burns. At last a man who happened to remember Stub's original patronym said: "Charles Burns? Why, Stub, that must be you."

"Well, I'll be dog-goned if it aint!" said Stub, "but why can't people write to a feller by the name he goes by?"

Part V.

Some Lies and Otherwise.

A bare record of the Sazerac Lying Club's doings as extracted from the minutes would be too monotonous for family perusal, so I have thought it better to make a choice selection of them, duly crediting each one to its author, and carefully guarding against the insertion of a truth. Not that such an adulteration ever occurred, for no member was known to be guilty of such a transgression; but my own regard for facts might unwittingly lead me into the pit-fall of interspersing the best stories of the Club with some of my own.

Matters had been very quiet in the Club for some time, but a member confidentially informed me that when the boys got paid off they would make Rome howl. Consequently an exciting session was to be anticipated that evening. They expected, he said, to initiate a new member, who was prepared to take his solemn oath that he saw a man fall 3,000 feet down an incline without touching its sides, top, or bottom, and that when his fellow workmen reached him he was lighting his pipe with his candle, which he had held in his hand, and which was not extinguished during the descent. The investigating committee had reported favorably on the man's application for admission, because they thought that was something like a reasonable lie. It should be remarked, that, by a rule of the Club, no member is allowed to tell a lie which might not have been true had such an occurrence taken place.

On the evening in question, I was on hand early, but although it was not yet seven o'clock the Club had already organized, Mr. G. Washington Fibley, the President, occupying his usual position in the chair. As it was the opening night of the session, after calling the roll, the President addressed a few remarks to the Club as follows: "Fellow-members of the Lying Club—I have noticed that it has of late become the custom with certain newspapers to propose for membership in this Club every scrub liar that turns up. This betrays a gross misapprehension of the objects of this noble order. As you are all aware, the objects of this Club are mental culture and mutual improvement; we do not lie for greed or gain, nor do we tolerate that class of liars who by word of mouth deceive their fellow-men for selfish or for wicked ends. No, members of the Club, while we permit a range of thought extending far away into the most distant depths of the realm of the impossible and the improbable, we do not stoop to the lie of deceit; we ask no man to place implicit belief in our lies—but if any man does so believe, he sustains no injury. There, hanging on yonder wall, is the picture of that noble man and illustrious patriot, G. Washington, Esq., in the very act of tackling the cherry tree. He could not tell a lie about who cut down that tree; but, my fellow-members, does any man here present, who possesses ordinary human reasoning, believe that if G. Washington had heard a man tell about catching an eleven-pound trout, he wouldn't have raised him a pound or two, even if he had never seen a trout in all his born days? The first lie of the evening is now in order, and I hope members will restrain their narrations within the bounds required by our constitution and by-laws."

These remarks being duly applauded, the President, by virtue of his rank, was called on for the first lie. This is a synopsis of what he said, and it is on the records under the title of

Oozed Into Him.

While on a recent journey to San Francisco, he shared a section in the sleeping car with one of the Comstock bonanza kings. The monarch occupied the upper berth, and the President of the Club the lower one. When the latter arrived in San Francisco he felt a peculiar heaviness in his body and limbs, his arms and legs especially being so weighty that he was hardly able to control their motions. He visited a prominent physician, who, after diagnosing his case, told him he displayed symptoms of metallic poisoning, and advised him to go to the Hammam, a bathing establishment of that name, and get "retorted." He accordingly went to that institution and took a Turkish bath; and when his pores began to open, silver oozed out of his body, like quicksilver going through a rag. Altogether, he cleaned up a bar valued at $417.92 and a fraction. He says the silver must have oozed into him from the bonanza king in the berth above, that night on the sleeper.

The admiration that this story aroused was almost enthusiastic, and when the applause had subsided, a member, hitherto unknown to general fame, broached the subject of

Cleopatra's Needle.

He said that he had seen the obelisk at Cairo, (Illinois) and declared that it was over two hundred feet long, and had an eye which even a camel could go through; at which statement the oldest member of the Club handed in his resignation. "There ought to be a limit to all things, and a story of a needle of that size was too much even for a lying club. Might he ask the size and shape of Cleopatra, and who in thunder Cleopatra was, anyway, that she required such a needle as that?" The President informed the indignant member that Cleopatra was a colored woman who nursed General George Washington when he was an infant; he (the President) was well acquainted with her, and had lived in the same town with her in Old Virginia.

This indorsement from the President calmed the ruffled feelings of the oldest member, and Cleopatra's Needle naturally suggested to another gentleman present

A Fossiliferous Lie.

He had been reading that newspaper paragraph which tells that a snail from the Egyptian Desert was found to be alive after having been glued for four years to a tablet in the British Museum; but said he, "There's nothing remarkable about that. It isn't a circumstance to an experience of mine. Once, while mining in the limestone over in White Pine, I blasted out a fossil snail, which I kept for a cabinet specimen, and one day it crawled out of the cabinet and bored itself back into the limestone where it had been imbedded for thirty thousand years before coming into my possession."

The impartial reader is left to judge whether the English or the American lie is the most entitled to credence.

Reading communications being next in order, the President arose and said that a gentleman residing in Virginia City sent in the name of an applicant for membership, and that his qualifications for admission were as follows: The applicant was riding on the Virginia and Truckee Railroad, between Virginia and Carson, when a lady from Ohio asked him if he had ever seen another railroad as crooked as the V. & T. "Certainly," replied he; "back in the Pennsylvania coal regions there is a railroad so crooked that on some of the curves they are obliged to uncouple the rear car to prevent its colliding with the locomotive." The lady bowed, and said that would do very well for crookedness; but she was heard to remark to her husband that if the bonanzas in Nevada were as big as the liars, it was no wonder there was a heavy discount on silver.

This lie was received in solemn silence, followed by a murmur of contempt; and on motion of Uncle John Gibbons the application was unanimously rejected. No other communication having been received, and the proceedings growing somewhat tame, the President asked if any one could name the author of the following, which he had seen in a San Francisco paper:

"While the P. M. S. S. *Orizaba* was on a recent voyage from Portland, Oregon, to San Francisco, during the recent gales, the vessel was carried on the top of a big wave as high as Mount Davidson, and came down with such force that the hull was buried eight feet deep in the sand at the bottom of the ocean. She stuck fast, and the sailors had to go down over the side and shovel her out before she could proceed on her journey."

As no one could place this magnificent specimen of nautical fiction, and several members pleaded prior engagements to a poker party, the Club adjourned, subject to the call of the President.

The Catfish.

"Has any member anything to offer under the order of business, 'Welfare of the Club'?" said the President, laying his pipe in the stove-hearth, and taking a "plug" of "sweet navy" from his pocket and biting off a piece.

"Mr. President, give us a chaw," remarked Mr. Thirsty.

"Sartingly," replied the Chair, as he handed the plug to him of the arid name, "but did the gentlemen present hear my observation about the order of business?"

"*I* heerd it," returned Mr. T., "and will take it up in due course as soon as I have disposed of the business in hand; I believe it was Solomon who said, 'No man can do two things to onc't.'" Then he carefully and deliberately bit off a "chaw" of the "navy," handed the plug back to the President, "posed" his feet on the stove, and proceeded as follows:

"Mr. President, you and all the members here present knows that there is a proposition on foot in this here town to plant catfish in Reese River. I don't s'pose thar's a gentleman now sittin' round this here stove what isn't acquainted with the catfish; they is not indigen-oo-us to this country, but we all knowed them in our childhood's days of innocence back yonder in the 'States.' The history of this movement about which I make reference—to wit, the plantin' of catfish in Reese River—is about the size of this: When the railroad was built from the States out here, the people what had been out here since forty-nine begin to have a hankerin' for the luxuries of their youth. It's a well-settled principle, Mr. President, that anything we was fond of in the eatin' line, when we was boys, tastes better when tasted through the vista of years than the most luxurious livin' a hash-house can afford when we have become men of the world and drained the cup of luxury down to its very dregs. I want to know if there is any whisky these days in this here country what tastes as sweet and contains as active a intoxicatin' principle as the clear juice of the grain we used to git back home when we was jest emergin' into manhood; is thar any cider seen now-a-days as is half so sweet as we used to git it suckin' it through a straw in the days gone by? No, sir; not much!

"Well, as I was a-sayin', the people of this coast, when they was placed in easy communication with the 'States,' commenced to hanker for the good things of their youth, and the result was a natural one, 'cordin' to the laws of supply and demand. There was a demand for certain things in this country, and people in the 'States' commenced a-shippin' of that class of articles to this coast over the railroad. The consequence was winter apples, ches'nuts, big oysters, eels, travelin' lecturers, catfish, and various other articles what this country don't produce of its own accord. Some fellers they brought out a lot of catfish and planted 'em in the Sacramento River, and the cats they growed and increased and multiplied the earth, so to speak, till thar was a surplus of 'em in Californy. Now when Californy has got more of a good thing than she wants herself, she sells the surplus to Nevada, at a pretty considerable figger of profit; and these fellers what was runnin' this catfish business, they advertised for sealed proposals from anybody who had any streams they wanted stocked with them kind of fish. This comin' under the eye of the enterprisin' citizens of this here town, they made up a purse and ordered a lot of the fish for plantin' in Reese River. This is the history of the case, and it remains for the members of this here Club to discuss the subjeck."

A profound silence reigned for a few moments after Mr. Thirsty had concluded his remarks; and then a member, who has been seven times defeated for the Presidency of the Club, on account of his disposition to cast doubts on the veracity of members, knocked the ashes out of his pipe, rested his elbows on his knees, and his head between his hands, and said:

"Gentlemen, I've got my doubts about the feasibility of this here project. S'pose they git the fish and put them in the river, how is they goin' to git a livin'? Thar's nothin' in thar for them to eat, and the whole fit-out will die of starvation."

"Sho!" exclaimed Old Dad; "catfish will eat anything, from a shingle-nail up to a horse-shoe. Why, when I was back home my father bought a catfish from a nigger for a picayune, and when we come to open it thar was a gold watch and chain worth two hundred and ninety dollars and a note of hand for sixty-three dollars, twenty-seven cents, ag'in the richest man in the county, inside of it."

"I s'pose your father got on a horse and searched the county to hunt up the owner of that watch and chain, didn't he?" sneeringly asked the Doubter.

"Not much," angrily returned Dad. "Look at me, and then tell me if you s'pose my father was a nat'ral-borned fool. No, sir—not much; he kept the watch and collected the note and the interest on it, which had been runnin' seven years."

"Niggers is great hands for ketchin' catfish," remarked the President, at this stage of the proceedings. "When I was a boy back yonder, we had a nigger on our place what could beat the oldest man in the country at enticin' of catfish. You all know that thar's a good many ways to ketch catfish, but this here darkey done it by charmin' of 'em."

"Charmin' of 'em!" exclaimed the entire Club, in chorus.

"Yes, sir, charmin' of 'em, that's what I said," resumed the Chair.

"You see this here darkey had a most pecooliar whistle, and he used to charm 'em with a whistle, and many and many's the time I've seed him do it. Our place was close to the river bank, and us boys used to go down thar and dig a big hole about ten feet away from the stream; then we'd dig a ditch runnin' from the river into the hole, and another runnin' out of the hole into the river. We'd fix gates to both ditches, and when we got all ready we'd shet the gate leadin' out of the hole, and open the one leadin' into it, and let the water run through it and fill up the hole. Then the black boy he'd squat on a log and whistle, and the catfish would jest come a-sailin' in through that ditch inter the hole; and thar they'd stay as still as a mice, with their heads a-stickin' out of the water, and list'nin' to that whistle as interested-like as if they was at a circus and it was the fust one they had ever seed. When thar was as many fish in the hole as the seats could accommerdate, one of the boys he'd run down and shet the gate leadin' from the river, and another he'd lift the gate leadin' from the hole, and of course the water would commence dreenin' out of the hole. But them thar bull-heads would stay right thar with their heads out of the water, never noticin' nothin' but that whistlin', till the first thing they knowed their tails struck gravel. They'd want to take the back track then, but twar'nt no use; they didn't have swimmin' room, and us boys we'd jest light inter the hole and capture every dog-goned one of 'em, and what we couldn't eat fresh up to the house we'd pickle down for the winter, besides havin' enough material from the insides to manure fifteen or twenty acres of 'taters."

"A valuable nigger," observed the Doubter, when the President had concluded.

"Yes, he was vallerble," replied the President, "but we never got no money out of him. The neighbors concluded that if that thar nigger was allowed to keep on, thar wouldn't be any more catfish left in the stream in a little while, so enticin' him out for a coon hunt one night, they hung him to a lim', and pinned a paper on his coat sayin', in big letters, 'A Warnin' to Whistlin' Niggers.'"

"Mr. President, have you said your say on the catfish?" inquired a member who to all appearance had been asleep during the foregoing narration.

"I've said my say," replied the Chair.

"Wal, Mr. President, and gentlemen, thar's more than one way of doin' the same thing, as you all will acknowledge, and now, with the consent of the Club, I'll tell how we used to ketch catfish back whar I used to live."

"Does the gentleman have consent?" queried the Chair.

"He do," returned one of the members.

"The gentleman has unanimous consent, and he will proceed on the catfish question," announced the Chair.

"Back in the States whar I used to live, the country was alive with ground-hogs, catfish, and niggers. We use' to set the niggers to ketchin' the ground-hogs, and the ground-hogs to ketchin' the catfish. A ground-hog is a animal which some people calls a porkypine, and they'll make a dog think he's stuck his nose inter a yaller-jacket's nest; they're stickier than them prickly pears what grows in the deserts around this section of country. Wal, the niggers they'd ketch a ground-hog, and us boys would take a hook and tie about three yards of line to it, and stick it inter the ground-hog's back and chuck him inter the river, and while he was swimmin' around and strikin' out for dry land, a catfish would come up and open that thar mouth of his'n, and down would go Mister ground-hog inter that fish's insides. He is a energetic cuss, is the ground-hog, and loves his liberty just like a human, and when he found hisself inside that fish, he'd commence lightin' out for freedom; he'd cut his way through that thar catfish in about thirty-three seconds. Of course, no fish ain't goin' to stand a hole the size of a ground-hog in his body, and 'tain't human natur that it could live up under it, and pritty soon the fish would come belly-up on the water, and we'd go out in a skift and yank it in, and the porkypine—as some people call it—he'd go sailin' down stream to do the thing over ag'in with another fish, and when we had all the fish we wanted, we'd row the skift up to the ground-hog and grab the piece of line, and snail him inter the boat and give him to the niggers, for their share of the ketch."

As the above narration drew towards a close, the Doubter's eyes began to twinkle and his lips to twitch, and every member present knew instinctively that there was something on his mind. There was. Addressing the Chair, he said:

"May I ask the gentleman who preceded me a trifling, unimportant question?"

The decision of the Chair being called for, it decided to suspend the rules and allow the question to be asked.

"All I want to know is, how much bigger and heavier that ground-hog was when he had got through catchin' catfish, than he was when he commenced."

The preceding gentleman didn't think he could answer the question, but would like to know what the skeptic was driving at by asking it.

"Oh, nothin' much," was the reply, "only I thought he must have swelled considerable from eating so much catfish, and I was a-wonderin' whether the darkeys what eat him didn't git about as much catfish to their meal as they did ground-hog."

Here the President's gavel fell. Rising to his feet, and taking his quid out of his mouth and sticking it on the under side of his chair-seat, he said:

"Gentlemen of the Sazerac Lying Club: You may, perhaps, have noticed that, during the discussion this evening, I have permitted a wider latitude than is actually rulable under our Constitution and by-laws. I have did it on this occasion in the hope that the gentleman what is continerly castin' doubts on the remarks of members might receive a rebuke what would make him forever after hold his peace; but I see it is leniency thrown away, and from this on, any member of this here Club what asks a frivolous question for the purpose of impeachin' the lie of a brother member, shall be considered as having been stuck for the drinks for the crowd. With these few remarks I now declare the Club adjourned for the evenin', and if any member has the wherewithal in his clothes, and feels inclined to make a jingle on the counter for that purpose, we will proceed to hold an informal session at the bar."

No member showing a willingness to make the jingle, the barkeeper said he guessed he would stand the "night-caps" if they would take them "straight," and not bother him to fix mixed drinks; to which proposition they all hastily assented, and, headed by their presiding officer, filed to the bar and denominated their stimulant.

An Affectionate Fish.

On the evening succeeding that on which the proceedings above narrated were had, the Club assembled around the stove at the usual hour, and the roll being called, the President opened the meeting with a few remarks, as follows:

"Gentlemen of the Sazerac Lying Club: We had a very edifying meeting last night—one which reflected the utmost credit on not only the members engaged in the debate, but on the Club at large, and which demonstrated to my entire satisfaction that as liars we are unapproachable; that interest in our organization is still maintained, and that notwithstanding that there is a prospect that death may one day enter our charmed circle and carry off its brightest ornaments, we still feel that the eyes of the world are upon us, and that we have a bounden duty to perform in keeping up the standard of American lying. The subject under discussion last night, as many of you may remember, was catching fish—catfish in particular. Gentlemen, there is nothing which affords so wide a range for the talents of the liar, which offers more opportunities for economizing the truth as the subject of fishing. Therefore, should members decide to continue the discussion under that head, the Chair will not only not interpose no objections, but will personally see to it that members are not annoyed with interruptions from any source, either within or without the pale of this Club."

The Chair, as it concluded the above remarks, hitched up its waistband, threw its coat-tail aside so as to display the ivory handle of its six-shooter, and bent its eyes on the Doubter, who shrank and cowered under the searching Presidential gaze.

"Gentlemen, are you ready for business?" asked the Chair.

"We are," replied the member who never makes any remarks except to answer the President's queries, call for "the question," and vote aye and no; but always tells on the outside what splendid arguments *we* had in the Club last night.

"Then proceed," observed the Chair.

Old Dad rose up, and scratched his head, and then sat down again, saying:

"I pass."

Then a newly elected member squirted a stream of tobacco juice on Uncle John's rheumatic foot, and said:

"Mr. President and gentlemen, speaking about fish and other animals, don't you know thar is some animals as knows as much as a human?"

"Some humans," interrupted the Doubter; but a glance from the Chair caused him to subside.

"Yes," continued the new comer, "some brutes knows a heap; and not only that, but they is capable of feeling attachment and affection. You all know how lovin' a dog or a horse can be to his master; but 'taint often you hear tell about an affectionate fish. Is it, Mr. President?"

The Chair said: "Not very."

"Wal, when I was a boy, I once run acrost a fish what was stuck after me worse than a boy after playin' hookey. I was visitin' over at an uncle's of mine what lived about fourteen miles from our house; and one day, when I was down to the crik, I seed a perch in the water. It was a awful pritty fish, with red speckles all over its back, and as shiny as a Carson dollar. I was goin' to run up to the house for a hook and line, when it stuck its head up out of the water, and looked at me kind of knowin' like. It didn't seem to be a bit afeared of me; and when I stuck my finger down to'rds it, it snapped and nibbled at it jest like you've seen a pet rooster do. I had a hunk of bread and 'lasses in my pocket—[I always used to go heeled with bread and 'lasses those days, for fear of accidents, jest as I go heeled now with a six-shooter, as you might observe by lookin' close]—and I broke off some crumbs, and give 'em to the perch, and he eat 'em out of my hand as tame as a kitten. Then I put my hand under him, and lifted him out of the water, and stroked him down the back, jest like you would a dog; but he never fluttered, but lay there kind of peaceful like, and lookin' up inter my eyes, as though he liked that sort of business. Wal, after a while I put him back inter the water, and went up to the house, and told about it; and my grandmother on my father's side, who was stoppin' at my aunt and uncle's, said I had a gift; that she once knowed a man who had a gift like that, who went to the Sandwich

Islands, and charmed rhinocerouses, so that they could drive 'em like horses in the king's carriage; and he'd a got rich at it, only the cannibals eat him up. His gift was only for dumb animals, and didn't have no effeck on cannibals. Wal, I used to go down to the crik every morning, and feed that perch; and when he'd hear me a-comin', he'd commence splashin' the water for joy and gladness. Finally, one day, my folks sent for me in a hurry to come home, and I had to take the back track and leave my fish. Gentlemen, you can imagine the affection of that fish for me when I tell you he follered me home. Yes, sir, actually traveled forty-three miles afoot to our house; and when I got up one mornin', thar he was, with a willow stuck through his gills, hangin' on to the latch of the front door."

"Was he still alive?" asked the Doubter.

"Certainly not," was the reply; "do you s'pose a fish could travel fifty-four miles afoot, and stand up under the strain? No, sir, he was dead; but a finer tastin' fish than that affectionate creeter was when he was fried, you never eat in your life."

The Doubter wanted the Chair's permission to ask how the narrator identified the perch which hung on the latch with the one in the stream; but was unanimously and by a large majority ruled out of order, and the Club declared adjourned.

Applications for Membership.

"Mr. Seccertary, be there any applications for membership?" inquired the President, at the conclusion of the roll-call.

"Yes, sir," replied the Secretary; "here is two applications on my desk."

"The Seccertary will read."

"Here is one from a feller in San Francisco, who says he's a newspaper editor, and therefore duly qual——"

"Hold!" exclaimed Old Dad; "them newspaper fellers can't lie."

"I beg to differ with the gentleman," remarked the Doubter; "I was readin' of an account in a paper this mornin' relatin' of a occurrence whereby a young lady run a needle into her foot a great many years ago, and after she had got married and her children had got married and had children, that thar needle one day came out of the top of one of her grandchildren's head—a leetle bit rusted, of course, but the same identical needle. Now if that aint a lie, I'd like to know what you call it."

"Sho!" said Dad; "that's a common occurrence; why, back in the States I knowed a woman what swallowed a——"

"I move the previous question, and call for the decision of the Chair on the newspaper man," interrupted the Doubter.

"Gentlemen," said the President, clearing his throat and winking at the barkeeper, who understood the hint, and proceeded to fix it up, with a little sour in it, "gentlemen, this here question of the admission of newspaper editors into this here Club, is one of the gravest as has ever disturbed our deliberations. It has been held by competent authority that editors can't lie. For myself I'm not prepared to speak on the subjeck; but in giving my decision on this here point, I will simply refer members to article hunderd and nineteen of our constitution and by-laws, which expressly forbids and prohibits the admission of professional liars into membership in this here Club. Them's my sentiments, and the Secretary will proceed with that there other application."

The Secretary, who had just had his "pedro" caught, arose from the table, and holding the remaining cards up towards the Chair, said:

"I hold in my hand an application for membership from a gentleman as signs himself Honorable Ananias Truefact. He's a stranger in town, but has jest caught my pedro nevertheless, and this is him settin' at this here table."

"Are his qualifications for membership stated in writing in his application?" queried the Chair.

"No," replied the Secretary, "but he has informed me in confidence that he was borned with an impediment in his speech which positively prevents his tellin' the truth."

The question was put on the admission of Mr. Truefact, and carried, with but one dissenting vote. That one was cast by the Doubter, who in explanation of his vote stated that he didn't "take no stock in natural but only in cultivated liars."

The New Member Speaks.

On the announcement of the vote, the newly elected member was invited to enter the charmed circle, requested to sign the constitution and by-laws, and questioned by the Chair as to his ability to comply with the rule requiring newly elected members to "set them up for the boys."

The stranger did not look like a Bonanza King, or a bloated bondholder or monopolist, or an aristocrat, and as he arose to answer the Chair's query as to his financial status, admitted that appearances were against him, which they surely were. His boots were down at the heel, his shirt (he wore no coat) full of holes, his hat battered and bent, and the seat of his pants patched with a quarter-section of a flour sack.

"G-g-gentlemen," he said, "I m-m-must admit th-a-at I'm imp-p-p-c-c-cunyus, b-b-b-but n-n-nev'r desp-p-pise a man b-b-b-cause he wears a r-r-r-ragged coat."

"We don't," spoke up Uncle John. "Stranger, its allowable in this here Club for a new member to have his treat paid for by a old member by proxy. I'll be your proxy on this glorious occasion; step up, boys, and nominate your pizen."

The Club here took a recess for the disposal of the poison, and that ceremony being over, were again called to order by the Chair, and as soon as the members were settled in their seats, Old Dad called for a lie from the new member.

"G-g-gentlem'n and M-m-mister P-p-president," stuttered Mr. Truefact, "I ain't m-m-much on the lie; b-b-but I'll relate a oc-c-c-cur-rence what t-t-took p-p-lace onc't when I was a b-b-b-boy, in th' earlier and p-p-p-purer d-d-d-days of this here Rep-p-p-public. You may some of yer p-p-perhaps have n-n-n-noticed that I've got a imp-p-p-ediment in my sp-p-peech. It was in the c-c-c-city of B-b-b-bosting, and I was a g-g-g-goin' along one d-d-d-day out in the outsk-k-k-skirts, when I s-s-s-seed a b-b-b-bildin' a-f-f-f-fire. 'T-t-t-was a tr'-m-m-m-mendous b-b-big b-b-b-bildin', m-m-mor'n t-t-t-two hund-d-dred f-f-feet high, and l-l-large otherw-w-ways in prop-p-portion. T-t-her' w-w-warn't n-n-n-nobody b-b-b-but me in s-s-sight, and I s-tart-t-ted t-t-ter g-g-g-give t-t-t'her al-l-larm b-b-by hol-l-lerin' f-f-fire, and——"

"And I 'spose the buildin' burned to the ground before you could get the word 'Fire' out of your mouth?" interrupted the Chair.

"T-t-that's j-j-j-just it," returned Ananias, "b-b-but d-d-d-does t-t-the r-r-r-rules of t-t-this Cl-l-lub p-p-p-per-m-m-mit t-t-th' C-c-c-chair t-t-to ant-t-ticipate a m-m-m-mem-b-b-ber's l-l-l-lie?"

A Picnic.

The President decided that the rules were capable of such a construction—when the member stuttered, and announced that the Club would now proceed to business under the head "Motions and Resolutions," whereupon a hitherto obscure member rose and said:

"Mr. President and gentlemen of the Club, you is all aware that the Fourth of July are almost upon us—that glorious day which witnessed the birth of him who was first in war, first in peace, and first in the hearts of his countrymen. I need not recount to you the history of that there man, or is it absolutely necessary that I should here repeat to you that touching and beautiful story about his cutting down the cherry-tree, and owning up to it like a little man, when he was as good as caught in the act, and knowed there was nobody else on the place what was liable to have got away with the fruit-tree. It is a story familiar to you all, and one which is impressed in letters of living fire on the heart of every true American. But in this connection, Mr. President, I wish to suggest that this Club ought to celebrate the anniversary of the Fourth of July in some fitting and appropriate manner; and, as we can't raise the money for fire-works, I move you, sir, that this here Club have a picnic. The Pest-house is now empty of patients, and anybody can hev' the use of the buildin'; I would therefore renew my motion that this here Club hev' a picnic on the Fourth of July at the Pest-house grounds, and that that thar buildin', in the absence of shade from which this locality is known to be sufferin', be used as a depositary to shelter the refreshments from the sun's rays."

"Do I hear a second?" asked the Chair.

"I second the motion," replied the member who answers all the questions of the Chair, and votes aye and no for the other members.

"And I," spoke up Mr. Thirsty, "move that the Chair appoint a committee to wait on the saloons and solicit contributions of refreshments for the use of the Club at the proposed picnic."

The Aye-and-No Member called for the question and voted aye, and the Chair declared all motions before the house carried, and the Club adjourned for the evening.

No Picnic.

When the Club assembled on the evening following the meeting above recorded, the President announced that he regretted to state that, owing to the sudden appearance of a case of small-pox, which now occupied the Pest-house, and an evident indisposition on the part of the saloon keepers to furnish the requisite refreshments, the Club would dispense with the picnic which had been resolved on at the last meeting.

Old Dad said he didn't like picnics, "no way."

Uncle John remarked that he was afraid of wood-ticks, "which was powerful plentiful down there to the Pest-house."

The President remarked that picnics—especially picnics without fluid refreshments—were a relic of the barbarism of by-gone ages.

Mr. Truefact got so far as to say that "p-p-pic-n-n-n-nics w-w-was a insti-t-t-tu——" when he was interrupted by the Doubter, who hinted that he had had all the picnics he "wanted in his'n" in the early days in California.

"Will the member be kind enough to relate his experience?" said the President.

The Doubter took a fresh chew of tobacco, straightened up in his chair, crossed one leg over the other, and proceeded to relate:

An Unpleasantness with a Bear.

"Onc't in Californy—I think it was along in fifty—me and five or six other fellers was minin' up on the south fork of the Yuba. Thar wasn't much in the way of amusements them days, as the boys worked pritty stiddy, makin' hay while the sun was a-shinin'—leastways, them as had good diggin's. Of course, thar was faro and Spanish monte for high stakes, and draw-poker for a big ante, and maybe an occasional fight or shootin' scrape, or that kind of recreations; but such divarsions as picnics, and camp-meetin's, and goin' to church, and school exhibitions, and concerts, and theaters, and them kind of rational amusements, such as is so common these days, was unknown in the mines in Californy in them early days, 'long in the fall of forty-nine and the spring of fifty.

"Up in a ravine in the mountings, 'bout three miles above our cabin, thar was one of the prittiest springs I ever laid eyes on, with willers all 'round it, and grass till you couldn't rest. Some of the boys what was inclined to put on airs used to go up there Sundays and take a wash, and they got to talkin' one day 'bout what a gay place it would be for a picnic, purvidin' thar was only some gals and other necessaries for such a institution.

"One of my pardners was a feller named Pike—they called him that 'cause he come from Pike County, Missoury. He was one of them fellers what aint afraid of nothin' what walks or talks, but the quietest, silentest critter you ever seed, and he had so little to say, even when he was drinkin', and was always so good-natured and smilin' like, that a stranger would a' thought thar warn't no sand in him, and he wouldn't fight nothin'. But he allers carried a big bowie in his boot-leg and a dragoon six-shooter in his shirt, and would fight a rattlesnake and give it the fust bite. He warn't quarrelsome a bit, but was powerful tender on his honor, and if a man would objek to his way of dealin' the keards, or allow that his folks wasn't one of the fust families of Missoury, Pike was liable to start in and make a starter for a graveyard. Thar couldn't nothin' excite him; I s'pose he could have cut a man's head off without ever crackin' a smile, and I actually b'leeve you might a' turned a cannon loose alongside his ear, and he wouldn't a' started, but jest turn 'round and say, in that quiet way of his:

"'Stranger, does your gun kick? It makes a powerful loud report.'

"Wal, to come down to the picnic, when Pike heard the boys a-talkin' on the subjeck, he spoke up and says, says he: 'Boys, s'pose we have a picnic next Sunday, instid of goin' to town on the usual hurrah?' And some of the other boys says: 'S'posen we do?' Wal, we talked it all over and concluded that a picnic wouldn't be a bad go; and afore we went to bed that night we had concluded all the preliminaries, as you may say. One of the boys was to go to town and git the fluids and a few decks of cards, another was to cook a pot of beans and bake a batch of bread, and the rest of us was to stand in and do all we could to help the thing along.

"At last the Sunday came along when we was to have the picnic. Some of the boys had been out the night before and borrowed a *burro** belonging to some Mexicans what was minin' down the river a piece, and though they was as quiet as possible about it, they did have to fire one shot, but only wounded the Mexican, and he didn't die for five days.

---

*A Mexican donkey.

They staked the *burro* out near the cabin, and next mornin' bright and early we tumbled out and got ready for the picnic. We got a aparayho* and put it on the *burro*, and packed on the whisky, and the bread, and the beans, and the cards, and a fryin'-pan and coffee-pot, and such other things as might come needful, and when everything was ready we started up the ravine drivin' the *burro* ahead of us.

"Boys, sometimes when I think of the disastrousness of that picnic, it makes me feel as if I'd like to go off some place and bag my head. But never mind!

"Wal, we got to the spring at last, and the fust thing to do was to 'unpack' the animile and git things in shape for a camp. Some of the boys went out to 'rastle' for some dry wood for a fire, others gathered and heaped up a lot of dry leaves, and me and Pike went to work to arrange the refreshments. The joltin' of the pack on the *burro* comin' up the ravine had disarranged the refreshments some, and I was tryin' to save some of the whisky into the coffee-pot from the broken demijohn, and Pike was a-fishin' some of the decks of cards out of the beans and a-scrapin' of them off, when Pike, he turned round and smiled, and says he in that quiet way of his, jest as easy and natural like as he'd say, 'Boys, let's take a drink,' and without ever crackin' a smile, says he:

"'GRIZZLY BA'R! TAKE A TREE!'

"And he got up and walked to a tree in his reg'lar, natural gait, never showin' no signs of excitement, and climbed up the tree as though he was a-goin' up stairs in one of them elevators you hear about in them fust-class hotels down to 'Frisco.

"I was too fur from a tree, and the ba'r was too clus' to me—that's the whole history of the case—and hap'nin' to throw my eye over my shoulder, thar he was, right behind me, not over three feet off, a genuine grizzly, and you fellers what has lived and mined in the Serry Nevadys knows what that means.

"One of the boys had brung along his double-bar'led gun, and it was layin' on the ground clus' to me, and I thought if I could only reach that thar gun I'd have something like an even show with the bar. The other boys was up in the trees, waitin' to see the circus open, and hollerin' to me to grab that gun. I knew she was loaded chock up to the muzzle with slugs and old nails and other rubbish, and if ever I got in the first shot on the ba'r I'd have the best of the unpleasantness; so, throwin' myself back-'ards, and turnin' a hand-spring, I landed on the ground right alongside the gun. You better bet yer boots, boys, I wasn't slow in takin' aim; but the consarned ba'r was 'bout as quick as me, and before I could turn loose he made a bounce at me, and grabbed the bar'l of that thar gun atween

---

*Aparejo—A sort of cushion used by the Mexicans and native Californians as a pack-saddle.

his teeth, with the muzzle pintin' down his throat. I was skeer't some, but I knowed enough to pull both triggers to onc't, and the way that old gun kicked lifted me out of all reach of danger, and separated me and the ba'r about forty-five feet. When I come to, which was in about a minnit, I raised up and looked for the ba'r, expectin' to see nothin' but little bits of him scattered on the ground. But I didn't. Thar he set, setten' up on his ha'nches, and retchin' kinder violent like, and pritty soon he began to puke up slugs, and old nails, and door-hinges, and other trash that had been loaded in that double-bar'led gun. Pike, he come down out of the tree and looked at the animal's tongue and felt its pulse, and remarked that it was the sickest grizzly ba'r he ever seed, and Jim Stackpole he held its head so's it could vomit easy, and the rest on us got the pack ropes and some lariats, and commenced tyin' up the ba'r to make a prisoner of him.

"We didn't have no picnic, 'cause when the gun kicked me I upset the beans, and the cards was all tramped out of shape by the ba'r, and the whisky, barrin' a few drops, had all run out on the grass from the busted demijohn; and we didn't feel as cheerful anyway as men ought to feel to make a picnic a success.

"When we got the ba'r tied up, we packed him on the *burro*, and took the back track, and on the way home we met some fellers what was huntin' a ba'r for a bull-and-ba'r fight up to Nevada City, and don't you know, Dad, (turning to that individual) that's the very same ba'r you had in that bull-and-ba'r fight up to Nevada City, of which you was tellin' about at a previous meetin' of this Club?"

"Very likely," said Dad, "I remember noticin' that the ba'r on that occasion seemed kinder sick like."

At this point the barkeeper announced that it was time to shut up for the night, and he hoped that in adjourning the stuttering member would take the usual thing, and not try to order some new-fangled drink, as this house didn't propose to run till daylight for no set of stiffs that ever herded a stove.

Mr. Truefact took the "usual thing," and the other members likewise took theirs "straight," and the Club was declared adjourned for the evening.

Rogers's Dog.

"Thar's good duck-huntin' over in Smoky Valley," said Uncle John, as he settled himself in his seat to take part in the discussion, in the Sazerac Lying Club, at a recent meeting of that organization.

"I like to hunt ducks," remarked Old Dad, "but this here dog of mine" (patting the animal on the head) "aint much on retrievin' ducks no more; but he's lightnin' on rabbits and kioties, or anything as runs on four legs."

"He aint no better at that than Rogers's dog is," observed the President.

"What can Rogers's dog do that nobody else's dog can't?" sneeringly asked the Doubter.

"Well, gentlemen," said the Chair, "if you'll come to order, and that member behind the stove will quit snappin' spittle off'n that quill tooth-pick into my eye, I'll tell you what Rogers's dog can do that nobody else's dog can't."

The censured member stuck his tooth-pick over his ear, and remarked that he didn't know she was shooting that far, and the President proceeded:

"Rogers, he took his dog and his gun and went down into the valley the other day, to see if he couldn't drum up somethin' to shoot. You all know his dog, and that it's a sizeable pointer. Wal, Rogers and the dog they beat around in the sagebrush for quite a while without seein' a hair or a feather, and was both on 'em gittin' kind of disgusted like, when up jumps a kioty right square in front of the dog. Rogers is a sportsman and a hunter, he is, and he wasn't goin' to waste his ammernishon and pros-titute his skill for the killin' of a mean, cowardly, sneakin', ornery wolf; so he jest sicked the dog on the animile and told him to seize him. Now, you all know that a kioty won't stan' up to a dog unless he's cornered, and if he's got runnin' room he'll run, and—bein' willin to give the devil his due—I will say it for a kioty that when he sets out to run he does the business right squar up to the handle. Wal, this here kioty, he looked up and he seed Rogers's dog, and heered Rogers tellin' of the animal to 'seize him,' and he had sense enough to know that thar was liable to be trouble in that neighborhood pritty soon. So he jest turned tail and commenced to light out, and Buster—which is Rogers's dog's given name—he lit out too, and away they went over the ground and through the brush, it bein' nip and tuck atwixt them, but the kioty havin' slightly the best of it on account of gittin' a little the start in the beginnin'. They must hev run that way for about a mild, with the dog's nose plum up agin the tip of the kioty's tail and not darin' to snap for fear of losin' ground, when the kioty thought he saw the hole what he occupied as his own family residence, and without stoppin' to make sure, he shot into that thar hole like he was shot out of a gun. Buster was a-goin' so fast, he wasn't noticin' no holes and he couldn't stopped himself if he had, and in he goes after mister kioty. Now, gentlemen, it so happened that this here hole wasn't a kioty-hole at all, but jest a squirrel-hole; but the kioty was so scart he wasn't particular, and Buster wanted that kioty so bad he didn't stop to notice the difference; and thar they was, both in the hole in the ground, and Rogers a-comin' up as fast as he could, and wonderin' what had become of his dog and that kioty. He don't believe in ghosts, cause he never saw a real out-and-out ghost, but ghosts is a subjeck open to a good deal of argyment, howsomever. As he didn't s'pose for a moment that them animals had gone inter the squirrel hole, and as he couldn't see 'em in sight, he sorter concluded they must be absconded some way supernat'ral like, and after huntin' around in the brush for a couple of hours, he concluded to go home, as he was powerful dry, his whisky hevin' give out, and likewise some hungry. The place whar he missed the dog was on one side of a little risin' ground what makes a little low hill in the valley, extendin' over a couple of miles to the slope on the other side. Wal, gentlemen, to come to the p'int, when Rogers got over in this other slope, he heer'd a kind of scramblin' noise, like as if it was underground, and he couldn't make out to account for it no way. But jest as he got to the foot of this low hill on the other side, he seed somethin' pop out of the ground, and in about a minnit thar was somethin' else came shootin out'n that hole. Them somethin's, gentlemen, was that kioty and Buster, which Rogers he recognized in a minnit, notwithstandin' that every bit of his hair had been rubbed off as clean as if it had been shaved with a razor. The kioty was plum give out, but Buster was jest gittin' his second wind, and he bounced that air wolf and held it down till Rogers could come up and beat it to death with rocks."

"Now," said the President, looking sternly at the Doubter, "can any gentleman here present tell me if he knows on another ninety-four pound pointer dog as can pursoo a kioty four miles and a half underground through a squirrel-hole?"

"I can't," spoke up the Doubter; "no more do I s'pose I could tell about anybody's kioty as could squeeze that many miles in front of a dog through a openin' and underground passage like that thar squirrel-hole."

The Chair looked as black as a thunder-cloud, and was reaching its hand around to the back part of its waistband, when the Secretary, one of whose duties it is to prevent bloodshed and smooth over the ruffled waters of any dissensions which may arise in the Club, spoke up, and said:

"Mr. President."

"The Seccertary has the floor," said the President, as he removed his hand from his hip and wiped his nose with his coat-sleeve, at the same time smoothing the wrinkles from his troubled brow.

"Mr. President," resumed the Secretary, "your account of that there dog of Rogers's reminds me of a incident I once knowed to happen to a cat."

"The Seccertary will relate," was announced from the Chair

Thereupon the Scribe proceeded to narrate as follows:

The Fate of a Cat.

"It gits pritty cold in this country sometimes, but it aint a patchin' to what it is back in the State of Wisconsin, whar I come from. It gits so cold thar that I've knowed it to freeze a river four foot solid in a single night. Well, durin' one of these cold spells our folks had a cat, and that air cat turned up missin' one mornin'. My folks set a good deal of store by the animile, and my little sister was afflicted more particular than the rest of us. But 'twarn't no use; the cat was gone, and all the huntin' in the country didn't have no effeck in findin' it. Thar was a pond close to the house, and we finally decided that the cat had somehow got in thar and the ice had froze over so quick it had froze her fast afore she could git out. And we wasn't *very* far out'n the way; for when that pond begin to thaw and the ice to break up in the spring, we found the cat, and, gentlemen, whar do you suppose we found the animile?"

The Doubter answered that he supposed the Secretary expected the Club to believe that they had found the cat in the pond; that it had been imbedded in the ice all winter, and when they gave it a little brandy and warmed it up by the stove, it ravenously devoured seven pounds of beefsteak.

"Not much," returned the Secretary; "we found the cat, when spring opened, down in the bottom of the well, which it had fell in; and though slightly soft, the corpse was in a good state of preservation, considerin' the circumstances. It was one of them kind of cats what didn't have no nine lives; otherwise, we might have found it in the pond, under the circumstances foreshadowed by the skeptical gentleman on the other side of the stove."

Whereupon the Club adjourned for the evening.

Deacon Toughly.

Deacon Toughly belongs to that class known in Nevada communities as the "Old Boys," which signifies that he is a Pacific Coast pioneer, and arrived in California in the golden days, when whisky was four bits a drink, and flour and other necessaries sold at rates in proportion. Why, where, when, and how he acquired the cognomen of "Deacon" I have not been able to learn, though I have made diligent inquiries of his friends, and tried to worm it out of the Deacon himself. Nobody in Austin ever saw him inside of a church, and he never had more than a mere bowing acquaintance with the preachers; likewise he was given to elaborate profanity at times, having a remarkable aptitude in the construction of novel oaths and expletives. His manner was always fatherly and dignified, but his marked disregard for cleanliness detracted somewhat from the dignity he constantly assumed. He may have acquired his deaconship from the following circumstance: When, if greeted by a friend or acquaintance, he was asked, "How's times, Deacon," his invariable reply was:

"My son, these here times reminds me of that air good old hymn we use' to sing back yonder when I was a boy,

> "'Shoo (shew) pity, Lord! O Lord, forgive,
> Let a repenting sinner live.'"

The exact connection between the words of the hymn and the state of business in Austin was something which no fellow could find out; but it is, perhaps, possible that this display of knowledge of religious literature was what earned for Mr. Toughly the title of "Deacon."

The Deacon had done a great deal of prospecting in his day, and at the time of which I write was enormously wealthy—in his mind. That is, he owned a lot of remotely situated mines which he believed to be fabulously rich, but which he could not have disposed of for ten cents an acre. He had no source of income, yet he managed to live, and was never known to ask anything in charity. His home was a little stockade cabin, with a dirt roof and a dirt floor, to which he only retired at night when the last light in town was extinguished, or in the day-time to prepare his simple meals, the greater portion of his time being spent in the streets and saloons. And the happiest moments of the Deacon's life were when he was comfortably settled in front of the stove in a saloon, with a crowd of "old stiffs" about him listening to the relation of his experiences. On such occasions the old gentleman was a whole lying club in himself.

Deacon Toughly was tall, but slightly stoop-shouldered, and his general make-up and appearance were not by any means imposing, and had it not been for the dignity which encompassed him, and his well-known capacity for taking up extensions on the truth, he would not have been a person to attract more than a mere passing notice. He had a pair of small, sharp, black eyes, which, however, owing to a habit of blinking his eyelids, were seldom visible; his head, save a few straggling gray hairs on top, and a lock on each side, falling down to his cheeks and hiding his ears, was destitute of hirsute covering, and as smooth and shiny as a new school-globe. His forehead was decorated with a pair of steel-bowed "specs," which the oldest inhabitant did not remember ever having seen the Deacon looking through, and that is why I designate them a decoration. His shirt was always dirty, and he on all occasions wore a paper collar that had been turned wrong side out, the right side having probably been utilized by some citizen of Austin other than the Deacon, who had cast the collar aside when too much soiled to longer contribute to his own personal adornment. A greasy and tobacco-stained vest, a rusty, snuff-colored coat that had once been black, a pair of pants turned up at the bottoms so as to make them somewhat in accord with the length of the wearer's legs, a dilapidated white plug hat, a stout stick, and a stream of tobacco juice running from each corner of his mouth, completed the Deacon's costume.

Deacon Toughly had never attended the re-unions in the Sazerac; he had his favorite houses, and this saloon was not one of them. But when the Sazerac Lying Club began to be "agitated" in the REVEILLE, he read the accounts of its proceedings in that sheet, and accosted me on the street one evening and questioned me regarding that organization:

"Look here, my son," he said, "what's all that you're puttin' of in the paper about that air Sazerac Lyin' Club?"

I assured the Deacon that there was such an institution in Austin as that to which he referred, and pointed with my finger to the Sazerac Saloon, informing him that it was in there that the nightly lying sessions were held.

"And them there fellers think they can *lie?*" questioned the Deacon, with emphasis.

"They most assuredly do," I replied.

"Wal, my son, I'll drap in there some night and jest go 'em a rattle; you never heer'd me tell how, when I was a boy, I tamed a lot of grasshoppers and harnessed 'em up for a team and hitched 'em to a little wagon and made 'em haul, did ye?"

I confessed that I had never experienced that pleasure.

"Wal, then, my son, I'll tell it to ye now."

Just then I saw a man down street who I thought would be looking for me in a couple of hours, and begged the Deacon to excuse me for a moment, and rushed off before he had time to frame a reply.

True to his word, the Deacon one evening dropped into the Sazerac, to "go them fellers a rattle." When he entered, the usual crowd was sitting around the stove, but business had not yet commenced, and several of the members were dozing in their seats. The Deacon first walked up to the bar and remarked to the barkeeper that it was a "fine evenin', but jest the leestest mite cold."

The barkeeper concurred, and inquired of the Deacon if he wouldn't partake of a little stimulant.

"Don't keer if I do, my son," replied Deacon Toughly, "it's not adzactly my time of day for drinkin', but bein' as the air's a leetle sharp on the outside of the house, a leetle stimulatin' beverage mought brace me up a bit."

A bottle and glass were set out on the bar-counter; the Deacon filled a glass to the brim, and holding it up and blinking at it furiously, said:

"My son, here's hopin' you may live a thousand years."

This said, he tossed off the liquor, and then stooping over the counter, and bringing his lips close to the barkeeper's ear, he "whispered" loud enough to be heard by all in the room:

"See here, my son, be there anything in this here Sazerac Lying Club, or aint it only one of them 'joshes' they gits up in the REVEILLE sometimes?"

The reply was, that the Club was an actual, positive, solemn fact.

"Wal, I've a noshun of tryin' my hand with them fellers," resumed the Deacon, in the same loud whisper.

By this time all the members of the Club were thoroughly awake, and the attention of all was riveted on the Deacon. Old Dad pressed on Uncle John's rheumatic foot, causing him to utter an exclamation that would have done credit to Deacon Toughly himself; the President poked the

Secretary in the ribs, and Mr. Truefact winked a stuttering sort of a wink to the Doubter, who drew up a chair and invited the Deacon to "sit by."

"Thank ye, my son, thank ye," said the Deacon, as he took the proffered seat. Then pushing his specs up a little higher on his forehead, and blinking at the rate of two hundred revolutions a minute, he said:

"Gentlemen, be this the Sazerac Lying Club?"

Mr. Truefact started to reply, but before he could frame the first syllable of the first word he wanted to utter, Old Dad broke in with:

"I reckon you've struck the wrong streak of gravel this time, Deekin; thar isn't a gentleman sittin' round this here stove as could lie, if he tried for a week."

"I'm satisfied, my son, puffickly satisfied!" exclaimed the Deacon. "I've hed my doubts about this here Sazerac Lyin' Club, but now I'm satisfied, puffickly satisfied that it do exist in dead, squar', sober earnest. I did intend comin' over here to go you fellers a rattle, and I wouldn't mind doin' it yit, but I'm a leetle bit doubtful of myself—a leetle bit doubtful."

"You can stand in with the boys, and take your chances like the rest of us," spoke up Old Dad.

"Wal, my son, I'll stand in, as ye say; so here goes:

"'Onc't on a time ——'"

"Hold on, thar, Deekin!" exclaimed the President. "Mr. Seccertary, what order of business is we workin' under now?"

"The Lie of the Evening," responded the Secretary, as he slapped down a queen and took the other man's jack of trumps.

"All right, Deekin, go ahead," remarked the Chair.

The Deacon "Stands In."

Deacon Toughly brought his chair round facing the President, so as to get a blink at that official, coughed three times to clear his throat, and proceeded to narrate as follows:

"When I come acrost the plains in forty-nine we had a powerful hard time; the stock got runned down, and the most on it give plum out. Consekently, afore I struck the borders of Utah Territory I was left afoot, my horse hevin' passed in his checks, and the train I was travelin' with hevin' lost all their animils but one yoke of cattle through dyin' or bein' stampeded by the dog-goned, dod-rotted —— —— —— —— —— of Injins; —— their —— —— ornery souls to ——ation."

The Deacon was here interrupted by the Chair, who informed him that a rule of the Club positively prohibited an indulgence in profanity in the deliberations of the Club.

"I aint much used to swearin'," apologized the Deacon, "but when I think of them Injuns, blast their —— ——"

A rap of the President's stick on the stove warned the Deacon to desist, and he resumed the thread of his narrative.

"As I was sayin', my son, I was left afoot, and I didn't hev' no money to throw at the birds nuther; likewise not much what the preachers call earthly goods what I could swap for a horse. I left home kind of sudden like, and in course, bein' as I was goin' to Californy, whar the gold was strowed around thicker than chawed chestnuts, (leastways I thunk so them days, bein' young and green) I didn't carry along a very big load of the effecks what my father had in the States. Consekently, when I got to the Mormon settlements, I was busted flatter'n a cold slap-jack, and no means of continerin' the journey to the gold diggin's The man what had the one yoke of cattle, he give me the privilege of walkin' alongside the train till we'd strike some place whar thar was sumthin' like civilization, but he kept a-warnin' of me that he had a fam'ly of his own back in the States to support. Wal, one night, 'bout sundown we camped on the edge of a Mormon settlement, and while I was a-b'ildin' a fire with some brush and thinkin' of some way to trade a Mormon out of a horse, one of the Mormons belongin' in the settlement come up to look around and see if he could observe any broke down stock he could trade us out of for little or nothin' and recooperate it and swap it or sell it for a big figger to the next passel of emigrants as come along that way. Seein' as how we didn't have nothin' wuth tradin' for, the Mormon got to talkin' to us, and I let out that my fix was such as I couldn't travel much furder unless a horse was to drop out of Heaven right alongside of my tracks, bein' as I was already powerful footsore.

"The Mormon spoke up, an' he says:

"'Pard, us Latter Day Saints bean't much in the habit of hirin' Gentiles, bein' as its agin our creed, and positively forbid except in cases of needcessity, but if I could strike up a fa'r bargain with ye, I'd take the chances on hirin' ye to help dig a ditch.'

"I axed the cussed sinner as called hisself a saint, and actooally was that fool enough to think he was, what he'd call a fair bargain on the ditch business.

"'Wal,' he said, (countin' over his fingers like he was figgerin' in 'rithmatic) 'if you want to go to work at helpin' me at diggin' that ditch, I'll give ye thirty dollars a month, in trade, and your board.'

"Thirty dollars a month and board was powerful big wages them days for a young feller jest from the States, and I was half thinkin' the best thing would be to stay thar with them Mormons and git rich workin' for wages, and not take any chances on Californy. But, howsomever, that trade business was somethin' I didn't exactly understand, and not wishin' to be exposin' of my ignorance I didn't ask no questions, but jest said to the Mormon:

"'Pard, its a whack!'

"So, gittin' my few traps together out of the waggin and sayin' goodbye to the man who had let me walk alongside his ox-team, me and the

Mormon started for his ranch. As we was walkin' along I spoke up and I said to him:

"'What kind of trade be you goin' to give me for wages?'

"'Wal,' says he, 'you kin hev your choice of ruta-baga turnips, or sorghum syrup, or pun'kins.' I kind of begin to understand what was his meanin' of trade by this time, and was some dis'pinted, but didn't say nothin', only that I'd see after a while which of them produce thar was the best market for.

"Them days, the Mormons didn't hev no money, and the most of 'em didn't know what money was like when they seed it. If one of 'em was to git hold of a silver half-a-dollar from a emigrant he'd think it was as big as the hind-wheel on one of them big prairy schooners, and he'd take it down cellar and bury it for to keep for a hair-loom in the family. There warn't no money 'mongst 'em, and they did most of their business by this here trade system.

"I didn't hev no use for ruta-bagas, or sorghum syrup, or for pun'kins, but I could trade em off, and keep a-tradin' and go on transactin' business till I got hold of somethin' I could swap for a horse and a little flour and bacon and a few matches, so as I could continner my journey to Californy; cause I'd come to this country to git gold, and didn't want to stay thar 'mongst them Mormons and git rich in vegetables, and, maybe, in the course of time hev several or more wives on my hands."

At this point in his narrative the Deacon stopped, and simultaneously every member of the Club straightened up in his chair. Corrugating his brow and blinking indignantly at the Chair, the Deacon said:

"My son, I hope my story aint gittin' teedjus?"

"Not much, Deekin—what made you think that?" returned the Chair.

"Wal," resumed the Deacon, "I thought I heerd a snore."

"'Twarn't me"—"nor me"—"nor me," spoke up the members, one after another, all except Mr. Truefact, who was trying to stutter out those words, when the President cut off his part of the debate by saying:

"Deekin, I'm surprised at you, thinkin' that any member of this here Club would go to sleep on you, when you was a-tellin' of such a int'restin' story."

The Deacon apologized for his suspicions by saying that his hearing was not what it was in days gone by, and resumed his lie:

"As I was sayin', I hired out to this Mormon for thirty dollars a month, in trade and board, hopin' one day to git a horse and jump the country.

"It was one of them grasshopper years in Utah, when the hoppers was swoopin' down on the country and eatin' up the last green thing on a ranch inside of a single night. They hadn't got to this here Mormon's ranch yit, but he knew they was comin', and which way they was trav'lin', and his objeck in hirin' me was to help him stand off the hoppers. He had an ijee, which was to dig a big ditch around his ranch, and when the grasshoppers come, to git out all his wimmin and childrin and the hired hands, and fight the insecks inter this ditch, and turn his chickins in among 'em.

"I caught hold of his ijee, and he showed me how it was as much int'restin' to me to keep off the hoppers as 'twas to him; so bein' as if they ate up all the craps, whar was my trade he was goin' to pay me?

"Wal, we got that ditch finished two days afore the grasshoppers come in sight, but you bet we could see 'em comin', and lookin' like a great big black cloud, what was hidin' the sun and makin' the air as dark as if it was jest comin' on night. We could see 'em before they got to us, but when they got thar we was ready for 'em.

"The Mormon, he had all his family out, guardin' the ditch at the side whar the hoppers was comin', and they was all heeled with a big bunch of willers tied to a stick, so as to bat at the insecks and fight 'em inter the ditch—and the chickens was all on the ground waitin' for the trouble to start, and cluckin' and crowin' and lookin' up inter the sky, jest like they knowed what was comin'.

"My boss was somethin' of a family man, hevin' sev'ral wives, and consekently a few children, which, bein' as they're Mormons in that country, nobody don't make no objection to. And when all the wives and all the children and me and the boss was all out on the ground together, with our brooms, we made quite a 'spectable outfit, what was enough to scare the grasshoppers and cause 'em to slew 'round to the next ranch, purvidin' they had as much sense as a last year's bird's-nest, which, in course, grasshoppers aint.

"When the hoppers come near enough for the queen hopper to see that thar was somethin' green on the ground, she give the order to light, and the whole raft of 'em commenced droppin' t'ords the ground."

[The Deacon was so absorbed in his story that he did not notice a s'norous sound that filled the room, and failed to observe that every member of the Club was, to all appearance, sound asleep.]

"But we was ready for 'em, and commenced fightin' 'em off and knockin' 'em inter the ditch as soon as the front ranks got in reach.

"The chickens was thar, too; thar was a band or 'bout two hundred layin' hens and sev'ral roosters, to say nothin' of a lot of pullets, and they jest waded inter them thar grasshoppers.

"Happenin' to git tired, I stopped beatin' a minnit to git my wind, and see how them chickens was makin' it with them hoppers.

"My son, you may b'leeve it or not, jest as you like—'cause this is a free country—but right thar afore my eyes them chickens was *turnin' inter grasshoppers*.

"Yes, sir, sure's you live, they was eatin' so many of them thar hoppers that they didn't have time to die-jest in 'em, and they was absorbin' of the elements of them hoppers and turnin' inter great big grasshoppers. big as a layin' hen, right afore my very eyes.

"I give the alarm, and the fam'ly quit fightin' the hoppers what was in the air to look at the hoppers what had been chickens; and when the man seed what was going on he said he didn't care nothin' 'bout the chickens 'cause the grasshoppers was concentrated anyway; and so, 'cordin' to his orders, we all pitched in and killed them grasshoppers what but a short time before was hens.

"Now, gentlemen, I'd like your opinion on that lie, which, howsomever, it aint, bein' a sollum, actooal, positive fact."

The only reply was a concerted snore, from the entire Club, so deep and loud that it seemed as if it would lift the ceiling off the room; which, as Old Dad avers, did actually move up a couple of inches.

Deacon Toughly arose from his seat, and blinked at each member of the Club in turn. Then he struck his cane violently on the floor, and his eyes opened, and he absolutely glared upon the sleepers; and when his terrible wrath found vent in words, he said:

"I wish I may be —— into —— in a minnit if I was twenty years younger if I couldn't whip every —— —— scrub as belongs to this here dod-rotted, dod-blasted, —— —— little old one-horse —— —— Lyin' Club with one hand tied behind me, the hull —— —— dod-blasted raft of 'em from A to izzard."

Echo answered but a snore; several of them, in fact.

And the Deacon stalked out of the Sazerac, and never again entered its portals during the remainder of his stay in Austin. He don't live in Austin now. He left here for San Francisco to sell his mines, failing in which he secured an engagement as a "frightful example" to a street vendor of a marvelous soap, that would take grease out of cloth in the twinkling of an eye; and for all I know he is still the center of an admiring crowd on some San Francisco street corner, while the soap-vendor displays the wonderful effects of his compound on the lappel of his (the Deacon's) coat, and illustrates by the contrast between the clean oasis, and the other portions of the garment, the detersive qualities of his wares.

Rejected.

When the Deacon was out of the room, and the door closed behind him, the Club awoke as by a common impulse.

"A little warm, aint he?" remarked the President.

"I wouldn't be as hot as him, no, not for all the mines in Lander Hill," observed the Secretary.

There was a general expression of sentiment on the Deacon's case, all of which was to the effect that, though a good and an original "cusser," he couldn't take a joke worth a cent, and his lying qualities were very far below par.

The question being put on the election of the Deacon, he was unanimously rejected, and the Chair, returning the Secretary's pipe, which he had borrowed for this occasion only, announced that the Club stood adjourned for the evening.

A Communication.

"If the Club isn't got no objection, I'd like to read a little communication," said the President, at a recent meeting of the Sazerac Lying Club.

Every member of the Club, with the exception of Mr. Truefact, responded in a moment by saying, "read ahead, old man," and while Mr. T. was struggling to signify his acquiescence in words, the Chair took from his pocket a newspaper, and unfolding the sheet, said:

"Gentlemen, I want to read a communication contained in this here paper; I want you all to lissen to it and not be interruptin' of me, and when I conclood I want you all to give an opinyon on the merits of the case and decide if you believe it, even if 'tis printed in a newspaper," whereupon he proceeded to read as follows:

"'A rancher in this vicinity planted some parsnips on his ranch, and while the vegetables were growing they threw out such enormous roots that when they were ripe he found it impossible to pull them by the ordinary method. As an experiment, he rigged a four-fold purchase to one of the plants, and when by this means he succeeded in pulling it, its exit was followed by a strong flow of water, and the fortunate rancher found that he had developed a valuable artesian well.' "

"That aint nothin'," exclaimed Dad, before the Chair could complete the sentence, "I pause for a reply."

"D-d-did y-y-you ev-v-v-er s-s-s-see s-s-such a oc-c-c-c-ur-r-rin-ince?" spoke up Mr. Truefact.

"I don't believe a word of it," growled the Doubter.

"Oh, shet up, you fellers," resumed Dad, "and I'll convince you that that thar communication as was jest read by the Chair don't amount to a hill of beans.

"The most of you's bin in Californy, and you know it gits away with the world for big vegetables, and all that sort of bizness. Why, when I was farmin' in the airly days in Sacramento Valley, we used to plant beets, so's we could make sure of water to irrigate the craps in the dry seasons. Some years thar's plenty water in Californy, but they has 'bout as many dry years as they has wet ones, and when thar comes a drought the hull face of the country's burnt up like a Arizony desert. Wal, we used to plant these here beets, and when we didn't have no water we'd jest rig a block and tackle to the branches of the vegetable, and put from four to six yoke of cattle to the other end of the string, and commence proddin' and punchin' and yellin' at them oxen, and they'd yank out that thar beet and a stream of water measurin' from fifteen to twenty miner's inches, and we'd chop the beet up inter cord-wood and pile it away for winter."

"Why that aint much different from the newspaper yarn — the facks in the case bein' 'bout the same," sneeringly remarked the Doubter.

"S'posin' it aint?" returned Dad; "don't it corroborate what the paper says, and show to a sartainty that such things aint impossible?"

The Doubter said he couldn't see it; but the Chair interposed and prevented an exhibition of feeling among the members by putting his hand on his hip, and saying:

"Gentlemen, don't forgit that you be gentlemen."

But there was not that fraternity of feeling which the Chair said it would like to see existing among members of so high-toned, moral, and respectable an organization as the Sazerac Lying Club. He was sorry to see a disposition among members to question the veracity of each other's lies, and as he didn't believe there could, under existing circumstances, be a free interchange of opinion, and a fitting communion of sentiment, and as the congeniality which in the past had so happily marked the Club's discussions seemed "a little off" this evening, he would declare the Club adjourned, and hoped members would drown whatever feelings of rancor they might possess, in the flowing bowl, at his expense.

And the rancorous feelings were duly drowned.

Indisposed.

Before calling the Club to order, at a recent regular meeting, the President pointed to a strip of red flannel which was bound around his neck, and explained to the members that he was troubled with a sore throat. It was not an ordinary sore throat, but he experienced a feeling as of some obstruction having lodged in his swallowing department.

"P-p-p'rap-p-s its one of-f-f y-y-your l-l-l-lies s-t-t-uck c-c-cross-w-w-ays," remarked Mr. Truefact.

"Mebbe he was tryin' to tell the truth," said the Doubter to Old Dad, *sotto voce.*

"Nothin' of the kind, gentlemen, nothin' of the kind; no insinooations if you please. The affliction under which this here Chair is now sufferin' is easily accounted for; it arises from an act of improodence on the Chair's own part. I went to bed last night without takin' of my yoosual 'night-cap' of a little stimoolant, with some sugar into it, bein' as such negleck allers makes a diff'rence and affects my physical constitooshun for the worser. If the Club is ready for bizness we will dispense with callin' the roll, and proceed with

"The Lie of the Evening."

"Did you fellers see or hear anything of that whirlwind to-day?" asked Dad, as a preliminary to the "regular lie."

"I noticed somethin' of a disturbance of the atmosphere," remarked the Chair.

"She was pritty bad up on Lander Hill," observed the Aye-and-No Member.

"I was out-doors all day," said the Doubter, "and seed sev'ral small whirlwinds, but none of 'em big enough to amount to much."

"I didn't expect you to know anything about it," said Dad, (addressing himself to the Doubter) "you never do happen to see anything that other people sees. But I ask this here Club as a body if they knowed there was a big whirlwind in town to-day?"

All the members present, with the exception of the Doubter, said they "knowed."

"Wal, then," resumed Dad, "none of you didn't see the worst part of it. I was over to Marshall Cañon doin' some assessment work on an old claim I located over thar in sixty-three, and I happened to look over to'rds a ranch that's close by, and I see that whirlwind comin' over the hill from town. It was gainin' and gainin' every foot it traveled, and was comin' straight for whar I was workin', and I made up my mind it was about time for me to git. So I got. I went straight for that ranch as fast as I could travel, but the whirlwind kept gainin' on me, and kept growin' taller and taller, and by the time I struck the door of the house on the ranch the top of the whirler was clean out of sight, and the foot of it must have been as much as a hunderd foot through. Whirlwinds is a common enough thing in this here country, and you've all on you seed lots of 'em, but I don't think any of you's ever seed one like this as I'm tellin' about. When I got to the house I was out of its track, and thar was a red-headed woman standin' in the door, skeer't so bad she couldn't talk straight, and I told her if she had any children or other portable articles lyin' around loose, she better corral 'em quick, 'cause whirlwinds aint no respecters of persons. But she said she didn't have only one baby, and that died of the measles over in Californy two years ago. Gentlemen, you've all seen these here whirlwinds pick up pieces of paper, and shingles, and small children, and loose wagon-wheels, and such trifles, and it stands to reason that if a common, ordinary whirler can pick up such things as them, a bigger one can carry off bigger things, can't it?"

The Philosopher said that such a hypothesis was strictly in accordance with the rules of logic, besides being in accordance with the inexorable laws of cause and effect.

"Certingly, certingly," continued Dad. "Wal, you see, this here whirler was a good deal bigger than ordinary, and as it come swoopin' along the ground, me and the woman being out of its track, and consekently out of harm's way—it was makin' straight for a cow that was grazin' on a little grass patch close to the house——"

"D-d-d-did it c-c-c-carry up t-t-he c-c-c-ow?" interrupted Mr. Truefact.

"Who said so, smarty?" returned Dad, angrily. "No, it didn't carry up no cow; it missed the cow by about a sixteenth of a inch, and tackled a great big quartz-wagon that had been abandoned in the cañon on account of the tire on the off hind-wheel comin' off. And it jest lifted that thar wagon. Me and the woman stood thar lookin at it, and it commenced to mount and mount, whirlin' around like a cork in a eddy, and a-trav'lin' a lively gait to the top of the great big column of dust. And all this time the whirler was a-goin' to'rds the summit of the range, and the last me and the woman see of it, it was crossin' the range and goin' straight for Smoky Valley, whar I s'pose it busted and dumped the wagon."

"Wal, I'll be blowed!" exclaimed Uncle John, who had come into the room and taken his seat during the course of the preceding narration.

All eyes were instantly turned on Uncle John, with a look of wondering inquiry; and the Chair inquired if it might take the liberty of asking the cause of the exclamation of surprise on the part of Uncle John.

"I'd jest as lief explain as not," said the old stage-driver; "you see, I thought it was a yearthquake. As I was drivin' the stage along over the road in Smoky Valley this afternoon, at a pi'nt 'bout two miles this side of the salt-marsh, thar suddently come a shock of the yearth, which lifted the coach clean off the road, with five passengers, the mail and express, and nine bars of bullion. We all thought it was a yearthquake; but since hearin' Dad tell about the whirlwind and the wagon, thar's a natural conclusion to be come to regardin' of the cause of the trouble. It must hev been that thar wagon strikin' ground what shook up the yearth in Smoky Valley, so's to make things that warm for the stage. Thar aint most nothin' but can't be accounted for, when you know the circumstances as caused it."

When Uncle John had concluded, Dad cast a triumphant glance at the Doubter, who muttered something about Uncle John not being any better than other folks, even if he was a stage-driver; but the Chair poured oil upon the troubled waters by the relation of a reminiscence of

How the San Francisco Vigilantes Originated.

"Mr. Truefact," said he, addressing himself to that individual, "don't you know you've got a mighty bad habit of anticipatin' the lies of members of this here Club? Now I actually b'leeve that if it hadn't been for you interruptin' of Dad when he was tellin' 'bout that whirlwind, that cow would hev' went up in it over the range inter Smoky Valley, instead of that air wagon, and we'd had Uncle John tellin' of a shower of meat, like the newspapers say they hed back in Kaintucky a short time back. Yearthquakes isn't uncommon in this country, but showers of meat is; so jest see what a phenomena (I b'leeve they call it) a little interruption can spoil!"

The Philosopher explained that "phenomenon" was the correct word to use in such connection.

"Wal, I know what I mean, anyway," observed the Chair, with an indignant look at the Philosopher; "and my remarks about interruptions can be taken by one member jest as well as another. But to resume:

"Now, Mr. Truefact, p'raps you're not aware of it, that jest such a man as you was the starter of the Vigilance Committee in San Francisco in the early days."

Mr. Truefact endeavored to stutter his surprise at such a statement.

"Yes, sir, jest such a stutterin' cuss as you started the Vigilantys to work. It come about in this ways:

"In the airly days in San Francisco thar always used to be a terrible big rush to the Post-Office when the steamers come in — 'cause the pioneers, bein' young them days, was in angziety to git letters from their folks to home, and to git little billy-duxes from the gals they left behind 'em in the States when they come out here to pick up gold by the bushel off the top of the ground, with no trouble only the stoqpin' over for it. But you all know how that was yourself, and that when we got whar the gold was, it took some powerful hard work to git sight of a color; that is, in most cases, bein' as I've knowed men to take out as much as six hundred dollars to the pan, and a long ways to bed-rock, to say nothin' of what's bin taken out with rockers, and toms, and sluice-boxes.

"Wal, as I was a-sayin', thar always used to be a great rush to the Post-Office when the steamer come in from the States; and so's thar wouldn't be no confusion, every man as was expectin' letters was compelled to take his place in a long line, and stay thar till his turn come to git to the winder whar they handed out the letters. I never lived much in 'Frisco myself, but I've heern tell from the boys what used to go down thar to git a chance to spend their dust, that sometimes a man would be 'bleeged to stay two hull days in that thar line afore his turn would come at the winder. I s'pose they used to carry grub in their pockets to last 'em the shift. Likewise I've heern tell that many a man made a homestake those days by standin' in the line till he got up pritty close to the winder and then sellin' out his chance for all the way from an ounce up to five hundred dollars to fellers as had more money than time and was in a big hurry for their letters, and then resoomin' his place ag'in at the tail end of the line, and sellin' out ag'in when he got close up—like you've seen fellers sell their chance for a shave on a Sunday mornin' in a barber shop, only the figgers isn't so big.

"One mornin' the steamer come in 'bout ten o'clock, and thar was the usual rush to the Post-Office, and long afore the winders opened thar was strings of men reachin' way off for as much as a dozen blocks, ev'ry man waitin' his turn to ask for letters. The fust man to git to the 'M to Z' winder was a Slavonyon, (Sclavonian) which was mighty thick in Californy in the airly days, hevin' come in with the first rush. This here Slavonyon kep' a fruit-stand down on the wharf close to the office, and consekently got thar one of the fust. He hed a name as long as a shovel-handle, and stuttered so bad he couldn't even sneeze without stammerin'. When the winder was shot up, and the clark stood thar ready to hand out letters, this here Slavonyon started to say his name, and commenced a-stutterin' and a-stammerin', but he couldn't make it. He hed his rights, like any other man as wasn't a nigger or a Injin or a Chinaman, and so the crowd didn't kill him then and thar, but kep' on patient like, waitin' for him to purnounce his name. Twelve o'clock come, and he hedn't managed to purnounce only the fust letter, which was a V, and the clark was a-holdin' of the V letters in his right hand, a spittin' on his left thumb, ready to sort over the bundle for this Slavonyon's letter. But the clock stroke twelve, and a post-office clark is like time and the tide—don't wait for his lunch for no man—and down come the winder.

"The crowd was pritty riley by this time, and a merchant what had a lot of goods on the steamer, and didn't know how much profit to charge on 'em till he'd got his letters about 'em, offered the Slavonyon a thousand dollars in good, clean, bankable dust for his chance; but the Slavonyon wouldn't lissen to no offer of money, and when the winder opened ag'in he resoomed tryin' to purnounce his name. But 'twarn't no go; and when six o'clock come and the office shet up for the night, he'd only got as fur as the fust syllable of that forty-rod name of his'n."

"This was more'n the crowd could stand, and that night they held a citizens' meetin' on the plaza and adopted resolutions that the city's safety was in danger, and 'pinted a committy to take that Slavonyon out and hang him. 'Cordin'ly, the committy went down to the Post-Office, whar that Slavonyon was standin' with his face agin' the 'M to Z' winder, waitin' for the office to open next mornin', and snatched him bald-headed up to the City Hall, and runnin' a beam out from the roof of the buildin', they hung him as dead as a nit.

"This was the starter of the Vig'lance Committy, and hevin' their blood up from the hangin' of this stutterin' Slavonyon, they waded in and hung and druv out all the other dangerous characters out of the State. And now, Mr. Truefact, let this be a warnin' to you in the future!"

"Yes, let it be a warnin'," said the Aye-and-No Member solemnly.

Mr. Truefact rose to his feet and commenced working his lips, as if striving to give utterance to the emotion which was evidently working within him; but the Chair brought its cane down on the stove in so emphatic a manner that it woke up the Philosopher, who had fallen asleep during the relation of the history of the Vigilantes. Then looking sternly at the struggling stutterer, the Chair announced:

"No explanation is necessary from Mr. Truefact nor no other member, and I declar' this here Club adjourned for the evenin'."

The Chair's *fiat* in the matter of adjournment is, by a rule of the Club, unquestionable and undebatable, and the members sadly arose from their seats, and as the barkeeper began to turn down the lamps, they departed through the door in a mournful procession.

A Lie-Brary.

On calling the Club to order, the Chair announced that, as the subject of a library for the Club had been broached, he would like to hear an expression from the members as to the most feasible plan of raising the money for the purpose—whether by assessment, or by voluntary contributions from the members. During the discussion which arose on this point, there was considerable feeling manifested by the springing of the question as to who should act as Lie-brarian, each member claiming that he possessed the peculiar qualifications necessary for that office; and the Chair, being appealed to, decided that, as the Club in itself constituted all the lie-brary required, and each member was a natural born lie-brarian, further debate was unnecessary on the subject, and the Club would keep on in the old groove, relying, as before, on the newspapers and religious tracts for inspiration.

This discussion being ended, the Chair announced that the Philosopher had recently been making some scientific experiments, and if he (the Philosopher) had no objection, the Club would like to hear from him as to their object and the degree of success attending them. Whereupon, the Philosopher took the floor, and related the details of

A Scientific Experiment.

The Philosopher stated that he had recently become impressed with the idea that there was some reason in the theory that the discharge of gunpowder created conditions in the atmosphere which resulted in rain, and had therefore set his mind to work to perfect a machine which, at small outlay, should accomplish this end. In pursuance of this plan, he purchased a quantity of detonating powder, gunpowder, blasting powder, nitro-glycerine, and gun-cotton. His idea was that by mixing these various explosives he would create a compound which, while occupying a small space, would exert a greater force than a much larger bulk of either operated with singly. Procuring an old quicksilver flask and some fuse, he started for Birch Creek to make his first experiment. Arrived on the ground, he placed his explosives in the flask, which he set on top of a high mountain, and attaching a fuse about a mile in length he went to the other end of the fuse and touched her off. Pretty soon he thought he heard something, *and he did.* The mountain was lifted just fourteen feet from its foundation, by actual measurement, and it came down with such force as to jolt him off the rock on which he was seated. In a few moments a cloud appeared in the sky, which each moment grew heavier, until in a little while the weight of the water it contained was too great for the atmosphere to bear up, and it came down with a thud. After the experimenter had noticed how the entire bed of the cañon was washed out, and saw four or five hills jumbled up together in the valley below, he realized that he had created a cloud-burst instead of a shower. The experiment had satisfied him, however, that his principle was correct, and he was convinced that the fault of the machine was that its effect was too concentrated—that it must scatter more. He announced to the Club that he intended to resume his experiments at the first favorable opportunity; but the Chair said he hoped the member would not insist on continuing. He (the Chair) believed in the theory, and thought it might be accomplished if a man would go to Death Valley or the heart of Africa to try the experiments. But here in this inhabited land it was dangerous; there was a liability that in attempting to create rain the experimenter would desolate the country with cloud-bursts; and he, (the Chair) for one, would frown down and rebuke in his sternest tones any further attempts at interference with the ordinary course of nature's affairs.

The other members unanimously coincided with the President's view of the case, even the Doubter declaring that there was already more water in the country than was actually needed for home consumption; and as for him, he had got along without it for years, and thought he could keep on doing without it till the cold finger of death beckoned him to his heavenly home.

Whereupon, the Philosopher said: "'A prophet is not without honor save in his own country,'" and that he had thought the tendency of the age was to seek for more light through the revelations of science. But as for him, he'd like to know what show Darwin, or Herbert Spencer, or Draper, or Tyndall, or "any of them scientific cusses" would have in a Club like this, and he did not know but he had a big notion to resign.

"Small favors thankfully received, large ones in proportion," sarcastically remarked the President.

"Yes," returned the Philosopher angrily, "you'd like me to resign so that you fellers could go on deridin' science, and tellin' of yarns which is in contradiction of all scientific truth, and puts to the blush any man who has read and studied and sought to probe into the depths of the illimitable that he might yank out therefrom some great and startling fact that would inure to the benefit of our posterity for ages and ages yet to come. But I won't quit; I'll jest keep on settin' here, listenin' to your outrageousness, and your contradictions of science, jest so's I may act as a check upon the miserable fallacies you're in the habit of puttin' forth to the detriment and injury of the good, the noble, the true, and the great, which aint found in nothin' but the revelations of science."

"Does the gentleman desire that Mr. Truefact—a brother member, and as good a man of his inches as ever made a track on top of the green yearth—does he desire that he shall git the lock-jaw?" sternly inquired the President.

A glance at the Stuttering Member revealed him with his arms extended and his mouth wide open, with jaws firmly fixed, and eyes protruding from their sockets.

"You see, gentlemen," continued the President, "Mr. Truefact, in attemptin' a reply to the Philosopher, has got stuck on one of them big words made use of by the gentleman in that thar unparliamentary language of his'n to'rds the Club. Swaller it, Mr. Truefact, swaller it, if you can't git it out."

By a motion of the hand, Mr. Truefact indicated that he required some fluid with which to wash it down; and the Club went into Committee of the Whole to lead him to the bar, where Mr. T. soon recovered sufficiently to announce that he would take it "straight."

The other members, also, renewed the assurances of their distinguished consideration, and the President, after warning the Philosopher against the use of unparliamentary language in future discussions, declared the Club adjourned for the evening.

Artificial Incubation.

"We was discussin' of science the other evenin', when brother Ananias Truefact come near to gittin' the lock-jaw, and would a' got it, too, if it hadn't been for remedies bein' handy."

Thus spoke the Secretary, as the sound of the words "I'm here, you bet," from the member whose name came last on the roll, died on the air.

"Yes," said the President, "and I hope, Mr. Seccertary, that you aint goin' to forgit yourself so far as to go out of the strict line of your dooty, as laid down in our Constitution and By-laws, and ring in no jaw-smashin', confusin' words onto this here Club."

"Not much," replied the Secretary; "that aint my style. Still, at the same time, as I may here remark, I'm somethin' of a stoodint of science myself. Has any of you gentlemen read in the papers about that thar preacher over to Reno as has throwed up preachin' the Gospil to go to raisin' chickens by hatchin' of 'em himself, bein' as it pays better?"

Several members responded that they had read concerning the matter to which the Secretary referred; and then that official, addressing himself to the Chair, said:

"Now, Mr. President, I want to ask you if you think this here thing can be did?"

The Chair announced that it had no knowledge of any provision in the By-laws of the Club which compelled the presiding officer to commit himself for or against any particular theory that might be advanced; but at the same time, for his part, he preferred chickens that had been produced in the natural and old-fashioned way.

"Wal," resumed the Secretary, "I don't believe it can be did, 'cause I've tried it myself, and it wouldn't work.

"As I was standin' in the door of my cabin a few weeks back, this here member as calls hisself the Philosopher, and slings dictionary around like as if he was the man as made it, come along, and we got to talkin' about hatchin' chickens in what they call the artifishal way. I didn't take no stock in the thing, but he said it could be did as easy as rollin' off a log. So I ask't him how they did it, thinkin' that what one man could do might be did by another, and I couldn't lose nothin' by tryin' of it, and might afore long have chicken three times a day for jest buyin' the eggs. 'Wal,' he said, 'the eggs must be exposed to a certain temperature'—them's his words, not mine—'and in the course of the proper time they would go through the pro-cess of incubation, and when the chicken was done it would, 'cordin' to the natural law that everything in this here world has a instink to struggle for existence—come bouncin' out'n the shell like it was shot from a gun.' He said he b'leeved a good way would be to get a egg and put it in a bottle and cork it up tight, so's the chicken couldn't git away when it was hatched, and to keep the business at a hundred and thirty degrees of heat by one of these common, ordinary thermometers, such as you can see round most any place.

"Now, gentlemen, my eddicashun aint bin neglected so's I can't read how cold or how hot it is by the thermometer; and as I'm a man what himself is somewhat given to reas'nin' from cause to effeck, I pritty soon dropped on it how I could run the thermometer up to a hundred and thirty.

"I told the Philosopher I was goin' to try of this here experiment, and tell him how the old thing worked, and I'm tellin' of it to him this minnit."

"I s'pose you succeeded in achievin' a scientific triumph, and in demonstratin' the fact that an incubatin' heat applied to a egg must, of necessity, and strictly in accordance with immutable laws, incubate somethin', didn't you?" inquired the Philosopher.

"Yes," replied the Secretary, "it incubated somethin', but let me continner my story.

"Procurin' of some Salt Lake eggs—ranch eggs is dear, but Salt Lake eggs is good enough for om'lets and tryin' experiments—I put one of 'em inter the bottle, and set it on a box, and rammed the cork in tight.

Then to fix the thermometer up to the right figger was the next question. I found by holdin' a lighted match up ag'in the quicksilver in the little glass ball in the bottom of the thermometer, I could run her up to a hundred and thirty pretty quick, but I couldn't be standin' thar holdin' a match for three weeks. But I got a bright idee.

"I hired two Injins, and divided 'em into a day shift and a night shift. Then I pasted a piece of white paper on the wall 'long side of the hundred and thirty mark—cause Injins can't read figgers, as you all know—and then I lit a candle and showed the Injins how the quicksilver would run up to that thar paper, instructin' of 'em to take away the candle when it tried to crawl up higher, and put it back when it dropped down lower. After drillin' of 'em a while they dropped on the bizness, and onc't they got their hands in they could keep her rangin' about a hundred and thirty quite reg'lar.

"Wal, I kep those Injins at this bizness for three weeks stiddy, one on the day shift and the other buck on the night shift; and when the time come when thar ought to be a chicken or a addled egg under the old system of hatchin' with hens, I went to look for my chicken, but it wasn't thar."

"May I ask the gentleman a question?" interrupted the Doubter, at this point.

"Certainly," responded the Chair.

"Wal," resumed the Doubter, "Mr. Seccertary, how did you git that thar egg into that thar bottle?"

"Jest oiled her and crammed her in," was the reply.

"Ah, I see," interposed the Philosopher, "by so doin' you brought the constituents of the egg under a certain compression, as it were, thereby destroyin' of its incubatin' capacity."

"I don't know nothin' 'bout what you're talkin' about," said the Secretary to the Philosopher, "but I do know mighty well that the experiment produced somethin' as wasn't in the bottle when I put the egg in thar."

"Ah, now we're comin' at one of the results of science!" exclaimed the Philosopher triumphantly. "What was it, Mr. Secretary, that the experiment produced in the bottle, as wasn't in thar when you put the egg in?"

"Yes, what was it?" cried the entire Club in chorus.

"*It was a powerful bad smell,*" replied the Secretary, with emphasis, and as he spoke he drew from his pocket a bottle. Extracting the cork, he held up the bottle and said:

"Those as don't b'lieve it can smell for hisself."

But the Club needed no evidence beyond that which came into their possession simultaneously with the drawing of the cork. It was the evidence of their own senses—that is, of one of their senses, the sense of smell; and as the odor from the bottle began to permeate the air of the room, there was a general stampede of the Club for the door; and the barkeeper stood not on the order of his going, but cleared the counter at one jump and went out of the door as if he had important business with a man in the street, and only the sixteenth part of a second to go.

After the members of the Club had induced the Secretary to come outside for a minute, and they had talked with him, and argued the case, and remonstrated with him for about an hour, and he had been carried home on a mattress by his friends, the barkeeper said he guessed he would take the adjournment into his own hands to-night, and thereupon declared the Club adjourned.

And as the members moved away from the door, the President told the Philosopher that this was all his fault, and he might, between then and the next meeting, consider himself a standing committee on disinfectants.

A Martyr.

At the meeting succeeding the one last recorded, the Secretary appeared with his head swathed in bandages, and a very woe-begone expression on so much of his countenance as was not covered by sticking plaster and blue marks.

"Mr. Secretary," said the Chair, addressing itself to the scribe, "'pears to me as if you must hev been engaged in a animated argument with the crank of a windlass."

"Looks like he'd been run up into the sheaves in a h'istin' works at some of the mines, yanked round up thar a few times, then drapped a few hundred feet down the shaft and come into contact with the piston of a steam pump," observed Old Dad.

"Mebbe he's bin examinin' of a thrashin' machine while it was a-goin', to see what constituted its active principle," suggested the Philosopher.

"Gentlemen," spoke up Mr. Thirsty, "you's, all of you, clean out of the way. *I'll* tell you what our worthy Secretary looks like—he looks like a man as hasn't had a drink for upwards of two mortal hours; and actin' on that hypothesis, I move you, Mr. President, that afore calling' this here Club to order, we all adjourn in a body to the bar and partake of a little refreshin' stimulant—me standin' the expense."

And the Club adjourned as requested.

When the members resumed their seats the Secretary rose to a question of privilege.

"State your question of privilege," said the Chair, "and if you've got anything ag'in any member here present, you better wait till you git inter fightin' condition afore makin' a detailed statement of your grievances to this here Club."

"Mr. President and gentlemen of the Club," answered the Secretary, "I only wish to state that in gazin' upon this here noble form which now stands afore you, you're lookin' at a martyr to Science."

"I b'leeve, Mr. President," here interposed the Doubter, "that the meanin' of a martyr is one of them fellers what gits the worst of a fight, aint it?"

"Somethin' to that effeck," replied the President, "but I must put a end to personal explanations and take up the regular order of bizness, which is under the head of 'reports of committys'; be thar any committys ready to report?"

"As cheerman of the Committy on Disinfectants," replied the Philosopher, "I beg leave to submit a report."

"Does the gentleman have leave?" asked the Chair.

"He do," replied the Aye-and-No Member, unanimously.

"The gentleman will proceed with his report."

The Disinfectant Report.

"Wal, then, Mr. President and gentlemen, 'cordin' to the instructions of the Chair, which 'pinted me on this committy at the last precedin' meetin' held previous to this one, I hev made a investigation of the subjeck of disinfectin'. On consultin' the authorities, I find that one of the most powerful and at the same time most innercent and rejuvenatin' of stuff for disinfectin' purposes is whisky."

"Taken in'nardly, I s'pose?" interrupted Mr. Thirsty.

"That's 'cordin' to the circumstances," resumed the Philosopher; "thar be cases whar it's bin known to hev a grat'fyin' effeck by rubbin' of it in through the pores of the skin."

"I'd like to know," angrily interrupted the Chair, "if the gentleman knows what he's talkin' about; he was 'pinted a committy on somethin' to remove the bad effecks of ancient eggs from this here room, and here he's reportin' on stimulants. Do you know, sir, that you're so fur out of order that you'll hev' to step 'round powerful lively to git in ag'in?"

The Philosopher humbly explained that he supposed whisky was good for most everything, and the Club by unanimous consent sustained him in that opinion, and politely requested the Chair to "shut up."

And the Chair said he always gave way to the verdict of the majority—but that there was not a member of the Club who could get away with him single-handed; and then he asked:

"What's the next order of bizness, Mr. Seccertary?"

The Secretary replied that, so far as he was concerned, the order of business was to go home to bed; for he was suffering so with the headache that he was liable to tell the truth at any moment.

This the Chair decided to be a sufficient excuse for absence; and he hoped that all members who might at any time be similarly afflicted would not endanger the integrity of the Club, and strike a fatal blow at the principles on which it was founded, by continuing to take part in its deliberations while in such an irresponsible condition.

The Secretary was thereupon excused, and took his departure for his virtuous couch.

Pioneer Prices.

"Has any member anything to offer for the 'Good of the Order'?" asked the Chair, after the Secretary had taken his departure.

"I don't know of anything, unless some of us orders the drinks," ventured the Aye-and-No Member, who felt that it devolved on him, and him alone, to answer this question.

"The gentleman has unanimous consent to adopt his own suggestion," decided the Chair.

The Aye-and-No Member duly made his jingle on the bar, and when the members returned to their seats he made his maiden speech in the Club. He said:

"Gentlemen, times aint what they used to be in the airly days. I remember when I was minin' on the north fork of Feather River, I had a sack that full of dust and that long that I could treat the house and pay four bits a drink easier than I can treat this Club and put up only two bits a drink now."

"Yes, prices have degenerated since then," sighed the Chair, as he sadly drew out the "draft" of the stove, and blew his emotion into the ashes. Then, running his coat-sleeve across his nose, he said:

"Why, many's the time I've paid a dollar in dust for jest one plug of tobacker."

"Yes," spoke up Mr. Thirsty, "but what you had to pay for tobacker and whisky, and them necessaries, warn't nothin' compared to what you was charged for the luxuries. Jest think of flour at a dollar a pound! And for such a thing as green truck—why a load of vegetables was worth more as a claim what was payin' an ounce a day to the man! You know the boys in them days used to think that if they didn't git some kind of vegetables to eat onc't in a while they was liable to git the scurvy; and I've knowed some fellers gittin' of it, too, and a powerful tough sickness it is, fust thing you know. These days, when we can git the best Kaintucky whisky they can make in San Francisco for two bits a drink, right up here in the mountains, and taters is as plentiful as grasshoppers in Missoury, we don't stop to think how it was them times, when everything was so high."

"But thar was more money to the man than there is now," interrupted the Doubter.

"Yes, that's so, sure enough. A twenty-dollar piece warn't bigger nor a bit them days," replied Mr. Thirsty.

"But, as I was sayin', things was high. When I was livin' up at Dead Man's Flat, in Siskiyou County, some of the boys concluded to send down to Frisco by express for some ingyuns. Ingyuns, as some of you might be aware, was one of the biggest luxuries them days, bein' as they was skase in the country and good for keepin' off the scurvy. Finally the ingyuns come along by express C. O. D., and us boys what had made up the pool to send for 'em, went down to the express office, and I weighed out the dust to settle the bill, and it warn't no small dab of dust either, you can jest bet your life. Wal, we took the fruit up to my cabin, and the boys got around and we divided them squar and even, thar bein' one odd one over, which we put on One-eared Sam's pile, bein' as he was crippled, hevin' hed his ear bit off in the dog-gonedest, gamest, rough-and-tumble fight you ever seed. After the boys had gone, I counted my ingyuns and found I had nine of 'em, weighin' about three pounds apiece, and I commenced figgerin' on the cost of 'em. They cost three dollars a pound in Frisco, and the express freight on them was seven dollars a pound, and the more I kep' figgerin' on what them ingyuns cost for one of 'em, the madder I got, and finally I got so mad at myself that I went to town and got drunk, and got to buckin' at monte, and the fust thing I knowed I was strapped as flat as a shingle."

"I wish," said the Chair, "that our worthy Seccertary didn't have such a head put onto him, 'cause we might got him to figger how much each one of them ingyuns cost."

"I aint much at figgers myself," said Mr. Thirsty, "but bein' as I lost nine thousand dollars at monte, and was out sev'ral dollars in the fust place, I've bin figgerin' ever sence that them thar nine ingyuns costed about a thousand dollars each, sayin' nothin' of fractions."

"I s'pose," sneered the Doubter, "if it hadn't bin for them ingyuns you might have beat the monte game."

"I might if it had bin on the squar', which some of the boys told me when I got sober it wasn't.

"But these here remeniscences makes me dry; let's liquor up, and then I'm goin' to adjourn."

And they all liquored and the Club adjourned.

The Club Goes Behind the Record.

The following sketch, which appeared in the deliberations of the Club under circumstances hereinafter related, was written by Dan De Quille, author of "The Big Bonanza," and first appeared in the columns of the Virginia (Nevada) *Enterprise:*

He was a little old man with a restless black eye, and an equally restless jaw, the latter being constantly employed in the mastication of "fine cut," while the former found business in more directions than there are points to the compass. Iron-gray locks projected from under his slouched wool hat, and a beard of the same color straggled far down over the front of his blue woolen shirt. His tongue was about as active as his eye; his voice was shrill and piercing, and all his assertions were of the most positive description.

He carried a small bundle in a handkerchief, and shortly after taking his seat in the cars at Reno, for this city, he turned to the passengers nearest to him and said:

"Boys, there are some curious ups and downs in this country. One day you see a man's breeches half-soled with a flour sack, and the next he is a millionaire, rolling in his coach and four, lolling back and smoking a Havana cigar a foot long. There is a flip, a flap, and a flop, and he is back into his old breeches, driving a bull team.

"Three days ago I was not only well-to-do, but fixed for life, as I thought; but bang! she went, and I was flat on my back again. Not my fault—not a thing I could foresee and guard against—jist a reg'lar dispensation of Providence, as you may say. Never heard of such a thing before in my life."

"Bottom drop out of yer mine?" asked a passenger.

"Mine be blowed! No, I had a ten-pin alley, and was doing a land-office business—jist a-coinin' money, as you may say—when all went to smash in an instant."

"Burn out?" said a listener.

"Burn out! No, worse than that—blowed up!"

"Blowed up?"

"Yes, blowed up! It was the most terrific explosion, and one of the most curious you ever heard of. Some fellows come in one morning to roll a game for the drinks—my first customers that morning.

"My Chinaman, Hop Sun, set up the pins for 'em. One of the men took up a ball—one of the biggest—he took a short run and let drive—I can see him now. The ball no sooner struck the alley than there was a report that shook the whole building, tore up the planks, and shattered the glass in the windows. Each bound made by the ball down along the alley was followed by the same kind of report, and the same kind of reck and ruin. The ball reached the pins and made a 'ten-strike,' but at the same instant there came such an explosion as shook the whole town. All the pins were shivered to pieces, and splinters from them filled the wall and the roof. Nothing was left of my Chinaman but the soles of his shoes, about a foot of his tail, and a few strips of his blue cotton blouse. Not enough of him could be found for the coroner to sit on—he was literally exterminated by the shower of splinters from the alley and the pins."

"What caused the explosion?" asked some one.

"Well, you see, they had a certain kind of a club in my town that they wanted me to jine. I refused, tellin' 'em I wasn't qualified, and couldn't conscientiously become a member. This got the club down on me, and some of 'em slipped into my place at night and greased my alley and all the balls and pins with nitro-glycerine. Blast sich a town as Austin, and sich an organization as the Sàzerac Lyin' Club, anyhow! By their doin's I am ag'in a poor man—ag'in a wanderer, roamin' the wide world without a dime. Will any gentleman present please let me have the price of a square meal and a night's lodgings?"

The above was submitted by the Chair, who requested the Secretary to read it, and at the conclusion of the reading there was not a dry eye in the room.

"What do you think of that, gentlemen?" asked the Chair.

"I think it a slander on this here Club, and that there ain't a word of truth in it," answered the Doubter.

"And I'm of the 'pinion," said Mr. Thirsty, "that it's a bigger lie than was ever told in this here Club."

"What should be done to the man who perpetuates such a outr'jus insult on this here Club as that?" asked the President.

"Elect him a member," responded Dad.

"Gentlemen," observed the Chair, "you must remember that it's ag'in accordance with the most positive rules of our Constitution and By-laws to elect a editor a member of this Club."

"Let's go behind the record, then," returned Dad, "and elect him a member by unanimous acclamation."

"That would be a bad president, sir, a bad president," remarked the Doubter.

"Look a' here," said the Chair, while an angry frown darkened his forehead, "I thought I'd stated to this here Club on many previous occasions that any personal allusions to this here Chair was always out of order, and would be considered as liable to lead to serious consequences. What do you mean, sir, by a bad President? Haven't I always tried to do the squar thing since occupyin' of this here chair?"

The Doubter hastened to apologize, and to explain that he meant it would be a bad *prec*-e-dent for the Club to go outside of the Constitution.

"Ah, I see," said the Chair blandly, "the gentleman means a bad pre-*ce*-dent. We must make excuses for the way his eddication was neglected when he was a boy. But what is the will of the Club about 'lectin' this newspaper feller as wrote that article, as you've jest heerd read, to be a member of this here Club?"

"I renew my motion for his election by acclamation."

"Do I hear a second?" asked the Chair.

"I second the motion," replied the Aye-and-No Member.

"Then," announced the Chair, "I declare the newspaper feller duly 'lected as a member of this here Club, and the Secretary is instructed to notify him of his election as a member of this here Club, and to send him the bill for his 'nitiation and monthly dues; and Mr. Seccertary, you might say in a kind of a postcript to hurry along the coin, as the boys is powerful dry."

When the Chair had finished, the Doubter arose and wanted to know if the Club proposed to "take off the bridle" and "let down the bars" for the admission to membership of all the newspaper liars who might apply.

"Why," said he, "we might as well let in stock-brokers to onc't, and hev done with it. But if we let in the newspaper liars even, what show's a lot of old pioneers goin' to hev alongside of them when it comes to lyin'?"

The Chair explained that the present case was an exceptional one, and that hereafter no newspaper man would be admitted as a member on any sort of provocation whatever.

"They be good liars," he said, "but the trouble is, they be too good, on account of their hevin' had more practice at it than we'uns, and I don't b'leeve in encouragin' competition what is liable to drive us fellers out of the field as a lyin' club."

There was a general concurrence by the Club in the sentiments above expressed, and, on motion of the Aye-and-No Member, the Club adjourned.

Mr. Bottomfact's Boy.

Mr. Bottomfact is a member of the Sazerac Lying Club not hitherto introduced to the reader of these chronicles. The reasons for omitting previous mention of this gentleman are many, the principal ones being that he is not a good liar himself, and lacks the qualifications necessary to a thorough appreciation of the lies of others, and by unanimous consent of the Club is voted a dreadful bore, in which particular the reader may think he resembles this book. To sum up his characteristics it is only necessary to repeat the opinion of one of the members of the Club concerning him:

"He's so matter-of-fact, he'd b'leeve the devil was askin' him to drink whisky instead of liquid brimstone, if old Cloven-Foot askt him to jine him at the bar, and he can't talk 'bout nothin' but that boy of his'n."

This description fits Mr. Bottomfact to a nicety. He is so confiding and innocent that he believes anything he is told, and never for a moment even thought of questioning the truth of the most outrageous lies told in the Club, accepting them all as perfectly true and eminently reasonable. He was usually an interested listener, seldom taking part in the debates, but when he did speak it was always to relate some marvelous exploit of "that thar boy of his'n," though on one occasion he related how he had lost his fortune by purchasing a salted claim in California, on the strength of appearances. The full name of Mr. Bottomfact's son and heir is George Washington Bottomfact, but in speaking of him his father usually calls him "my boy Wash." Mr. Bottomfact's hobby is that "my boy Wash" is a genius, and that he is destined to make his mark in the world; and he never misses an opportunity of inflicting his "weakness" on the Sazerac Lying Club. The least allusion to a boy is sufficient to set him going on "Wash," and his long harangues have frequently seriously interfered with the Club's debates, and either put all the members to sleep, or driven them out of the house. Consequently, all the members were very cautious about touching on the subject of boys, which was usually scrupulously avoided. But one unfortunate night a member happened to relate a lie about a boy, only six years old, who knew the multiplication table by heart, and could read the first three chapters of the Lord's Prayer, and this put Mr. Bottomfact in his element and set him going on his favorite theme.

"Talk about smart boys!" he said, "thar aint none on you ever seed a smarter boy than my boy Wash. Why, here he aint been goin' to school nigh onto two year, and the teacher's puttin' him to writin' compersitions a'ready. Jest look a' here."

Then Mr. Bottomfact drew from his pocket a roll of paper, and proceeded to unfold it, and the members were getting ready to depart, but were arrested by the voice of the Chair, who requested them to wait and see what "old B'leeve-it-all" had to offer, and not pass a hasty judgment on something with the merits of which they were unacquainted. Accordingly, the Club resumed their seats, and Mr. B continued:

"This here, Mr. President and gentlemen, is a compersition my boy Wash writ up to the school, and I think it's one of the best things I ever heerd on the subjeck. What I want to ask is, that the Seccertary be instructed to read it to the Club, and if they find it satisfactory—as I know they will—that it then be deposited in the Arkives of this here Club, and voted to be printed in the REVEILLE."

"I'm willin', if the paper don't charge a cent for it," said the Doubter.

"Wal, gentlemen," decided the Chair, "if nobody aint got nothin' better to offer for the consideration of this here Club, I'll order the Seccertary to read."

No objection was offered.

"The Seccertary will purceed to read, and he is instructed to give the compersition to the REVEILLE for publishin', requestin' of the editor to print it jest as it is, spellin' and all, and not make no hifalutin' alterations."

And the Secretary then proceeded to read as follows:

6

Snaix.

[BY GEORGE WASHINGTON BOTTOMFACT.]

"The snaik is a animal what is all tail but his hed. He dont hav no legs, but walkes on the ground on his stummick. They is a grate menny kinds of snaix, but rattil snaix and snaix what is in butes is bout the only kind of snaix in these parts, ceptin water snaix, which aint pizen and cant bite. I onct knod a boy whos muther told his farther thet if he didnt let up hed have snaix in his butes, and Jimme, which is that boys name, he luked in his pars butes and didnt find no snaix, caus they must a dide in there, caus Jimme he sed tha smelt like sumthin hed crorled in ther and dide. Ther aint no snaix in Austin, ownly them bute kind, and I never see nun of them; but out in the mountings they is rattil snaix two plentifle. Rattil snaix isnt afeard of a man, but tha is skeert of a hors-hare rope. My father he knod a man what wunst went out prospektin, and he lade a hare rope rownd his blankits, and when he waiked up in the mournin tha was as menny as 15 hunderd snaix stickin of tha heds over that rope and a waitin of him to cum out. His dorg et them all up and saved his life, and rattil snaix tha aint good to ete fur a man. Tha is a grate menny kind of snaix as I hev heerd tell on wich I haint never seed. Won of them kind is corled a bo-constructor, caus it bo's up its back when it gits mad, and tys his selfe inter bo-nots. Tha grows in Nu York and them uther forrin countrys ever so menny miles from Austin, and tha has them in surkises. Tha aint no boy in Austin as ever seed a surkiss. I kno a boy what his farther keeps a sloon, and he sez his par sez he is orfle glad no surkiss kant cum to Austin caus they brake the town and noboddy dont hav no munny left to spend for the drinks. I heerd a man say that if we had a raleroad maybee the surkiss and the bo-constructor and the elefint would cum to Austin. But I never seed a ralerode, no more didnt no other boy in Austin, ceptin three or fore who is bin to skule in Californy, but a Austin boy dont git no chance to see surkisses and ralerodes and trees, and them kind of wonderfull things, ceptin the locuss trees, and they was brot here by sum mens. A boy onct told me that a ralerode could run faster nor 3 quarter-hosses, but I dont believe that, caus tha aint no animal not even a zebray could do that, and tha just put that in the skule books like sum of them uther lys, to skare us boys so we will be goode wen we dont want to. This is all I kno about snaix."

"What do you think of that for a compersition?" triumphantly asked Mr. Bottomfact when the Secretary had concluded the reading of the above.

"I think, Mr. Bottomfact," said the Chair, "that, while it's a fust-class literary effort for a boy of your Wash's age, it aint got no bizness in this here Club. The objeck of this organization is lyin'; and, not sayin' that thar aint no lies in Wash's compersition, still, what he says 'bout the jim-jam snakes hes a great deal of truth inter it. Thar'fore, Mr. Bottomfact, I decide that in future you won't be allowed to ring in Wash and his compersitions onter this here Club, and I would advise you to jine some lit'rary society, whar sich things is better appreciated."

Mr. Bottomfact seemed very much crestfallen over this decision of the Chair, and did not ask anybody for the loan of a chew of tobacco for full five minutes, and in a short time he arose and said that he guessed he would go out and hunt up Wash.

As the door closed on Mr. Bottomfact's retreating form, Mr. Whisky said he had a "good notion" to make a motion for the expulsion of "that air Bottomfact."

"He aint no 'count, no way; he can't lie wuth a cuss, and nobody never knowed him to treat the house yit."

The Chair said that as for himself he had never recognized Bottomfact as a member of the Club, but merely as a spectator at the meetings; and in his (the Chair's) opinion a formal expulsion would be tantamount to recognizing Bottomfact as a member.

"'Cause how can you expel a man unless he's a member; and if a feller aint a member, how can you expel him? That's what I'd like to know."

The members unanimously "gave it up," and Mr. Thirsty said he would not press the motion for expulsion; but "had the members of this Club ever heard what the Governor of North Carolina said to the Governor of South Carolina?"

"I know," hastily exclaimed the Aye-and-No Member; "he said, 'It's a long time atween drinks.'"

"That's jest what he said, and that's jest what I say," returned Mr. Thirsty. "S'pose, gentlemen, that we sashay up to the bar."

And they all "sashayed."

A Saline Atmosphere.

At a point in Smoky Valley, some forty miles distant from Austin, there exists a deposit of salt, in what is commonly called a salt marsh. Similar deposits are found in numbers of the valleys—or deserts—in Nevada and Utah. The particular salt marsh in Smoky Valley has for a number of years been the source from which the silver reduction mills of Austin and Belmont have obtained their supply of salt for the chlorination of ores—a process absolutely necessary to their successful working, and which can only be practiced on a large scale by the aid of salt.

The method for a long time in vogue in gathering this salt was to shovel it up from the marsh as it was deposited on its surface by the natural evaporation of the water which holds it in solution. This was a tedious process, only practicable in good weather, and the salt thus obtained contained many impurities. The parties owning the marsh finally adopted a plan whereby the process of evaporation was hastened and a better article of salt obtained, and to this is due the lie which Uncle John related in the Club on the subject, and which is here recorded.

The improved mode of salt gathering may be thus described: A bed of hard clay was found a few hundred yards from the marsh, and in this a number of tanks or vats were cut. A pump and steam machinery were placed at the marsh, the pump being connected with the tanks by a pipe, from which the saline water was discharged into the tanks, and there allowed to evaporate by nature's process.

The salt-works lay close by the road which Uncle John's stage daily passes over, and each evening during their construction he would report their progress, and explain their principle to the Club. At last the works were finished, and running successfully, and the subject of salt and salt marshes dropped out of the Club's deliberations, till one evening a member happened to say:

"Uncle John, how's them salt-works getting along?"

"Bad, rather bad," was the reply; "that is, bad for the salt company, which are losin' a considerable of salt, but good for the ranchers and some other people."

"How's that, Uncle John?"

"Wal, you see, the pipe leaks."

"What of that?"

And in reply Uncle John related thus: "The salt water that runs through that leak evaporates as soon as it strikes the air, and the wind—which is always blowin' in the valley—ketches up the salt and carries it over the valley in clouds. For a mile each way from the marsh the air's so thick with salt that half the time I can't see the stage team, and it jest keeps rainin' salt all the time. When the ranchers in the valley wants salt, they jest set an open sack out in front of the house, and in less than twenty minutes it's filled chock up to the mouth with the finest kind of cookin' salt."

"Very singular," remarked the Doubter.

"Not at all," returned the Philosopher. "It is only in accordance with a natr'al law of evaporation and specific gravity, that when thar's salt in water, the water dries out and leaves the salt, and when the salt's in the air, it comes down on the ground, on the principle of what goes up must come down. Don't you see?"

"Don't the men what owns the marsh shovel up the salt as lays on the ground?" asked the Chair.

"They'd like to," replied Uncle John; "but the stock camps round thar and eats it up afore they can get a chance to shovel it; and losin' salt's cheaper than hirin' men to herd fifteen or twenty thousand head of cattle away from it, sayin' nothin' of sheep and horses."

Mr. Truefact was trying to say that the story was wonderful, when Uncle John took the word out of his mouth and said:

"Yes, it is wonderful; but I ain't told all of it yit. That thar salt air is the surest cure for rheumatism I ever seed."

"Did it cure you?" asked the Doubter.

"No; I aint hed the rheumatiz sence that leak started, but I know it's a sure shot. There is a feller has got a ranch over in Monitor Valley, and he tried the hot springs over thar, and used up four bottles of my horse liniment, and it didn't do him no good. He was so crippled up he couldn't use his arms and legs, and couldn't talk straight; and that thar man he walked thirty miles to the marsh, and sot down in that thar salt shower, and in seventeen minnits after the salt fust struck his lungs he held four jacks ag'in an ace-full, and stood his wife's mother off in a two-hour talking match."

The Chair here remarked that Uncle John was going outside of the subject-matter of his lie, and inquired:

"What has four jacks ag'in an ace-full got to do with curin' the rheumatiz?"

"Nothin' particular," replied Uncle John; "only four jacks ag'in an ace-full, specially when thar's money in sight, is a healthy hand, and it takes a healthy man to hold 'em, and I only mentioned the circumstance to show that the man didn't have no more rheumatiz; 'cause if he had, he'd bin layin' round home cussin' and howlin', instid of playin' poker with the boys."

The apology was deemed sufficient, and Uncle John remarked that talking about salt had made him dry, and inquired if the gentlemen of the Club would jine him.

The gentlemen all jined.

Fixing a Dog.

It was at the time of year that, under a city ordinance existing in Austin, an annual tax on dogs is collected. By a provision of the law, each dog must be provided with a tag attached to its collar, and all canines found at large without such tag are arrested and impounded, and after a few days of grace for its owner to redeem it in, the unlucky animal, if not redeemed, is shot. The dog question being the current topic, it was being discussed by the Club. The exploits of the city dog-catcher were criticized, and, by a natural sequence, the thread of the argument merged into kettling and other outrages on dogs. The most approved hitch for fastening the kettle to the dog had been elaborated on, the cruelty of turpentine denounced, and the merits of fire-crackers argued; various members had related their experience in that line, and Mr. Truefact had just started in to try and tell a funny dog-kettling incident which occurred in Pioche, and had stuttered as far as, "Mr. P-p-pres-s-id-d-ent; d-d-down t-t-to P-p-p-pioche——," when a stranger walked into the room. He did not wait for an invitation to be seated, but sat right down in a vacant chair in the midst of the group that constituted the Club. This intrusion was not by any means relished by the members, and there were mutterings of a storm of indignation, and stage whispers that "some people didn't have no more manners than a hog," and "whar I come from, people used to wait till they was invited," and other remarks of that nature. But the stranger did not seem to heed these disparaging utterances, but tilted his chair back, cocked his feet on the stove, and took a paper of fine-cut from his pocket and took therefrom a chew, and, without the formality of addressing the Chair, said:

"I b'leeve you fellers was talkin' about kittlin' of dogs, when I come in."

The President observed that if, in speaking of "fellers," the stranger referred to him, he wanted it understood that he called himself a gentleman, and that people who did not desire a fight on their hands must address him as such.

"Fellers, indeed!" exclaimed the Doubter.

The entire Club arose to its feet as by a common impulse; but the Chair interposed and said:

"Hold on, gentlemen, he looks like he might be a pretty good liar, and let's give him a chance. Thar's many a rose as is born to be cast afore swine, and many a jewel as don't shine till it's cut down to a fine p'int. Let's give this man a chance, notwithstanding he calls us fellers." Then turning to the stranger he said:

"Stranger, go on with your rat-killin', and let's hear what you've got to offer on the subjeck of kittlin' dogs."

The stranger said he meant no offense by speaking of the members as "fellers"; but he had been in the country a long time, and was not used to putting on airs. However, as he had heard them talking of the various methods of annoying canines, and as it was a subject on which he considered himself well posted, he had taken the liberty of chipping in.

"Wal, you've chipped," observed the Chair, "now make your play, and let us see if any of us can call you. And if none of us can't, why, then, you're a member of this here Club, which is the Sazerac Lying Club, which mebbe you might have heerd of afore."

The stranger replied that he had never before heard of the Club; but when it came to lying, he could hold his own with the oldest man in the country. He then "chipped" as follows:

"Over in Virginny City, in sixty-four, I see the dog-gonedest thing about fixing a dog. The animile was one of those big, yaller curs, and some feller had fixed a giant powder ca'tridge to his tail, fuse, cap, and all. I was a-standin' in front of the big hotel, smokin' a four-bit cigar that Kettle-belly Brown had just treated me to in the Sawdust Corner, when along come Mr. Dog, trottin' ahead as though he didn't have no giant powder ca'tridge fastened to him plumb up ag'in the terminus of his spinal column. Jest as he passed me I see a puff of smoke, then a flash, and then an explosion that shook up the big hotel like a Shoshone wickiup in a whirlwind. As soon as I got my wind, and rubbed the dust and splinters out of my eyes, I began lookin' around to see if I could see any pieces of that yaller dog."

"Did they find any of him?" eagerly interrupted the Doubter.

"Never you mind," replied the stranger; "this is *my* dog story. Find any of him! Why, bless your soul, they found all of him. There he was, on the sidewalk, not six inches from where he stood when the shot went off, a-playin' with his tail, and snappin' at the sparks that was stickin' to it."

"You're electid!" enthusiastically exclaimed the Chair, when the stranger had concluded the above lie.

"Thank ye kindly," said the stranger, "but that thar aint no lie; but as I'm a member of this Club, I'll make out to tell you a lie one of these days."

"Yes, I'd like to see you try your hand at lyin'," remarked Old Dad. "I think after you had some experience that way, you might make out to tell a pretty solid lie, on an average."

At this point Mr. Thirsty arose, and called the Chair's attention to the fact that the new member had not yet complied with the rule in reference to members initiating themselves.

The Chair thanked Mr. Thirsty for the suggestion, and informed the new member that under the rules he was required to put up for the drinks for the boys.

The new member replied that he had not come prepared for any such emergency. "But," said he, smiling at the dispenser of liquids behind the bar, "if the bar-creetur don't mind takin' my face for the drinks, I aint no objection to treatin' the crowd."

The bar-keeper, who had listened to the stranger's lie about "fixing" the dog, observed that, as he (the stranger) seemed to be such a truthful man, he would trust him for the drinks if he would promise to pay the next time he came in.

The stranger promised, saying: "You better bet your boots that thar bar-keep's a judge of human natur. I never told him so, but he knows by my looks I'm Old Reliable himself."

And by the name of "Old Reliable" was this member thereafter known in the Club, at the sessions of which he was a constant attendant from this time on.

Uncle John's Dog.

When the members of the Club, after the interview with the bar-keeper, had resumed their seats, and the Chair announced that "we would now re-open under the head of dogs," Uncle John took the floor. He said he was not much of a dog-sharp, but had seen some powerful smart dogs in his time. He once knew a dog that could tell a newspaper from a piece of beef with his eyes shut, and in his boyhood's days he had seen in a circus a dog that could beat a man at seven-up, and give him two points in the game.

"Dogs over here in the sagebrush," said Uncle John, "knows more than dogs does in Californy, 'cause they've got a better chance to learn things and post themselves. Over to Californy a dog's time is mostly taken up fightin' the fleas, and they haint got no time to waste on their education. You've all of you lived in California some time or other, and you knows how it is yourself about fleas. I had a dog thar once, and he was about as good a dog as ever made a track, but the fleas bothered him that bad that he'd go into the river and stay thar a week at a time to git shet of them. But the fleas they didn't mind that, but used to swim off to shore and camp on the bank, and wait for that dog to come out, and then they'd bounce him ag'in, and stick to him closer than a gal to a feller that she's clean gone on. Finally the thing got so bad that that thar dog was actooally thinkin' of suicide. I hed a double-bar'l'd shotgun in the barn whar I used to keep the dog, and that poor animile would, every once in a while, go smellin' at the muzzle of that gun, and a-feelin' of the trigger with his paw, like as if he was figgerin' how he could have his head at the muzzle and his paw on the trigger both at the same time. But he was a short dog—leastways he wasn't long enough to reach that fur. Finally the hostler in the stage barn he took pity on that thar dog, and he fixed him up a collar with a lot of long iron spikes stickin' into it, with the pints outside, and that worked two ways. The dog could scratch hisself with the spikes, and when the fleas would come lightin' down to tackle the dog, they'd strike on the spikes and stick there; and when the collar got full of fleas, the hostler he'd take 'em off one at a time, and chop their heads off with the ax, and feed 'em to his chickens."

"Is that all?" asked Old Reliable, when Uncle John had concluded.

"All! Did you expect I was goin' to say the hostler killed the chickens and fed 'em to the fleas, or the fleas eat up the dog, or any such improbable lie like that? No, sir, not much; though I didn't calkerlate to stand off that thar lie of yours about the giant powder."

Old Reliable attempted to explain that his story was "gospel truth," but the bar-keeper commenced to turn down the lights, and thus the debate was shut off for the evening.

A High Fever.

"I miss the cheerful countenance of our stutterin' friend, Mr. Truefact," said the President, casting his eyes over the members before calling the Club to order.

"Mr. Truefact's a little under the weather," responded the Secretary, in reply.

"What's the matter of him—bin pressin' his tansey too heavy ag'in?" inquired the Chair.

"That aint what's the matter of him this time," returned the Secretary; "he's laid up with a pritty bad dose of mounting fever."

"That thar mountain fever's a tough thing," said Uncle John, "but it aint a patchin' to rheumatiz when it gits a good hold onto a feller."

"I don't know about that," observed the Doubter, "I had mounting fever so bad onct that they had to carry me out doors and lay me on the ground so's the heat of me wouldn't set the blankets afire."

"That *was* a hot fever, sure enough," spoke up Mr. Thirsty, "but 'taint much alongside of a fever I onct knowed a boy to have back in the States. He was the all-firedest cussedest boy as ever I seed—always robbin' hen-roosts and orchards, and a-suckin' of other folks's milch cows, and them kinds of devilment. He used to suck eggs and drink milk when he wasn't the leestest bit hungry, jest to be doin' of somethin'; but one day he got his dose, and it come pritty near curin' of him. He'd eat up a hull lot of eggs one mornin', and drinked a power of milk, and 'long about noon he was the sickest boy ever seed in that section of country. His folks sent for the doctor, and when he got to the house that thar boy was in a rip-rarin, ragin' fever, and jest a-burnin' up by inches. The doctor talked to the folks, and felt his pulse, and axed what he'd bin eatin' for breakfast, and the folks said they didn't know, cause he always was eatin' of somethin' as didn't agree with him and laid heavy on his stummick. Then the doctor looked at his tongue, and said the fever was mostly inside, and he guessed he better give him a emetic. So he went down in his saddle-bags and got out some truck, and while three or four of 'em held him, he rammed the stuff down the boy's throat. 'Twarn't mor'n a few minnits till the boy begin to git pritty sick, and afore long he commenced throwin' up, and for about half an hour he throwed up nothin' but the nicest lookin' custard you ever seed in all your borned days. Now I'd like you to show me a mounting fever as is so hot that it'll bake a custard in a boy's insides what will swaller a lot of eggs and milk."

"Pritty warm; pritty warm," remarked the President, at the conclusion of Mr. Thirsty's remarks.

"Yes, it's hot," observed Old Dad, "but not so hot as I've seen it in Californy."

A Hot Country.

"You don't mean to say it's hot in Californy, do you?" hastily spoke up the Doubter. "Why, down in Southern Utah it's as much hotter as Californy, as a Eureka smeltin' furnace is alongside the North Pole. Why, me and a lot of fellers was prospectin' in Southern Utah onct, and it was so hot we didn't used to build any fire when we camped, but jest cooked our grub by the heat of the air. We used to buy eggs of the Mormons, and we had lots of bacon ourselves, and we jest used to put the eggs and bacon on a hot rock in the shade, and they would fry brown in about three minnits. We didn't dare to put 'em in the sun, cause if we did the grub would sizzle to a coal afore you could bat your eye."

"Sho!" exclaimed Old Reliable. "That aint nothin' to Arizony! Why, I've seen horned toads and lizzards git sun-struck in the shade down thar. Hot! Why, you fellers don't know nothin' bout hot. What would you say if I was to tell you that it was so hot down thar that the only way they could git to tell anything about how hot it was, was to splice two thermometers together, and even then the quicksilver would spirt over the top of the top thermometer, sometimes."

"Wal, I don't know what the rest of the Club would say," observed Uncle John, as if replying to Old Reliable's question, "but as for me, I'd say that's about as big a lie as any of the oldest members of this here Club ever told, and I can't help sayin' that its doin' mighty well for a new member, and I aint a bit surprised at your callin' yourself Old Re-*lie*-able himself; for you're *able* to *lie* with the best of *us*."

The Chair Speaks.

On calling the Club to order, the Chair arose, and said if the gentleman over in the corner would quit plaguing "that thar dog of Dad's," he would make a few remarks. The member designated ceased teasing the dog by sticking a broom straw in his ear, and the dog lay down on the floor with his nose between his paws; silence reigned in the Club, and the expectant members bent their heads in an attitude of earnest attention towards the President, to hear the words of wisdom which they felt sure would fall from his lips, like the gentle dew of heaven on the morning mushroom.

The Chair said he felt it his duty to congratulate the Club that recent events have brought to light the fact that some of the greatest men of the United States are, or were, liars, and eligible to membership in the great and glorious Sazerac.

"Gentlemen," he said, "you're all twenty-one years old, free-born and white, and the majority of you know how to read. Of course, you all read the newspapers, and you know about this here affair of Grant sayin' that the late lamented Charles Sumner was a nat'ral-born, constitutional liar afore he died. Sumner is dead and buried, true enough, but, gentlemen, it's a consolin' reflection to us, as good, squar', honest, consistent, and conscientious liars, to know that a man as has been set down as one of the greatest statesmen of these here times was, when he was alive, as one of us—that he could lie like a house afire. S'posin', howsomever, for the sake of argument, that Grant's bin lyin' about Sumner, then the state of the case is thuswise: A ex-President of the United States stands before you in the attitood of a liar. Take either horn of this here bull, my fellow-members, and in any case it sticks out like a sore thumb that somebody's lied, and that somebody one of the great men of this here country. I tell you, gentlemen, this here Club has a cause for congratulatin' of itself, when it stops to consider that the greatest of great men *can* lie."

At this point the Chair was interrupted by Old Reliable, who remarked that "when it comes to lyin', the best of em's on it." The Chair rebuked the interrupting member, and observed that if he did not know that Old Reliable had not "settled for them last drinks," he would impose the fine the rules inflict on a new member as a penalty for interrupting the Chair. Then resuming the thread of his discourse, he said:

"There are a record of one man in the United States, who, so the hist'ries claims, couldn't tell a lie, which his name it was George Washington—same as mine and Mr. Bottomfact's boy's front name."

The Doubter here said something about G. W.'s namesakes not resembling him much in one particular; but the Chair, without deigning to notice the slur, asked the Club if any of them had ever heard the story of George Washington and his little hatchet.

There was a unanimous response in the negative, and several members expressed a desire to hear the story, which the Chair consented to tell.

The Champion Lie.

Pointing his finger to a picture on the wall, he said

"Up yonder thar is the picture of George Washington, Esquire, sometimes called the Father of his Country, 'cause he was first in war, first in peace, and first in the hearts of his countrymen. When this here George Washington was a chunk of a boy, he lived on a farm, and one day his old man went to town and bought him a hatchet for a birthday. When George got the hatchet he went pirootin' round the ranch, cuttin' and slashin' at everything in sight, and one day he got into the orchard and tackled a cherry tree that the old man set a heap of store by—'cause it was a new kind of cherry as didn't grow no pits. Young George he clapped eyes on this here tree, and commenced slashin' at it, kind of absent-minded like, and the first thing he knowed he'd busted his hatchet clean through the middle of it, and it was a sure thing thar would be no cherries without pits on that ranch that season. When the old man come home from town and seed the tree cut down he was as mad as a hornet, and commenced rampagin' round askin' of the niggers who was the feller what had chopped that cherry-tree. George was in the barn hackin' away at an old board, and heerd his dad askin' of these questions, and he knowed, bein' as he was the only boy on the place as had a hatchet, that the old man had him dead to rights. So he rushed out'n the barn, and drappin' at his father's feet, sung out: 'Father, forgive me this onc't; I did it with my small ax!' The old man couldn't stand this; it was too much for human natur' to bear, and he busted out cryin' and said, 'Bless you, my children,' like they does in the theater shows."

The Club's eyes were moist (and their throats otherwise) when the Chair had concluded the above affecting narration, and a deep silence reigned in the room for some moments. The Doubter was the first to recover his composure and his voice; when he had done so, he said to the Chair:

"Mr. President, do you b'leeve that thar yarn?"

"I must b'leeve it, 'cause it's handed down in hist'ry," was the reply.

"Wal, as for me, I think it's the dog-gonedest biggest lie as was ever told in this here Club, and I'd like to hear the sentiments of the gentlemen here present on the subject."

"We'll take the sentiments of the Club then," announced the Chair.

The question was then put to the vote. As stated by the Chair it was thus: "The question now before this Club is: Are the story about G. Washington and the cherry-tree a lie, or are it gospel truth? Those in favor of its bein' a lie, will say 'Aye,' and those opposed, contrarywise."

The response was a unanimous 'Aye.'

Thus did the Club, at one fell blow, demolish one of the great truths of American history.

The Quadruplex System.

The Western Union Telegraph Company are now using the quadruplex system over the Virginia and Salt Lake circuit, by means of which four messages may be sent simultaneously over a single wire. The wire over which this system is in use passes through Austin, and has of late given considerable trouble to the operators. They have been unable to find any break, and a close examination of the wire has failed to reveal any cause for the difficulties, which for some time past have been experienced in the transmission of messages over it. The mystery is now solved, however. In the Sazerac Lying Club, at the last session, Old Dad interpreted the cause of the trouble. After describing the quadrup ex system, he explained that the strain on the wire was increased beyond the wire's carrying capacity. He said he was out at Dry Creek the day before, and that in that vicinity the wire was just humping itself, and groaning and straining and dropping words off in chunks. He examined the wire and found a knot in it, and came to the conclusion that a quadruplex message had struck the knot and got tangled up, and stuck at that point. He tried to straighten the wire out, but a section of an account of a battle between the Turks and Russians struck him on the ear and knocked him down, and he concluded that it was not advisable to fool with the thing. He had informed the manager of the telegraph office in town, as to the cause of the difficulty, and stated to the Club that a man had already been sent out with a crowbar to pry out some of the biggest words and smooth the knot down, so that the words could pass each other.

Mosquitoes.

"Has any gentleman anything to offer?" asked the Chair, when the members were all comfortably settled in their seats, a few evenings after.

"I can't offer to treat," said Old Reliable, "'cause I aint got no bullion in my clothes, and the bar-keep aint quit lookin' crosswise at me yit, on account of that thar 'nitiation fee of mine; but as the boys has been talkin' 'bout warm weather, can't some of the members tell us somethin' about skeeters — which goes together with hot weather?"

"I don't know much 'bout skeeters, myself," spoke up Old Dad, "but they do say that in Jersey the skeeters is so big they light down onto the face of the country and scoop up young calves and small children. But I was never in Jersey myself."

"I s'pose," said the Philosopher, "that in speakin' of skeeters, the gentleman refers to that well-known American bird, the *miss*-keeter."

"That's the animal as is bein' referred to," decided the Chair.

"Skeeters ain't bad in this country," remarked Mr. Thirsty, "owin' to the altitood and the light air, which doesn't agree with them. But up north in Idaho, they is wuss than rats in Sacramento. Why, I knowed a man as was camped out in that country onc't, and durin' the night a band of skeeters come down and eat the shoes clean off'n his mule's hoofs."

"You're sure you aint made no mistake, Mr. Thirsty," said the Doubter; "'cause I've heerd that lie afore, and the way it was told to me, the mule eat the shoes off of the skeeter's hoofs."

The Chair bent a look of sternness on the Doubter, and asked him if he was aware that such frivolity was a discourtesy to the Club at large.

"Don't you know, sir, that skeeters don't hev shoes, and to be throwin' out of insinooations that they does, is to cast the suspicion of doubt onto the remarks of the gentleman as preceded you? You be a old enough member of this Club, and the Chair has cussed you often enough for you to know by this time that castin' doubt onto another member's lie is plum, dead, square agin the rules of this here Club."

The Doubter, with much meekness, replied that he did not desire to cast doubts on Mr. Thirsty's statement, but the mosquitoes he referred to were the kind that Old Dad had mentioned as infesting the wilds of New Jersey, and he did not know but it might be the custom of the people of that country to "lass"(lassoo) the "varmints" and break them to harness and, of course, in that case, they would have to be shod

The Philosopher said that the Doubter's supposition was a perfectly natural one; but, speaking of mules, had any member here present ever investigated the characteristics and studied the mental traits of

The Mule?

The Chair said that, for himself, he had once met with a blasting accident, and since then had been strongly disinclined to fool with explosives. Uncle John remarked that once, when a man tried to sell him a mule, he consented to examine the animal. He got the man to drive the animal into a corral, and then got on top of the roof of a barn and examined it with a spy-glass.

The Philosopher here observed that he did not mean to refer particularly to the leg-power of a mule; that subject had already been exhausted in the newspapers, and the American people are perfectly familiar with it. Said he:

"Mr. President and gentlemen, what I'm tryin' to git at is this: I advance the propersition that mules don't never die. You all think you've seen a dead mule, don't you? But you never did. They lay down and look like as if they was dead, but it aint so. Sometimes they're turned into newspaper editors, and book agents, and other kind of animals as has cheek; but the active principle of the mule is somethin' as never dies. Why I know a mule as is now puttin' in its reg'lar ten-hour shift workin' on a 'whim' on a mine over in Humboldt County, that you couldn't no more kill than you could the snakes a man sees when he's got the jim-jams. The fust account any hist'ry gives of this here mule, he was put up for a breastworks at the battle of New Orleans, and the Britishers didn't dare to come near enough to shoot at him with a cannon. One cannon-ball *did* accidentally come pritty close to him, and he let out at it with his off-hind foot and sent it scootin' back amongst the English troops, and it went clean through three regiments of soldiers, and the wind of it knocked one of them 'high-you' muckamuck English lords clear out of his saddle. This here mule was brung to Californy in the airly days, and Grant—the same as used to be President—he got hold of him by winnin' of him at a horse-race. When Grant went back to the States, he took that thar mule with him, and took him all through the war; and I've heerd it said that Gin'ral Grant has been heerd to say that if it hadn't bin for that thar mule, the chances was the South would hev bin victorious. After the war was over, Grant sold the mule to Governor Stanford, who was buildin' of the Central Pacific Railroad them days; and that mule was blowed clean out of sight one day by a nitro-glycerine explosion. The man as found the mule, when he come down, was on his road to the Black Hills; and when he got out on the plains he traded it to a Gov'ment contractor, who sold it to Gin'ral Custer, and it was all through that battle what Custer was killed in, and come out without a scratch. Gentlemen, that mule has a history. It went to Africa with Stanley, has bin through a tidal-wave on the coast of South America, taken a hand in the famine in China, was saved by a scratch from a Mississippi steamboat explosion—'cause he was at the Centennial at the time—and has been more or less connected with every calamity as has happened durin' the present century—and thar don't nobody know to a certainty as he isn't one of the pair of mules what old Noah druv' inter the Ark when he was a-savin' of two of each kind of animiles for seed, when he saw that cloud-burst a-comin.' "

"Can you show the papers for that?" asked the Doubter, when the Philosopher had concluded the mule's biography.

The Chair rose right up in its seat, and frowned its darkest frown upon the Doubter, and requested that gentleman to state if he was courting forcible expulsion from the Club.

"The idear of one member askin' another gentleman if he's got the papers to support his remarks at one of these meetin's! It's the most outrageous thing as has ever occured in this here Club; and no matter how much I may think of you as an old pard of my own, and one of my best friends, my duty is plain, and I've got to enforce the rules, even if I knowed we wouldn't never be friends no more. The gentleman as asks for papers to be produced, is fined the stimulants for the crowd; and this here Club stands adjourned for the present evenin'."

A Clear Atmosphere.

At the meeting following the one recorded above, when the Chair announced that "lies is now in order," Old Reliable opened the evening's exercises by remarking that during the discussion at the preceding meeting, in referring to the effects of this climate on the health of mosquitoes, something had been said about the "lightness" of the air. It is a fact well known that in mountainous countries, owing to the rarefaction of the atmosphere, the range of human vision is very wide. A hill or other object which in less elevated localities would be distant from the point of observation say a couple of miles, and which appears to be about that distance away, may in reality be from seventy-five to one hundred miles distant. There are places in Nevada where mountain peaks are plainly discernible at a distance of over two hundred miles. The fact in regard to the clearness of the atmosphere, and the extent to which the vision can reach, is commonly known to the people of Nevada; and it was in reference to this that he spoke of the "lightness" of the air.

"I b'leeve somethin' was said on that subjeck," said the Philosopher, "but has the member as referred to it ever bin in Colorado?"

Old Reliable answered that he had never visited the particular State in question.

"Then," said the Philosopher, "he don't know nothin' about light air. Why, up on some of them high peaks of the Rocky Mountains, when the weather is clear, a man can stand and see the ships comin' in through the Golden Gate at San Francisco, purvidin' he's lookin' westward."

Old Reliable drew a sigh that seemed to come from the innermost recesses of his boots, as he said:

"That raises me clean out. What I was goin' to remark don't begin to come up to the remarks of the previous gentleman."

"Let's have it, anyway," demanded Uncle John.

"No," said Old Reliable, "I lay down my hand and quit. For onct in my life I've got to holler enough. The gentleman as knows all about them scientific things has got me in the door, and my hand sinks down inter absoloot insignifercance."

"Cheer up, cheer up, Mr. O. R.," said the Chair, sympathizingly; "there's as good fish in the sea as was ever yanked out of it. Let's hear your little lie; and this here Club will be the judges."

Thus implored, "Mr. O. R." proceeded to recite his little tale, which was as follows:

"I'd heern tell so much about the light air in this country, and how a man could see a deer on top of a mountain a hundred mile off, that I made up my mind to try somethin'. The other mornin' I climbed up onto the summit of Mount Prometheus to take a peep and see what I could see. The mornin' was clear, not a cloud bein' in the sky, and when I began to look over west, the fust thing I seed was Virginny City, strung along the side of old Mount Davidson jest as nat'ral as life. I thought at fust it was a mirage, 'cause Virginny is a hundred and eighty miles from here in a air line; but I soon seed that the thing was as real and honest as the Methodist Church steeple, which was a pritty considerable distance off, as you may know, but didn't seem mor'n twenty foot away from me. Wal, I got to lookin' around to see what was goin' on in Virginny. I seed the quartz wagons goin' through the streets, and the minin' superintenders drivin' around with their spang-up teams, and all the population bowin' and scrapin' to 'em; and I seed a couple of fellows havin' a shootin' scrape on C street, and all the p'licemen runnin' down to Chinatown to arrest the Chinamen for firin' fire-arms inside the city limits; and I seed the ladies steppin' across the street and holdin' up their dresses—and most of 'em had on striped stockings. I couldn't hear the steam whistles on the histin' works at the mines, but I could see when they tooted 'em, and I could see 'em changin' shifts at some of the mines, and the night-shift comin' up on the cage and the day-shift goin' down. But the most important thing I seed was in the court-house. I looked into the county jail, and I seed a feller what was in thar for stealin' a bronco horse, sittin' in cell Number Four filin' off his irons. He was red-headed, hed a wart on his nose and checkered pants and a Californy gray shirt. I come down as quick as I could, and told the sheriff up here to the court-house, and he sent a telegraph to the sheriff over at Virginny, tellin' of him to look out for cell Number Four. Pritty soon he got a answer, and the Virginny sheriff said that cell Number Four was a awful criminal and had jest escaped by blowin' up the court-house with nitro-glycerine, and him and a man as was in for murder, and who was actin' as deputy sheriff, was goin' out in a couple of days—soon as a reward was offered—to hunt up that feller what had escaped from Number Four."

"I call for the decision of the Chair!" exclaimed the Doubter, when Old Reliable had concluded.

The Chair decided as follows:

"Gentlemen, in the humble opinion of this here Chair, the Nevady lie is ahead of the Colorado lie. The Colorado lie only showed the ships comin' into the Golden Gate at 'Frisco, but we all knows a ship is a big object, and can be seed a long distance off; but when a atmosphere exists as will make a man able to see clear through a brick wall a hundred and eighty miles off, I say that it's a pritty clear case."

"A clear case of the jim-jams," growled the Doubter.

"I thought I'd told you afore about indulgin' in personalitics to'rds members," said the Chair, angrily, addressing himself to the Doubter; "but, howsomever, I would suggest to our friend as tells about what he seed up on the mounting, thet he goes up thar ag'in, and watches for that feller what escaped, and p'raps he'll see him streakin' it across the country, and can corral him, and come in for that thar reward."

Old Reliable replied that he would wait till the reward was offered, and might "take a hand in that game" if the amount was big enough to make it an object to a gentleman to exert himself to the extent necessary to climb the mountain and look for the escaped prisoner.

Fish Lies.

The debate for some little time after the occurrence of the proceedings narrated above seemed to lag for want of material, and things looked favorable for a dull and spiritless session. The President yawned, and the Secretary actually "threw off," so that the other man might make high, low, jack, pedro, and the game. The members smoked their pipes and chewed on their quids, and were seemingly wrapped in their own thoughts, or sleeping the sleep of the just, and dreaming the happy hours away; and it seemed as if all the life had suddenly gone out of the Club. At last Old Dad came to the rescue. He knew that the subject of fishing is one which affords so wide a scope for the talents of the liar that the mere mention of fish or fishing was enough to excite the Club to action, and to cause the old fire to again burn in the eyes of its members. Stamping his foot on the floor to attract the attention of the Club, (though he apologized for the action by saying that he actually thought his foot must have gone to sleep) he said:

"Gentlemen, you've all on you done more or less fishin', and no doubt every man of you thinks he's the best fisherman as ever made a track along a stream. I'm a pritty good fisher myself, and can yank as many trout out of one hole—providin' they're in thar—as the next man; but from all I can hear, and from what's been told me, thar is a fisher as discounts any of us."

"Whar does he live?" inquired the Doubter.

"Over to Virginny City and in that neighborhood," was the reply.

"What's his name?" asked Mr. Thirsty; "he's got to be a pritty good fisher if he can git away with me when I'm at myself."

"Oh, you've all heard of him," said Dad, after keeping the Club in suspense while deliberately cutting a pipe-full of tobacco from a plug of that article, and filling his pipe.

"Who is he? Who is he?" asked a number of members simultaneously.

Dad struck a match and lit the pipe, and then taking several long whiffs, he looked up at the curling smoke and said:

"This here fisher is p'raps the greatest fisher in the world. As I've said, you've all heard of this fisher. Mr. President, the fisher to which I'm makin' reference is *the great Comstock fissure.*"

A look of blank amazement came over the faces of the Club, and it was at least a minute before the Chair could subdue its feelings and find words in which to rebuke Old Dad for what it characterized as his levity.

"I'm sure," said the Chair, addressing the culprit, "that you're the last man in the world that I'd have thought would have undertaken to catch this here Club on a sell."

Dad said he had not meant to hurt anybody's feelings; and sooner than that anybody should feel aggrieved over his little joke, the Club could "sashay" to the bar at his expense.

Thus was the bloody chasm bridged over with kindly feeling, and the era of conciliation again resumed its sway in the Club.

When the members resumed their seats, Mr. Thirsty took the floor, saying:

"Gentlemen, speakin' of fishin', I've got a little fish story myself."

"Propel!" said the Chair.

And Mr. T. "propelled" as follows:

"I was up Reese River fishin' last week, and a very curious occurrence occurred to me. I'd fished along up and down the bank all mornin', without hevin' any luck wuth tellin' of, and was gittin' kind of disgusted like—'cause the fish wouldn't bite, and my bottle was as dry as a powder-horn, I myself bein' pritty much in the same condition. I was trampin' along the bank, droppin' my hook in here and thar whenever I saw a likely place, more jest to be doin' somethin' than expectin' to get a bite, when I come to a big, deep hole, whar the water was clear as a lookin'-glass. Peepin' over the bank, I seed the biggest trout I ever laid eyes on. It was a-swimmin' round in the pool, and there was up'ards of four hundred little trouts follerin' it around, like a lot of chickens follerin' of the old hen.

"'The mother of all the trouts in Reese River, by thunder!' says I to myself.

"Wal, I baited my hook, and sneaked my pole over the bank, and drapped the line inter the pool; and the fust thing I knowed, I got the most all-powerful bite——"

"Was it a skeeter?" interrupted the Doubter.

"Skeeter be blowed! No; it warn't no skeeter, but jest that big fish, the mother of all the trouts in Reese River. I jest braced myself, give one yank, and landed that old trout high and dry on the grass behind me."

"Did you bring it home?" hurriedly asked Uncle John, who has a weakness for fish, and hoped to come in for a portion of the trout.

"No, I didn't fetch it home," returned Mr. Thirsty; "it went ag'in my conscience to do it. When I looked back inter that thar hole, thar was them little fishes a-swimmin' round and round, and a-takin' on orful, 'cause their mother was gone. Gentlemen, you all know I'm a kind-hearted man, and I couldn't stand by and see the distressful actions of them fish; so I jest took the hook out of that nineteen-pound trout, and chucked her back inter the water. You jest ought to seed them little trouts when the old she-one struck the water; they felt as glad as if forty bushels of worms and a lot of grasshoppers had drapped down on them from heaven. The old gal she jest throwed herself over on her back, and the young ones they begin to suckle her, jest like a lot of kittens; and when I left thar she was feedin' some of the smallest ones with one of them thar nursin' bottles."

"Your heart's a heap bigger than your appetite for trout," said Uncle John, sarcastically.

"Mebbe that's so, and mebbe it aint," returned Mr. Thirsty; "but, gentlemen, I actooally believe that in chuckin' of that thar fish back into the stream, I've been a public benefactor. If, as I'm inclined to b'leeve, she was the mother of all the trouts in the river, why it follers as a nat'ral consequence that if I'd have killed her, all the other fishes would hev died for want of a mother's care; and then what would all you fellers do for fishin'?"

"Eat mackerel," growled Uncle John.

The Chair here interposed, and stated that while it did not take much stock in Mr. Thirsty's fish, the discussion between him and Uncle John had extended to the utmost limit of propriety; and, for fear of accidents, he would now declare the Club adjourned for the evening.

A Conundrum for the Club.

The members were all in their seats, and the Chair was just in the act of taking his chew of tobacco out of his mouth, that he might the better have the use of his voice in calling the Club to order, when a stranger entered the room.

The new-comer walked straight to the bar, and then, facing toward the Club, nodded to the Chair, and said:

"Come up, gentlemen, and wet your whistles."

Each member of the Club jumped to his feet and started for the bar to accept the stranger's invitation; but the Chair rapped on the stove with its stick, and demanded order.

"Gentlemen," said he, "you're actin' like a lot of hogs; don't you know the rules of this here Club about the members drinkin' with strangers?"

Mr. Truefact, who appeared in the Club this evening for the first time since being attacked with the fever, attempted to stutter out that as he understood the rule it was never to refuse to drink with *anybody;* but the Chair shut off debate from the convalescent fever patient by saying:

"If we'd wait for you to interpret the rules, we'd die of thirst afore we got a chance to drink."

Then, again addressing himself to the Club, he said:

"Gentlemen, this here thing must be put to a vote, and I caution you that there must be unanimous consent. All those as is in favor of drinkin' with this gentleman, please say 'Aye'—contrary-minded, 'No.'"

A prompt "aye" from every member present attested the "unanimous consent."

"Gentlemen," said the Chair, "you have so decided, and we'll purceed to drink with this here stranger. All promenade to the bar."

The members promenaded, and as they stood ranged along the bar, each, glass in hand, awaiting the signal from the President to chorus, "Here's luck," the stranger said:

"Gentlemen, why am I a musician of the first order?"

The President said this was not a conundrum society, and on behalf of the Club he gave it up.

"Because," continued the stranger, "I have waked to ecstacy the living lyre (liar)."

"Can't see the point," said the Doubter, swallowing his liquor and walking away from the bar.

"Best thing I ever heard in my life," said the Chair.

"I s'pose you mean the invitation to drink," whispered Uncle John to the President.

The Chair trod on Uncle John's foot, for the purpose, as it (the Chair) afterwards expressed it, of cautioning Uncle John not to "give away the business." But it happened to be Uncle John's rheumatic foot that was trodden on, and the old man said some bad words, and hopped around on one leg. This gave all the members something to laugh at; and the stranger thought they were laughing at his conundrum, and said:

"Thank you, gentlemen, you're the most appreciative lot of cusses I ever saw. But I can't stop; I've got to go up town and ask a man why an old maid is like a buzz-saw running at four thousand revolutions a minute."

"Give it up," said the Secretary, from the little round table over in the corner.

"Then I take down the pot," said his opponent.

This gave rise to a dispute between the Secretary and the man he was playing with, the latter contending that the former had given up the game, and the Secretary insisting that it was the conundrum he meant to give up; and during the confusion the stranger escaped. The disturbance which arose in the arbitration of this matter by the Club caused the stranger and his conundrum to be forgotten, and prevented its merits being discussed, as it otherwise would have been. The President decided the Secretary's dispute by ordering the pot confiscated to the use of the Club, and the money appropriated to the purchase of the "drinks for the crowd."

"Further Business."

After the ceremonies of confiscation and appropriation, the members resumed their seats, and further business was transacted as follows:

Uncle John related that where he used to live in the States there was a dog-breeder, who, by means of crossing various kinds of dogs, finally became possessed of one so small that when ten feet off she could not be seen except by the aid of opera-glasses. The man had been in hopes of getting the thing down so fine that he would grow rich by the sale of dogs of a suitable size for microscopic watch-charms; but he failed on that. When this animal became a mother, she gave birth to seven bull-pups, each of which weighed eleven pounds at birth.

Nobody expressed any doubts of the truth of this story; but the Doubter was heard to mutter: "Seven times 'leven's seventy-seven. Seventy-seven pounds of bull-pup, and the mother no bigger'n a peach-pit!"

When Uncle John had concluded, the Chair asked if anybody could "call that." There was no answer to this question, but Mr. Truefact said: "S-p-p-osen w-wee t-t-talk 'b-b-bout g-g-g-gras-s-s-hop-p-p-pers?"

"S'posen we do," assented several members.

Then the discussion was opened under the head of "grasshoppers."

All the old stories about grasshoppers eating mules and stopping railroad trains and bridging over rivers were related, and recorded by the Secretary, and it looked as if nothing new on the subject was to be advanced, and one member had even essayed to make a motion to adjourn by saying that the times were too dull and money too scarce for good, square, honest, lying, when Old Reliable interrupted, and said he hoped the gentleman would withhold his motion for a moment. This request being acquiesced in, Old Reliable cocked his feet upon the stove, borrowed the President's pipe, and spoke as follows:

"Mr. President, and gentlemen of the Club, what I am about to relate aint no lie; it's a true and actual positive fact. Once, when I was in Salt Lake, during one of the grasshopper years, they had br'iled chicken marked on the bill of fare at the restaurant I boarded at. I'm sort of partial to 'yaller-legs,' and I told the waiter to bring me half a br'iled chicken, which he did, as soon as the cook had fixed it up in shape. I proceeded to eat the bird, but noticed a kind of peculiar taste to it. So I questioned the waiter about it; and, gentlemen, what do you suppose I had been eating?"

"Grasshopper!" cried the entire Club in chorus.

"Not much; it was jest chicken. You see it was so long since I had eat chicken that it tasted kinder peculiar to me."

"Sold, by thunder!" was all the President said; but those words fitly expressed the sentiments of the entire Club.

"Speakin' of chickens," said Old Dad, when the Chair announced that the Club was again ready for business, "speakin' of chickens reminds me of somethin'"; and then he related a narrative, the substance of which was as follows:

Back in the Shenandoah Valley, when he was a boy, the whole country was covered with Methodist preachers and "yaller-leg" chickens. The former used to visit the people who owned the chickens, generally accompanied by an umbrella and a pair of saddle-bags, and when any one of them took his departure many less chickens lived on that farm than when he arrived. His uncle was the possessor of a yellow hound, which had been taught to chase and catch the feathered bipeds when any were wanted for the table, and the animal got to know the preachers so well that whenever a man appeared on the farm with an umbrella and a pair of saddle-bags, he would not wait for orders, but would make a straight break for the chickens, a number of which he would catch and carry to the house. To save their poultry his uncle had either to turn Presbyterian, or kill the dog; and he chose to change his creed.

Dad concluded the hour had grown late, and the Chair said he "reckoned they had better adjourn," and was about to declare the evening's session at an end, when another stranger entered the room. He was ragged and dirty, and as he passed the bar he looked imploringly at the bar-keeper. That individual pretended not to see him; and the stranger walked right up to the stove, lifted his coat-tails, placed his hands behind his back, and braced himself so as to catch the warmth on the reverse portion of his anatomy, while the obverse faced the Club.

"Gentlemen," said he, "was any of you fellers ever in this new minin' country, the Black Hills?"

There was no answer.

"I was thar nigh onto twenty year ago," continued he of the rags and dirt, "but was druv out by the Injuns, and they come mighty nigh nailin' my skelp, too, you bet your life."

"What kind of a country is it for timber and water?" asked the Chair, who felt that it devolved on somebody to notice the stranger.

"Timber and water! Blazes! Thar's a water stream every hundred yards, bunch grass at every step, and more and bigger pine timber to the squar' foot than to the squar' mile in the Sary Nevadys, and just alive with game at that. All a man needs in *that* country to git a livin' with is a shotgun and a sack of salt. Now ef any of you gentlemen's got a few dollars to invest in a good prospector, and a miner sence forty-nine, jest put yer trust in me. Gimme an outfit—a ridin' animal, a pack animal, a Henry rifle, tools, and about two hundred dollars' wuth of pervisions—and I'll go to them thar Black Hills and locate every one of you a claim that'll pan out to make yer all richer than Rosschild and Creesus put together. Does any of you gentlemen wish to invest?"

Echo answered "nary invest," and the President thereupon declared the Club adjourned.

The Club Perpetuated.

The President arose from his chair in front of the stove, and sighed. His classic features had a care worn look, and all the members present mentally noted that their beloved presiding officer seemed sad and cast down; and Mr. Thirsty was heard to mutter in an undertone that the Chair looked as solemn as he (Mr. Thirsty) did on the occasion that he met with a misfortune by swallowing a fly in his whisky.

The Chair simply said: "Gentlemen of the Club, jine me at the bar."

And the Club jined.

The Chair informed the bar-keeper that he would take "the same old thing"; and as he poured the fluid from the bottle into the glass, it was noticed that he made his allowance considerably in excess of the usual "three fingers"—that he filled the glass nearly level with its brim. The bar-keeper looked at him reproachfully, and remarked something about there being a wholesale liquor store down town, and the Chair took the hint, and said, in an apologetic tone:

"I need a big snort, to brace me up; I'm rastlin' with a mighty problem."

"A bar-glass level-full of straight whisky at one gulp is a mighty problem for any white man to rastle with," returned the bar-keeper, in a sarcastic tone of voice.

"Yes," meekly replied the Chair; "like assimulates to like, and I'm sendin' of this here mighty problem to meet the mighty problem as is now agitatin' of my brain." So saying, he swallowed the whisky, as the bar-keeper had described the process in advance, "at one gulp"; and as soon as he had regained his breath, he said:

"Gentlemen, let us resume."

"The way to resume is to resume," remarked the Philosopher.

"I hope members won't indulge in no triflin' to-night," said the Chair, with the tears welling up into its eyes—from the effects of his overdose of stimulant—"we hev on hand the most important business as has ever come afore this Club; so please resume your seats and come to order, and I'll state the sittywation."

The members, whose curiosity was now thoroughly aroused, hurriedly resumed their seats; and the Chair, having secured order, arose and said:

"Gentlemen of this here Club: As I hev stated afore, we hev most important business afore us to-night. You are goin' to be called on to deliberate the gravest question as has ever come under the consideration of this here flourishin' organization from the minnit of its commencement to date. I, as I hev said, hev rastled with the problem, but it knocks the spots off me. In fact, I give it up. I onc't heerd a man say that in a multitude of counselors thar is safety; and I'm goin' to submit this here question to the whole Club, not feelin' like takin' the responsibility of decidin' it single-handed, which, howsomever, I hev power to do under our Constitution and By-laws, bein' as I'm President."

"State your p'int of order," interrupted the Aye-and-No Member, who was evidently growing impatient.

"If you're goin' to state this question, you better come up here and do it, and you be President instead of me, and I'll step down and out into the obscurity of private life," returned the Chair, in a reproachful tone, and with his eyes bent on the Aye-and-No Member.

"Mebbe I could do it as well as some folks as I knows on, and not be all night beatin' round the bushes at it, either," snappishly returned the official voter for the Club.

"Gentlemen," said the Chair, in a sad tone, "you all know me well enough to know that at any other time I should resent the remarks of the galoot as has preceded me. But this is no time for quarrelin', and, considerin' that we hev important business on hand, and that this is the fust debate in which the gentleman has took part, I overlook his unpoliteness to his presiding officer on this occasion. Now to the p'int. The Seccertary will please read this, which explains itself, and durin' the readin' let every member sit still as a mice."

So saying, the Chair handed the Secretary an envelope, from which that official extracted a sheet of letter paper, and read from it as follows:

AUSTIN, Nevada, Nov. 20th, 1877.

TO THE PRESIDENT AND MEMBERS OF THE SAZERAC LYING CLUB —Gentlemen: As you may be personally and officially aware, I have, in my capacity of editor of the Daily Reese River REVEILLE, been divers and sundry times called upon to record in my valuable, widely circulated, and strictly family journal, some of the proceedings of the Club of which you have the distinguished honor to be President and members. This circumstance has caused the fame of the Sazerac Lying Club to spread abroad over this land of liberty, and even across the great waters to the effete monarchies of the old world, and all up and down the earth, and to the ends thereof. Yes, Mr. President and gentlemen, your fame and renown have spread like the exhalations of the upas tree, or a Chinese umbrella, or a Chicago girl's feet, or a church scandal, or anything else that has a habit of spreading; until at last it has even reached unto San Francisco.

I am in receipt of a communication from a firm of San Francisco publishers, requesting me to endeavor to obtain access to the archives and records of your Club, and to extract therefrom such matter as I, in my judgment, may select, the same to be published by the said firm in the form of a book, that the Sazerac Lying Club may be perpetuated unto our children, and our children's children, and to other generations yet unborn. My object, therefore, in thus addressing your most honorable body, is to obtain the permission as herein set forth for the purpose above stated, and to enable me to comply with the request embodied in the preceding.

Respectfully,

EDITOR REVEILLE.

P. S.—The publishers state that their object in desiring to publish the book aforesaid is not for mere speculative purposes, or to make money; but simply that a light may be given to the world that shall guide the step of youthful innocence in the walk of virtue, and lead the tottering feet of age through a path that shall be a fitting close to an eventful life.

"I vote aye!" shouted the Aye-and-No Member when the Secretary had concluded the reading of the above. "I want to be perpetuated to rising—may I say self-rising?—generations."

"Gentlemen," said the Chair, solemnly, "this is not a matter to be decided in a minnit. We must deliberate on it—calmly, deliberately, dispassionately; without fear or favor; with charity towards all, with malice towards none, and irrespective of age, sex, or previous condition of servitude. I would like to hear a expression of the sentiments of the Club on this here subjeck."

Mr. Thirsty spoke up and said, for his part, he didn't want to be "cremated"; he had read in a paper recently an account of the cremation of a woman in Pennsylvania, and concluded it must hurt.

"N-n-not c-c-c-rem-m-ma-t-t-ted, b-b-but p-p-p-p-p-erp-p-p-p-et-tuat-ted, you d-d-d——"

Before Mr. Truefact could finish the sentence given in part above, the Chair called him to order, and explained to Mr. Thirsty that he had not heard the word aright—that it was perpetuation and not cremation that was under discusssion.

Mr. Thirsty replied that if "the rest of 'em" could "stand it," *he* could.

A running discussion now ensued, in which every member of the Club took part. There was great diversity of opinion as to the proper course to pursue, the Doubter strenuously protesting against the granting of access to the records. He became so heated in the course of the argument that it became necessary for him to retire to the bar to recuperate his wasted energies; and Uncle John took advantage of his absence to move the previous question.

The question was put; the Aye-and-No Member hurriedly voted "Aye," and the Chair decided that the previous question was carried unanimously, and that the Club had resolved as with one voice to give access to its archives and records, that material might be selected therefrom to constitute matter for publication in a book, to be known as "THE SAZERAC LYING CLUB."

The Doubter, who returned to the stove just in time to hear the decision of the Chair, immediately tendered his resignation, which was accepted by his being fired out by unanimous consent.

Uncle John then offered a resolution that reporters should not be admitted at future sessions of the Club, and that all future records of proceedings be chucked into the stove as soon as recorded. This was unanimously adopted, as was a resolution by Old Dad, that the sessions of the Sazerac Lying Club be conducted with closed doors, NOW AND FOREVER AFTER.

Part VI.

FRONTIER SKETCHES.

Marcus.

The subject of this sketch was never a member of the Sazerac Lying Club, although he possesses, in a marked degree, the peculiar qualifications for eligibility to membership in that organization; and had he resided in Austin since the formation of the Club, would have been one of its most prominent members, and proudest ornaments. His full and true name is Marquis de Lafayette Shoults, but since his residence on the Pacific Coast he has been generally known as Marcus Schultz, and commonly called "Marcus." He is a native of Missouri, and emigrated from that State to California some twenty-five years ago, coming "the plains across" in an ox-wagon. From the time of his arrival in the Golden State until his emigration thence to Nevada, in the year 1862, Marcus was generally notorious throughout the mining camps of California as a queer and original character; and to-day he is known as such, or known of, in every mining town in Nevada, Utah, Idaho, and Montana, but more particularly in far Eastern and Southeastern Nevada, in which sections he has resided for ten years past.

Like all who went to California in the first rush, Marcus went there to seek his fortune. He failed to find it, and has long since given up the search. He is not wealthy, nor is he ever likely to be so; but no Rothschild or no Bonanza King is happier or more contented than he. He belongs to that class of men who deem that the world owes them a living, and that they are bound to have it; and if Marcus gets his regular meals and stimulants, and a few rough, comfortable clothes to wear, without being compelled to work for them, he asks nothing more of the world or its people. It is related in a sort of traditional way that when he first arrived in California he sought his fortune through the avenue of manual labor; but that was so long ago, that, even if the story is true, there is now no means of verifying it, and it would be hard to convince the majority of those who know him that it has any foundation in fact. But that for twenty-five years on the Pacific Coast he has lived and flourished without work, is sufficient evidence that he possesses talents of a peculiar order. The reader is not expected to understand that Marcus is a deliberate fraud; for he is not such. By his odd ways and original sayings he has a faculty of making everybody his friend, and in whatever town he may be living, there are few who have any means to spare but who see to it that he does not lack for the necessaries of existence; and the free and open hospitality so common in the mines prevents him from suffering for that liquid comfort which is now the chief consolation of his life.

When he left Missouri to go to California, the portion of the former State in which he was "borned and raised" was little better than a wilderness; so it can readily be conceived that his ideas were somewhat crude, and that he did not possess the education, refinement, and culture now so characteristic of the natives of the State of Missouri. To quote his own words, he had only a "*common classical education.*" But contact with the world, aided by a naturally sharp wit, and a faculty for observation, made him as good a judge of character and reader of human nature as though he had deliberately devoted his whole life to the study of those subjects. He has failed in these particulars somewhat of late years, owing to the too frequent putting of "an enemy into his mouth"; but there have been times when, by some sarcastic, but at the same time ludicrously witty remark or repartee, he has made men in high social or political position squirm as if they had been bitten by a tarantula. He used to be quick to detect hypocrisy or toadyism, which qualities he hated with his whole heart; and many a hand-shaking, smiling candidate has he made to feel as if he wished he had never been born. Not by abuse, or blackguardism, but simply by some comical allusion which would instantly bring its object into ridicule. He used to say:

"These here office-seeking cusses can stand all the blackguardin' you've a mind to give 'em; you can abuse 'em all you want to, and they won't kick; call 'em the meanest names on earth, and they'll ask you to drink; insult 'em, and they won't even talk back: but laugh at 'em, or make other people laugh at 'em, and they'll weaken like a dog on a desert and forty miles to water. They can't stand ridicule no mor'n a man can live on the smell of a dish-rag for nineteen days."

In his palmy days Marcus was a man full of resources, and possessed a great deal of a certain energy. He has roamed over the deserts and mountains on foot and on horseback from Arizona to Montana, always in search of the "better camp," and his efforts for a "stake" have to a limited extent at times been crowned with success. His means for the acquirement of money was principally through cards, or gambling of some sort, in the tricks of which he was an adept, in the earlier portion of his career. He never deemed it wrong to cheat at cards, and when caught in the act would own up like a man, and tell the cheated one:

"This here's a world whar every man in it is tryin' to git the best of somebody else. Some does it by smooth talkin' and lyin', others by merchandisin', and others by keards. I'm one of them last, and if you can't purtect yourself and keep off advantages, you aint got no business to try conclusions with a man that's made the subjeck a study. We all has to pay for our experience, and these here few dollars what I've beat you out of is only the price of one lesson."

In his earlier and purer days, Marcus was something of a dandy, and when he made a raise would get himself up regardless of expense. On one occasion, in Austin, when he had accumulated quite a sum in the business of banking, (he was banker of a rondeau game—a game played on a billiard table with a number of small ivory balls, the banker getting a certain percentage for keeping the game) he went to a tailor and ordered an expensive and elaborate suit of clothes, made strictly in accordance with his own peculiar ideas of style. In his views of dress, Marcus somewhat resembled the Chinaman, who, in buying Melican boots, buys the largest size in the store, so as to get as much leather as possible for his money. There was a time in the mountains of California when the "shanghai" coat was the prevailing mode for "dressed up," and Marcus always clung to this style. On the occasion in question his coat was of fine broadcloth, reaching nearly to his heels, silk-velvet vest of a gorgeous pattern, pants of a large plaid, stuck into a pair of high-heeled, stub-toed boots, the bottoms of the heels being tapered down to the size of a silver half-dollar piece, one of these coins being fastened by a screw to the bottom of each. A white shirt with a big "specimen" gold pin, and a broad-brimmed slouch hat, completed his outfit. When thus arrayed he presented a somewhat imposing appearance. He was large of stature, and of full figure, with something of an aldermanic development of body, which, added to an assumed important strut in his daily walk, and a dictatorial speech, was calculated to impress a stranger with the idea that he was one of the magnates of the town—a mining superintendent at the very least.

The writer of this well remembers the day on which Marcus first appeared in the gorgeous array above described. It was a Sunday morning, and Mr. Shoults walked into a barber shop, which was crowded with men waiting their turn for their Sunday shave. He stepped directly to a long mirror which was fastened to the wall, and which reflected his full length, and surveyed himself therein. Then, as if talking to himself in the glass, he said:

"Marcus, you're the best dressed man as ever stepped across the bound'ry lines of the State of Missoury." Then, turning and addressing the crowd in the shop, he said:

"Gentlemen, if I was to go back to Ralls County, Missoury—whar I come from to this country—the people for two hundred miles round would flock to our house to see the best dressed man in the State. Back thar they never seed a man dressed up as fine as I am, cause most of the people thar wear tow-linen shirts till they grow up, and then if they git one suit of linsey-woolsey homespun in a year, they think they're fixed for life. And look at me, in broadcloth and fine linen, and money in my clothes to throw at the birds! Why, I s'pose, fixed up as I am now, I could go back to Missoury and marry the best and richest gal in the State by jest crookin' of my finger at her."

But the days of Marcus' splendor have gone by; it is ten years since he has had a "shanghai" coat, and a white shirt, and a specimen pin; but he is as happy and cheerful in a pair of blue overalls, "stogie" boots, and a California gray flannel overshirt, as he used to be in his purple and fine linen. As illustrating his liking for good clothes, the following anecdote is related:

It was when Marcus had started down hill, and had got pretty well along towards the foot. Winter was coming on, and he had no overcoat, and it was in the bleak climate of White Pine, in which a heavy overcoat is an actual necessity for at least eight months in the year.

A gentleman hearing Marcus remark that it would not be long till the winds whispered an inquiry into his ear as to what he had been doing all summer, and where was his overcoat, volunteered to purchase and present him with that necessary garment. Of course Marcus did not refuse the kind offer, and the two started across the street to a store to select the article. On the way over, the gentleman asked Marcus what kind of a coat he would like.

"Somethin' warm, and at the same time becomin'. I go about as much on style as I do on comfort," was the reply.

"Don't you think a blanket coat would fill the bill?"

The blanket coat is a very commonly worn article of attire in the mountains, but is much more comfortable than elegant. Marcus wanted something better and more expensive, and replied that he did not think he should like a blanket coat, and would prefer one of broadcloth.

"But," said his friend, "a blanket coat is about as comfortable a garment as can be worn in this climate."

"Yes, I know it's comfortable," was the reply, "but the truth is, I never could play cards out of the sleeve of a blanket coat."

He got the broadcloth.

The Bank Exchange.

Marcus has been a business man in his time, having once been the proprietor of a "first-class" saloon. It was in a little placer-mining camp in Montana, named Indian Creek, but more commonly called "Hog'em." The camp was new, and there was, as is usual in such cases, a considerable floating population—though the actual resources of the place were not adequate to the support of one hundred persons, all told. One day Marcus came to the writer, who was working for wages in the diggings, and said:

"I want you to come up to my saloon to-night, and paint me a sign."

"My saloon" was a new revelation; and as for painting a sign, that seemed entirely out of the question in a place where there was not a brush or a drop of paint to be procured. But, as has previously been stated, Marcus was a man of resources, and assured the sign-painter that he need feel no uneasiness as regarded the materials for the proposed work.

When evening came, no difficulty was experienced in finding the "saloon," for there were not to exceed a dozen houses in the camp, at best, and the loud tones of Marcus' voice, which could be heard from one end to the other of the little street, soon indicated the precise locality of his establishment.

The "saloon" was in a little log cabin, with a dirt floor, a wide door in front, and no windows. The furnishing consisted of a couple of rude benches, a rickety table covered with a dirty blanket, two barrels on which rested a board, which answered the purpose of a bar, a pair of dilapidated gold scales, and a few bottles with lighted candles stuck in their mouths. The stock in trade consisted of a couple of greasy decks of cards and a gallon of cheap whisky, subdivided into four bottles, respectively labeled, Whisky, Gin, Brandy, Sherry—displayed ostentatiously on the "bar," and fenced in with a row of dingy glasses. After extending to the sign-painter a hospitable invitation to "take somethin'," Marcus went to the rear of the saloon and produced a board and a number of charred sticks. "I put in half a day makin' of these paint-brushes," he said, "and I want you to go to work and paint me a sign on this board, to stick up in front of the saloon."

There used to be in San Francisco a very popular drinking saloon known by the name of the "Bank Exchange." At one time it was the principal and most generally patronized saloon in that city, and its fame extended into the most remote mining camps. The name was as popular as was the establishment, and was adopted as a saloon title throughout California, and subsequently in the other mining States and Territories—mainly settled and developed by original Californians; and to such an extent was it carried, that it is doubtful if there is, or has been, a town or mining camp from Arizona to Montana, and from Oregon to Colorado, in which there has not been a "Bank Exchange Saloon."

What more natural, then, than that Marcus should choose the name "Bank Exchange" for his establishment?

And that was the name the artist painted on the pine plank with the charred sticks. And when the sign was completed, and fastened in place across the front and over the door of the log cabin, Marcus pronounced it a work of true artistic merit, and defied the world to produce its superior in the way of a saloon sign.

The "saloon" actually flourished for a few days, and Marcus was kept busy dealing out his stock, which he was compelled to frequently replenish by means of water and fresh purchases of whisky—a gallon at a time. He felt that he had "struck it" at last, and was on the high road to fortune, and was elated accordingly. But a reaction came, and he was plunged into the lowest depths of despair.

It was soon demonstrated that the diggings would afford work and pay to but a small number of men, and when this fact became unquestionable, there was a "stampede" for some other new camp, and the Bank Exchange was left without customers, or so nearly so that there was no longer any money in the business. Marcus, erstwhile so busy in dealing out poor and watered whisky at two bits a drink, now put in his time in bewailing the decadence of the camp, patronizing his own bar, and berating the Territory of Montana as a country not fit for a white man and a gentleman to live in. He was not the man to stay by a dead or dying camp, and when it became evident that Hog'em was gone in, Marcus determined to join the other rats that were leaving the sinking ship, and seek fresh fields for his talents, this determination necessarily resulting in the closing of the Bank Exchange. He had tried to sell out, but nobody wanted the property; and when all efforts in that direction had failed, he concluded to shut up shop and leave the place. When he had made up his mind to this course, he went behind the bar, and addressing himself to two or three old soakers who were lounging on the benches, said:

"Step up, gentlemen, and finish the stock in this here establishment."

The invitation was accepted with alacrity.

Marcus set a glass before each of the "gentlemen" ranged in front of the bar, and with his hand on the last bottle of whisky (labeled sherry) in the saloon, thus held forth: "Gentlemen, I come here to Hog'em to do bizness; I brung capital here; but you see how the camp's gone down. In the last ten days I've sunk twenty-one hundred dollars in this bizness, and this here bottle's the last of it. Help yourselves, gentlemen!"

The "gentlemen" helped themselves, and Marcus joined them; and when the bottle was emptied, he upset the bar-counter, chucked the gold scales into a corner, and said:

"Good-bye, gentlemen, and good luck to you all. I'm off for a better camp." Then he went out of the door, in front of which his horse stood saddled, and mounting the animal, turned once more to the "gentlemen," who had assembled at the door to see him off, and casting his eyes and pointing his finger at the sign, said:

"Gentlemen, you all know I've lost twenty-one hundred dollars in this bizness in the last ten days, and I want to tell you all, right here, that I think the Territory of Montany's a fraud. Why, gentlemen, I'd rather run an ice-cream cart in the State of Nevady than a first-class saloon in the Territory of Montany; and I'm now on the back track for the sagebrush. Good-bye!"

So saying, he put spurs to his horse and was off.

The truth of the matter was, that Marcus started the saloon without any capital whatever, getting credit for such stock and furniture as he purchased, and during his flush time he had taken in several hundred dollars, which was nearly all profit. This money (in gold dust) he carried sewed inside of his shirt when he left Hog'em. But his object in declaring and reiterating that he had lost $2,100 in the business was to prevent any of the impecunious individuals of his Hog'em acquaintance from asking him for a loan.

How They Got Grub.

Several years ago, before the building of the Pacific railroads, and the consequent introduction of railroads into Utah Territory, Marcus and a companion, who shall be here called Mr. Brown, were traveling through the Mormon settlements in Northern Utah, *en route* to Montana. The two men were on horseback, and had a pack-horse for the transportation of their provisions, blankets, and camping outfit. They had traveled many hundred weary miles over mountain and plain, and not having had a very large supply of provisions to start with, were on short rations most of the way, and when they reached nearly the northern borders of Utah their stock was completely exhausted. They were traveling through the Mormon settlements, where provisions were easily procurable for money or for barter; but they had neither one nor the other to offer in exchange for the articles they needed. Riding along the road one day, when they were down to their last allowance of bacon and flour sufficient for a meal, Brown suggested that at the next settlement they came to they swap the pack-horse for the needed provisions, pack them on one of the saddle-horses, and "ride and tie" with the other saddle-horse the rest of the journey. To "ride and tie" is for two men with one horse between them to take turn about at riding and walking. This plan Marcus instantly and strenuously opposed. He said he was not "stuck after walking, anyhow," and urged that the saddle-horse could not carry as large a quantity of provisions as the pack-horse ought to bring in the exchange. He admitted that it was positively necessary that a supply of provisions must be obtained that day; but as for him, he would rather live on sage-brush for the balance of the journey than to part with one of the animals.

The two men rode along in silence for some time, each absorbed in his own thoughts, and each probably trying in his mind to devise some means to procure the necessary food, when the houses of the settlement appeared to view in the distance. Reining up his horse, Marcus halted, and, pointing to the collection of houses, said:

"Yonder is the settlement. I'll ride ahead and see how the land lays, and you lead the pack-horse, and come along slow."

"What do you propose to do?" asked Brown.

"Oh, I'll ride in thar, and make myself at home with them Mormons, and talk sweet to the women folks; and if we don't git the grub we want, they'll give us a squar meal, anyway. You be sure and ride along slow, and give me a chance to git my work in."

Brown assented to the plan, but he had only slim hopes that Marcus would succeed in wheedling the Mormon women out of the required provisions; for he knew that the Mormon settlers were very suspicious of Gentiles, and also exceedingly avaricious, and that it was part of the creed instilled into them by their leaders never to assist a Gentile, and never to have any dealings or business transactions with them, unless they (the Mormons) were sure of getting the best of the bargain. Marcus spurred his horse into a "lope," and soon reached the settlement; and alighting at the first house in his road, dismounted, and knocked at the door.

The door was opened by a young, pleasant-faced Welsh woman, with a baby in her arms, and Marcus asked her for a drink of water. She hastened into the house to procure him the water, leaving him standing at the door, and soon returned with a tin cup filled with water. Marcus took the cup, and while he was drinking, the baby in the woman's arms set up a piteous wail, which attracted his attention to it, and he noticed that its head was a perfect mass of sores.

"What's the matter with your baby, ma'am?" he asked.

"I'm sure I don't know, sir," she replied. "These sores came and covered its head all over, and the poor wean haven't had no rest nor comfort since. There beant no doctors among we people, and naught I can try seems to do it any good. Does thee know anything I could do for the wean?"

"No, I aint no doctor," replied Marcus, "but back here a piece, trav'lin' with me, is one of the finest and smartest doctors on the Pacific Coast, and what he don't know about doct'rin' aint wuth talkin' about. You see, ma'am, he's got a big band of cattle what he's takin' up to Montanny to sell for beef, and me an' him is ridin' ahead horseback, and the droviers is behind with the cattle. He's a very rich man and don't practice any only to accommodate his friends; but bein' as he's a little consumptive himself, me and him is travelin' ahead for his health. He can cure your baby, but you mustn't offer him no money, for he's that hightoned he'd git insulted in a minute. Thar he is; that's him comin' now," and Marcus pointed to Mr. Brown, who was slowly riding up, leading the pack-horse.

"Will you ask him to do something for my wean?" said the woman.

"Certainly," replied Marcus, "but don't you say nothin' to him, 'cause then he'll know you've found out he's a doctor. Leave it to me, ma'am, and I'll git him to fix your baby up as sound as a new dollar."

Mr. Brown had now approached within call, and Marcus said:

"Step this way, Doctor Brown."

Mr. Brown was puzzled to account for Marcus' reason for applying the title "Doctor" to him, but felt that it had some connection with the plan to procure grub. Therefore, he said nothing in reply to the call, but determined to await events. He rode up to the door, and as he dismounted, Marcus said, in a loud tone of voice:

"Doctor, step in here and look at this lady's baby, and see if you can't do something for it."

Dr. Brown's appearance was not calculated to impress the beholder with the belief that he was a man rolling in wealth. Long travel through all kinds of weather had played sad havoc with clothes not originally of the best, and sleeping on the ground and other hardships had not given to him the cleanly aspect which even a Mormon woman might expect the "finest and smartest physician" on the Pacific Coast to present. But well-dressed men were not common in the Mormon settlements in those days, and the Doctor's ragged attire and unkempt condition did not impress the woman unfavorably, or cause her to doubt the statements of Marcus concerning him.

She politely invited the Doctor into the house, and laid her infant across her lap, with its head toward him, that he might the more readily inspect it.

The only thing Dr. Brown could think of for the moment as the proper and professional thing to do under the circumstances, was to grasp the child's wrist, look wise, and feel its pulse. Then he looked at its head. And such a head! It was one mass of scabs, and its appearance was absolutely revolting, and the Doctor was forced to turn his eyes away from it, in fear that it would sicken him. In thus turning away his eyes, they encountered a table on which stood a number of tin pans filled with new milk; and he was struck with a happy idea. It seemed eminently proper that such a disgusting spectacle as that child's head ought to be covered from sight, and he at once conceived a plan for so concealing its hideousness from view.

"Madam," said he, turning to the woman, "have you any fresh milk in the house?"

"A plenty—a plenty of it."

"Have you likewise some wheat flour?"

"Oh, yes, sir; a plenty."

"Bring me some fresh milk and some wheat flour, then."

The woman hastened to comply with these orders, and in a few moments set before the Doctor one of the pans of milk and a wooden platter filled with flour.

Dr. Brown, with the flour and milk, mixed up a compound of the consistency of thick paste, and whittling a paddle out of a piece of wood, plastered the child's head over with the mess, and entirely concealed the sores from view. The stuff, which must have had something of a cooling effect, seemed to relieve the infant's pain, and it quit the crying it had up to that time kept up ever since the Doctor's entrance.

"Thar, I told you!" exclaimed Marcus, addressing himself to the woman. "I knowed he could cure your young-un in a minnit and a half by the watch."

The woman evidently believed that the Doctor had applied a sovereign remedy to her child's cranium, and began to utter expressions of gratitude, and wound up by inviting Marcus and the Doctor to stay to dinner. This invitation was unhesitatingly accepted by the two travelers, as was the permission to put their animals in the corral, and give them some hay and a feed of grain.

While the woman was preparing the meal, Marcus and Dr. Brown went out, the former to attend to the horses, and the latter to prepare some "powders." Among the cherished possessions of this worthy pair were a few lumps of white crushed sugar, contained in a cylindrical tin box, such as butter is packed in for the use of prospectors. It was the last sugar they were destined to see until Gentile settlements were reached; as the Mormons knew not sugar in those days, sorghum syrup—which was plentifully produced in Utah—answering their purposes for "sweetening." This sugar the Doctor proposed converting into "powders," but Marcus entered a feeble protest against its being so wasted; but the Doctor succeeded in convincing him that it was absolutely necessary that the child should have medicine.

While Marcus was looking to the comfort of the stock, Dr. Brown sat on the ground in the corral, and, with the tin box for a mortar, and the handle of a knife for a pestle, was crushing the sugar into powder. He felt some misgivings as to the course they were taking with the woman and her baby, and suggested to Marcus that it would hardly be the fair thing to accept anything more than the meal and the horses' feed for services of such little value.

"Thunder!" exclaimed Marcus, "they've got grub to throw at the birds."

Then he explained that he had learned from the woman, while awaiting the Doctor's arrival, that she was wife number five of a Welshman who owned six little ranches at different points along the stream which ran through the valley in which this settlement lay; that he had a wife at each ranch, and visited each one at stated intervals. This husband, he had learned, was wealthy in live-stock and produce, and he urged that from such a man it was not wrong to accept enough food to enable them to continue the journey. He then requested that all matters pertaining to the procurement of provisions be left to him, and, this being agreed to, he again entered the house.

When Dr. Brown had completed the pulverization of the sugar, he took from his pocket a note-book, from which he tore a number of leaves.

Dividing these into pieces of a suitable size, he placed a portion of the sugar in each, and folded it up as he had seen apothecaries put up "powders." When his task was completed there were upwards of one hundred of the powders, and he gathered them up and returned to the house.

As he approached the door he heard the child screaming at the top of its lungs, and on entering, observed that the poor little thing's head had turned completely black. A closer inspection soon revealed the cause of this sudden change in color, from white to black.

The flies were very numerous, and, attracted by the sweet mixture on the child's head, a myriad of them had settled on it. When once a fly lit on the mass, there it stuck; and the result was, the little one's skull was covered with flies.

The Doctor directed the mother to procure some warm water and a soft cloth, and wash the mixture from the child's head. This done, he applied a fresh coat of the paste, and directed the woman to cover it with a soft wet cloth. This being complied with, the infant soon became quiet, and the flies were unable to settle on its poor, disgusting, sore little head, and in a short time it was calmly sleeping in a cot in a corner of the room.

The woman was delighted with the success of Dr. Brown's treatment, and grew profuse in expressions of gratitude; and when the Doctor handed her the bundle of powders and told her to administer one every two hours, she so far forgot the caution Marcus had given her as to say that if there was anything on the place he would accept in payment, she would give it to him.

Dr. Brown thanked her, and said he had quit practicing medicine "for pay" many years before, and only rendered medical services now as an act of kindness. Marcus, however, had already interviewed the woman on the grub question, and spoke up, saying:

"Doctor, I don't know but we're a little short of some things; and as this here lady won't take pay for nothin', and we've got to have 'em, anyway, or else wait till your cattle comes up, we might as well take 'em, and done with it."

Dr. Brown replied that as the commissary department was entirely under the control of Marcus, and as the question of subsistence stores was too trivial for his (the Doctor's) consideration, the entire matter was left to his (Marcus') discretion.

Nothing more was said on the subject for the time being, and soon the hostess announced that dinner was ready. And the two travelers lost no time in getting to the table, where they seated themselves, and did ample justice to the first square meal they had eaten in over five hundred miles of horseback travel.

When the meal was concluded, the travelers expressed an intention of soon resuming their journey; and then Marcus and the woman conversed on the provisions question.

"We don't need much of anything," said he. "A little flour, and some bacon, and perhaps a little butter and a few taters, and some cheese."

The grateful woman placed her cellar at the disposal of Marcus, and he was not at all backward in making his selections, so he soon had the pack-horse loaded with flour, bacon, and the other edibles mentioned, to the full extent of the animal's carrying capacity. In fact, the pack-horse fairly staggered under its load.

The packing completed, the Doctor gave the woman directions concerning the treatment of the infant's head, cautioning her not to let the paste harden, but by constant washing with warm water, and renewals of the application, keep the head constantly covered with moist milk-and-flour paste. The woman promised strict compliance with this order, and the additional one, to be sure and give a powder every two hours, and bade the Doctor and his traveling companion a grateful adieu, and the two travelers went on their way rejoicing.

The incidents above related occurred in the spring of the year. In the fall of that year Marcus again passed through the Mormon settlement, where this had occurred, on his return to Nevada from Montana. Dr. Brown also returned to Nevada, but by another route.

When the two met in White Pine, for the first time since they parted in Montana, Marcus informed the Doctor that he had passed through that settlement and stopped and had a talk with that Welsh woman. He averred, and offered to take his oath to it, that when the child whose head had been treated was shown to him, its head was covered with a profuse growth of hair at least a foot in length; that the woman had assured him that the child had commenced to mend from the moment of taking the first powder, and had continued to improve, until at the end of a few weeks it was entirely well; and its hair commenced to grow, and had continued growing at the rate of an inch per day. And further, that she had given some of the powders to the mother of another of her husband's wives, who by their use had been entirely cured of a severe case of inflammatory rheumatism, and concluded by asking kindly concerning the health and welfare of Dr. Brown, and showering blessings on his head, and wishing her "man" could only see him to thank him for the salvation of their child.

Not Worth Killing.

The adventure herewith related is one which befell the author of this work some eleven years ago, and though it appears in this book of lies, it is as one grain of wheat in a bushel of chaff, as the account here given is strictly true.

I was on my way on foot to the Salmon Basin diggings (called also Lemhi mines) in Montana Territory. Many miles of weary and footsore travel over mountains and deserts, and through a wild and almost uninhabited country, had brought me into Eastern Idaho, and at the time of meeting this adventure I was some forty or fifty miles north of Snake River.

[I cannot be particular as to the exact distances after so great a lapse of time.]

My equipment consisted of the clothes on my back—which were coarse, ragged, and travel-stained—a pair of blankets which I carried in a roll slung over my shoulder by a rope, and in which were enclosed a few pounds of flour, a small sack containing ground coffee, a small piece of bacon, a box of yeast powders, a little salt tied in a rag, a tin plate, and some matches. The rest of my outfit consisted of a pocket knife and a tin cup, the latter slung to a leather belt around my waist. Thus equipped, I was on my way to seek my fortune in a new camp, situated over 1,200 miles from the point from which I had started.

The Salmon Basin diggings were placer gold mines, about the extent and richness of which marvelous tales had been told and circulated throughout the mining camps of the Pacific Coast; and at the time of which I am writing there was in progress a movement towards them popularly called a "stampede"—that is, people were rushing in there from all directions. The diggings, however, cut no figure in this story beyond answering mere introductory purposes.

One evening I arrived at a station on the Salt Lake and Montana stage road, along which my route had lain after leaving Salt Lake. At this station, which was called the Junction, two roads met. One was the regular traveled stage road from Salt Lake City to Helena, Montana, and the other the Holliday road to the same point *via* Bannock and Virginia City, and which merged into the traveled road at this point. The Holliday road north from the Junction had been abandoned, and the only travel on it was occasionally by Mormon trains bound with produce for Bannock and other points in western Montana.

The station at the Junction stood out in an open plain, and consisted merely of a barn for the horses, and a shanty for the hostlers. I do not distinctly remember, but it may have been a "home station," in which case there was also a larger house for the accommodation of the drivers whose "routes" ended here, and where meals were furnished to the stage passengers.

On my arrival, I laid my blankets on the ground a short distance from the station, and, unrolling them, took therefrom my provender and cooking traps, built a fire with some brush, and proceeded to prepare my simple meal. The tin plate served me as bake-oven and frying-pan, and the tin cup as coffee-pot and drinking vessel. My method of cooking was thus: Filling the tin cup with water, I set it on the ground; then opening the sack in which my flour was contained, I made a depression in the flour with my fist. Into this I dropped a pinch of salt, and a small quantity of yeast powder. Then, kneeling beside the sack, I poured water from the cup into the depression in the flour with my right hand, while with the left scraping flour from the sides and stirring the mess I was forming. When the proper consistency was attained, I gathered the dough and kneaded it in my hands. Then, greasing the plate with a piece of bacon, I patted the dough down on it in a rude loaf, and, drawing some coals from the fire with a stick, I set the plate on them, and thus baked the loaf. The coffee was prepared by setting a cup of water on some coals, and when the water boiled, dropping the proper allowance of coffee into it, and after allowing it to boil a few seconds, taking the cup from the coals and setting it on some ashes, where it could keep warm and "settle" at the same time. When the bread was done, it was taken from the plate and laid on the ground, and the plate made to do duty in frying the bacon.

I am thus minute in describing my cooking operations that the reader may better understand what follows.

After disposing of my meal, I went over to the station and asked permission of an hostler to spread my blankets in the haystack that night. This was ungraciously refused, the man giving the excuse that I might set the hay on fire. That I should have done so was out of the question, for I had already built my camp-fire at quite a distance from the station, or stack, which he could not help seeing, and would have no use for fire in the vicinity of the hay. However, I did not argue the matter with him, but went back to my camp-fire, spread my blankets on the ground, and turned in.

Next morning, while I was preparing my breakfast, the man of whom I had asked permission to sleep in the hay, and another whom I had not before seen, came to my fire, and, after bidding me good morning, in a pleasant tone, asked me which road I intended to take.

I replied that my intention was to continue on the stage road.

One of the men then asked me where I was bound for.

"Salmon Basin," I replied.

"You are going to take the longest road, then," he said.

I requested an explanation, as I knew nothing of the Holliday road, and supposed there was but one road, and that the stage road.

He then, assisted by occasional suggestions from his companion, explained to me that by traveling the Holliday road I should save sixty miles of travel.

I knew enough of the geography of the country to realize that he was telling the truth—though I did not doubt him—and that the Holliday road must be a shorter cut to my destination.

"But," I said, "are there any stations on the road, or is there anybody living along it?"

In reply, he stated that the road was abandoned, but that there were good camping places at easy stages of travel, besides the deserted stations, in which I could take shelter for the night when reaching one of them.

"How are the Indians on that road?" I asked.

He answered that I need have no fear of Indians, as there were very few of them in that vicinity, and those were peaceably disposed.

I afterward learned that these men at the station *knew* that two white men had been killed by Indians on this Holliday road but a few days before. What their object was in endeavoring to induce me to take that route, I have never been able to conceive; for it is hard to believe that two civilized beings would attempt to induce a fellow-creature, alone in a wild country, to take the chances of death and capture at the hands of Indians, except through pure, heartless wantonness.

I had no reason to suppose that the men were actuated by any sinister motive in advising me about the roads, and a saving of sixty miles was a great object for a man in my situation. So, packing my blankets and slinging them over my shoulder, I thanked the men for the information they had imparted, bid them good-day, and started out on the Holliday road.

I will here digress to state that the Bannack and Snake Indians, portions of which tribes inhabited and roamed the section through which I was traveling, had for some time been very warlike, and it was only the presence of soldiers in the country that kept them at all within bounds and protected travel on the roads. The redskins had suffered frequent severe chastisements at the hands of the troops under the command of General Connor, and were so far subdued that they would not attack armed parties, but continued to murder and rob in isolated cases, where the attacked parties were incapable of adequate resistance.

On the evening of the first day out from the Junction I arrived at one of the deserted stations on the Holliday road. It was situated in a beautiful, grassy cañon, through which ran a pretty little stream, its banks fringed with willows and quaking aspens. The station consisted of a large barn structure, built of rough planks, and at one side of it was a long, narrow house, or cabin, with a shed roof sloping from the roof of the barn. To sleep under cover was a luxury which of late I had not had many opportunities of enjoying, and I entered the cabin—which had served as hostlers' quarters when the stage line was running—and proceeded to arrange for quarters for the night. At one end of this cabin there was an excavation about four feet in depth, which had probably served the purpose of a cellar when the cabin had been occupied, and along one of the walls was fastened a board, which had been used for a shelf. Unrolling my blankets on the floor in the front part of the cabin, near the door, I took out my provisions and laid them on the shelf, and then went outside to build a fire with some chips from a large pile which lay near the door. While thus engaged, I noticed a movement of the willows on the bank of the stream, and presently there emerged therefrom two Indians.

They were Bannacks, and handsome fellows withal. They were tricked out in garments of fringed buckskin, with their hair decorated with feathers and bits of brass, and each carried the blanket which is every Indian's inseparable companion. For arms, one had an army musket, and the other a bow and a quiver of arrows, and each wore a knife slung at his waist.

Their sudden appearance from the willows nearly took my breath away; but before they reached where I was kneeling, in the endeavor to light a fire, I had managed to partially recover my composure. But I was dreadfully frightened; though I did all in my power to avoid the betrayal of any signs of fear or surprise, and when they reached me I made out to utter the salutation common in addressing an Indian:

"Hello, Jim."

"Hello, Jim," they both echoed in chorus.

They then both entered the house, and I arose and followed them in. One of them jumped into the hole at the rear end of the cabin, and the other stood on the edge, and for a few moments they remained thus, grinning at me and conversing in their own language.

This gave me a few moments for thought, in which I realized that I was in a bad scrape. If the Indians were disposed to be hostile, they had me at their mercy; and the odds were that, finding me alone and incapable of resistance, they would not be disposed to extend to me any great amount of merciful consideration. With the exception of an insignificant jack-knife, I was unarmed. At one stage of my journey I had possessed a Colt's five-shooter, but had dropped it in the water while jumping across an irrigating ditch in one of the Mormon settlements, which had rusted it so that the cylinder refused to revolve, and I had traded it to a Mormon for some flour and bacon. And as I stood there smiling in return to the grins of those Indians, the only thought I could summon was:

"Oh, if I only had that five-shooter!" With a revolver I could hold my own against both Indians, and if I could only exhibit such a weapon, they, with their crude arms, would never dare to attack me in close quarters, and if they attempted to shoot me at a distance, I could fortify myself in the house, and having some provisions and they none, could hold out longer than they could on that kind of a siege.

As I stood in the cabin, with these thoughts passing through my mind, the Indian in the cellar vaulted out on to the earth floor, and deliberately walked to the shelf on which lay my provisions, and picked up a remnant of a loaf of bread left over from my morning's baking at the Junction, and breaking it in two, gave one half to his companion and walked laughing out of the cabin. The other Indian then lay down on my blankets, and proceeded to eat his portion of the bread.

He had a pair of green blankets, and the color of mine was red—a hue particularly dear to the Indian heart. He felt of the texture of my blankets, and then of that of his own, and looking up into my face, said:

"You like him schwap?" (swap).

The only thing I could think of to say was: "How much schwap?"—meaning how much boot he was willing to give me, as mine were the best blankets.

"No got any how much," he grunted in reply.

Then he joined his companion outside, and they walked to the willows by the stream, and disappeared in their thickness.

I hardly dared to hope the savages had left me. I knew the Indian character pretty well, and that treachery was its predominant trait. They had no assurance that I was unarmed; I might have a revolver in my shirt—in which manner that arm is frequently carried by mountaineers and prospectors—and they might have concluded that it was unsafe to attack me then and there, and had pretended to leave, but intended to come back at night, and either kill me in my sleep or set fire to the station and burn me alive.

My predicament, however, did not destroy my appetite. I had footed a matter of thirty miles that day, and, despite my fears and danger, was intensely hungry. It would be bad enough to be killed by Indians, away out in the wilderness, metaphorically a thousand miles from anywhere; but it could but add to the pang of death to die on an empty stomach; so I set about preparing my evening meal. By the time I had eaten my frugal fare it was growing dark, and as the Indians were not in sight, there was nothing for it but to turn into my blankets. I was terribly tired and needed rest; for, if the Indians did not molest me, I must travel on the morrow. I thought I was too frightened to sleep, but I would lie down on the blankets and rest, and keep a sharp lookout for the Indians, and if attacked would at least die with my eyes open.

The air had grown cool, but I hesitated about closing the door of the cabin, for fear I could not keep sight of the Indians should they approach; but while debating in my mind what was best to do in this respect, my eyes fell on a piece of a board which lay on the cabin floor, and the sight at once inspired me with an idea. Picking up the piece of board, I closed the door—which opened toward the interior of the cabin—and placed it slanting against the door, so that one end rested under the rusty and catchless latch and the other against my left hip as I would lie in my blankets. I then lay down and adjusted the board; and it was but a few moments till my fears were overcome by my fatigue, and, notwithstanding the peril, I slept.

I must have been slumbering thus a couple of hours, when I was awakened by the end of the board pushing against my hip. Like a flash I assumed a sitting posture, and, trembling and perspiring with fear, while the beating of my heart was as audible as the ticking of a clock, bent my eyes on the door.

The door had been pushed open a space of about two inches, and gleaming through the interstice was a pair of glittering Indian eyes, shining like twin stars.

I felt that my hour had come, and again the wish for my unfortunate five-shooter was my uppermost thought.

But wishes were futile; and as the savage gazed, and his eyes seemed as if they were burning into mine, my hand encountered an object in the pocket of the overalls I wore.

It was a tobacco-box.

A tin tobacco-box, with a strong, loud-snapping spring to the cover.

By mere impulse I drew this box from the pocket, and first raising the lid, then shut it down with all the power of my strength. The spring gave a loud snap as the lid closed. In the dark, and under the circumstances, the sound was like that made by the cocking of a pistol.

Mr. Indian thought so too, and lost no time in getting away from the door.

My hip was not disturbed again during the night. I slept fitfully, and with the first streak of dawn through the cracks of the cabin, I was up and outdoors, hurriedly preparing my breakfast, and anxious to resume my journey as quickly as possible.

While thus engaged, the willows by the stream moved, and out therefrom came the two Indians. They approached me smiling, and running their hands through their long hair, as if making their morning toilet, and coming to the fire squatted down over it and shivered, and said:

"Heap cold."

I replied in terms: "Heap cold."

When my breakfast was cooked, they watched me eat it; and when I was through, one of them said:

"Heap hogadi; tower heap gib 'em me."

"Hogadi" is Indian-English for hungry, and "tower" is the nearest they can come to saying flour—under which head they include food of any description.

As they showed such a disposition to be polite, I emptied the remnants of my breakfast into their hands, and gave them the coffee-cup with its remaining contents, and proceeded to do up my blankets, preparatory to taking up my line of march.

It did not take the Indians long to consume the food; and this done, one of them climbed up on the roof of the cabin, and thence crawled up the roof of the barn to the comb, spread himself on his breast, and, shading his eyes with his hands, looked intently down the road in the direction which I had come the day before. Meanwhile, the other went out into the road and lay down, placing his hand to his ear, and the ear to the ground.

I did not know what to interpret from these maneuvers; but soon the Indian on the roof came down, and the one in the road arose, and they both came toward me.

"Heap waggin," said the one who had been on the roof.

I caught the idea in a moment. There was a train of Mormon wagons on the road, a short distance behind, and the Indians, with their delicate sense of hearing and far-sighted eyes, had become aware of the fact.

"Yosh," (yes) I replied. "Heap waggin, me waggin"—pointing my finger at my breast to indicate that I belonged to the train, and leaving them to infer that I was traveling ahead to spy out the road, which was at times the custom by a man on horseback.

My pack was now ready, and I slung it over my shoulder and started ahead through the cañon. The Indians followed behind in a dog trot, but I kept close to them, and with my hand inside my shirt, as if holding a weapon, eyed them closely. The three of us continued on in this way for a distance of about three miles, till the mouth of the cañon, where it opened into a wide valley, came in view; then they suddenly turned and trotted off on the back track, and were soon lost to view in the windings of the cañon.

And that was the last I saw of my two Bannack braves.

I trudged along through the valley, which was nothing more than a desert, with prickly-pears (cactus) for its only vegetation, congratulating myself on my lucky escape of the night before, wishing my journey was ended, or that I had never undertaken it, and occasionally building up a beautiful air-castle, such as many a fortune-seeker, on his way to a new mining camp, has builded, and will build, so long as there are mines and men to seek them, when I observed a great cloud of dust in the valley. My first thought was that the dust might be created by a train of wagons; then, that perhaps it was soldiers, as I know that troops were moving about the country. But I was soon enlightened as to the cause. A short time sufficed to bring me near enough to the object to see that the dust was occasioned by a large body of mounted Indians moving across the plain.

Here I was, afoot and alone, one insignificant human being, in a great valley, with upwards of two thousand Indians moving down upon me. I suppose I ought to have felt very important, but I didn't. I felt as if I wanted to run; but that would have been folly. The Indians could see me as plainly as I could see them, and plainer. They were mounted, and I was afoot; it was a long distance to the hills, and on their fleet ponies they could overtake me before I could reach the hills, and even if there, they could kill or capture me without resistance on my part. So there was nothing for it but to keep right on in the road and meet them, and take the chances on what might turn up. I trudged along, each moment bringing me nearer to the savage horde, and as I walked I counted on my capture as sure when I should reach the cavalcade. I knew the Indians tortured all prisoners, without exception, and I pictured myself tied to a tree as a target for the young Indian idea to learn how to shoot close to a man's heart without hitting it, or lying on the ground and serving as a cushion for the old squaws to sit down on, or sitting in a lodge on a buffalo skin, acting the part of doll-baby for the pappooses to stick arrow-points in to hear it holler. I did not dream of any Pocahontas running to my rescue to save me from the fury of the cruel chief, her father. Pocahontii don't exist among the Indians in these degenerate days; and the prettiest young squaw takes as much delight in the torture of a prisoner as does the most hardened brave, and all these facts I knew. But, whatever my thoughts and fears, the only course to pursue was to keep right on and face the music. The gap between the Indians and myself gradually closed, and soon I stood face to face with the chief. As I approached, the entire body of Indians halted.

As it stood there on the open plain, the cavalcade was a magnificent sight. Upwards of two thousand Indians, in their fringed and beaded buckskin and feathers, and with painted faces, all mounted, with the exception of a few blear-eyed old hags who were leading the ponies of favorite squaws. Piled on the backs of some of the ponies were packed the tanned deer-hides which formed the lodge-coverings, and the skins which served for beds; and slung at the sides of the animals, with one end trailing on the ground, were the lodge-poles. On the ponies thus laden, sitting on top of the packs, were the young squaws and children, and on other horses rode the braves, some seated in saddles and others bareback.

As the body of Indians halted, I advanced toward its front; and as I approached, I was greeted with the salutation, uttered in as plain English as I myself could speak:

"Good morning, Captain."

Replying in kind, and feeling reassured by the peaceful greeting, I surveyed the man who had addressed me. He was mounted on a magnificent, coal-black, American horse, decorated with gorgeous barbaric trappings, and what with the height of his horse, my own embarrassment, and his stature—which was extraordinarily tall—he seemed to me a veritable giant, as I stood before him on the ground, gazing up into his face. The very first impression I formed of him was that he was a renegade white man, who had worked his way into authority in the tribe, and no Indian at all. He had handsome Caucasian features, of a regular mold, and lacked the aquiline nose and high cheek-bones characteristic of the Indian race. Besides, the tones of his voice, and his pronunciation of English words, were as much as possible unlike Indian utterance. He was clad in Indian costume—buckskin pants and hunting-shirt, ornamented with beads, deep fringes, and beaded moccasins. His hair, which was black, fell to his shoulders; but his complexion, though naturally dark, and tanned to a still deeper hue, was not the tawny red color of the Indian skin. I thought then, and still think, that I had never looked upon a more magnificent specimen of physical manhood than this pretended Indian; for that he was a real Indian I can never believe. By his side, mounted on a pony, sat a very pretty, girlish-looking squaw, and resting across the pack which served her for a saddle, was a wicker frame, such as the Indian women carry their children in, and out from it peeped a cunning little face, with rosy cheeks, and keen black eyes, and soft, silky hair, very much unlike the coarse hair of the full-blooded Indian.

When I had answered his salutation by replying: "Good morning, sir," he asked me where I was bound for.

"To Salmon Basin," I replied.

"What made you take this road?" he asked.

I then related to him the circumstances which had transpired at the Junction, whereby I was induced to take the Holliday road.

Applying to the men who had persuaded me to take this route an epithet reflecting on their maternity, he said:

"Are you aware that in persuading you to take this road they were sending you to your death?"

During the conversation my timidity had departed, and I had gained confidence that I would be allowed to pass on without molestation; but when he said these words my courage failed me, and I could distinguish a tremor in my voice and feel a quaking of my limbs, when I answered that perhaps they did not know the Indians were bad on that road.

Noticing my agitation, he said: "Don't be afraid—*I* won't harm you, nor will I let my people touch a hair of your head. But the Indians are *not* bad on this road, because they have no interest in being bad."

He then explained that the band of Bannacks which he headed was then on its way to a stream known as Ross' Fork—a tributary of Snake River—where they were to meet the United States Indian Agent and receive from him annuities in the shape of flour, blankets, arms, ammunition, cooking utensils, soap, beads, tobacco, boot-blacking, patent medicines, condensed milk, pickled oysters, canned jellies, and the various other necessaries and luxuries which the Great Father at Washington is in the habit of occasionally bestowing upon his red children.

"And," said the chief, "it aint worth our while to kill an occasional traveler and thus make trouble in the securing of our annuities."

I then recounted to him my adventure of the night before in the cañon with the two Indians. He smiled while listening to my narration, and when I had concluded, he said:

"Do you know why they did not molest you?"

I answered in the negative.

"Because," said he, "YOU WERE NOT WORTH KILLING."

Just about this time, I did not have a very exalted opinion of myself, to think that I should be so insignificant that a couple of miserable Indians did not think me worth the killing. But I ventured to ask him why they considered me so valueless.

"Because," said he, "it is evident that you possessed nothing which could tempt their cupidity. You had only your pack, and they had seen the contents of that, and there were too many chances involved for them to attempt to kill you for the sake of seeing you kick. They did not know but you might be armed; they knew that wagons were a short distance behind, and presumed that you belonged to the trains; also, that it must be known that you were on the road, and that if they should kill you and you be missed, the fact might cause an investigation to be made by the agent, which might interfere with the prompt issuance of our annuities—and then they would incur *my* displeasure. But, on the whole, if you had been worth killing, I don't think they could have resisted the temptation to take the chances on attacking you."

After this explanation, my heart throbbed in thankfulness for the good luck that had rendered me not worth killing.

While the conversation between the chief and myself was going on, several of the old squaws who were afoot crowded around me and kept continually tugging at my pack and ejaculating:

"Tower—lead!"

I had not sufficient flour to last me to the end of my journey; and as for lead, all I possessed in that line was three or four bullets, which I carried to put in my mouth to stay thirst while crossing stretches of country where the distances were great between water. The chief saw that I was annoyed by the persistent begging of the women, and shot out at them a few Indian words, which caused them to shrink back dismayed. Then rising in his stirrups, he placed his hand at the side of his mouth, and turning his horse so that he faced his followers, uttered some words in a voice so loud and distinct that he must have been heard very plainly by every one of them.

As he finished speaking, the band of Indians opened ranks, leaving an aisle through its center, from one end to the other. Then again addressing me, he said:

"Pass right on through my people; none of them will harm you. Good luck to you, and may you make your everlasting fortune in the mines, and never again have such a close game with Indians as you had last night."

Thanking him for his courtesy, and bidding him adieu, I started on through the lane made by the movement of the Indians in obedience to his order. They all eyed me closely, but none offered to molest me; and as I passed between their ranks, I thought of the Children of Israel as they crossed dry-shod over the Red Sea, with the waters bounding them on each side, and considered whether after all there might not be more or less truth in that phenomenal yarn. At all events, I breathed freer when the last Indian was passed and I was again trudging along the road on my way to the new diggings, with none to molest or make me afraid.

The First Fourth in White Pine.

The spring of the year 1868 witnessed the inception of the great mining craze known as the "White Pine Excitement." At the time of the discovery of the then rich mines there, Austin was the nearest town to the district, and it was from that place that White Pine was first settled. The discoverers of the mines were Austin prospectors, and on making their find brought their specimens here for assay and testing. I was living in Austin when the first ore from the Hidden Treasure and the famed

Eberhardt mines was brought in. It was not necessary that a person should be an expert to determine that the rock was rich. A man who had never in his life seen a silver mine, or never before handled a piece of silver ore, could tell at a glance that it was metal. It came pretty near being pure silver, some of the "horn-silver" specimens being so heavy and metallic that they could be converted into bullion by the simple process of melting in a crucible. Ever on the alert for a new camp, I had no sooner seen these specimens than I determined to go to White Pine. And to White Pine I went. It is situated 120 miles from Austin, and I made the trip on horseback in two and a half days; but there was nothing in the journey in the way of incident that could interest the reader of these pages in its relation.

The mines, which were destined afterward to make such a stir in the world, were contained in a high mountain called Treasure Hill, whose peak rises to an elevation of 9,000 feet above the level of the sea. At the foot of the western and southern slopes of this mountain lies the town of Hamilton. It was then called "the Caves," owing to numerous caves in the dolomite of which the geological formation of the locality consists—and a few ambitious miners even went so far as to call it "Cave City." The city I found, on my arrival at the Caves, consisted of three or four stone cabins, a tent in which a couple of gentlemen from Austin had started an establishment combining store, saloon, restaurant, lodging-house, post-office, and express office, a few tents used for dwellings, a number of prospectors' open-air camps, and about seventy-five inhabitants. There was also a city on the mountain, at the mines, to which the description given of Cave City is likewise applicable.

At the time of my arrival there was considerable rivalry as to which of the two camps should be the future metropolis of White Pine. The mines were marvelously rich, and the prospects were that they were extensive; and it was evident that the district was destined to receive a large population ere long—so, of course, it must have a city. The hill people based their claims for metropolitan prominence on the fact that they were "squatted right down on the top of the mines." The Cave fellows knew the city would be at the foot of the mountain, because there was not a drop of water on the hill, and no likelihood of there ever being any found in that limestone formation. Besides, it was a straight pull of three miles up the mountain to get there; and again, there was not as much room for a large city on top of the mountain as there was at its foot, where the slope gradually spread out, and ended in a level plateau. Time proved both parties to be right. Cities sprung up on both sites, and, though their existence was short, they were "lively camps" while they lasted. "The Caves" was located for a town-site, and named Hamilton, after the man who made the location. Treasure City kept its original name through the varying fortunes of White Pine, and keeps it yet—but it is only a name.

The opening of the month of July, 1868, found the rivalry described

9

above existing in bitter intensity, and so strong was this feeling that a man who owned a town-lot in one survey hardly felt like speaking to the possessor of a similar piece of real estate in the other. The Fourth of July was approaching, and the propriety of celebrating that day in a manner befitting the patriotic founders of two great cities began to be broached. The inhabitants of each town held a public meeting, at which committees of arrangements and officers of the day were appointed, and resolutions adopted that each town would hold a celebration on its own hook, independent and entirely oblivious of even the existence of the other. Better counsels prevailed, however, when on "counting noses" it was found that there was not a sufficient number of men in each camp for two celebrations, and that the only way in which an air of respectability could be secured to the occasion was by fusing the forces and holding a joint celebration. A compromise was effected, by the terms of which Treasure City was to have the poet of the day and the chairman to preside over the literary exercises. Hamilton was to have the other offices, and the meeting and the "ball in the evening" were to be held in that town; but it was stipulated that the citizens of Hamilton were to march in procession up to Treasure City, meet the citizens of that metropolis drawn up in line to await their coming, and escort them in procession back to Hamilton.

At the meeting held in Hamilton to perfect arrangements for the celebration, it was my fortune to be appointed a member of the Committee on Flag, Music, and Ball in the Evening. It was the most difficult position with which an admiring constituency have ever honored me during the whole course of my checkered career. I may say it was a position of impossibilities—but some fellow has said nothing is impossible. It was just because there was nothing in the way of material from which to fulfill my duties as committeeman that made the position such an impossible one.

As to the flag, there was not such an article to be had nearer than Austin, and that was 120 miles distant, and the time lacked only forty-eight hours to the morning of the Glorious Fourth.

The "ball in the evening" was an easier matter than the flag, though even that was attended with many difficulties. There was a man called "Pike," who could play one tune—the "Arkansaw Traveler"—on the violin, and call a few of the simpler figures of an easy quadrille; but there was danger that he would succumb to the "spirits" of the glorious occasion before Night cast her sable mantle over the earth, and he be thus incapable of disseminating melody for the revelry. This danger was overcome by appointing a sub-committee to follow in Pike's wake during the day we celebrated, and to prevent him, even by the use of force if necessary, from imbibing more than three drinks of whisky an hour. The combined female population of the two camps numbered but two, and they both belonged in Hamilton. They could "stand in" on the round dances, and help fill out one quadrille set, and such other sets as might be formed on the floor could be "stag" dances—that is, dances in which only men take part. So the committee could see its way clear on the music, and the "ball in the evening" questions; but the flag was the poser.

Add nothing to nothing and you've got nothing, is a logical conclusion from the axiom, "Take nothing from nothing and nothing remains." There was not an American flag in the district, and the best rider in the camps could not ride to Austin to procure one and return in time for the Fourth. What would a celebration of the Fourth of July amount to without an American flag? was the question that agitated the minds of the pioneers of White Pine, and nearly drove the Committee on Flag, Music, and Ball in the Evening to hard drink. But an attempt must be made. The committee could manufacture a flag, if they could only procure material with which to build it; and the said committee passed a resolution, resolving each member thereof into a sub-committee to scour the camp for flag material. The stuff for the stars and the white stripes was easily procurable, because there was a quantity of drillings at the store, which was used for "lining" houses and making tents. We might even find some red shirts, which we could cut up for the stripes of that color; but how and where to obtain the blue for the field was the grand puzzle.

In my capacity as sub-committee on searching for flag material, I came across an aristocrat who had a quilt on his bed. This article was lined with red calico, and was confiscated forthwith, thus doing away with the necessity of calling for donations of red shirts. The evening preceding the Fourth arrived, and a thorough search of both camps by the committee had failed to discover and procure any textile fabric of a blue color; and the committee sat in solemn council, debating the propriety of making the field of the flag out of a gray shirt, and taking the chances that the vivid imagination of the beholder might give it a blue hue, as the emblem of our liberties floated from the ninety-foot pole which the Committee on Pole had already erected and fitted with halliards. While this important matter was under discussion, a courier arrived at the council and announced that a family of Mormons had just arrived and were making camp in a little ravine below our embryo city—and there were four girls and an old woman in the outfit, too. This was glorious news. Four girls and an old woman could not fail to have among their aggregate possessions a blue dress, or some other garment of cerulean hue; besides, the four girls—to say nothing of the old woman—would fit in splendidly in the "dance in the evening." The committee immediately passed a resolution that I was the best-looking member, and instructing me to forthwith wait on the Mormon family and interview them as to their possession of "something blue," and if found, to not only make a note on't, but to purchase it instanter, without regard to cost. In pursuance of these instructions, I wended my way to the spot where the family of Saints and Saintesses were camped, which was but a short distance from the collection of huts and tents that we called "town." It was dark when I arrived there, but a big sage-brush fire was burning, which rendered surrounding objects distinct. The father of the outfit, assisted by a couple of lads, was engaged in constructing a habitation for his brood, by driving poles into the ground in a circle and enclosing them with bits of carpet, horse-blankets, and pieces of cloth; poles laid across the top of the upright poles, and covered with brush, constituted the roof. The mother and girls were at work around the camp-fire, preparing supper.

Approaching the fire, and advancing to where the old lady was kneeling in front of it, holding over it a long-handled frying-pan, in which were some slices of bacon, I raised my hat from my head, made my best bow, and said:

"Good evening, madam."

The old lady was very large, fat, and ungainly. She was so busy with her cooking that she had not noticed my presence in the camp till I addressed her as above stated. Whether it was my handsome features or my good clothes that so forcibly impressed her, I know not, but when I spoke to her she started as if somebody had called "fire!" in her ear through a fog-horn; and in attempting to get up from her knees and assume a position of dignity befitting the reception of so evidently distinguished a stranger as myself, she lost her equilibrium, and keeled over on her back at full length on the ground, while the frying-pan described an arc of a circle and landed in the brush about twenty feet behind her, in its flight shedding a shower of slices of sizzling bacon, one of which struck the oldest girl on the back of her neck, and slid down inside her dress. The girl set up a yell that would have done credit to Sitting Bull when urging his warriors on to victory with the war-whoop of his tribe, and I commenced to take up the line of a masterly retreat. I was intercepted, however, by the *pater familias*, who confronted me with an uplifted ax, and demanded to know what I had been doing to his "folks." Tremblingly I explained my mission; and while I was talking, the old woman and the girl with the hot bacon down her back recovered their composure, and the entire family gathered about me, wide-eyed and open-mouthed, and stared at me as if I was the first handsome man they had ever seen. When I had concluded, the man said:

"Mother, aint you got some blue stuff among the traps you can let this gentleman have?"

"Le's see," replied "Mother," "that thar blue gownd of Brigamette's we traded off to them Injuns would have been jest the thing. Heberine, what's gone of that blue apron of yourn?"

Heberine, who was one of the daughters, replied she had "tored up" the blue apron into strips to tie round "Orsie's" foot when he was "snake-bit that time back yander."

"Say, marm," spoke up the girl who had undergone the "moxa" operation with the bacon, "don't ye mind we brung along thet thar big blue veil of yourn, that you used to wear going to Conference to Salt Lake, so's the sun wouldn't spile your complection?"

"Sure enough! Sure enough!" exclaimed "Marm;" "whar is it?"

"Down in the bottom of the big hair-chest," answered one of the smaller girls, in a piping voice, and shrinking away as if she had said something awfully wicked, and I was an ogre who was going to eat her for it.

The entire family then "adjourned" to a hair-covered trunk that stood on the ground by the wagon in which they had made the journey from Utah to White Pine, and after the unknotting of sundry ropes and the cutting of various strips of raw-hide which bound it, the trunk was opened, its contents taken out and laid on the ground, till at last, by the light of a fagot, held by one of the boys, my expectant eyes beheld that "big blue veil."

A bargain for the purchase of the "blue stuff" was soon concluded. The old lady said she had owned the veil for a long time and did not like to part with it; she had "brung" it from the States when they first "jined the Mormons," and it was to her a souvenir of happy days gone by; but if I did not mind paying five dollars for it I could have it and welcome; and that ought not to be too high a price in a new country, where the mines were so rich that the silver was sticking right up out of the top of the ground, so she had heard.

I paid the five dollars, took the veil, and hurried back to town, and hunted up the members of the committee; and that night was put in by the Committee on Flag, Music, and Dance in the Evening, in manufacturing an American flag for the celebration of the first Fourth of July in White Pine.

While the committee were seated on the floor of my tent, sewing on the flag by the light of a number of candles, it was resolved to invite the Mormon family to be present at the literary exercises to be held on the morrow, and also at the ball in the evening; and that the committee should wait on them in a body and tender the invitation. Accordingly, early the following morning, the committee visited the camp and extended the invitation in due form.

In response, the mother said: "I'd jest as lief the gals would go, but thar aint one of them got a shoe to their foot."

This was a very embarrassing situation. The boards which composed the floor of the ball-room were unplaned and full of splinters, and it was impossible that the girls could dance on it in their bare feet, and it was not a supposable case that women's or girls' shoes could be found in the stock at the store. However, the committee said they would "look around," and if they could find suitable shoes, would buy each of the girls a pair, and the old lady said they could go up town and look for the shoes, but she wanted it understood right there that the girls were to dance only "square" dances; for round dances were against their faith, and they had not "apostatized" from the Mormons just yet, if they had come amongst the Gentiles to try and better their worldly condition.

The promise about the "square" dances was given, and the committee went back to town to seek the shoes. They succeeded in finding in the store a sufficient number of men's cowhide brogans to shoe the Mormon girls, and thus was another difficulty overcome.

The morning of the Glorious Fourth broke bright and beautiful. The day was ushered in with a salute fired from anvils, and the flag was hoisted to its place on the pole midst the shouts and cheers of the multitude—and as it floated up there, ninety feet above ground, it was a pretty respectable flag, and the beholder would never have guessed the materials of which it was composed, or that it was not a regular, Simon-pure, store flag.

At the appointed hour the male inhabitants of the future city of Hamilton formed in line of procession—two and two—and marched up the trail to Treasure City. There was not a brass band at the head of the procession, but two of the best whistlers in camp walked in front and whistled "Yankee Doodle" till the steep ascent and light atmosphere took away their breath. Arrived on the hill they were met by the citizens of Treasure City, who, after the formalities of reception were gone through with in the nearest "saloon," also fell in line, and the combined forces of the two towns marched in procession back to Hamilton.

On the return to Hamilton the literary exercises were inaugurated. They consisted of an oration by the orator of the day, a poem by the poet of the day, and the singing of patriotic songs by the congregation.

At the conclusion of the exercises, a White Pine Pioneer Society was formed, and a resolution adopted that the flag then flying from the pole outside should form a part of the Society's archives, that future generations might know the difficulties, hardships, and privations with which the pioneers of White Pine District and the founders of the city of Hamilton had been beset in their endeavors to properly celebrate the anniversary of the nation's independence.

This stage of this narrative is probably as good as any other at which to record the fate of the flag.

As times began to get lively and people poured into Hamilton, the parties owning the store where the archives of the Pioneer Society were deposited, added a lodging-house to their establishment. This department consisted of tiers of bunks ranged along the sides of a room in the rear of the store, each bunk being furnished with a coarse, straw-filled tick, two pairs of blankets, and a rude pillow. These bunks were rented out to weary travelers and hopeful pilgrims to the new mines at the reasonable rental of two dollars per night, with the privilege of a free cocktail at the bar on arising in the morning. One night an aristocratic capitalist from San Francisco put up at the lodging-house, and had the effrontery to demand a pair of sheets on his bed. The proprietor of the establishment was almost struck dumb with amaze at this outrageous request; but then the man was a capitalist, and was from San Francisco, and it might be against the interest of the mining resources of the district for him to become offended. He might get mad and go back to San Francisco without having purchased a mine. The landlord had no sheets, and there were, in all probability, none to be had in the camp; but he was equal to the emergency. He went to the archives of the Society of White Pine Pioneers, and took therefrom its only archive—to wit, the flag—and tore it in half and spread the two pieces on the bed to be occupied by the high-toned capitalist. The dismembered flag of our country did duty as bed sheets for many months afterward, and the particular bunk in which they were laid was kept in reserve for the occupancy of San Francisco capitalists, who were charged half a dollar extra for its use, because it had sheets on it. The last that I saw of the starry emblem which had thus been prostituted to such base uses, a couple of Shoshone squaws were wearing each a piece of it over their shoulders for a shawl.

Before entering on a description of the "ball in the evening," it is necessary, in order to aid the reader to the better understanding of some of the incidents connected therewith, which I am about to attempt to describe, that descriptive mention be made of the "hall" in which this social event was held. The said hall was an incomplete house, one of those mushroom board houses such as are usually constructed in new camps. It was intended to be used as a store, and was in dimensions about 40 x 20. The floor was laid on posts set in the ground, and as the ground sloped off abruptly from the front to the rear of the lot, the back part of the building was some six feet above the ground, while at the front it was but a step from the floor to the ground. Only the sides of the building were up, the ends and roof not yet being completed, so that it merely consisted of a floor and two board-sides. It was intended that the building should be ceiled and lined with cloth, and the material for this purpose had all been sewed together into one large piece. This canopy was spread over the top of the two standing sides, making a roof, and the end surplus was dropped down over the rear opening, making a rear wall, the front of the building being left open on account of lack of material. Pike, fiddle in hand, was seated on a little three-legged stool in the rear end of the hall, next to the unsubstantial and deceptive wall. His guard had kept him tolerably sober, and he fiddled away at the "Arkansaw Traveler" and called the figures with an energy worthy of the day that was being celebrated. There was a large attendance at the ball, the Mormon girls and their brogans being on hand, and taking part in all the square dances. The costumes of the men were not full-dress, being principally gray shirts, overalls, and "stogie" boots; but everybody seemed to enjoy the occasion, till an unforeseen and calamitous incident cast a pall of gloom over the festivities, and broke up the affair. The watch on Pike had been relaxed, and during the intervals between the dances he visited the tent next door. The constant worship at the shrine of Bacchus unsettled the musician's nerves and unsteadied his brain. The dancers were in the midst of a quadrille, when suddenly the music grew faint in sound, and the "calls" ceased. The fiddler had suddenly and mysteriously disappeared. Wonder and curiosity were depicted on every face in the ball-room, but the overturned stool, which had been the orchestra stand, and notes of the "Arkansaw Traveler" welling up faintly from the rear of the building, told the awful tale. Pike, in an effort to put some artistic variations, had leaned back against the treacherous cloth wall, lost his equilibrium, and dropped out of sight through the wall to the ground below. A number of men rushed out to the rear of the house to recover the orchestra, but when they got to him he was just passing into a peaceful sleep, his right hand spasmodically working the fiddle-bow, which lay across his left shoulder, and the expiring notes of the "Arkansaw Traveler" dying on the air. All efforts to arouse him were fruitless, and as he was the only man in the camp who could fiddle, the "ball in the evening" was at an end.

Shortly after the Fourth of July, 1868, the big rush to White Pine set in, and from that time till the autumn of 1869, all was excitement in the new district. Town lots, which could have been bought during July, 1868, for merely nominal sums, were valued in September of that year high in the thousands, many selling as high as $25,000 a lot 25 x 100. The mines were panning out big, and money was the most plentiful article to be seen in the two cities. Buildings went up in a night, streets were laid out, banks and express offices established, stores opened with immense stocks of goods; the streets were blocked with freight teams and crowded with people; and it was exultingly proclaimed on every hand that "forty-nine" had come again, and the old flush days of California were about to be repeated. The Fourth of July of 1869, compared with that anniversary of the year preceding, was like the transformation scene in a spectacular play in a theater, or, better, a veritable fairy tale. Where the handful of coarsely-clothed prospectors had marched in procession the year before, now marched a grand pageant—military companies, a fire department, with handsome and costly and beautifully-decorated engines and hose carriages; a car of state, containing bright-faced and gaily-attired girls, representing the various States in the Union; brass bands, streamers, brightness, and beauty; and where but one short year before had waved the solitary home-made flag, the starry emblem now kissed the breeze from a hundred staffs. The line of the procession of the year before, over a mere trail through the brush, with a few poor tents and cabins only marking the site of the town, was now a broad street, with handsome two and three-story structures of brick and stone, built compactly on each side. A thousand women and children gazed on the procession from the upper windows of stately structures; and at the "ball in the evening" there were hundreds of richly dressed and jeweled women, in contrast to the two Gentile women and the four Mormon girls in their homespun dresses and charity brogans, that had graced with their presence the "ball in the evening" of the Fourth of July a short twelvemonth before.

White Pine went down almost as rapidly as it came up. The mines petered and the bubble bursted. To-day, Hamilton and Treasure City are both insignificant and nearly depopulated camps; the few who remain in them have clung on, hoping on, hoping ever, for a strike in the mines that shall bring a return of something like the good old times of the early days. Their hopes will in all probability never be realized; though both places have a reasonable prospect that sufficient mineral wealth will be developed in the deep workings which for several years have been energetically pushed in Treasure Hill, to make them prosperous small mining camps. But they will never again see the rush, the excitement, the money, the wild speculation, and the rapid gain and loss of fortunes that characterized their career for a year succeeding the "First Fourth in White Pine."

Under the Gallows.

In the course of the journey during which the incident detailed under the head "Not Worth Killing" transpired, I arrived at a mining camp known as East Bannock, sometimes called "Grasshopper Creek." I reached the edge of the town at night, when all the lights were extinguished; and, knowing it to be what was called a "vigilante town," I did not care to enter it during the night. It might not be healthy for a stranger to be caught prowling around East Bannock at night, and he might experience considerable difficulty in convincing any of the watchful inhabitants who might be abroad of the honesty of his intentions. I therefore concluded to camp at the outskirts of the town that night, and enter it in the morning. I accordingly spread my blanket on the ground, lay down, and was soon sleeping the sleep of the tired.

When I opened my eyes in the morning, the first object they encountered was a gallows. I did not know it was a gallows at first, but was soon enlightened as to the true nature of the beast. The night preceding had been very dark, and when I made my camp I did not notice the instrument of execution of the death penalty, and had laid my blankets directly under the cross-beam, and between the uprights, and there I had slept. There was a small piece of rope dangling from the center of the cross-beam; but still it did not strike me that the machine was a gallows. I lay there in my blankets, looking up at it, and wondering what it could be, until at last the sun began to mount in the heavens, and I arose. As I looked about me, I observed, a short distance to the right, what appeared to be a small cemetery—a row of head-boards and small, grave-like mounds, situated on a little knoll. The first thought was that it must be the town-cemetery, and I wondered that a town of the size of East Bannock should, at its age, (it was then probably four or five years old) have so small a graveyard. In new mining camps, about the first work of public utility performed is to lay out a graveyard, and there is almost invariably some public-spirited citizen who contracts to provide occupants for it. In most mining camps, a graveyard can boast at least twenty graves before it is six months old, the majority of the occupants being obstinate men who thought they had a better title to a town-lot or a mining claim than the man who had established the precedence of *his* claim with a bullet, or men who had unfortunately held the opinion that they were better fighters and surer shots than the individuals who had convinced them of their error with a six-shooter. However, I walked over to the cemetery, and approaching the first head-board, read thereon the name, "Henry Plummer," and the date of the aforesaid Plummer's death.

The whole thing was now plain to me—this was the private graveyard of the East Bannock Vigilantes.

The story of the execution of Henry Plummer and his band of "road agents" was familiar to me then. I had heard it in Nevada, and at intervals, at different places all along, during my journey to Montana. It is not very fresh in my memory now, as I have forgotten some matters of detail; but the story substantially is about as follows:

Plummer had been City Marshal and a prominent local politician of Nevada City, California; but, if my memory serves me, killed a man there, and escaped to the then Territory of Nevada. He did not linger long in the sage-brush, however, for fear of arrest by the California authorities, but made his way "up north," as the section now comprising Montana and Idaho was then by a general term designated. There had been some placer-mining discoveries in British Columbia, and it was to that country that he first went; but as other mines were found to the eastward, in what is now Montana and Idaho, Plummer followed the "rushes" till he at last brought up in Bannock, under which designation a large section of the eastern portion of the present Territory of Montana was then known. I am not familiar with much of his career during the earlier portion of his residence in Bannock, except generally that it was a wild and desperate one.

The Territory of Idaho was formed and divided off into counties, and county governments organized. Each county covered a large area; for the country was new, and the population small and scattered. Of one of these counties—the one in which East Bannock was situated—(it is now in Montana) Plummer was chosen sheriff. He had married, and apparently reformed, and abandoned the life of a desperado, and was looked upon as a good citizen for a new country. He was known to be a determined, and was thought to be a brave man; and having had some experience in a police capacity, was deemed just the man for the position.

The country was infested with cut-throats and highwaymen, jocularly called "road agents." These "agents" stopped the stages and robbed and murdered passengers, killed men on the trails and roads for pure wantonness, and committed murder, robbery, and outrage on every hand, and with the utmost impunity; and not an arrest was made, or an effort put forth to bring one of them to justice. Every man was his own law, and his pistol the only peace officer to which he could look for protection. The agents were banded together, and usually went in gangs, and no man was safe from them, even in the towns. They would enter a camp, and after filling themselves with liquor, would "take the town"; that is, they would be masters of the situation, do as they pleased, and maltreat and abuse peaceably disposed persons as their humor moved them. In short, they ruled the country, and had everything their own way, apparently safe from all danger of arrest or punishment.

This state of things could not last forever. The patience of the law-abiding and peaceable men of the country was exhausted, and a Vigilance Committee was quietly and secretly formed. At first they made no move to visit punishment upon any of the suspected or notoriously bad characters, but quietly busied themselves, each man acting as a detective, in posting themselves as to the ramifications of the road agents' organization, finding out their haunts and learning their mode of operations. During the course of these investigations it was learned, and the discovery created the utmost surprise among the Vigilantes, that Henry Plummer, the Sheriff of the county, was the head and front of the road agents' organization. He personally took no part in their exploits, but knew all their plans, and received a certain share of their spoils. He posted them when there was gold dust on the stages, and when he learned that a man or a party of men were traveling with large sums of money or batches of dust, he informed the agents as to the route taken, and consulted with them as to the best method of accomplishing the robbery and disposing of the victims. Besides this, he protected them from arrest, and aided them to get out of the country if the facts implicating them were so plain and glaring that his failure to arrest them if they stayed would tend to betray his connection with the gangs.

A watch was put on Plummer, and the Committee satisfied themselves that he saw there was no chance for a mistake about his connection with the road agents; and on a certain night, which had been agreed on, he was arrested. Plummer had not dreamed that he was suspected, and the arrest was a complete surprise to him. He blustered considerably at first; but when he saw that the Committee had indisputable evidence of his guilt, he "weakened," and offered to tell all he knew. This offer was rejected, as enough was known to show that he was undeserving of mercy. He was placed under a strong guard that night, and a detachment of the Committee proceeded to arrest others of the road agents.

If I remember the circumstances aright, several of the gang were Mexicans, who, learning that a vigilance committee had been formed and was after the road agents, took refuge in a stone cabin situated on the outskirts of the town of East Bannock. This cabin was visited by a detachment of the Committee, who demanded the surrender of the occupants. The Mexicans made answer by firing a volley on the Vigilantes, without, however, hitting any of them. The Vigilantes then set fire to the cabin, and when at last the heat grew so intense that they could no longer remain inside, they made a rush on the party of Vigilantes, but were all shot down before they could do any mischief. Thus one portion of the gang was disposed of.

In the meantime, another party of the Vigilantes had arrested several Americans who were known to have been active participants in the robberies, murders, and outrages; and others who were suspected managed to effect their escape. I do not remember the exact number arrested, but it was somewhere between six and ten.

In the days of vigilance committees in California, it used to be the custom, before executing the law of Judge Lynch, to give the accused a sort of trial, at which he was allowed to bring forward any evidence tending to establish his innocence which he might be able to procure. But this plan was not pursued in Bannock, and never in Montana, that I am aware of.

When the Committee had arrested all the known road agents they could find, a gallows was erected just outside the town of East Bannock, a resolution condemning the men to death having previously been passed, and the prisoners were conducted to the place of execution, and there hung by twos and threes, with the exception of Plummer, who, on account of his former prominence as a politician and county officer, was granted the courtesy of an execution all to himself.

It is stated that when Plummer became satisfied that the Vigilance Committee were determined to hang him, he cried like a child, and begged piteously for his life, but all in vain. There had been too many men murdered and mutilated, and life and property had been rendered too insecure for mercy to be shown to the man who, while holding an office of public trust, and one created to give protection to the people, had aided and countenanced the murderers and robbers. The hour of vengeance had come, and the people had arisen in their might to demonstrate to the ruffians and cut-throats that their sway was at an end; that they would no longer be allowed to ride rough-shod over peaceable and law-abiding men; and even while Plummer, with the rope around his neck, was pleading, and begging, and promising, the box on which he stood was pulled out from under his feet, and in a moment he was strangling and dangling at the end of the rope.

The gallows on which these men were hung was the same under which I had camped the night I arrived at East Bannock, and the little mounds with the boards at their head on the knoll at one side were their graves.

The formation of the Bannock Vigilance Committee was, I believe, the foundation of the great Vigilance Committee which in a short time extended in its ramifications over the entire Territory of Montana, which was soon afterward created. Springing out of the necessity for self-preservation, and starting off with the performance of a necessary act, it at last grew to be a curse, where at first it was a blessing. Bad men, to keep suspicion away from themselves, joined the Vigilance Committee, which came to be an oath-bound organization of the strictest secresy. There were good men also in its membership, nearly every merchant and business man in the Territory joining it; and it was even hinted that United States Marshals and Judges, Sheriffs, Constables, and District Attorneys were enrolled on its muster. It soon, however, fell into the control of the villains and adventurers, many of whom, for plunder, or to gratify malice and revenge, made accusations against innocent men—and to be accused before the Vigilantes was equivalent to being condemned. Sentence was passed in secret, and the accused was given no opportunity to be heard in defense, but the officers of the organization on whom devolved the duty of executing the sentence immediately proceeded to put it into execution. The unwarned wretch was surprised at night in his cabin, or on a road or trail, or even late at night in the streets of the towns, by a body of masked men, by whom he was overpowered, gagged, blindfolded, bound, and carried to the tree used as an engine of execution. There one end of a rope was tied around his neck, the other thrown over a limb of the tree, the victim hauled up and the rope made fast, a placard on which was written the crime for which he was executed being generally pinned to his breast. Murder was not the only crime for which men were executed. Horse or cattle-stealing, passing bogus gold-dust, or highway robbery, also met the punishment of death. But in the later days of the Vigilance Committee the mere suspicion or accusation of these crimes was sufficient to hang a man.

I remember hearing a story—in fact, it was generally current in Montana at one time—that the Vigilantes seized and hung a boy on suspicion of having stolen some work cattle, and while he was dangling from the rope the missing cattle, which had strayed, walked into the corral in which the boy was hanging.

Some of these Vigilantes themselves at last met with their just deserts at the end of a rope, pulled on by their fellow members of the Committee. There was one of these who went by the name of "Frenchy." He was a thief, a murderer, and a villain; but he gained admission to membership in the Vigilance Committee, which for several years he used as a cloak for his crimes. He was known as a Californian, and many members being from the Eastern States, Frenchy was relied on to furnish information concerning the antecedents of such Californians as came under the ban of the Committee; and it was afterward suspected that he gave evidence against men of whom he had never before heard or had never before seen, simply that he might appear to be well posted. If he took a dislike to or held a grudge against a man, he denounced him to the Committee as having been a horse-thief in California or Nevada; if a man refused to be blackmailed by him, he lodged an information against him before the Vigilance Committee, charging him with some crime, and in most cases the charge was equivalent to conviction, and resulted in execution. In some instances, all that was necessary to bring the executioners of the Vigilantes down on a man was that he should have money. In such cases the "stranglers," as they were called, would pounce on him at night, or follow him out into the country when he started on a journey, overpower him and hang him, take away his money or live-stock, and then report to headquarters with a trumped-up charge against him, and aver that they found it necessary to hang him to prevent his escape. Frenchy was particularly at home in this class of cases, acting the part of a detective to find out men who were going to travel with long sacks of gold-dust. At last Frenchy began to be suspected by the more respectable members of the Vigilance Committee, and a watch was set on his actions; and it was not very long till he was caught. One dark night, Frenchy fell in company with an old man from one of the outside mining camps, who was known to possess considerable money. The Vigilante spy and informer soon placed himself on friendly terms with the stranger, and the two visited the saloons and dance-houses, and dissipated until the old man became intoxicated. Frenchy then inveigled him into a dark street, and knocked him senseless, and proceeded to rifle his pockets. The pair had been followed during the night by a party of Vigilantes; and while Frenchy was engaged in robbing the old man, they rushed in on him, and captured, bound, and gagged him before he could make a move or utter a cry.

It was always swift work with the Vigilantes. After they had once suspected Frenchy, many things about him became plain, and facts were obtained showing his villainy; and now that he was caught in the very act, no time was lost in executing vengeance on him. He was conducted through out-of-the-way streets and over lonely trails to the execution tree in Dry Gulch, on the outskirts of the city, and was there given a short shrift and a long rope. I heard, several years afterward, that during the preparations for execution Frenchy got the gag out of his mouth, and screamed out that he was a Californian, and implored any Californians who might be in the party to help or save him, for the sake of geography, as it were. But if there were in the party any gentlemen from the Golden State, they said not a word in his behalf, nor attempted to put forth a hand to save him. And next morning the people of the good city of Helena beheld the body of the late Frenchy dangling from a tree, and on his breast a placard bearing the words:

A MURDERER AND A THIEF!

Swore Away Men's Lives.

Hoist by his Own Petard.

As the story goes, another prominent member of the Execution Band of the Montana Vigilantes also met his death at the hands of his former comrades. He had helped at the execution of so many that hanging men grew to be a passion with him; and it was said that he only knew happiness when he was pulling a rope over a limb, with a man fastened to the other end by the neck. Finally, this fellow gave offense to some of the other Vigilantes, and a party of them talked the matter over, and decided to hang him. He knew too much about some of them, or had failed to divide some plunder fairly, or they had come to dislike him. I don't know the exact reason for his execution, only that they strung him up, and that there was a sort of grim humor to the story.

The party were at Fort Benton, the head of navigation of the Missouri River, which was quite a busy little city in those days, on account of the travel and freight from the East; and numerous steamers which plied the river from St. Louis, St. Joe, and Omaha, tied up and unloaded their cargoes there, for transhipment by mule and ox-teams to various points in the Territory. Fort Benton is situated on a sand-flat on the bank of the river, a regular desert waste, and the view on all sides, as far as the eye can reach, is nothing but sand, without a tree or shrub to relieve the barrenness and desolation. This fact gave rise to some difficulty in the hanging of the doomed Vigilante; and the stranglers, in their dilemma, went to him and requested him to devise a plan for hanging himself. The matter was worked in this wise. Hunting up the victim and taking him aside, one of them said to him:

"We have got a fellow we want to string up, and don't know how to manage it, as there's not a tree, or anything big enough to hang a man on, growing within miles of this place. How would you manage it!"

"Manage it!" exclaimed the unconscious victim, "you just leave that to me, and I'll fix you up the loveliest contrivance that ever raised a man off the ground. Leave it to me, will you?"

The party consented to leave the construction of the "lovely contrivance" to their candidate for a noose, and he proceeded to business at once. Procuring three stout poles and some baling-rope, and a stouter rope for a noose, he packed them on a horse, and mounting his own horse he drove the pack-horse before him, and rode out on the plain to a point secure from observation from the town. Here he unpacked his gallows material, and with the baling-rope tied the three poles together fast at one end, and setting the other ends on the ground, spread them out in the form of a tripod. He then made a running noose with the other piece of rope, and fastened it to the top of the tripod, hanging inside of the poles. This done, he returned to town to hunt up his friends and invite them out to an inspection of his ingenious work.

It did not take long, and having got them together, he said:

"Come on, boys, and go out and look at her; she's just the sweetest thing in that line you ever laid eyes on."

In response to this polite invitation, the "boys" mounted their horses and rode out to view the "sweet thing," the victim accompanying them.

They had intended to hang him at night; but such a splendid opportunity for the work was now presented that they concluded to take advantage of it; and as they rode along they communicated with each other by whispers, and a plan was agreed on to hang their man before they returned to town. The gallows was handy, and they had him secure and safe from observation, and it seemed like tempting Providence to let this chance slip and take the chances of something happening before night to put him on his guard, so that he might get away.

Arrived at the tripod, the party dismounted, and after they had viewed it a few moments, the leader asked its architect how it worked.

"Easiest thing in the world," replied the victim of misplaced confidence; "you see, you walk your man in under here (pointing to the space under the noose); slip this thing over his head (pointing to the noose); then three of us each pick up one of these poles and shift its end inwards towards the center, and that raises the height of the machine, and draws the noose tight, and your man has nothing to stand on. Did you ever see anything smoother than that?"

"Suppose *you* get under, and let's see how it works," said the leader.

"Me get under it! What for? It's the simplest thing in the world, and a baby could understand it."

"*Get under there!*" exclaimed the leader, in a stern tone, drawing and cocking a six-shooter, and pointing it in the victim's face.

Simultaneously the other men drew their pistols, covered the fated wretch, and said, "*Get under there!*"

The face of the gallows-builder turned pale, and his limbs began to quake with fear.

"Oh, boys! you don't mean it. You're only joshing me, I know; but those pistols look wicked, and make me nervous. Put up your guns and go back to town and take a drink with me, and we'll fetch that fellow out here to-night and give him a lively send-off."

The only reply was the nearer approach of the muzzles of the six-shooters to his head, and the words: "*Get under there!*"

The poor devil begged, cried, and implored, but to no purpose; and at the very point of the pistols which surrounded him on every hand, he was forced inside the tripod and the noose slipped over his head, and he was duly hung in strict accordance with his own directions for the hanging of the other fellow. There he was left hanging, and a few days subsequently, after the carrion birds had made several hearty meals from it, his body was discovered by some men from Fort Benton, who cut it down and buried it.

Part VII.

Life in a Mining Town.

One day, while out in search of an item, I asked a fellow-citizen, "What's the news?" "Nothing startling," he replied. Nothing startling! That man would never do for a newspaper reporter in a small interior town. Nothing startling, indeed! Why, as he made the remark, two dogs were preparing to sign articles for a prize-fight right in front of his store; a wagon loaded with wood could be seen in the distance, which was sure to pass his way during the day, if something did not break down. Two women, whom he knew to be mortal enemies, were approaching each other on the corner above; a doctor was hurrying across the street, and a man who always kicks up a fuss and gets arrested when drunk was just entering the door of a saloon a block below. If that fellow-citizen had had the soul of a reporter within his bosom—or in any other part of his body where a reporter's expansive soul can find lodgment—he would have got out his jack-knife, picked up a chip, and, sitting down on the first convenient dry goods box, have whittled, and waited for something startling. Nothing came of all the incidents, however. The dogs signed a peace protocol and formed an alliance to bark at a passing horse; the load of wood was delivered lower down the street, the women merely swept their skirts aside from each other as they passed, the doctor only wanted to borrow ten dollars of the man on the other side of the street, and the fellow who makes a noise when he gets drunk simply went into the saloon to inquire what time the Battle Mountain stage started.

It is such disappointments as these that sour the reportorial milk of human kindness, and force the country newspaper man to fill up his columns with incidents evolved from his own imagination—incidents that are invariably tinged with the humor born of worldly wisdom, and the practical as opposed to the sentimental view of men, life, and things. I have before explained the origin of the Sazerac Lying Club; and to the same want of "local" the following actual occurrences owe their appearance in print:

High-Toned Folks.

A short time ago, a prominent citizen of Austin, criticising something which had appeared in the REVEILLE, complained that a majority of the characters introduced in our local sketches were people of rather a common order; that the language employed in the dialogue was coarse, and only such as is in use among the lower classes. This, he urged, was likely to make people outside of Austin think that there were not any aristocratic residents here, and that the Austinites on the whole were rather a common crowd. We accepted the criticism gratefully and gracefully, and there and then resolved to watch out for any little domestic incident transpiring among the "Upper Ten" that could be worked into a sketch. We had not long to wait.

A gentleman residing in this city, through whose veins courses the blood of a long line of ancestors, entered the portals of his palatial mansion just as the glorious orb of day was sinking to rest behind the western hills. He was met on the threshold by the partner of his joys and sorrows, who greeted him with a kiss of welcome. He entered the house, and throwing his weary form upon the luxurious sofa in the drawing-room——got right up again and howled.

The delicate fabric on which she had been engaged in embroidering the armorial bearings of her husband's noble house had three needles in it; she had thrown it on the sofa in her haste to greet her lord, and he had sat down on all three of the needles.

Instead of saying, "Dearest, thou art careless," as the reader has a natural right to expect, he just stood up on his toes and cursed till the air was blue.

She, on her part, instead of putting her hands on his shoulders and gently pushing him down on the sofa and saying, "Be calm, thou light of me soul," which any person with a grain of sense must concede was the proper thing for her to do under the circumstances, in a tone more in sorrow than in anger, told him if he didn't "shut up this minnit," she would faint.

"Faint and be d—rowned!" said he.

And then she called him an old brute and an unfeeling wretch, and told him he could go to the restaurant to get his supper; for she wished she might fall nine thousand feet down a shaft if she cooked a mouthful for any such old nincompoop as him *that* night.

And he went down town after his supper, and as he stood up against the bar while his appetizer was being concocted, he said to the bar-keeper: "I put it to you, as a man and a brother, if a man jumps eight feet and howls like a coyote, just because he has sat down on three insignificant cambric needles, can he with truth and propriety be designated an 'unfeeling wretch'?"

The bar-keeper said he thought not.

A Scared Citizen.

Mr. Thompson has just laid in his winter's wood, and a few evenings ago, on returning from his work in the mines, brought home some giant powder cartridges for the purpose of blasting up the big logs into stove size. He deposited the explosives on the kitchen table, intending to use them in the morning; but after he had gone to bed the thought troubled him that he had not exercised sufficient caution; and that he should have placed the dangerous articles in the cellar, or in some corner out of the way of "that boy Jim." But, being tired and sleepy, he felt a natural indisposition to get up and remove them to a place of absolute safety, and concluded to risk all chances for the night, and rise early in the morning so as to put them out of Jim's way before that mischievous young gentleman was out of bed.

Falling into a troubled sleep he had visions of explosions, saw the air filled with fragments of his house, his beloved daughter Clarissa sailing straight for the moon on a joint of stovepipe, the wife of his bosom shooting through the air carrying her severed head under her arm, and Jim—the pride of his latter days—sitting astride of the piano-stool, with the baby's arm in his hand, and grinning like a fiend as he put that innocent's thumb to his nose, and disappeared from view behind the summit of Lander Hill.

When he awoke in the morning it was with that sensation of weariness which usually follows a night of exciting dreams, and as he lay in bed in that drowsy condition, between sleep and awaking, which all of us have experienced at some time or other, Clarissa seated herself at the piano in the parlor to practice an operatic piece. Bracing her feet firmly on the pedals of the instrument, and fixing her eyes on the music, she raised both hands on high to get a good ready, and then came down with both fists on the keyboard with the vigor of a thousand music masters.

Crash! Bang! Rattletybang! Crashytecrash!

The air of the opera swept through the house in a hurricane of noisy melody, and Thompson shot out of bed as if he had been blown from a cannon.

"Great heavens, Maria!" he screamed to his wife, "we're blowed hellwest and crooked; quit your dog-goned snoring and say your prayers; Jim's got hold of the giant powder and we'll all be blowed to a thousand fragments in sixteen seconds by the watch!"

Maria merely turned over and yawned, and said: "Shut up, you cussed, excitable old fool! It's only Clarissa practicing the uproar of Travitroovatore, or some such stuff, on the pianner, and the instrument's all out of kilter owing to the dry climate."

The prominent citizen dressed himself and sadly wended his way to the nearest saloon to hunt up a man to tune the piano.

Story of an Ear.

Just for a change he thought he would spend one evening at home. His astonished wife met him at the door and asked him if he had forgotten anything.

"No, pet," he replied, "I just thought I'd come home and keep you company to-night; you must be lonesome sitting here all alone."

The wife was delighted; it was almost a new experience to have her husband at home at night, and she thought that at last her appeals against pedro for the whisky had taken root in his heart. Placing another stick in the stove and giving the damper a turn, she rushed into the bedroom and brought forth his slippers and dressing-gown, and turning over the pillow of the sofa, said:

"Here dear, lie down—you must be tired—and I'll get you a book, a new novel I've just borrowed from Mrs. Ginx, who borrowed it from Mrs. Smithers, whose aunt is well acquainted with the author's brother-in-law, and it's just perfectly splendid."

"Well, pet, after all there's no place like home," said the husband, as he stretched himself on the sofa, "bring along your book."

He was in a gracious mood, and after turning over a few of the leaves, said: "S'pose I read aloud to you, sis?"

"Oh, do, that's a dear, it'll be so nice."

Pretty soon he came to a paragraph something like this:

"'Standing in the archway, with the brilliant light from the chandelier playing about her golden hair, she looked a picture of marvelous beauty. The proudly poised head set on the queenly neck; her deep blue, liquid eye shining in tearful sympathy on the dyspeptic poodle that crouched moaning at her feet; her tiny ear, looking like some creamy-white, pink-tinted shell of ocean——'

"By the way, dear," said the husband, cutting short his reading, "that description reminds me of your ear; you have an ear like a shell."

It was the first compliment she had received from him since the early days of their marriage, and a blush of pride suffused her face as she asked:

"What kind of a shell, darling?"

"An abalone shell," he replied.

She had never heard of an abalone shell, but did not want to display her ignorance; so she silently made up her mind to hunt it out in the "Condensed Treatise of Conchology" that ornamented the center table. Next morning, as soon as her husband had left the house, conchology was in order. She found that it was described as a shell about the size of an ordinary wagon-wheel. She nursed her wrath during that day, and when her husband came home at night, she met him at the door with the towel-roller—and now *his* ear is as big as an abalone shell, but it looks like a piece of pounded beef.

Musical.

This is a musical community. Through every night, far on into the small hours of the morning, may be heard the sweet squeak of the fiddle, the enchanting tones of a piano with a cold in its head, the dulcet strains of the accordeon and concertina, the harmonious melody of the hand-organ, and the thrilling tones of the bass drum, occasionally set off and elaborated by the martial strains given forth by a brass band. Singing is usually added to the charming collection of sounds, which, from the peculiar acoustic properties of the cañon in which Austin is situated, can be heard throughout the town; and in what should be the still hours of the night, voices can be heard trying to outscreech a Chinese bagpipe, to the tune of "Little sweetheart, come and kiss me," or, "Who will care for mother now," which tunes, by the way, don't harmonize very well with the bagpipe's tune, which is a mile and a half long, and only contains three notes. All this is very pleasant for people who have murdered whole families and can't sleep, and instead of soothing the savage breast it sets the Indians in the camps on the surrounding hills to howling as if every mother's son of them was laboring under an attack of the cramp colic. Then the cats and dogs add their voices to the melody, and unmusical people lie abed and listen, and wonder how many cases of murder and suicide will be reported next morning, and reflect how easy it would be for them to bring in a verdict of justifiable homicide if they happened to get on a jury to try a man for killing two or three of the musicians.

Turning Over a New Leaf.

A prominent citizen, who had fallen into the habit of lying in bed till a late hour in the morning, made up his mind to turn over a new leaf. He told his wife that it was a shame for a man in the prime of life to be wasting the most beautiful hours of the day in bed, and gave her injunctions to awaken him at six o'clock the following morning, and to insist on his arising, and to be sure not to let him fall asleep again. Then he pictured in glowing colors the beauties of the morning—how he would go forth from the house and take a morning walk among the sweet-smelling sagebrush, and drink in the pure and health-giving morning air, and listen to the music of the birds, and come home vigorous and refreshed, with that appetite for breakfast which only healthful exercise can give. Next morning his wife awakened him promptly on time.

"Thunderation, can't you let a fellow sleep?" he growled, as he turned over for another snooze.

His wife was not to be discouraged, and persevered in her efforts to arouse him, reminding him of his directions given the evening before After considerable yawning, and stretching, and growling, the citizen managed to get up and dress himself. Then he started out for his walk. When he got to the first saloon he concluded to go in and take a cocktail—a man needed some little stimulant when he broke over old habits and got up so early. Just one cocktail, and not another drop before breakfast. When he got inside the saloon two men were engaged in an animated argument on the Eastern Question, in which he became so interested that he forgot all about his walk until it was time to go home to breakfast, and every time one or the other of the disputants would get the best of the argument, he would "treat the house." When the citizen got home the breakfast was cold, his legs unsteady, and his voice thick, and he spoke to his wife with a Russian accent. When she asked him how he had enjoyed his walk, and if he didn't know breakfast was cold, and what made him look and act so queerly, he said:

"Bin 'gaged in a nanimated scushion er Rooshin war and tookernextracocktailertwo."

His wife was surprised at the facility with which he had learned a foreign language, but expressed herself in effect that early rising and walks before breakfast were not as conducive to health as lying in bed till breakfast was ready.

Poker and Politics.

They were talking politics and playing bean poker—twenty beans for a quarter. There were three of them, all Democrats, and for convenience we will call them Smith, Brown, and Robinson. Smith was dealer, and while he was giving out the cards, Brown and Robinson were discussing the overwhelming corruption among the officials of the land—and shoving cards up their sleeves. The cards being dealt, Brown, who sat next to the dealer, passed, at the same time remarking:

"As I was sayin', the fearful corruption which runs through every branch of the public service is horrifying to every true patriot; the blush of shame mantles my cheek when I think of Grant, the President of the United States, lending himself to all kinds of thievery and jobbery, and surrounding himself with a horde of blood-sucking robbers what are draining the very life-blood of the people."

"It's perfectly awful—I chip," chimed in Robinson, as he neatly disposed of his hand, and got four kings out of his sleeve.

"I pass out," said Smith.

"Just look at Belknap, and Babcock, and Blaine, and the rest of them fellows—I raise you twenty beans," continued Brown, as he deftly got from his sleeve the four aces which were there concealed.

"Yes, and think of Bristow and them mules—le's see: I call that raise, and go you twenty better," returned Robinson.

"That sizes my pile. Just go back a few years in this Administration, and ponder on the Credit Mobilyer, the back-pay steal, the risin' of the President's salary, and the use of money to carry elections in New York; such things as them were never heard of in Andrew Jackson's time or when the Democrats was in power. I call you—what have you got?" said Brown.

"I've got pretty nigh an invincible—here's two little pair of kings," said Robinson, as he laid his hand on the table.

"Oh, I can just rake them—here's four bullets," said Brown, as he reached for the pot.

"Great snakes!" exclaimed Robinson, "you're a nice pill to be talking about the corruptions of the Administration, aint you? If I couldn't play poker honester'n you, I'd never talk about other folks. You and Mr. Smith continue the game while I go out and rustle some more soap."

Wanted a Puff.

"Throw your eye over that!" shrieked a voice behind us. And then a chunk of rock was slammed down on the table on which we were writing, just barely missing the "funny-bone" of our arm. Our first thought was that it was one of those fellows come to inquire "who wrote that article," and we were about to reach for our trusty mitrailleuse, when the voice said: "How's that for richness?" and then we knew instinctively that it was a prospector come to display a specimen of a rich find. We picked up the piece of rock, scanned it carefully, and then asked our visitor where it came from. "You can say it's an entirely new deestrick," he replied, "never afore trod by the foot of a white man. I call it the Fortunate William. You see, I go by the name of Lucky Bill; but that's too common and vulgar-like a name to slap onto a mine." The specimen was composed principally of granite, with here and there a speck of quartz, and looked as if it would assay about six bits a ton. "What do you think she'll go?" asked our visitor, as we concluded our examination of the specimen. We told him we were not a good judge of ore, and could not form an estimate of the value of the rock he exhibited. "Wall," said he, "I *am* a judge of ore; I've prospected every camp from Arizony to Montany, and I can jest tell you that that air rock won't go a cent under ten thousand dollars to the ton." Then he told us the location of the district in which his ledge was situated, declared that the vein was a "well-confined ledge," sixteen feet wide by actual measurement, free-milling ore, wood and water plentiful, and that he honestly believed it to be the second Comstock; and concluded by requesting us to "give her a h'ist in the paper," as he wanted to "attract the attention of capitalists." Then he unbuttoned his shirt, and, thrusting his hand under the bosom, rummaged around till he found a dilapidated cigar, which he handed to us, saying: "Thar, take that, and set her up as high as your language will go." We declined the cigar, (because it was such a poor one, and mashed besides) saying that we did not expect remuneration for representing to the world the mineral resources of Nevada, and particularly of this section. "All right," he said, as he returned the cigar to the place whence he had taken it; "but I want you to understand that I aint one of them ducks what wants editors to puff their mines for *nothin'*; thar aint nothin' mean about me, and if you want the cigar you're welcome to it." We again declined the proffered gift, and he left, after extracting from us a promise that we would "set her up high."

A Sunday-School Story.

"Yes, my boy, to be virtuous is to be happy. It gladdens your old father's heart and causes it to swell with pride when he beholds your name published in the REVEILLE as having attained the maximum figure awarded for deportment in your school. Keep on in the pursuit of knowledge; refrain from the vile practice of playing hooky; do not allow the example of bad boys to induce you to throw spit-balls at your teacher; never, never swear; and you will grow up worthy of the name handed down to you by your Puritan ancestors. Bring me my slippers, my son, and I will hear you recite your lessons, and see what progress you have made."

Johnny stood one hundred in deportment on the last roll of honor of the Austin Public School, which shows that he is a very good boy; and when he dropped a dozen tacks into his father's slippers, it was done in a fit of abstraction. He had worked out several abstruse mathematical problems on his slate since then, and his mind had been so absorbed that he forgot all about such a trivial matter as a few tacks in his father's slippers. He did not intend to be around when the old man put on the slippers, but the circumstance of the tacks having slipped his memory, he brought and laid them at his father's feet in all the confiding innocence of unsuspecting youth.

"As I was saying, my son—Ooch! Owch! Gewhilikens! Thunder'nlightnin'! Hellfire'nbrimstone! What'nthunder'sthat!"

"Did you step on a pin, sir?"

"'Step on a pin!' I'll pin you, you young rapscallion of thunderation, you! Come out here in the wood-shed, and I'll show you what I stepped on."

Then Johnny's father took him out in the wood-shed and talked to him, and the boy in the next house took his fingers out of the jar of jam in the pantry, and remarked, "Jersey District and the Black Hills, aint he a-catchin' it, though?" And Johnny remarked that he "wouldn't never do it no more."

Moral—The fact of a boy's name being on the roll of honor is not a sure sign that he is truly good.

A Toothache Cure.

Night before last, a prominent citizen was awakened from his peaceful slumbers by the pain of a raging tooth, and his sympathizing wife told him to go into the pantry and get some cloves, and put three or four of the spices in the hollow of the tooth. He tried to find the cloves in the dark, but the attempt was attended with unfortunate consequences. He knocked over a pan of dough which had been placed on a chair in the kitchen, and after he got his feet out of the sticky mass and was proceeding to the pantry, he suddenly sat down in a bucket of slops. He is a good-tempered man, but this circumstance ruffled him and wet the nether portion of his night garment. But he was determined to have those cloves. He got to the pantry, and, following his wife's directions, reached for the little crock in the right-hand corner of the third shelf. He was not discouraged because he pulled down a pitcher of yeast and a keg of brine. It is true, these liquids wet his hair and ran down his spinal column; but he didn't mind that—he had the crock. Then he reached down into it for those cloves, and his hand went into something soft; he didn't know whether it was preserves, or mustard, or tar, or jelly, or mud, but it was something very sticky and soft; and he called in a voice of suppressed emotion for his wife to bring a light. He called pretty loud, as he thought his wife was asleep; but she answered the call promptly, and when she reached him with the lamp, her remarks were to the effect that he was a nice-looking object. She had not complimented him in many years of their married life, and her words touched him. "Yes," he said sadly, "I'm in a hellofafix."

After getting some of the jelly out of his hair, and the dough scraped off his legs, and the brine washed out of his eyes, she said she guessed she'd just look for those cloves herself—"a man couldn't be trusted to do *anything*." There was not a clove in the house, and when she went back into the bedroom to tell him he had better go to a dentist and have that grinder snaked out, he said the bitter experience of that night had cured his toothache.

There is no cure for pain equal to diverting the thoughts with pleasant experiences.

No Quarter.

A man who looked as dilapidated as the last rose of last summer went into a Main Street saloon this forenoon, and, with confidence in human nature and himself depicted in his every movement, strutted to the bar and told the gentlemanly dispenser of stimulants to trot out some of his best whisky. The bar-keeper obeyed the order with alacrity. Millionaires in rags are sometimes to be found in a mining country, and the man of bottles and glasses had learned by experience never to despise a man because he wears a ragged coat. The stranger poured out and swallowed a glass of that best whisky. Then he went down into his pocket for a quarter, as the barkeeper and the bystanders supposed. But he didn't bring up anything but a piece of a pocket-handkerchief that looked as if it had spent seven years in the coal-bins at one of the Eureka smelting furnaces. Wiping his mouth and eyes with the rag, he drew a deep sigh, and said to the mixer of drinks:

"Have you heard about this terrible war in Europe?"

"Oh, that's too thin," replied the barkeeper, "hand out a quarter for that whisky, you old fraud."

"Patience, patience, my friend," he said, "can you tell me why I am like the barbarian Turk when he gets a Russian soldier in his power?"

"No, I can't," snapped the exasperated purveyor of liquors.

"Well, I'll tell you. It's because I show no quarter."

The barkeeper reached under the counter for his trusty six-shooter; but ere he could bring it to bear, the man who showed no quarter had vanished like the baseless fabric of a vision.

The War and Poker.

The hands were running small, and interest in the game was flagging, and a discussion on the Russo-Turkish war relieved the tedium of "ace-high" and single pairs, varied as occasion required by the utterance by the players of the technical terms of the game. It was Smith's deal, and as he dealt the cards from the pack he remarked that it was wonderful how the Turks had held their own at Plevna.

"Yes," said Brown, who was "next the dealer," "them Turks is fighters from the ground up; I Chipka."

"And I pass," observed Jones, who was next in say.

"Speaking of Chipka Pass," observed Tompkins, who was last in say, "it did seem at first as if the Russians was goin' to warm the Turks thar; but you see the Turks was on their own dunghill, and that give 'em a big advantage. I have my redoubts about this hand, but will call you, and raise you five."

"I Pasha out," said Smith, as he threw his cards on the table.

The discussion was now narrowed down to Brown and Tompkins. Then the dealer asked Brown how many he would take, and he said be-Kars it was Tompkins, he wouldn't be mean, and would take one; and when he was helped, Tompkins asked the dealer to reinforce his hand with four cards. Then Brown called up his reserves, and moved on the pot with five beans, and Tompkins remarked that he would raise the siege twenty.

"Aint you Russian it?" asked Tompkins, as he put up the twenty, and raised Brown the size of his pile. Brown rallied, and met the charge, and then they showed down their hands; and Tompkins had two pair of deuces, and Brown likewise had two pair, aces at the head, and when Tompkins took the pot prisoner Brown said he would have to go into winter quarters, 'cause he was "froze out."

Misplaced Confidence.

"Suppose," he said to the bar-keeper, "suppose you had four hundred and twelve dollars twelve and a half cents, and, holding the position you do, drawing a stated salary and having free access to the money-drawer, you would have just the amount of idle capital represented by them figgers, wouldn't you? Now when a man has idle capital what does he do with it? Why, he invests it where it will earn something for itself, don't he? Now, in casting about for some place to put it where it will do the most good, he naturally lights on a savings bank, as being something combining safety with profit, and he walks up to the cashier, planks down his soap and says, 'Give me a bank-book!' And he walks out, feeling that his idle capital is in a safe place and no longer idle, but producing something. Now this is what you would do with that supposable four hundred and twelve dollars and a half—but being a bar-keeper you *might* invest it in a diamond pin, but we're supposing you don't want your capital to remain idle—and the next morning you wake up and come down town and pick up the newspaper, and the first thing that strikes your eye is that your savings bank's busted, and the President's gone on a pleasure trip to the

Sandwich Islands, and you're a ruined community. Now, the natural result of all this is that you're a victim of misplaced confidence, aint it!"

While the harangue detailed above was being delivered, the barkeeper stood pensively turning a towel around the inside of a glass, and answered never a word until the last question was put; when he set down the glass on the bar, gave it a twirl with his fingers, and, looking the customer straight in the eye, said:

"My friend, you needn't unreel any more of that rope; I might as well tell you right here that if you expect to spar me out of a drink on that kind of lip, you're the worst victim of misplaced confidence between here and the north pole."

"I might a'knowed it; sweetness wasted on the desert air," was all the impecunious one said, as he turned sadly away and started out to "try the next house."

The Biggest Man in the State.

At a store in town, yesterday, a large lot of goods, consisting principally of heavy groceries, was being delivered on the sidewalk from a freight wagon, when a strapping young fellow, about six feet in height and muscled in proportion, came along and asked if they wanted help. The clerk, who was superintending the unloading, is rather a light-waisted looking individual—delicate looking, in fact—but has had considerable experience in handling groceries, and has got a knack of chucking around sacks of flour and barrels of sugar with a perfect looseness.

"Are you pretty stout?" said he to the applicant for work.

"Stout! I'm the biggest man in the State—why jest look at me!"

"Yes, you look pretty stout," replied the clerk, "but you'll have to work with *me*."

"Work with *you!*" said the biggest man, and he curled his upper lip, and cast a glance of withering scorn at the slim proportions of the clerk, "work with *you!* Jest peel yourself and start in, till you see how quick I'll wear *you* out."

They went to work, and the way that clerk slung bags and boxes up to the eighth and ninth tiers, and kept the store truck on a keen jump, was a sight for sore eyes. The biggest man in the State weakened early in the action, and, with the perspiration pouring in streams from his brow, sat down on a ham and watched the clerk as he tossed things right and left.

"What's the matter?" said the clerk, "I hope you ain't tired already; I'm only a delicate, sickly sort of a cuss, and *I* ain't tired yet."

"Sick be damn'd!" retorted the biggest man, "you're nuthin' more nor less than a donkey engine. I can hold my own agi'n muscle; but I'll be dog-goned if I can stand off steam."

"Young man," said the clerk, in solemn tones, "remember that the race is not always to the swift nor the battle to the strong; and never again go around blowing that you're the biggest man in the State."

A Cure for Hiccoughs.

A young gentleman who attends the Austin public school had been told that a sudden shock or fright would cure the hiccoughs, and the other evening, while he was studying his lesson for the morrow by drawing a picture of the schoolmarm on his slate, his respected progenitor was seized with a fit of hiccoughs. The old gentleman was tilted back in his chair, with his feet resting on the top of the stove, and the young hopeful concluded to try the cure on him. Just as the old man was "rastling" with a heart-breaking hic, the boy jumped up and yelled "Fire!" The old man was just getting out "cuh—cuh!" but he never got it out. He gave a jump which tilted over the chair, and in endeavoring to regain his lost equilibrium his feet flew up against a table, upsetting it and a student lamp which stood on it, and his head landed in the ashes on the stove hearth. The old lady, hearing the racket, came running in from the kitchen, and tripped over the old man's prostrate form, knocking down a what-not with a lot of glass and China ornaments. When that boy's father arose from the wreck, and shook the ashes and splinters of glass out of his hair and clothes, he was cured of the hiccoughs, but there was a look of sternness in his eye; the boy says he knows it was a "stern" look—feelingly "stern," as he can testify. He says fright is a splendid cure for the "hiccups"; but that the "stern" look it occasions is three hundred thousand times worse than the "hiccups." He can't play tag now, as he says his mother has forbidden him, and he sits on the edge of the seat at school, and lies on his front when in bed, and silently murmurs that the old man can hiccup his consarned old head off before he will ever again try to cure him.

The Sausage.

Reader, did you ever stop to mentally analyze the constituents of pork sausage; or when that article has been set before you, crisp and smoking from the frying-pan, have you trusted to luck and the theory that "where ignorance is bliss, 'twere folly to be wise"? Has it ever occurred to you that just about the time pork sausage begins to ripen, somebody's dog is missing? These are thoughts which should commend themselves to all, and questions which every head of a family should propound to himself about this time; for pork sausage is in season. We know of no sure test to detect the presence of dog in sausage. One of the oldest expedients is to whistle to the sausage, and if it tries to wag itself, there is dog in it. But if the dog has been put into the sausage-cutter tail first, the vitality of that member has been affected, and the test won't work. Some persons rely on the presence of hair in the sausage as a means of detection; but this is merely circumstantial evidence, and therefore entitled to but little weight. The most approved method of determining the exact constituents is laid down by Dr. Doggonimoff, chief surgeon of the Russian army in Bulgaria, in the following formula: Set a frying-pan on a hot fire and lay the sausage gently in it; then prod each link suddenly with a fork to see if it will emit any bark. Let them fry till done brown, then dish up and cram them down your mother-in-law's throat, and if you have any in excess of her carrying capacity take them to some deep mining shaft and dump them in. If, when they strike the bottom, a yelp is heard, as if somebody had trod on a dog's tail, then there is canine in them, and the test has worked to a charm.

Why They Quit.

A certain gentleman of this city has long been paying attention to a young lady, the daughter of a well-to-do rancher in one of the adjacent valleys; and his feelings were fully reciprocated by the lady, as she has frequently informed several of her lady acquaintances that she felt "a little sweet on Jim."

The other day, Jim paid a visit to the ranch where his Dulcinea abideth, in accordance with an invitation to "come over and stop a few days." The roads were very muddy, and when our hero arrived at the ranch he looked like the last remnants of a cloud-burst. The lady sympathized with the woe-begone appearance of her admirer, feeling flattered that he should endure all this for her sake, and exerted herself to her utmost to make him comfortable, preparing an excellent supper, and giving up her own apartment, so that he might rest comfortably after the fatigues of the day. In the morning, before Jim was astir, the young lady requested the hired man to go into the room and get Jim's boots, and scrape off the mud, and make them look presentable against he should be ready to arise. The hired man did as directed, and brought what he supposed to be the boots into the kitchen, where the lady was preparing breakfast. Noticing a peculiar odor, the lady glanced at the man, when, horror! he was blacking—not Jim's boots, but his socks. She ordered the man to return the pedal envelopes to the room, and sprinkled chloride of lime all over the house; and when Jim arose he commenced to intently examine the thermometer, and wonder what had caused the weather to turn cold so suddenly. He ate his breakfast without appetite, saddled his horse, and came to town; and now he says he don't go a cent on a girl whose warmth of affection is up to ninety-eight degrees at night and falls to zero in the morning.

Two men were shoveling snow from the roof; they were absorbed in their work, and did not notice the people who passed over the sidewalk on which they were throwing the snow. First came along a little girl; she tripped along gayly, humming to herself the words of that beautiful song, "Oh, how I love my teacher." Just as she got to "Oh, how I love my ——gracious!" two shovelfuls of snow came kerchunk on her innocent head, and she sputtered and spit, and thought there was a snow-slide. Then there approached a lady fair. She was tied back and had overshoes on, and was saying to herself: "Twenty yards for the dress; fourteen for the overskirt; six dozen buttons—eight and eight's sixteen, and nine's thirty-three—no—le's see——Owch!" A bushel or so of snow had been emptied down her back, and she wriggled and squirmed as though an army of fleas was making a forced march down her spine, and hurried home to change her clothes. The next was a pillar of the church—a God-fearing man, who never allows his lips to utter guile. He got a shovelful of snow square in the face, but he only rolled his eyes heavenward, and remarked something about the place of future punishment, and uttered the name of his Saviour. Three or four small boys were buried up by the snow which descended from the roof by the shovelful, but that little matter is hardly worthy of mention. They will probably be found when the big thaw comes.

She was fixed up in her prettiest, and had just started out to make her calls, determined to let her lady friends know that other people could wear new bonnets as well as themselves. The man who was going to wet down the street with the hose turned on the water just as she passed his store. For a moment she did not know whether it was a cloud-burst or the second deluge; but when the man humbly said, "Excuse me, madam," her emotion found vent in words. "Excuse you!" she said. "Yes, I'll excuse you when you go down in your clothes and bring up seventeen dollars for a new bonnet; when you pay four dollars for this dress; when you yield up eleven dollars and a quarter for this polonaise; when it ceases raining down my spinal column; when you purchase me a box of bronchial troches and a bottle of cherry pectoral and six patent mustard-plasters; when you recognize my claim to nine dollars damages for injury to my best and holiest feelings, then I'll excuse you." The man told her to make out a bill of items and he would settle it, if he had to sue her husband for his store bill to raise the money.

The price of fresh oysters in Austin is twelve and a half cents each. They were out walking, and she remarked that she had observed in the REVEILLE that there were fresh oysters in town.

"Do you read the papers carefully, my dear?" he asked.

She said she read all the fashion news, and all the murders, and the recipes for making cup custard and "floating-island," and the divorce cases; but she would just like to know what all that had to do with oysters.

"Well, you see, my dear," said he, "there's a terrible contagion broke out among the oysters, and the newspapers are advising people not to eat them; it appears that the bivalvular structure of the animal's diaphragm has become affected by a species of parasitical conglomeration, which, reacting on the vitality of the muscular forces of the alimentary canal, produces a paralysis of the oyster's nervous and digestive functions to such an extent as to render it unfit for human food."

She said he was the best husband in the world to be so careful of her health, and she would go home and tackle the cold pork and cabbage left from dinner, as she felt rather faint. He saw her home, and then went to the restaurant and had two dozen raw and a bottle of ale; and as he planked the money on the counter in payment therefor, he remarked that fresh oysters were a necessary luxury, but it was like swallowing silver coin to eat them.

A respectable-looking old gentleman, just arrived from the Eastern States, was around town to-day, trying to find a man named Smith. There are several members of the Smith family in Austin, so the old gentleman experienced some difficulty in finding the exact Smith he wanted, and we are not positive that he has found him yet. Probably possessed of the somewhat prevalent idea that boys know everything, the old gentleman accosted one, and addressing him as "my son," asked him if he knew anybody in this town by the name of Smith.

"Smith?" said the boy, "which Smith do you want? Le's see—there's Big Smith and Little Smith, Three-fingered Smith, Bottle-nose

Smith, Cockeye Smith, Six-toed Smith, San Joaquin Smith, Lying Smith, Mushhead Smith, Jumping Smith, Cherokee Smith, One-legged Smith, Fighting Smith, Red-headed Smith, Sugar-foot Smith, Bow-legged Smith, Squaw Smith, Drunken Smith, El Dorado Smith, Hungry Smith, and I don't know but maybe one or two more."

"My son," said the gentleman, "the Smith I am in search of possesses to his name none of the heathenish prefixes you have mentioned. His name is simply John Smith."

"All them fellows is named John," screeched the boy, as he drew his six-shooter and ran to the other side of the street to get a good shot at a passing Chinaman.

The old gentleman mused for a moment, and then walked into a blacksmith shop and asked to see a city directory.

He was seedy and battered, and he looked "powerful" dry. He entered a Main Street saloon, and approaching the bar, said to the barkeeper:

"It's a good ticket, aint it?"

"First rate," replied the bar-keeper.

"You betcher life, them's my men; Hayes'n Wheeler for me. 'Rah for Hayes'n Wheeler! Set out some o' yer 'Publican whisky, barkeep!"

"My friend," replied the bar-keeper, "you're a little off; this is a Democratic house."

"Thunder!" exclaimed the soaker; "the Dimmycrats aint got nobody to holler fur yit, and I'm as dry as a powder-horn, and not a cent 'twixt me and eternity."

"My friend," said the obliging barkeeper, "while differing with you in politics, I cannot resist your appeal—help yourself to some of this"; and he set out a glass, and the bottle of lightning kept for the special use of "stiffs." The "stiff" poured out a glassful of the stuff, and emptied it into his throat; and when he got through coughing, and wiping his eyes on his coat-sleeve, said:

"I aint got no money; but if I was the Comstock ledge, I'd bet myself ag'in a Lander Hill razor-blade that them durned Black Republicans don't git away with the ensooin' election."

An old lady of this city, whose daughter reads a great many dime novels, hearing some person conversing about the Centennial, said her Maria ought to know all about it, for she "just keeps the whole family busted buying them 'Tencent-ial' novels."

By a sort of freemasonry existing between natives of Missouri, they recognize each other as being from the same country "back thar." One of them came across the plains in forty-nine; and the other is a grasshopper sufferer, and has just got through the blockade on the railroad; but they know the same Jim Joneses, and Sal Smiths, and Nate Thompsons, and Si Perkinses, and Marier Tompkinses, and other Mary Annses, and Bills, and Jacks, and Sols, and Hi's. It was nine o'clock last night when they sat down by the stove in one of the principal saloons, and at two o'clock this afternoon they were still telling how Jim Jones married Mary Ann Perkins and had a whole raft of young uns, and how Jim "tu'k to drink," and stole horses, and died with snakes in his boots; and how Squar' Thompson he found a lead hill on his farm and sent his boys and girls to "collidge"; and Marier this ran away with Bill that, and divers and sundry similar reminiscences. In vain the bar-keeper carried them glasses of water; in vain were pictures of coffins held up to their gaze; in vain spectators muttered that the worst death in the world is to be talked to death. They are still at it, and it is expected that by to-morrow morning the forty-niner will be found cold in death, with the grasshopper sufferer, prostrate and dying, whispering in the ear of the corpse.

The talking match mentioned in Saturday's paper continued until yesterday morning, when it was brought to an end by the merciful interposition of outsiders. The forty-niner fainted twice during the night, but was restored to consciousness by his head falling against the hot stove. The grasshopper sufferer never showed the least sign of weakness, and when the forty-niner was dragged off by force, the sufferer was muttering, "An' Si Wallace he got killed in the war, and Bill Pearce married the widder, and the oldest gal she run away with——" but two stout men seized and held him, while several others bore the forty-niner from the scene.

A prominent citizen, as he calmly watched his hat wafted toward Emigrant Cañon by the zephyrs, this afternoon, remarked:

"Thar goes my wife's new bunnit!"

"Why, that ain't a bonnet," remarked a bystander.

"The blazes it aint!" replied the citizen, "d'ye s'pose I'm a Rosschild and can buy my wife a bunnit and myself a hat both in the same month, and it two weeks to pay-day, yit?"

It is evident that some woman in town won't get any new bonnet till pay-day.

It is a well-known fact that caterpillars are numerous—so numerous, in fact, that they are everywhere. They invade houses, crawl into the frying-pan and teakettle, play tag on the piano-cover, have games of hide and seek in gentlemen's pants, and run races on ladies' striped stockings, taking a stripe for a race-course. Last evening he called on her. They sat on the porch and drank in the beauties of the gorgeous sunset. Their souls were in the far away, and she was saying how she wished to be transformed into a butterfly, to fly through ethereal space and bathe her wings in the golden-tinged moisture of yonder cloud. They might have sat thus in the gloaming, engaged in sweet converse, until the shadows of night darkened the earth, and none can tell how much romantic thought she would have spoken, had not their conversation been brought to an abrupt termination by her feeling something crawling up her leg. She made a wild grab at the costly merchandise which concealed her beauteous limbs; and then, in tones of agony, exclaimed: "It's smashed!" It was only a caterpillar, but she had to go in the house and wash her hands and put on a clean pair of stockings; and the young man went home, more in sorrow than in anger, and wondered why a girl should think a butterfly such a beautiful object, and yet get sick and scared at the flattened body of a butterfly without wings.

The publisher of the *National Protestant*, a religious paper published in New York, has heard of the editor of the REVEILLE. He knows we are a Christian, and ever ready to lend a helping hand to the cause of religion. If he were not aware of this, he would not have made the very modest request embodied in a postal-card which we received from him this morning. He requests us to subscribe to his paper, canvass the town and rustle up other subscribers, and furnish his paper with contributions from our "able pen." The remuneration which we are to receive for these services is the reward of an approving conscience. We should like to oblige the publisher of the *Protestant*, but we are engaged in other work at present; we are bending our energies to the propagation of the Gospel among the Shoshones, and are endeavoring to organize a tract society, and are devoting our fortune to the purchase of grub and clothes, so that we have neither time nor money to spare for the *National Protestant.*

To show the power of mind over matter no stronger argument is needed than that which we heard advanced by a boy this morning. Said he to another boy: "You needn't be puttin' on no airs if yer is got a boughten sled; I'm in the third reader and you can't spell 'cat' without spellin' of it with a 'k.'"

The "Colonel" was warming his coat-tails by the stove at the Sazerac. His nose bore evidence of successful culture, and glowed with that rich ruby hue which only a steady and prolonged worship at the shrine of Bacchus can produce. There was a "dry" look about the corners of his mouth, which was readily noticed by the sympathizing bar-keeper, who good-naturedly asked the Colonel if he would not take a little stimulant.

"Certainly, certainly, sir," he replied promptly, as he briskly stepped up to the bar. Pouring out a tumbler level full of the fluid, he tossed it off, and as soon as he could regain his breath, assumed a deprecatory tone and thus addressed the bar-keeper:

"This, sir, is my sixty-fourth drink to-day. I must put on the brakes, or the first thing I know I shall degenerate into excess. Moderation, sir, moderation, the grand secret of health, has been the rule of my life. If I had but one more drink at this moment, Richard would be himself again."

The subsequent remarks of the bar-keeper indicated that, for all he cared, Richard might remain impersonal till the day of judgment.

His complexion denoted him a full-blooded member of the race that inhabit that section of God's footstool "where Afric's sunny fountains roll down their golden sands," and the rest of his *tout ensemble* was that of an overloaded pack-mule. On his back a bundle of blankets, surmounted by two pairs of boots; slung in front of him, a huge bundle; on one side a carpet-sack and a frying-pan; on the other a valise and a coffee-pot; in his right hand a stick, and in his left a basket. Halting in front of the court-house, he hailed a man sitting on the stoop of that building, and said: "Say, boss, which am de best hotel in dis hyar town?" The person addressed told him that the International was reputed to be the best house of entertainment in Austin. With a grin that opened a cavern in his face, and made it look as if his head was splitting in two in the middle, the overladen man and brother resumed his line of march, saying, as he stepped forward: "Yer see, boss, I aint 'bliged ter 'pend on dese hyar hotels; if der 'commodations don't suit dis hyar chile, I travels so's I can organize myself inter a fust-class hotel at a moment's notice, wid an elevator, hot and cold water in every room, barber shop in de basement, and all de modern improvements."

A diminutive chap, about four years of age, walked into Sower's store, this morning, and inquired for a sled. A bystander asked him what he wanted with a sled, telling him there would be no snow this winter.

"How do you know?" asked the youngster, "you aint God."

"What's the news up your way?" asked a down-town woman of an Upper Austin woman in a Main Street store to-day.

"Oh, not a thing in the world," replied the one questioned; "you see, we're awful quiet, peaceable people up our way, and of course I stay to home so much I don't know what's going on, anyhow, 'cause I have so much to do to 'tend to my children, and the sewing, and washing, and cooking; but they do say that Mrs. Bustem has got a brand-new silk dress, and nobody knows how she got it, and her husband only a common chlo-rider, and hasn't had a crushing in four months, and his last rock didn't pay for milling; and that Mrs. Gabble and Mrs. Tattle has had the worst kind of a fight, and when Mrs. Tattle made a grab at Mrs. Gabble's hair it was false, and all came out, and two-thirds of it was jute; and Mr. Squeezem chucked his wife out of doors 'cause she lammed the servant girl for letting him kiss her in the wood-shed; and that Mr. Sinchem drew a six-shooter on Mr. Bilkem for saying his wife said that his wife couldn't have no new bonnet this fall, 'cause her husband was poorer than Job's turkey, and couldn't pay ninety cents on the dollar if his creditors was to come down on him to-morrow and sell him out at forced sale. Oh, I tell you, we're awful peaceable people up our way; only it's tedious living in a neighbor-hood where there aint nothing going on."

In the REVEILLE reporter's wanderings about town last night, he heard a lady talking across the street to a neighbor, thus deliver herself on the subject of scandal:

"Of all the things I do hate in this world, it's a scandalizing woman. Now there's Mrs. Jingletongue, that everybody knows isn't a bit better than she ought to be, and whose two daughters cut up so shameful that no decent woman ought to speak to them, and whose husband gets drunk, and they do say he owes for the grenadine she puts on so many airs in over her betters. If I was to say mean things about people like she does, I would pull my tongue out by the roots, the nasty, scandalizing, stuck-up old cat."

A miner working in one of the mines of Lander Hill bought a new bedstead, the other day. His wife set it up in the bedroom, and the miner and the partner of his joys and sorrows occupied it last night for the first time. During the night he dreamed he was working in a drift, when suddenly he heard a timber snap. Looking up, he saw that the mine was caving in, and almost certain death staring him in the face. His only hope was to reach the shaft. Fear lent speed to his footsteps, and he reached the shaft in safety. Horror! the cage was not there! Behind him he heard the snapping of timbers and the rumble of great masses of falling earth and rocks, every second approaching nearer. If he could but ring down the cage he was safe, and grasping the bell-wire he gave a desperate pull. There was a piercing scream, a snapping and crashing and rumbling, and he felt himself going down, down—till he stopped. The slats of the new bedstead had broken.

"Am I dead?" asked the miner, hardly awake and conscious.

"I wish you were," said his wife, "you've pulled out every bit of hair I had in the world, and I'll have to go through life bald-headed; for false hair is going out of fashion, and besides it's almost impossible to get a shade to match."

A prospector passed up Main Street this forenoon, and halted his outfit at the watering-trough in front of the REVEILLE office. Said outfit consisted of a little two-wheeled cart—the body of the cart being composed of rough pine boards—and a pony about as big as an ordinary sized jackrabbit. At the end of the cart hung a blackened tin coffee-pot and a battered tin pail, and piled in the box were blankets, picks, shovels, and grub, the whole affair betokening that it was a prospector's. Approaching the owner of the horse and cart, we asked:

"Whither bound?"

"Don't know," he replied, sententiously.

"Where are you from?"

"Over yonder," he replied, pointing his finger toward the direction of Washoe County.

"Prospecting?" we asked.

"'Spect so," he replied. Then glancing up at the sign in front of the REVEILLE office, he remarked:

"I'd just like to see the shape of one of you newspaper fellers that could pump *my* true-inwardness dry."

We gave him up.

Some little girls were playing tag on Court Street last evening, when one of them, who had been "tagged" seven times in succession, got tired, and proposed to change and play house.

"What kind of house will we play?" asked another.

"Oh, play calling," replied the first speaker. "Mary, here, she can be Mrs. Brown, and set on the step, and me and Julia will call on her, and ask her how she is, and how her husband is, and if baby's got over the measles, and tell her how nice she looks in her new wrapper, and hope it won't hurt her much when she has that tooth filled. And then we'll say, 'Good bye, Mrs. Brown; come and see us some time or other, and bring the children and your sewing; and you're *such* a stranger, we don't see half enough of you.' And then me and Julia, we'll c'urtsey, and walk off a piece, and I'll say to Julia, 'Did you ever see such a horrid old fright as she looks in that wrapper?' and then Julia, she'll say, 'The *idear* of anybody having *false* teeth filled!' and then I'll say, 'Yes, and what a homely lot of dirty little children them young ones of her'n is.' Let's play it; what do you say?"

There was unanimous consent, and the play went on.

A man sat for an hour and a half in a Main Street saloon this morning, without saying a word to anybody, and then he arose, faced the bar-keeper, spread his arms, struck an attitude, and said:

"Peace, white-robed Peace, again spreads her wings over distracted Eu——"

But the bar-keeper interrupted him, and said:

"P. U. or S. U.! You got a drink on the Silver Bill day before yesterday, played the Chinese question on me yesterday, want to ring in Peace in Europe to-day, and the chances are that to-morrow you'll be trying me on a disquisition on the non-existence of a material Hell. But it won't do; I won't have it. More coin and less hyperbole is my motto from this on."

And then the man went into a corner and ruminated, and after a while he stealthily approached the bar-keeper, and whispered in his ear:

"'P. U. or S. U.' means put up or shut up, don't it?"

"You couldn't have hit it nearer if you had guessed for a thousand years," said the barkeeper.

And then the man said this was a cruel and unfeeling world, where one's best and holiest feelings were trifled with to an extent that rendered life hardly worth the living.

We are in receipt from a friend in Virginia of a novel French contrivance, called the "Centennial Telegraph." It consists of two tin tubes, with one end covered with parchment, to which is secured a string connecting the two tubes. It is operated by one person placing the open end of one of the tubes close against his or her ear, and the party at the other end of the string places the open end of the other tube to his or her mouth, and whispers such words as are desired to be communicated to the party at the other end of the line. While the persons operating can distinctly hear and understand all that passes over the line, nobody else can hear a word that is said. The string which forms the telegraph line is about fifty feet in length, but can be shortened at will. This is a very useful invention, and supplies a want long felt by hen conventions and ladies' sewing circles. By its means two ladies can sit in opposite corners of a room which is filled with company, and exchange their sentiments about the other women present, without those who are being talked about having the least idea of what is going on. It is a great improvement on whispering, which is often in danger of being overheard. It will also be found useful as a means of communication between husbands and servant girls.

We were sitting where we could watch all his movements. He came up the street with an unsteady gait, his legs now and again acting contrary, one foot trying hard to cross the path of the other. At last he reached a railing that stood by an open cellar-way, and here was a haven of rest for his weary and Fourth-of-July-racked soul. He grasped the railing to steady himself; then gradually his head sunk down on the rail, and there was a bending of the knee-joints. Slowly, carefully, he slid down the cellar stairs; the bottom step was reached; one long drawn sigh, ending in a deep bass snore, and, away from the gaze of men and the City Marshal, the tired soul was at rest—a rest so perfect that all the firecrackers on earth could not have recalled him to the scenes of unrest of the day after the Fourth. He was there this morning, lying on his back, with the bright sun shining on his upturned face, and several blue-bottle flies sipping the sweetness from his parted lips. Reader, that man was once a little boy, and went fishing on Sunday, and robbed orchards and birds' nests, just like many and many another innocent boy; and had it not been for the demon of whisky, he might have grown up to be a member of the Legislature.

A tall, gaunt-looking individual, who at first and last glance would be taken to belong to the noble brotherhood of bull-punchers, walked up to the bar in a Main Street saloon, this forenoon, and laying down a smooth quarter, called for whisky. The bar-keeper set out the bottle, and the customer, crossing his legs, placing the forefinger of his left hand firmly on his coin, and grasping the neck of the bottle with his right hand, asked:

"Is this here stuff strained?"

"Strained!" said the bar-keeper, with an astonished look, "strained of what?"

"Look a' here, mister," returned the ox-manager, "I've got an ajid mother back in Missoury; I cum out here to make a stake for the old gal, and I haint got it yit. Besides, I was brought up relijus, and my old marm told me never to die till I was perpared to face the music. I aint perpared to die; and what I want to know is, if the snakes is strained out of them air whisky."

The bar-keeper assured him that the snakes were strained out, and he poured the glass level full and threw down the liquid as if it was mother's milk.

Now that the ground is covered with snow, the boy and his sled are as inseparable as a young lady and her newest beau. If the baby swallows concentrated lye, or runs a clothes-pin up its nose, and Johnny's mother says, "Run, quick, Johnny, and bring the doctor before that clothes-pin gets into the baby's brain," he has to drag his sled out of the woodshed and slide on it to the doctor's office; and if he should get spilled over a bank and delayed, the baby is liable to die before the doctor can reach it. If there is company at dinner, and it is suddenly discovered that "there aint a bit of butter in the house," and Tommy is dispatched to the store to get some, with an injunction to "hurry up," he must, of course, haul it home on his sled; and if he happens to meet another boy he is sure to have a race, in the excitement of which he forgets all about the butter, and either comes home with it distributed on the seat of his pants, or it has slid off the sled into the snow. Of course, Johnny or Tommy gets licked for these little misfortunes; but the licking diminishes not his love for his sled, which is part of himself so long as the snow stays on the ground.

Music, besides having power to soothe the savage breast, has the quality to make a sleepy man get up and howl, and wish he was deaf. For instance: Last night the air was just running over with music. Piano, violin, French horn, guitar, Chinese fiddle, flute, Chinese bagpipes, accordeon, violoncello, hand-organ, toot-horn, musical box, bass-drum, and harmonica, and vocal renditions of "Pull down the Blind," "Hear me, Norma," "The Piute Death-Song," [by the Medicine Man] "Lannigan's Ball," the "Slave's Lament," "I wish she was my Mother-in-Law," operatic selections, and "Old Dog Tray," all being banged, and scraped, and pounded, and ground, and tooted, and howled simultaneously, and shedding harmony on the air thicker than the buzzing of flies round a fat infant. The acoustic properties of the cañon in which this town is built are such that sound is carried to a great distance very distinctly; and a man lying in his bunk in his cabin on the summit of Lander Hill could take in every note of the grand musical combination in question. Too much music hath charms to make a man savage.

He caught pedro a good many times during the night, and was a "little off" when he got home; but he felt good—he felt poetical. As he entered the bed-room some familiar lines came into his head, and on the impulse he commenced to recite. Said he:

"'Oh for a lodge in some vast wilderness, some boundless contiguity of——'"

At this point he was interrupted by his wife, who remarked:

"I should think you belong to lodges enough; here you are a Mason, and an Odd Fellow, and a Knight of Pythias, and a Red Man, and an Ancient Hibernian, and a Pioneer, and an Irish-American, and a Fireman, and if you join any more lodges there won't be nights enough in the week to go around. And riding them goats, and climbing them greased poles, and sleeping in them coffins unsettles your nerves, and you come home excited every blessed night."

He thought he was getting off pretty easy, and promised her he would not join any more lodges.

County Assessor Spires discovered a mouse in his office in the court-house, yesterday. Instead of getting up on top of his high desk-stool and gathering his skirts about his ankles and screaming, he took down the assessment-roll and let it drop on the mouse. As this was only a one-hundred-and-forty-two quire book, it merely stunned the animal; and as it lay on the floor unconscious, he pounded it on the head with the bullion-tax book and Vol. 1 of the Compiled Laws. Then he went out and got a broom and shovel to remove the corpse, and just got back to the office in time to see the mouse's tail disappearing in a hole in the base-board. The remarks addressed to the retreating mouse can be found in almost any orthodox prayer-book, but not connected in the exact sequence in which Spires framed the words.

A gentleman having charge of a mine in this vicinity recently invited a friend to visit and inspect the mine. They descended the shaft and passed through various workings, the superintendent explaining matters as they went along, till they came to the bonanza of the mine.

"Here, you see," said the superintendent, "is where we first struck it. We run that cross-cut from yonder drift through solid granite, without a streak of quartz, as you saw; then we encountered a small seam of vein-matter, and sunk that little winze; here we are; now look; here's the foot-wall; there's the hanging-wall, and here we have our ore. The streak's kind of narrow right here, but we'll go up this chute in a minute, and ——"

He thought his friend was listening very intently, and was surprised that a stranger to mining matters should take such a deep interest; for during the entire explanation the friend had not said a word. Turning around, he saw that his friend was not with him; and retracing his steps to look for him, he found him stretched out on the bottom of a drift, fast asleep, and snoring the tune of Old Hundred, as if he were practicing for the bass in the opening chorus at the Centennial.

There is no doubt that the Germans, as a class, are a very enterprising people. In most cases they come to this country poor, and by dint of hard work, perseverance, and economy, establish themselves in business, which with good management gradually expands, till in the course of a few years they are wealthy and influential citizens. As their wealth increases, they engage in new and more extensive enterprises, always using their capital to advantage, and making every dollar of it count. We are reminded of this by the fact that a German gentleman of this city, who was born in the region of the historical Black Forest, and who came to Austin poor, and by industry and economy has accumulated as much as three hundred dollars, is about to return to the land of his birth, with the intention of purchasing the Black Forest and opening a lager-beer garden therein. We do not care to mention names in this connection, as it is advisable that Bismarck and Bill Three should not be made aware of the gentleman's intention till the purchase is completed.

Before they were married he used to tell her that she was the sunshine of his life, the one bright star of his existence. The scene shifts. They are married. The sunshine of his life and the bright star of his existence leaves a pail of water standing in the middle of the kitchen floor. Tableau: All is dark in the kitchen; he moves cautiously, to avoid contact with the stove; a wild crash, as of a bursting torrent; he staggers to his feet, rubs his shin, groans, and utters some Scripture quotations. A flash of light breaks upon the scene; she comes, clad in robes of white, and bearing a candle. She speaks:

"You 'ornery old fool, you'll catch your death of cold standing there, as wet as a dish-rag."

The sunshine of his life has gone out, the bright star of his existence has faded, and he mournfully asks:

"Was there *ever* a woman that had as much sense as a yaller dog?"

Curtain falls, while he puts on dry clothes and anoints his shins.

A little boy who lives in this city spent a few weeks on a ranch last summer, where he witnessed the branding of a number of cattle. The operation seems to have greatly impressed him, and he has been continually talking about it ever since his return from the ranch. A few days since his mother smelt something. The odor seemed to come from the kitchen, and on entering that department of the domestic economy, she beheld her beloved son engaged in the operation of branding the family cat with the kitchen poker. He had the cat securely tied, and with the red-hot poker was endeavoring to trace his full name on its body. Had he not been interrupted but been allowed to carry out his original design, the name would have gone clear around the cat, longitudinally, and its hide would have been pretty much all brand. The lady released the cat from the torture, and took her hopeful son into a bed-room to talk to him about the wickedness of cruelty to dumb animals; and when she got through with him he thought *he* had been branded, and wondered whether the cat wished it had a soft pillow on its chair, like he did.

A prominent citizen of Austin, who is suffering with a severe cold, was advised to put a mustard plaster on his breast. He was not much posted on mustard plasters, but he knows a good deal more about the properties of mustard now than he used to. He bought a bottle of mustard, mixed the contents with water, spread the mixture on a pocket-handkerchief, got into bed, and laid the plaster on his breast. In a few moments he fell asleep and slept soundly for a couple of hours, when his slumbers were disturbed with horrid dreams of fires and coal-oil explosions. He dreamed that while kindling a fire with coal-oil, the can exploded and set fire to his breast, and in the midst of his agony he woke up to find that it wasn't only a dream—there was considerable reality about it. He made a wild grab at the plaster, and flung it across the room; and yesterday he was going around with his spine arched up like a Reese River cow's in a snow-storm, so as to keep his undershirt from rubbing against his breast, and ever and anon he was heard to mutter, "Behold, how great a matter a little fire kindleth."

There can be no doubt that the exhortations of Moody and Sankey are extremely powerful, and that the means used by them for the conversion of sinners are effectual; for they have actually converted a bullwhacker. The convert is a man who drove an ox-team in this section for many years, who has just returned from a visit to his friends in the East, having left this place last fall for that purpose. We met him on the street this morning, and among other sights which he related having seen, he mentioned Moody and Sankey.

"Did they convert you?" we asked, jokingly, not for a moment supposing that a bullwhacker could be converted.

"You bet your life they did," he replied. "When first I went to hear them I went for the fun of the thing, but when I heard the preaching and singing it made an impression on me; I began to consider that I had a soul to save; I went every day to hear them, and before three days had passed, I wish I may be damn'd eternally if they hadn't made a Christian of me."

A seedy customer entered a restaurant this morning, and ordered "the best in the house"; and after finishing a hearty meal, told the proprietor of the establishment to "charge it." The indignant proprietor said never a word, but his actions talked louder than any words could speak; one lunge of his strong right foot, and the customer landed on the sidewalk. Turning around, and facing the hash-dealer, he said:

"My friend, Seligman used to go to school with my brother; and when your action in excluding me from your house is made public, it will raise a storm of indignation that will convulse this broad land, and threaten a social revolution."

He commenced quickening his steps, when the proprietor called out:

"Jim, fetch that stomach-pump here, quick."

And in the twinkling of an eye his form had vanished into the dim distance.

A prominent citizen, desiring to beautify the yard in front of his residence, procured some slips from some trees on the premises of a friend, and planted them. The directions given were to attach each slip to a potato and plant it in rich soil. These directions were followed, but the result was, that the slips died and the potatoes flourished like a green bay tree. The potato vines are now in blossom in the midst of a luxurious growth of alfalfa, and are much admired by visitors to the gentleman's residence, few of whom suspect their real character. When ladies ask, "What kind of plants are these?" the answer is, "*Solanum tuberosum*," which is botany for potato; and the fair inquirers elevate their eyebrows and say, "How beautiful! Never saw anything like it before; must be of tropical origin." And then the host says, "Certainly; it is very generally cultivated in Ireland and other tropical countries."

In addition to the ordinary games played by boys in other places, the boys of this city have a game created by their surroundings, and therefore peculiar to this and other communities where the conditions are similar. When marbles are out of season, when it is no longer top-time, when kites have lost their charm, when there is no snow for sledding, and the weather is too hot to play tag or horse, then the little boys play mining. Under a bank on one of the upper streets, last evening, we observed a number of little fellows engaged in this play. With bits of wood they were digging an incline into the bank, and when they came to a piece of rock they separated it from the earth and put it in one of those thin wooden boxes used for packing strawberries, and when this was full the smallest boy would carry it off a piece and empty it on the dump. In reply to the question, "What are you all doing here?" the little carman said: "Dittin' out wock for de mill."

A gentleman who runs a ranch not many miles from Austin was in town last Sunday, and during the day indulged in divers and sundry games of "pedro" for the drinks, and when evening came he was feeling pretty comfortable, but somewhat oblivious. As the church-bells commenced to ring for divine worship, our rancher concluded that going to church and hearing a sermon would be a good way to taper off; and accordingly he made his way to the sacred edifice, entered, and seated himself in a pew. During the sermon the minister gave a glowing description of heaven and its delights, describing it as a city paved with gold—its ways covered with beautiful foliage, and the air redolent with the perfume of orange blossoms; but in the midst of the description, the congregation were startled by our rancher, who, nudging his next neighbor and winking knowingly, whispered in a whisper that was heard throughout the church, "I've been there; *that's Californy.*"

A fellow-citizen hunted all over the house for his spectacles. He kept on repeating to himself, "Don't let your angry passions rise"; then he kicked over the rocking-chair, and said "dammit." That didn't bring the spectacles; so he went into the kitchen, and told his wife she had "better keep an eye on them brats, and not let them be packing off everything useful there was in the house." "A man couldn't even call his soul his own" in that domicile, he said, and here "them cussed young-ones" had carried off his spectacles, and perhaps even now had started a Lick Observatory with them in the back-yard.

"Why, you old fool," replied his patient and loving wife, "there's your spectacles right on top of your clumsy old nose."

"Well! I wish I may be—transplanted into glory," was all he said, or words to that effect.

She was from the country, and she went into a Main Street store and asked to look at some stockings.

"What number, ma'am?" inquired the polite clerk.

"Only one pair this time," she answered, "but if I like them I may buy some more next time I come in."

"I mean, what number do you wear?" explained he of the yard-stick.

"What number do I wear! Young man, aint you ashamed of yourself to ask such a question? Do you suppose jest 'cause I live in the country that I go scooting around with one stocking? The number I wear is two, of course. Do you think I'm a heathen, and do I hobble around like a woman with only one leg?"

Then the clerk managed to make her understand that he wanted to know the size of the stockings she required, and she said she guessed about eleven inches would do for the foot, and as to the rest it didn't matter much.

In a certain restaurant in this city, the proprietor has refrained from putting up the stove, his idea being to freeze out the flies. The temperature of the room don't appear to have as much effect on the flies as it does on the human patrons of the restaurant; and at the breakfast hour this morning numerous shivering individuals sat at the tables with their forms encased in blanket overcoats, their feet in Arctic overshoes, and their hands in seal-skin gloves. When the waiter went around among the boarders to get their orders, one man said, "Bring me a blanket on toast"; another said he would take some flannel cakes for his feet; a third wanted a broiled buffalo robe; and still another called for a red pepper smothered in coals. But one man was reasonable. Said he: "Bring me anything and everything you've got; I owe seven months' board, and I'll bet another month's that no freeze-out game can't win with *me*."

"Do you take trade dollars at par?" asked a stranger of a bar-keeper in a Main Street saloon this morning.

"Certainly; take anything," replied the accommodating tumbler-slinger.

"Well, then, give me some whisky," said the stranger.

The bar-keeper set out the bottle and glass, and the stranger poured out and swallowed his drink, and started for the door.

"Hold on there, where's that trade dollar?" said the bar-keeper.

"Oh, *I* haven't got any trade-dollars," replied the stranger, "I only asked if you took them at par for information."

A shade of sadness stole over the bar-keeper's face as he discovered that somebody had borrowed the pick-handle he keeps under the bar for such emergencies—and the soda-water bottle that swished through the air only came within about six feet of where the stranger had stood the moment before.

One of the County Commissioners having sent a supply of provisions to an "indigent," was shortly after accosted by the individual with:

"You sent coffee, but not an ounce of sugar."

"Sugar!" exclaimed the county dad, "what in blazes do you want to do with sugar?"

"Sweeten my coffee, of course," replied the indigent, "how in thunder do you suppose I'm going to drink coffee without sugar?"

"My friend," returned the Commissioner, "you don't appear to be aware that Rothschild, and A. T. Stewart, and the Marquis of Lorne, and Boss Tweed, and Flood & O'Brien, and Dives, and Julius Cæsar, and Billy Sharon, all got rich by economy on the sugar question. Had any of these men indulged in sugar in their coffee, there wouldn't one of them have a slick quarter to-day. Economy is wealth, my friend, and if you can't drink coffee without sugar, you'll have to do without coffee."

A prominent citizen, on entering the parlor of his residence, yesterday, found lying on the center-table a beautiful bouquet, pinned to which was a card bearing his name. Looking about cautiously to assure himself that no person was in hearing, he pressed the flowers to his Roman nose and exclaimed:

"Who has sent me them beautiful flowers?"

"That's just what *I'd* like to know," said his wife, as she crawled out from under the sofa, "and I'd pull every hair out of her head by the roots, if I did—the hussy!"

The neighbor woman, who came in and rubbed his head with arnica, said, as she went out:

"Oh, no, of course not! How could you ever think of such a thing? I aint one of them women what goes around telling everything I hear; you may be sure I won't mention it to a living soul."

But, somehow or other, by last night the entire neighborhood knew all about it.

A teamster was driving a ten-mule team, hauling a load of wood, up Main Street to-day, when the leaders started at a passing wagon and swayed around toward the sidewalk. Instead of cracking his blacksnake and using profane language to his animals, as most teamsters would do under similar circumstances, the driver merely remonstrated with them. Taking the nigh mule by the bridle, he led it around so as to straighten the team, and whispered in its ear: "—— —— your —— —— soul to —— nation, if you ever do that again I'll shoot you right here in the street." The threat seemed to have an effect on the mule, and it made no attempt to repeat the performance for the next three blocks

---

At the ball last night the floor was quite sticky, owing to its having been newly waxed and the wax not being evenly spread over and worked into the boards. A prominent citizen who was present suffered considerable inconvenience from this circumstance, and had half determined to refrain from dancing during the remainder of the night, when he was struck with a happy thought. Approaching his wife, he asked her to waltz with him. Surprised at such an unusual condescension from her husband, who generally when he attends a ball dances with every lady present except his wife, the lady asked him the cause of such unexpected gallantry as he displayed to her on this occasion. "Oh," said he, looking down at her feet, "I want you to waltz with me so as to spread this grease over the floor." She didn't dance with him.

The setting of the sun last evening presented a truly magnificent sight. The western sky was o'erspread with waving, billowy clouds, rendered transcendently beautiful by the glow of color from the reflection of the retiring god of day. Here, a faint blush of rose tint; there, a gorgeous purple; beyond, a cloud fringed with a glitter of golden color, or enriched with the subdued hue of amber. It was a sight to move the soul of a painter to its innermost depths; and to the poetic mind it brought the thought that even then, far down in the peaceful valley, the reflection of the dying day might be casting a halo of glorious light about the head of a red-headed girl milking a brindle cow, and that in the vast and varied economy of nature, even a red-headed girl may have her uses.

We were accosted on the street by a small boy last evening, who thus addressed us:

"Say, mister, will you put somethin' in the paper?"

"What is it you wish inserted in that family journal, the REVEILLE, my son?" we said in reply.

"Well," he said, "some of the boys up to the public school is a-cuttin' the other fellers out of their gals."

Poor little boy! In the freshness of his innocent youth he little knows that getting cut out of a "gal" by another "feller" is a sorrow not confined to school-boys alone. He does not dream that boys of a larger growth know the deep poignancy of sitting on the fence and seeing another "feller" escorting their heart's idol home from church. That boy has more to learn than is taught in schools.

An Austin young lady, who "follows the fashions," read in one of the fashion magazines that the "classical" outline of feminine attire is produced by the following process: "A strong elastic is attached to one garter, just above the knee, carried over and fastened to the other garter; thus the length of the steps taken by the wearer is regulated, and the classical folds of the costume remain undisturbed." Not to be "behind the age," our young lady rigged the elastic as directed; and an old lady acquaintance, whose house she passed while her limbs were thus fettered, remarked to her daughter:

"Wal, I declare! I've knowed Mirandy sence she was an infant, and I never knowed afore that she was pigeon-toed."

Passing down Main Street, this morning, we overheard the following colloquy between two little boys, neither over four years of age:

First Little Boy (anxious to display his knowledge of Mother Goose)—"Little Tommy Horner, sittin' in a corner, eatin' a piece of Chris——"

Second Little Boy—"Oh, shore, I know that."

First Little Boy—"But I seen him a-eatin' it."

Second Little Boy—"That ain't nuffin; I seen him stuck in his fum."

First Little Boy—"Le's play tag."

Both those boys will be eligible as members of the Sazerac Lying Club when they grow to be men.

He had some six bits' worth of gold dust in a small glass vial, and he said it was some he had taken out of the Black Hills twelve years ago.

"Why didn't you stay there and get more?"

"Oh, the Injuns druv us out, but thar's slathers of gold in that country, you bet."

"Going back there?"

"No, thar's too much of the yaller thar. Ye see, thar's goin' to be a stampede, and they'll rush in thar and take out so much gold that the demand won't be ekal to the supply, and the discount on gold will be so big that it won't pay a man to prospect fur it. As a business fur steddy follerin', both gold and silver minin's gettin' to be stale, flat, and unprofiterble. Whisky-straight, *ef* yer please."

We have heard a number of people complain that this has been a dull day; but we have failed to see it. A freight team arrived; several loads of wood passed up Main Street; seventeen dogs were all barking at once at a cow, on Court Street; a woman stubbed her toe against a plank, on Union Street; a man dropped a four-bit piece through a crack in the sidewalk, on Cedar Street; a clothes-line full of clean linen was blown down, on South Street; a cat had fits, on Overland Street; two little boys had a fight, on Sixth Street; a cow ate up a whole garden, on Pine Street; and there was a whirlwind on Virginia Street. If the day was dull with all these stirring events, we would like to see what some folks call a lively one. But some men would say times were dull if their grandmother was to fall three thousand feet down a mining shaft.

A four-year-old hero related to us the details of a desperate encounter which a party of boys and girls had with a lizard on the hillside this morning. It is so thrilling that, in order to keep the printers in copy till the telegraph news comes in, we give it to our readers:

"I seed the lizard first, and all the girls was afraid. I frowed a great big stick at him, and he wun up on a wock and laid down dead. Then a little girl hit him with a wock, and didn't hit him, and I went up and poked him with a stick, and he got alive again and wun away, and we all wun'd after him and he wun in a hole, and I fell down and skinned my nose, and one of the girls she lost her shoe and her mother spanked her when she got home, and we're all goin' up this afternoon to kill that lizard."

One of the most beautiful sunsets on which it has ever been our lot to gaze decked the western sky last evening. It appeared as an open sea viewed from the shore, the fleecy cloudlets which flecked the surface seeming like the white caps of old ocean. So remarkably brilliant was the scene that it attracted general notice, and Main Street was filled with people, who gazed enraptured on the glorious sight, one lady becoming so enthusiastic as to declare that she would give seven dollars and five bits for a dress as gay-colored as that. How true it is that the beauties of nature stir within our breasts the noblest and most exalted thoughts and aspirations!

Last night was truly a glorious night. The sky was cloudless, and the round-faced moon shed its refulgent rays o'er mountain and valley, while bright Venus stared down on the Citizens' Mill like the headlight of a celestial locomotive. The air was still as death, but cold enough to freeze the nose off the statute of the Greek Slave; all nature was hushed, and no sound disturbed the stillness save the rattle of the stamps of the Manhattan Mill, and the cooing of three or four dozen gentle tomcats. It was a night to awaken all the finer feelings of the human breast, and to cause the reflective mind to ponder on the infinite mysteries of nature and the cost of a livery team for a moonlight ride.

A young gentleman of this city called on a lady friend last evening. At the time of his visit she was engaged in darning stockings, having an egg in one of them to keep the hole in shape, or for some similar purpose. When the caller made his appearance, she hurriedly dropped her work on a chair and invited him to be seated; and, although he does not cover a great deal of surface when he is seated, he managed to sit down on the stocking and the egg and the darning needle all at once. Then he got up and darned the stocking and the egg and the needle; and when the pain had subsided a little and he got the egg wiped off his pants, he said it was one of the richest and at the same time most pointed experiences he had ever met with in the whole course of his long and eventful career.

An individual of the genus "tramp" accosted a brother last evening on Main Street with, "Say, Jimmy, let's take a walk."

"Walk!—what do I want to walk for?" asked the other.

"For exercise, to give yer an appertite."

"Appertite! Appertite! Well, that's good! Why, consarn it, I've got appertite to throw at the birds; I waste more appertite on the desert air every day than would surfice for all the bloated millionaires in town for a week. If yer can walk me up to a squar' meal then I'll walk, but otherwise I prefer standin' on this yere corner and watchin' the chances for a drink."

A cruel parent in this city placed some spikes, point upwards, in the gate in the fence fronting his residence. He forgot to tell his daughter about it, and she never noticed the spikes till the young man who comes around to inquire how her mother liked the sermon at church last Sunday intimated that somebody had done a darned mean trick. Then she took in the situation; but the breach in his clothes was too wide to be bridged over by mere words, and he will accept of no explanations till he can find some cloth to match the pattern of the pieces he left on the spikes. Thus were two loving hearts and one pair of pants sundered by the act of this hard-hearted father.

An upper Austin man refuses to allow his daughter to attend church any more. A few Sundays ago the preacher said in one of his sermons, "Love thy neighbor"; and the daughter followed the injunction and fell in love with a young man who lives in the house adjoining her father's, who only earns sixty dollars a month and board as engineer of a wheelbarrow in a livery stable, and sits up till three o'clock in the morning playing pedro. The father says if the preachers can't preach any better doctrine than for the girls to love every scrub who happens to live in the next house, he would rather his daughters would grow up without the consolations of religion.

A well-known Austinite, while on a recent visit to San Francisco, went into a barber-shop to be shaved. The workmen in the shop were all colored men, and when one of them had shaved him and was about to commence dressing his hair, the Austinite pointed to the few straggling hairs on the top of his head, which just save him from positive baldness, and told the barber to distribute them around on his head to the best advantage.

"Yes," said the man and brother, stepping off a step, and cocking his eye on the lonesome looking hairs, "we is got to be ecomnomical wid dat 'air ha'r."

A young lady walking along Court Street, this morning, was caught in the center of one of those whirlwinds which spring up so suddenly, and which are now so prevalent. She braced her feet firmly to the ground, and the whirlwind toyed with her store clothes, the effect being very pretty, and resembling two candles surmounted by the American flag, being spun around at the rate of seventeen hundred revolutions a minute. When the dust had cleared away, she commenced ejecting the granite from her mouth, and said it was only to be expected that when a whirlwind wanted to tackle anybody it would go for a poor, weak woman; it was the way of the world (wind).

Marriage works many changes in men. Before marriage he would lift her across the muddy places for fear she would get her little tootsey-footseys wet, and would insist on carrying her fan home from the ball, for fear it might tire her to carry it herself. After marriage he looks on with supreme indifference when she steps into a mud-hole, and tells her he thought her feet were big enough to bridge across it, and wants to know if she thinks a man is a Chinaman that she asks him to carry bundles through the streets. She is big enough and ugly enough to carry them herself. This state of things does not prevail in Austin, however.

The magnificent appearance of the sky was a common subject of remark last night. Not a cloud marred the clear blue of the heavens, the stars shone with unusual brilliance, and the beauteous moon shed its soft light upon the earth, gilding the pile of bricks in the brickyard like refined gold, and casting a halo of glory about the head of a red-headed girl as she whispered the parting good-night to the idol of her heart up in Upper Austin, besides effecting a great saving of candles in the residence of a prominent citizen, who has nine marriageable daughters and who has just been sold out on stocks.

She had just returned from a visit to a married couple, and as she threw her hat on the sofa, she turned up her nose, put on a look of disgust, and said: "If there is anything on this earth that is hateful, it is to see married people kissing and hugging and gushing before folks." Her little brother crawled out from under the sofa, where he had been hunting a stray marble, and, addressing his sister, said: "You and George is all the time kissing each other before me; but you isn't married yet, and then I s'pose I'm too small to be folks." That little boy told another little boy next morning that it wasn't always a sign when your ear burned that somebody was talking about you.

A man who believes that this is an era of conciliation and a year of compromises was out on Main Street this morning, trying to borrow fifteen dollars. One man told him times were too hard; another said that all his money was in stocks; another wanted to know if he was popularly supposed to be a member of the Rothschild family, and still another said he wouldn't loan fifteen dollars to a bonanza king. The would-be borrower, as he turned sadly away from the last "refuse," said there must be some mistake; the era of good feeling had not yet arrived, and the lamb had better keep its usual distance from the lion for a year or two longer.

An Austin man, who was visiting in one of the adjacent valleys recently, tells the following. He stopped for the night at a ranch, and while sitting in front of the house with the rancher's daughter, the planet Mars rose up over a high peak, looking for a time like a fire on the mountain. The Austinite contemplated the sight in silence for a few moments, and then broke into a rhapsody on its magnificence, when the girl interrupted him by saying:

"Stranger, that thar aint nothin' but a star; we see it 'round here frequently. You town folks ought to come out and live on a ranch, and you can see more stars than you can shake a stick at."

There was a mining accident yesterday, which, while it was not attended with any loss of life, was disastrous, from the fact that an entire mine was demolished and obliterated at one fell swoop. The miners had sunk an incline in the hill in the rear of the court-house, and had commenced drifting from the bottom of the incline, to follow the ledge up to the Indian camp, when suddenly, and without warning, incline and drift caved in, burying the unfortunate miners out of sight. They scratched out with their hands, and mmediately located and commenced to open another mine. Age of the superintendent, six years. The other miners are still of spankable age.

Early this morning, the hills surrounding Austin were hid from view by a dense pogonip, but as the sun struggled through the mist over the summit of Lander Hill, the wall of cloud that enveloped Mount Prometheus rolled up like a huge drop-curtain, revealing the upper slope of the mountain clad in a mantle of snow. It is such a sight as this that brings the human heart in close communion with nature, and instills into the soul the consciousness that there is another and a better land beyond the vail of cloud and mist and fog that shuts from view the roads to Belmont and Eureka.

A predatory cow made a raid on a clothes-line in Upper Austin last evening, and before she was detected had succeeded in eating two frilled skirts, three lace-trimmed chemiwhatyoucallems, and several pairs of striped stockings. As the cow stumbled down over an embankment, an angry woman could have been seen at its top, waving a broom in the air, and with an expression on her countenance which said, in language as plain as words could express it:

"What wouldn't I give if I could cuss like a man!"

The story is told of an old lady who asked one of our physicians how a certain patient of his was getting along, and when the Doctor informed her that the person in question was convalescent, she said:

"That's rough. Back yander, in the States, I knowed two wimmin and a crippled boy to die of convalescent. On one of the wimmin it broke out all over her in a rash, and it struck in and she died afore you could bat your eye. But she made a beautiful corpse. They make nice corpses when they die of that, don't they, Doc?"

The Doctor said he believed so.

It's "strange, but true," that the industries of a locality exercise a marked influence on the dreams of the inhabitants. To illustrate: Mr. Happytite ate a can of lobster, half a ham, and two loaves of bread, just before going to bed, the other evening, and he dreamed that he was falling down a shaft seven thousand feet in depth, that the cable had parted, and the cage was coming down after him at the rate of three thousand miles a minute. Now, if that man had lived in Cincinnati, he would undoubtedly have dreamed that he was a hog, and was being salted down for use in the navy.

They were lovers, but trouble had arisen between them, and he was about to bid her farewell, never, never again to speak to her while life lasted. He had but a few words to say at parting, but in these were included a request to return the presents he had given her in happier days, the most valuable of which was a gold chain and cross. "Not much!" said the maiden, as he preferred the request for the return of the trinket; and pointing to an embroidered motto which hung in a frame on the wall, and read, "Simply to thy cross I cling," she observed, "them's my sentiments exactly." And she clung.

A woman went into a Main Street store this morning, and purchased a pick-handle. No question was asked her by the polite clerk, and he did not even intimate a desire to know if she was going prospecting. But she volunteered the information that she intended to make her husband and that carroty-headed old cat understand that she was not dead yet, even if she did have a consumptive cough, a weeping eye, false teeth, a big bunion, and symptoms of the hip complaint. There is one man in this town who will hear the tocsin of war sound pretty soon.

Business is dull with the doctors as well as with other people. A prominent physician sat for several hours on a rock to-day, intently watching a house on the opposite side of the street. When an acquaintance passed and asked: "What are you camped there for, Doc?" his only reply was: "The man who lives in that house got a present of a box of green cucumbers from a friend in California, this morning," and he resumed his gaze at the door, with an evident determination to be on hand at the first indication of family suffering.

The following touching lines were written by a little girl in the Austin public school, only eleven years old, and with warts on her hands and deaf in one ear. For touching pathos and deep sentiment they are equal to anything ever written by Byron or Captain Jack Crawford:

Oh, the flies, the flies, the horrible flies,
Creep o'er your nose and tickle your eyes,
Glide up your neck and crawl on your head,
The flies, oh, the flies, I wish they were dead!

A few days ago, a stranger at one of our restaurants asked for a napkin at dinner. The landlord refused to give him one.

"But," said the guest, "that man at the other table has one."

"That man is a regular boarder, and has just got back from San Francisco, and I have to pander to him for a day or so; but it won't be long before he will be wiping his mouth on the table-cloth, and cleaning his nails with a fork, like the other gentlemen. No, stranger, we don't allow any style here as a regular thing, but we can't help ourselves sometimes."

Paradise Valley is a farming section of Humboldt County, reached from Winnemucca over a stretch of desert and sagebrush. A traveler visiting the valley a short time since stopped at a farm-house, and his host, pointing out the country, said:

"This is Paradise, and the next valley beyond here is Eden."

"Yes," returned the traveler, "and it's hell between here and Winnemucca."

It is by such remarks as this that Nevada gets its reputation for profanity.

A sure cure for a boy's toothache is to start with him to the dentist's office. The tooth will cease to ache when he gets in sight of the dentist's sign. We witnessed a case in point this morning. The boy said he hoped he might never die if his tooth ached one teeny little bit; but his mother insisted that the tooth was as decayed as a frozen potato—as though the boy didn't know about his own tooth. A wild shriek of agony that rent the air in the vicinity of the dentist's office, a few moments afterward, testified that the fearful forceps had done their awful work.

A prominent citizen of Upper Austin was advised to take a "rum-sweat" for a severe cold with which he was suffering. The directions were to seat himself on a cane-bottom chair, incase his form in blankets, and let his wife place a vessel containing rum under the chair, she to light the spirit, and he to remain on the chair and let the fumes which should arise play about his manly form. The experiment was tried a few evenings since; but the citizen did not remain on the chair more than two seconds after the match was applied to the rum, and now he is unable to sit on a cane-bottom or any other kind of a chair, even with his clothes on.

A New York advertising agency sends the REVEILLE an offer of ten shares of the capital stock of a certain gold and silver reduction company, and two cases of gin, in exchange for $136 worth of advertising. We now hold more corporate shares than we can pay assessments on; and as for gin, there is a spring on a mountain near here that flows pure Holland gin at the rate of forty-two gallons a minute. If the agency will offer us a yellow dog and a dozen bottles of hair restorative in exchange for advertising, it may perhaps be able to make terms with us.

He was being questioned by the assessor as to his personal property.

"Got any jewelry?" said the official.

"No."

"No watches, chains, or silver plate?"

"No."

"No diamond studs?"

"No, nor mares either."

The assessor thought he saw a man running up the street to pay his poll-tax, and he went to meet him.

"Are them Mormon eggs, Mister?" asked a woman, in a Main Street grocery-store this morning.

"No, ma'am," said the polite store-keeper; "since the exposure of the dreadful atrocities at the Mountain Meadows, and the revelations of the cruelties practiced by the Mormons, we have, as a matter of principle, quit importing eggs from Utah."

"I don't care nothing about that," she replied; "but lately them Salt Lake eggs has been running about eight bad to the dozen."

An Austin young lady said good night to her beau, at the front door, last night, and went into a room where her sister sat reading Mark Twain's book, "Tom Sawyer."

"What are you reading, sister?" she asked.

"Tom Sawyer."

"I don't care a cent if he did; I guess I've got a right to kiss Jim if I want to, and Tom better mind his own business."

It was a new revelation to "Sister."

The season for hauling wood and charcoal being about to set in, a saloon-keeper, who is up to the times, has invented a new drink, which he calls "Coalburner's Ecstacy and Teamster's Rejuvenator." One drink of it makes a man forget all his earthly troubles; two drinks make him think he's a smarter man than Brigham Young; the third causes him to fancy himself General Crook on the war-path against the Sioux; and the fourth is calculated to land him in the august presence of Justice Logan, with the danger of thirty dollars' worth of "painful duty" staring him in the face.

An Austin young gentleman, who has been an intimate friend of a family in this town for several years past, was forbidden the house by one of the young ladies of the family, had the dog set on him by the old woman, and got struck in the back of the neck with a dead cat thrown by the youngest boy, simply because he asked the young lady whether this was her fourth or fifth eighteenth birthday. The young lady had previous to his question joyfully remarked to him:

"I'm eighteen to-day; just think of it!"

"I believe you're traveling the straight road to hell," said a pious church member to his wife, in the presence of witnesses, last night. "Finery and furbelows are vanities of the spirit as well as of the flesh; besides, stocks are down, and I lost six dollars and six bits playing pedro for the drinks night afore last, and you'll have to wait till next fall before you can get that spring bonnet, unless you can find some other dog-goned fool to pay for it." She said she would go home to her mother if she only had money enough to pay her fare to the interior of York State.

A poor man applied to a citizen for relief to-day, and was referred to the woodpile. The unfortunate individual declined to tackle the saw and ax, on the ground that Friday is an unlucky day, and that he would rather starve to death than take chances of spoiling his luck. He said he had a rich aunt back in the States, and would cut off his finger-nails or wash his face before he would risk losing her fortune at her death by commencing an industrial enterprise on an unlucky day.

A little boy was noticed standing on the sidewalk on Main Street this morning, and crying bitterly.

"What's the matter, sonny?" asked a gentleman who was passing.

"Matter! Matter enough, I should say! Dad's got busted on stocks, mother's got the neuraljy so bad she couldn't cook breakfast, sister's run off with a bullwhacker, baby's swallowed my top, and I've got à short bit so far down this here crack in the sidewalk that a feller with sixteen eyes in his head couldn't see one edge of it. *That's* what's the matter!"

An Austin gentleman, who served through the war of the rebellion, told his wife that the 30th of this month will be Decoration Day.

"I hope, then," she said, "you will decorate me with a new bonnet."

"My dear," he replied, "this is a year of compromises; I'll compromise on ten yards of calico."

The spirit in which this offer was met has convinced him that the era of good feeling has not yet arrived, and he thinks he will adopt a policy of conciliation.

A correspondent asks us if it is in violation of the rules of the Orders of Good Templars or Red Cross to eat mince-pie. We don't know; but we saw a young man resting himself on the curb on Main Street the other evening, who said he had been eating mince-pie, and it didn't agree with him. We have seen exactly the same effect produced by whisky; but this young man assured us that he belonged to the Red Cross. We never knew before that mince-pie could make a fellow so tired.

A gentleman walking along Main Street in company with his wife, last evening, was lost in admiration of the beauty of the sky, and was uttering such exclamations as: "How beautiful!" "Aint she perfectly gorgeous!" "What a grand and magnificent sight!" "How beautiful are thy works, O Nature!" when his rapture was interrupted by his better half ejaculating: "Oh, dry up, and come in here and plank out three and a half for a pair of shoes for Johnny."

An Austin young lady was complaining to a gentleman friend that some work which she was compelled to do was very tiresome, from the fact that she had no assistance in it and it took nearly all her time.

"You ought to have a change of shifts," said the gentleman.

He is now wondering what made her mad, and she has ceased thinking that he wandered from the subject, since she has learned the signification of the word shift, in mining parlance.

Two little boys on Main Street:

"Say, Johnny, is yer goin' to church to-night?"

"No; are you?"

"Bet yer life I is; there's a whole lot of folks goin' to be confined, and I want to see what it's like."

We suppose the little boy had reference to the fact that a number of ladies and gentlemen were to be "confirmed."

How man's boasted superiority fades before the reflection that the howling of one little, insignificant dog can upset the nerves of all the old maids within sound of its voice, and cause stern-visaged men, who would face an empty cannon without blanching, to kick off the covers, and sit upright in bed, and curse and swear till the air of the room is one sheet of blue flame! There was that kind of a dog in the Pound last night, and it kept up its doleful wail for seven hours without stopping to take breath.

"My husband is my idol," observed Mrs. Rubyrock to Mrs. Batterystamp, at a recent hen convention in this city.

"Well," returned Mrs. B., "if he's any more idle than my old man I'd just like to see the shape of him. Why, my husband is that lazy that if he saw a twenty-dollar piece a-laying in the big road, he'd lay down alongside of it and go to sleep till I came along to pick it up for him."

The other woman said that was not her ideal of what a man should be.

The stars shone brightly, last night, and the pale light of the moon shed a luster on their humble cottage, as, leaning on her husband's arm, she stood in the open door, and casting her eyes heavenward said:

"Dearest, how beautiful the heavens look; oh, how I love to gaze up into the blue vault and watch the tiny, twinkling stars, which shine like so many jewels in——Oh! you nasty, careless brute!"

He had pulled the door to, and her thumb was in the crack.

A little boy, chasing grasshoppers on Main Street this morning, pounced on and picked up a bee by mistake for a hopper. The boy let go before the bee did, but as the bee soared away heavenward, the boy commenced to cry, and when asked what ailed him, he whined out between his sobs:

"I picked up a hot grasshopper, and it burns wuss'n bein' spanked with an old slipper with fourteen holes in the sole of it."

In a Main Street saloon, last evening, we overheard a miner telling one of his friends that his wages had an ornament on them.

"How's that?" asked his friend.

"Well, you see," replied the miner, "a fellow I owed a little money to, put a garnishment on my wages, and I looked in the dictionary and found that the definition of garnishment is an ornament, or ornamentation."

A charcoal teamster stopped his team in front of a popular Main Street saloon this morning, and went into the saloon to get a drink. The bar-keeper happened to be playing a game of billiards at the rear end of the saloon, and there was nobody behind the bar; and when the teamster saw his own image reflected in the big mirror on the wall back of the bar, he turned away, and said he wished he might be blowed if he was going to drink in any saloon where they had a nigger for a bar-keeper.

We overheard the following dialogue between two small boys, on Main Street, this forenoon:

"Johnny, you's on the roll of honor this time, isn't yer?"

"Bet yer life.'

"It's the fust time since you've bin goin' to school, isn't it?"

"Yes, but yer better bet yer boots, I went through like a dose of salts this time."

We received this morning from a Philadelphia publishing house a printed list of questions about Austin, with a polite request that we would write answers to the questions and return the list to the parties sending it. One of the questions was: "What are the manufactures of Austin?" The only reply we could truthfully make to this question was: "Silver bricks and children."

A cynical young man, who has been taking items on clothes-lines, declares that the reason the ladies put lace and embroidery on their underfixin's is that they may hang them on the line as an evidence to the woman in the next house, or across the street, that they can afford just as good clothes as anybody, and are not so poor as to be obliged to wear underclothes made of 000 canvas, like some folks they know of.

There is no living creature so helpless as is man. We were led into this train of thought by seeing a colt scratch its nose with its off hind-foot to-day; and the chapter thus opened in nature's book led us along the thread of reflection till we thought how man, with all his boasted power and superior intelligence, cannot scratch his own back, or see for himself whether a boil on the back of his neck is coming to a head.

She was obliged to lift her dress as she crossed Main Street, as the street was muddy and she had on striped stockings. They were yellow stripes and green, and looked like a lot of crawling snakes; and a prominent citizen gazed on them in horror as he remarked, "Jehosaphat, I never had 'em that bad before," and right there he registered a vow that he would join the Murphy movement at its next meeting.

A German gentleman residing in this city has received a letter from his aged father in Germany, stating that the American potato bugs, which are visiting that country, are already able to converse fluently in the German language. The visitors are thought so much of in the German Empire, that the government has had their pictures taken, and distributed in every household in the rural districts.

"What's flour to-day?" she asked in a Main Street grocery store. "Eight dollars, ma'am," replied the polite store-keeper. "Flour's riz, aint it?" she asked. "Yes, ma'am, flour's gone up." "What makes flour raise?" she questioned. "Yeast, ma'am," he replied. She went out, and going to another store ordered a sack of flour, and told the store-keeper that that man over to the other store was too smart to live long.

Two little boys were quarreling in front of the court-house this morning, when one said to the other:

"Your father aint got no wood contract, like mine has."

"I don't care if he haint," replied the other; "your mother aint got no carbuncle on her neck, neither; and mine has."

This was a clincher.

A prominent citizen remarked, in a Main Street saloon, this morning, that this town is so distressingly quiet that it must be an immense labor for the reporter of the REVEILLE to think up lies to put in the paper. While we repel with scorn the insinuation that we would give publication to a lie in the columns of the REVEILLE, we admit that facts on which to base local items are as scarce as preachers at a horse-race.

The earlier birds of the season, such as caterpillars, stink-bugs, mosquito-hawks, and grasshoppers, have given way to large brown beetles, which are now quite numerous. When one of these insects lights on the back of a young lady's neck, the neighbors all say:

"The presumption of that hussy! The idea of *her* trying to sing Italian opera!"

Last evening was a beautiful one; the sky was clear, the stars twinkled brightly, and the crescent-shaped moon, as it rose over the hill-tops, cast a mellow light on the Indian wickiups, reflecting the profiles of the beautiful squaws against the star-lit sky, and giving them the appearance of ghostly forms arisen from the dead to taunt mortality with the fickleness of earthly life. It was a poor evening for stage-robbers and cats.

A wee little bit of feminine humanity was taken to a certain church in this town, last Sunday. It was her first visit, and she kept as still as a mice, but took in all the surroundings with wide-eyed wonder. When she got home, somebody asked her what she had seen at church, to which she replied: "I seed a man wiz his night-down on; but he didn't doe to s'eep."

A single lady, whose sands of life are beginning to run low, while recounting to a friend one of the sorrows of her early life—the loss of the only lover she was ever blessed with—was told by the friend:

"Never mind, there are as good fish in the sea as ever were caught."

"Yes," replied the disconsolate one, "but it takes fresher bait than I am to catch them."

The young gentleman that called on a young lady the other evening, and was invited into the kitchen, asserts that he had no intention of stealing the chair he was sitting on. He says he didn't know the varnish wasn't dry, and he thinks it's trifling with a man's noblest feelings, and making a direct attack on his heart-strings, to allow him to ruin a pair of eight-dollar store pants in such a manner.

A Boston lady, who had recently arrived in Austin, told a young man who works in the mines that she could indulge in the ecstacy of osculation with an adult male of the genus homo with feelings of gratification analogical to quaffing the nectar of the gods; and after he had consulted the authorities he was mad at himself because he had not kissed her.

She was a young lady from Reese River Valley, and her beau treated her to ice cream in one of the restaurants. She tried to eat the cream with a knife and fork, and because she did not succeed, said it was the most "unsatisfyin' truck" she "ever seed," and asked the waiter if he wouldn't please warm it up a little.

A young lady who went on an excursion to the country, yesterday, had both her pleasure and a beautiful pull-back dress ruined, just because a little boy hollered "snakes!" And then the little boy went home and told his mother that "that 'air gal's" legs were painted. The poor little innocent had seen striped stockings for the first time in his young life.

A lady passed down Main Street this morning, tied back so tightly that she could only step about three inches at a step. A man of horsey mien and air, who was standing on the sidewalk, eyed her intently for a few moments, and then turned to a bystander and asked "if that critter was hobbled?"

A prominent citizen, who had just eaten three dozen Eastern transplanted oysters, which cost $1.50 per dozen, told his wife he had been eating silver. She said that "back thar in Missoury, where she came from," anybody, to smell his breath, would suppose he had been eating whisky.

A man who found a chicken in one of the eggs set before him in a Main Street restaurant, this morning, called the waiter's attention to that fact, when the waiter grumbled out that some people are never satisfied; they growl when you board them for eight dollars a week and throw in poultry for breakfast.

Two dogs had an argument over a bone on Main Street this forenoon, and all the other dogs thought there was an alarm of fire. In three minutes from the time the first yelp sounded, Main Street was a raging sea of dogs, through which teams were unable to force their way. Traffic on the street was suspended while the blockade lasted.

Two little boys were playing in front of the REVEILLE office this morning, and one said to the other: "My mother's got a guitar, and yours aint!" "The blazes she aint!" replied the other; "my mother's had the catarrh for three years, and it makes her snort like a wind-broken horse going up hill."

A man on one of the back streets, last night, who saw a red-headed girl running for the doctor, mistook her for a shooting-star, and wished seventeen wishes before she was out of sight. The mistake was a natural one, as shooting-stars are very plentiful these nights.

A prominent citizen, who had been taking spring medicine, reading that there was a general movement of the Russians, remarked that he could sympathize with them, as he knew how it was himself.

A little boy was talking to another little boy about cats, on Main Street this morning. Said he:

"Cats is got nine lives, and you've got to kill 'em nine times afore they's dead. You can't pizen 'em, 'cause they like pizen, and the only way my dad says you can pizen a cat is to chop his head off, and throw him down a shaft, and pile rocks atop of him so he can't climb out."

A floating newspaper paragraph says that Mrs. Denison, the authoress, has made enough money out of "That Husband of Mine" to purchase a Washington residence. There is a woman in this town who has made enough money out of that husband of hers to purchase a set of furs on the installment plan. She did it by going through his pockets while he was asleep.

"Boys, let's all take a drink," said a man in a Main Street saloon this morning, and immediately there was an overturning of chairs in the vicinity of the stove, and a scurrying toward the bar; but when the stranger put the finishing touch on his oration by uttering the words, "of water," the "boys" returned sadly to their seats, and resumed their discussion on the evils of Chinese cheap labor.

An Upper Austin woman, who heard that a Cedar Ravine woman had been talking about her, told all her acquaintances that she intended to spit in that hussy's eye the first time she caught sight of her, and when they met, she walked right up to her, put her mouth close up to the "hussy's," and——kissed her right on the lips, and said:

"Oh, my dear, I'm so glad to see you; and how's all the children, and has baby got through teething yet?"

An Austin man who deals in stocks through a San Francisco broker, received a note from the broker the other day, which read: "Stick to your Julia; she will do to tie to." Of course, his wife found the note in his pocket; and now the man is putting in regular ten-hour shifts in explaining that Julia is the name of a mining stock. But she will be satisfied with nothing short of documentary evidence, and he has had to send to San Francisco for the stock certificates.

A young gentleman of this town called upon an Upper Austin young lady, a few evenings since, and requested the loan of one of her old shoes, saying he had invited a party of ladies to go sleigh-riding, and was unable to procure a sleigh. By the time he recovers from his injuries a genial sun will have melted the snow from the hill-tops, the grass will be springing fresh and green, and he will be preparing to negotiate the purchase of a straw hat and linen duster. But the doctor says his wounds are not necessarily fatal.

Charles Napier, an English scientist, prescribes a vegetable diet as a cure for intemperance. He says that if the lovers of strong drink will eschew all meat, and masticate cabbages and turnips for the space of six months, all desire for alcoholic stimulants will depart from them. That this will work has been demonstrated in Austin. A resident of this city, having read Mr. Napier's suggestion, confined himself to a diet of cabbages and turnips for six months, and at the end of that time he had no further desire for strong drink. He had a splendid funeral, and the doctors said he died of cholera.

A prominent citizen went into a store on Main Street this morning, and purchased a broom. The clerk asked him if he should send the article home in the store's delivery wagon.

"No," he replied, "I might as well pack it home myself; but don't you know, whenever my wife sends me to the store to buy a broom it always reminds me of the time when I was a boy going to school?"

"How is that?" asked the clerk.

"Well, you see, when I was going to school and I used to cut up any didoes, the teacher used to give me his jack-knife and send me out to cut birch switches for him to whale me with. See the point?"

The clerk said he thought he saw it.

The occasions when silver bullion is shipped from the Express Office in this city open a social problem which commends itself to the consideration of the scientist and the attention of the student of human nature. Prominent citizens will congregate on the sidewalk where the bullion is piled, awaiting loading on the stage, and will pick up and "heft" the heavy bars, with scarce any apparent exertion. And yet when the wife of any one of those same prominent citizens tells him to "bring in an armful of wood, you lazy brute," he swears, by all the gods above, that stooping and lifting give him a crick in the "spine of his back."

The extraordinary weather of this morning is dangerous to our institutions. It threatens to introduce the umbrella in our midst. The last man who ventured on our streets with an umbrella was promptly shot, but his corpse was not mutilated, like that of his predecessor. Since the completion of the Central Pacific Railroad the manners and customs of an effete Eastern civilization have one by one encroached upon our isolation, driving the old pioneers further and further back into the fastnesses of the mountains; and now that showers in March threaten to foist the deadly umbrella on an unwilling people, men look into each other's faces and ask: "What *is* this consarned country coming to, anyway?"

One of the most glorious mornings that ever dawned upon the Toiyabe Range was that which ushered in this day. The air was as soft as the young man who thinks that all the girls in town are stuck after his moustache, and as mild as boarding-house coffee; the skies were as clear as that a year's desertion constitutes good grounds for divorce in this State, and the sun shone as brightly as the spick-span new twenty-dollar piece that a man hates to change in paying for a two-bit plug of tobacco. It was one of those mornings when all Nature smiles, and the responsive heart of the bar-keeper gives down its milk of human kindness, so that Nature is not the only thing that smiles.

A certain gentleman of this city had for a considerable length of time been "keeping company" with a young lady, and on the occasion of her birthday, recently, sent her as a present a beautiful album. The lady was not at all satisfied with the gift, as she had expected something which would be significant of matrimonial intentions on the part of the gentleman—an engagement ring, or something in that line. She confided her dissatisfaction to her bosom friend, and said she thought her beau might have sent her "something binding." This remark the bosom friend communicated to the gentleman in the case, who was equal to the emergency, and immediately sent the dissatisfied lady a present of seven pounds of cheese

---

"Is it a crime to shoot cats?" asked a prominent citizen of an eminent jurist, in the International Restaurant, this morning. The lawyer said he could not answer till he had searched the statutes and ascertained what bearing the common law had on the subject. Though not a lawyer, we think we can satisfactorily answer the citizen's question. In our opinion it is not a crime to shoot cats, providing you hit them square between the eyes, and stun them so that they will lie still till you can get to them and chop them into small bits with an ax. We do not hold that walking into a sitting-room, and turning the contents of a six-shooter into a cat as it peacefully slumbers in an old maid's lap would be strictly within the law; but we contend that the murder of a cat that is attending a musical rehearsal in the still watches of the night under your bedroom window is within the pale of the Constitution.

There is a Boston lady in this town who is a great stickler for refined language, and who has a perfect horror of vulgarisms, in which she includes many familiar terms. Recently a successful chlorider, who resides in Upper Austin, gave a swell dinner, to which this lady was invited. After disposing of a couple of pounds of roast turkey she passed her plate to the host.

"Some more turkey?" queried he.

"No, thank you," she returned, "but please be so kind as to introduce a spoon into the interior recesses of the frame of the turkey, and extract for me therefrom some of the insertion."

"Some of the *what?*" gasped the unfortunate man.

"Why, some of the stuffing she means, you illiterate old fool," suggested his wife.

"Oh!" And then he fainted and was borne on a shutter to his chamber, where he now lies in all the dreadful delirium of brain fever.

In a large city there are industries and modes of obtaining a livelihood which in smaller places are impracticable. An instance of this came under our observation during our recent visit to San Francisco. Walking along Kearny Street one day, in company with a city friend, we noticed a remarkably and extraordinarily ugly woman, and called our friend's attention to her.

"Yes, she is frightfully ugly," he replied; "but she makes it pay—makes big money at it."

"Makes it pay! Makes big money at it! How?" we asked in surprise.

"Well, you see," was the reply, "the town's chock full of garroters; and wealthy men hire this woman to walk home with them nights, to frighten away the garroters and hoodlums."

Such an industry were not possible in Austin, on account of lack of material—no garroters and no homely women.

The most surprising and at the same time exasperating accident that can befall a young lady is to have a sled shoot out from under her while she is coasting down hill, and leave her sitting in the snow in solitary contemplation of the heavenly bodies. It is at such a moment as this that her soul is filled with bitterness and her mind with the contemplation that this is a cold, cruel, and heartless world—particularly the cold part; when romance or sentiment find no place in her thoughts, and she takes nothing on trust. A young lady who was one of a coasting party met with an accident of this nature last night, and when her companions, on their return up the hill, found her sitting in the snow, and sympathizingly inquired if she was hurt, she replied:

"I have not investigated as to that as yet; but that I am mad, and disgusted with coasting, is the cold bottom fact of the business."

A rancher brought his family into town for a holiday a few days since, and leaving them at a hotel, went out and took a bath, purchased and put on a new suit of clothes, and otherwise improved his personal appearance. When he returned to his family's apartments at the hotel, he was a transformed man in appearance. His children failed to recognize him, and when he attempted to kiss his wife she threw a wash-pitcher at him, and told him she would scream if he did not leave the room "this minute," and would tell her husband when he came home, anyhow. He was obliged to go out and get a friend, to go with him to his wife and identify him; and when she finally became convinced that he was really her husband, she said that if she had known his true complexion before her marriage to him she would never have married him in the world. She thought he was dark, and here, after taking a good, square wash, he had turned out to be light. She was a blonde herself, and believed in contrasts in marriage.

An aged man, with the snows of many winters upon his venerable head, and his body bent under the accumulated weight of years, was hit plump in the eye with a snow-ball yesterday afternoon on Main Street. There was something of the fire of his youth in his uninjured eye, and tears and redness in the other, as in his virtuous indignation his form towered erect and he shook his fist at the retreating bad small boy, and exclaimed:

"I wish I may be —— into —— in a minute if I wouldn't make you think an earthquake had landed athwart your ear, if I had you within reach of this good right hand, you young cub of the devil!"

But when the *gamin* derisively placed his thumb to his nose, and spread his fingers like a fan, it was more than human nature could bear; and the poor old man, whose sands of life were running so low, went into the nearest saloon, and in tearful accents requested the bar-keeper to fix him a hot Scotch, and "be sure to put lots of sour in it."

According to some medical authorities, more quarrels arise between husband and wife from their sleeping together than from any other cause. It is held that the eliminative nervous force of one person is absorbed by sleeping with a person of absorbent nervous force, and that the absorber will sleep, while the eliminator will be restless, nervous, and sleepless. The electrical qualifications of the cerebro-magnetic concatenations, the one being a positive and the other a negative pole, so disturb the nervo-vitality of the eliminative functions, that two persons possessing these attributes in an opposite degree are uncongenial in magnetic equilibrium; and thus quarrels in bed between husband and wife are the inevitable result. We have frequently noticed this phenomenon in our own experience, and the only remedy we can suggest is for husband and wife to each sleep with somebody else.

Several years ago, in this city, a gentleman prominent in bull-punching circles was arrested for some slight infraction of the laws, and taken before a justice of the peace, by whom he was found guilty and sentenced to pay a fine. The ox-steerer was very indignant at the result of his case, and very bitter against the judge for the severity of the sentence, which he claimed was greater than the circumstances justified. Revenge rankled in his heart, and he determined to get even on the judge, and this is how he did it. He named the off leader of his team after the judge, and whenever he was driving the team past his enemy's office he would run up to the off leader and sock the goad viciously into the poor animal, and cry:

"Git up, you Judge Blank, you —— —— son of a ——, —— —— your —— —— heart into ——ation."

When the judge would go to the door of his office and gaze down street and see that man's ox-team coming up, he would retire to the privacy of his back room and stuff his ears with cotton.

The Austin Post-office has been doing a rushing business to-day in the distribution of valentines, of which a very large number have passed through the mail. The scene at the Post-office during the day has been exciting in the extreme. The varied expressions of hope, despair, joy, or chagrin on the faces of the applicants for letters was enough to move the stoutest heart. The most touching incident of the day was when a young man who had applied the fifty-fourth time at the window for "a volumtime for me," at last received the coveted missive. It was enclosed in a richly-embossed and perfumed envelope, and as he broke the seal his hand trembled and his eye shone in joyful expectation. He unfolded the valentine. Alas for bright hope! It was a picture of a man with a small head and exaggerated feet, and the words "Brainless Fop" printed in large capitals, under the picture, seared his brain like letters of living fire. The bystanders thought he would faint, but he didn't. He only raised his hand on high, and said:

"I'll bet forty-five to fifteen I can lick the stuffin' out of the dog-goned, ornery, consarned critter what sent me this volumtime."

We draw the curtain on this painful scene.

Tramps abound in Austin at present. They are depredatory, larcenous, and burglarious; and it would be well for owners of portable property, such as hot stoves and steam-hoisting works, to keep a lookout on their goods, wares, and merchandise. A few evenings since, some of these pedestrians entered a saloon and broke open the till in the bar-counter, and the same evening a robe and overcoat were stolen from a livery stable. When the tramps come around residences, pretending hunger and asking charity, invite them to an interview with the wood-pile. If they accept the invitation, it shows that they are willing to work for a living; and after they have sawed and split eight or ten cords of wood into stove size, it would be as well to offer them something to eat. If they refuse to tackle the wood-pile, then they are the tramp, in all his native cussedness. In this case set the dog on him, or stand him up against the fence and pour hot water down his back, or get a six-shooter and make a true fissure lead ledge in his carcass. This last is the most effectual method of dealing with him; and if you lodge three or four bullets in his brain, or increase the weight of his heart by the addition of a couple of pounds of slugs and horse-shoe nails inserted therein, he will not be liable to trouble you again. The best protection of all, however, is to keep your doors locked.

A stranger passing through Churchill County recently, had the misfortune to lose his team of mules, they having become alkalied by the water of that section. The mules died within a few miles of Stillwater, the county seat, and one of the solid men of that place went over to where the stranger was camped, to sympathize with him. He drove over a span of mouse-colored mules, of about the dimensions of jack-rabbits, and, in order to help the unfortunate traveler out of his plight, offered to sell them to him at about twice their value. The man examined the mules, inspected their teeth, and twisted their tails to test their kicking powers. Then he said to the Churchillian:

"Can these mules draw well?"

"Draw!" exclaimed the man of the desert. "Draw! Stranger, you aint much of a judge of hoss-flesh. I use these here mules for plowin', and I'm 'bleeged to hitch 'em to two plows. If I only used one plow they'd yank it through the land so fast that the friction would burn up the face of the yearth so's thar wouldn't nothin' grow on it. I should say they *could* draw."

The stranger said he guessed he wouldn't buy the mules, as they were too energetic for his purpose, because he wanted to travel slow, so as to view the scenery.

"Put some perfumery on my moustache," said a young man to the barber, who was putting on the finishing touches, in a popular Austin barber shop, yesterday afternoon.

"Must be going to make a call," said the polite tonsorial artist.

"Yes, going to drop around to see some folks," was the reply.

"Going to see some of your many young lady friends, of course," insinuated the knight of the razor.

Then the young man rose up out of that barber chair, and said:

"See here, my friend, do you suppose I put perfumery on my moustache because I'm going to see a man, or a boy, or an old woman, or a baby in arms? Do men gather grapes of thorns or figs of thistles?"

The barber said grapes were out of season, and figs were dear in this country on account of the freight; but long observation in his profession had convinced him that perfumery on a moustache possessed a certain significance in most cases; but there were instances where the man who wanted the hair on his upper lip strongly scented knew to a certainty that the girl he was going to see that night was in the habit of eating onions for dinner. And the customer laid down a quarter to pay for his shave, and said that the barber business must afford a magnificent field for the study of human nature.

Initial Conversation.

In the play of "The Mighty Dollar," the Hon. Bardwell Slote economizes his conversation by using only the initial letters of certain words, and when the play was introduced in San Francisco, the populace caught up Mr. Slote's plan, and initial conversation became a common thing in that city, as a species of slang. Like all other fashions, sayings, and doings, which reach Austin after they are played out everywhere else, this practice has got here. An Austin store-keeper, who visited San Francisco some time ago, has got it on the brain, and inflicts it on his friends and customers at every opportunity.

Yesterday, an old lady from the country walked into his store to make a purchase, and he, observing her from the office, called out to a clerk:

"Here, Augustus, S. A. lively and wait on this lady."

"'Gustus S-A'd to wait on me last time I come in, and kept me waiting about two hours," remarked the lady.

"That's just it, ma'am, and that's why I told him to S. A. lively (stand around lively). T. is M. (time is money) just as much with us as with you, ma'am."

"I don't want no tea of no kind, but I want two pounds of your best coffee at your lowest cash rates."

"That's it, ma'am, C. T. in this establishment."

"I told you I didn't want to C. no tea, but coffee."

"Oh, I mean C. T.—coin talks—in this establishment."

"It does, does it? Well, then, I'll just G-O-P-H across the street, where I can get all the credit I want to."

And as she went out, the storekeeper muttered:

"G-O-P-H—let's see, yes, that means goph (go off) and she's S. U. (slid out), and I'm a D. O. G. (danged old galoot) for L. A. K. (losing a customer)."

Caring for a Baby.

A woman from the country came into town the other day on a shopping expedition, bringing her baby along with her. She carried the infant into a store at which she is in the habit of trading, and setting it in a chair asked one of the clerks, who happened to be the only person in the store at the time, to look out for it for a minute, while she ran up to the drug store to buy a few articles. Without giving the clerk time to frame a speech in acceptance of the trust thus reposed in him, she bolted out of the store, and he, a lone, lorn bachelor of the most correct habits and principles, was alone with that infant. The sense of responsibility he felt crushed him as if the fat woman in the circus had sat down on him; he gazed on the babe, as it lay placidly sleeping in the chair, and the thought came over him, what if—just then the child let out a yell that went rippling and cavorting through the store as if the rumbling of an impending volcano was shaking up the hams and sides of bacon and boxes of lard and candles and canned fruit.

"Oh, oo ittle pootsey tootsey," said the alarmed clerk, "don't oo ky, oo muzzer will be back in a minute."

This only caused the cherub to increase the vehemence of its yells, and to grow black in the face with the intensity of its emotions.

"Shut up, you consarned, ornery, squalling, nasty little brat. Do you want people on the street to think I'm trying to murder you?"

But the baby refused to listen to argument, and opened up a fresh series of yells, with variations.

"Look on this manly breast, thou sweet cherub; tell me if you see there any outcroppings of the consolation thou most desirest. I am powerless to help thee. Thy mother will return ere long. Still, I pray thee, still thy lamentations."

Another howl, louder and more prolonged than any that had preceded it, was all the answer that mite of humanity vouchsafed.

"Dod rot and dog-gone a baby anyhow! Shut up, or I'll be the death of you!"

And in the agony of his despair the clerk sat down on the lovely babe. He sat there on that infant three hours before the mother returned; and when, looking through the window, he saw her coming down the street, he got up and went to his desk and commenced to post his books. As the mother entered the office she apologized for her long absence; but said she had got into an argument with another woman as to whether polonaises would be cut bias and gored, or whether they would be knife-pleated and scalloped, and had forgotten all about the child.

"But how had baby behaved itself, anyhow?"

"Quietest baby I ever saw in my life," replied the clerk; and then he excused himself and went out. The woman picked up her baby, which was mashed flat, and she had to take it to a blacksmith shop and hold its mouth to the nozzle of the bellows, and have some more breath pumped into it; and she says if her husband don't buy a shotgun and kill that clerk she will sue for a divorce and go home to her mother. But the clerk has not yet returned. The latest news concerning his fate is that he was footing it across Death Valley, and striking out at his best pace for Mexico, with which country there is no extradition treaty for sitting down on babies.

Part VIII.

INDIANS AND CHINESE.

Indians and Chinese are usual constituents in the population of every Nevada town. The principal tribes of Indians in the State are the Piutes, Shoshones, and Washoes. The Washoes live in the western portion of Nevada, near the California line, and are probably an offshot of the California Digger Indians, whom they resemble somewhat in stature and feature, and whose counterparts they are in squalor, filth, and dullness of intellect. The Shoshones occupy the territory east of a given line from the center of the State to a point near the Utah boundary, out of which limits they seldom venture. The Piutes, being numerically the strongest and most powerful, besides much superior to the others in both mental and physical attributes, roam where they please, their lines extending into Idaho and Oregon on the north, nearly to Arizona on the south and east, and west from the eastern base of the Sierra Nevada to the Territory of Utah. There are certain places in Idaho and Nevada which serve as head-quarters for the various subdivisions under the lesser chiefs, or "captains"; but, except at particular seasons, when dance festivals (called fandangos) are held, or excursions are made to the hills for the purpose of gathering the crop of pine-nuts which forms a large part of their winter subsistence, they hang about the towns—as do the Shoshones in their own territory. There are other but insignificant tribes in the southern portion of the State, and the eastern part of Nevada and Western Utah is inhabited by the Goshutes. This tribe, which was once warlike and powerful, is now almost extinct, and numbers but a few hundred souls, it having

been almost exterminated by the troops under command of General P. E. Connor, in 1864–5, as a punishment for and to check their attacks on emigrants and stages on the Overland road. At one time, all these tribes warred with each other; but now the hatchet is buried forever. They have occasional tribal troubles on account of the Piutes stealing horses or squaws from the weaker tribes, and there are frequent quarrels among them caused by whisky and gambling—but these are as likely to occur among members of the same family as with neighboring tribes. In the majority of cases, the differences are submitted to the arbitration of some white man whom the Indians conceive to possess authority—justices of the peace, sheriffs, town or city marshals, and frequently the editor of the local paper. It is a common occurrence for Indians to call at the REVEILLE sanctum with statements of their grievances, and a request that I "heap put 'em in paper." They fancy that a publication of their wrongs in a newspaper is a sure method of obtaining redress.

In the towns, the Indians perform various menial offices. The men chop wood and dig, act as street scavengers, dish-washers in the restaurants, and in divers other capacities of simple labor; the squaws do washing, and some of them make very good house servants. The money they obtain in this way is used in personal adornment and playing poker—an amusement to which all Indians, male and female, are passionately addicted.

There is a strong antagonism between the Indian and the Chinaman, principally felt by the Indian, and the races have frequent quarrels, in which the Indian, owing to the Chinaman's superior cunning, usually comes off second best. The Chinaman lives in quarters, apart from the portions of the town occupied by the whites, the streets of which look like a slice cut from China; and to Chinatown the Indians resort for a miserable compound miscalled whisky, which is furnished them by the keen "Johns" at an enormous profit. They are dependent for the gratification of their alcoholic tastes almost exclusively on the Chinese, as it is seldom that a white man will supply liquors to them, being restrained by the strict State laws prohibiting it. Therefore, Lo, who hates John with a bitter hate, cannot afford to quarrel with him; for, though he despises the Chinaman much, he loves liquor more. As this purports to be a Nevada book, and as the Chinese and Indians form so large an element of Nevada's population, I here introduce a few sketches of incidents in connection with those races, many of which were published from time to time in the REVEILLE.

The Indian, stripped of the romance with which he is clothed in the imagination of those whose estimate of him is based on novels, poems, and histories which treat on the "noble son of the forest," stands forth merely a crude, dirty, vicious savage. This is his best aspect. Until subdued by force he is cruel and treacherous, with a nature little better than the wolf that prowls the plains. He is cunning, and politic to the extent that when he is whipped, and feels himself in the power of a superior race, he grovels and toadies to that superiority—accepts its cast-off clothes, does its chores for a consideration, and copies its vices. Its good traits he seldom or never learns or practices. An Indian is a coward. Liquor or excitement may render him desperate, but true bravery is something foreign to his nature. He will only fight when he has the best of it, and even then he skulks, and shoots from shelter; and it is seldom that he will battle man to man with the whites, except when cornered—then he turns at bay like any other wild beast. He is a stranger to the feeling of gratitude, and if a favor is done him he can conceive no other motive for it than fear. Do an Indian a kindness, and he is sure you are afraid of him. I have seen members of nearly all the tribes of Indians between the Rocky Mountains and the Pacific Ocean, and this description applies to one equally with the other, except in some isolated cases in Montana and British Columbia, where intermarriage with whites and the teachings of the Catholic fathers have taken some of the wolf out of them. But even the best of those classes are not the equals in moral attributes of the lowest grade of white men. Nobody who has ever been brought in direct contact with the Indians as they are, ever knew or heard of one of them performing an act of magnanimity or of charity. Among themselves, in their own social life, they are brutes. They compel the women to carry all the burdens and to perform all the labor, and when the females grow old they are neglected, starved, beaten, and abused, and frequently stoned to death to get them out of the way. Cleanliness they know not of, and the proudest looking Indian that ever stalked in fringed buckskins and beads, with painted face, and hair adorned with army buttons, is covered with vermin, from which he never makes an effort to free himself.

The Indians in Nevada, having been cowed and subdued by frequent chastisements by the military and settlers, after for several years pursuing a cruel and diabolically torturing warfare, are now merely a collection of nomadic loafers. They have head-quarters of subdivisions of the tribes at certain points—but few consenting to live on Government reservations—and from these they roam the country, some picking up a precarious subsistence in hunting jack-rabbits, sage-hens, and such other small game as the country affords, and others hanging about the mining towns and the towns along the line of the Central Pacific Railroad. A few are induced to work on ranches at certain seasons. In the main they dress in clothes which have been cast off by the whites, but a few of them wear robes made by sewing together the skins of jack-rabbits.

The town Indians subsist by begging at the kitchens of residences, hotels, restaurants, and miners' cabins, and the majority of them pass their time in sleeping in the sunshine or gambling at cards. With all, gambling is the chief aim of life—whether it be at Indian poker or monte, by day on the street corners, or at night in their miserable wickiups, or playing marbles "for keeps" among themselves, or with small white boys. Some of the men work at odd jobs, such as cutting firewood, scavenger work, wash-

14

ing dishes in restaurant or hotel kitchens, and other odd chores, while many of the women do rough washing for families and perform various easy menial services. The women are much more industrious than the men, but all their earnings go to their lords and masters, to furnish them with gambling capital.

The women of the Piute tribe are, except in isolated cases, virtuous; but in the other tribes they do not know the significance of such a word. Among the Piutes a lapse from virtue is punishable by death, by burning, or by stoning; but in the other tribes, the husbands, so-called, pocket the proceeds of the women's prostitution, and shame is a feeling which neither man nor woman of them ever experienced.

There is a humorous side to the Indian character, however; and it is in the endeavor to portray this, that the sketches which follow are embodied in this work.

The Chinese.

The Chinaman is a problem. He is all over the Pacific Coast, in every State and Territory which comprises that region, and forms the most undesirable and disturbing element of the population. His good qualities are very few, and may be summed up in three words: Industry, frugality, and patience. His vices are legion, and comprise, in part, dishonesty, cruelty, filth, idolatry, and opium smoking. He has no home ties, and seeks none; he lives in a hovel in the villages and towns, and, crowded like sheep in a pen, in filthy buildings in Chinese quarters in the large cities. His women are all prostitutes, brought from China as slaves. To steal is his creed; to lie, his religion. I will not say that there are no Chinamen whatever better than this picture; but where there are such, they form notable exceptions to a general rule. John, like Lo, has his humorous side, and an attempt to depict it is the cause of his introduction in these pages.

The Origin of the Fandango.

The fandango, or dance, is a species of thanksgiving festival, held in accordance with instructions from a source which will be mentioned below. The Shoshones and Piutes, unlike Fennimore Cooper's and Ned Buntline's Indians, have no belief in a "Great Spirit" or "Happy Hunting Ground." Their idea of a hereafter is a place where there are millions of fat crickets always roasting, and thousands on thousands of ponies roaming around on grass-clad hills, with red blankets strapped to their backs; and the being they worship, and in whose honor these festivals are given, is a traditional Indian, whose history the medicine-man gives as follows:

"Heap sun-ups, maybe long time ago," a mountain in the Goose Creek range suddenly became very much disturbed. It rocked violently to and fro, sending forth loud noises resembling exaggerated human groans. The Indians, who at that time flocked in large numbers to that locality to gather pine-nuts, were greatly terrified at the actions of the mountain; but they could not flee—they were chained to the spot by a sort of fascination, and all their efforts to tear themselves away were fruitless. They huddled in groups at the foot of the mountain; the men pale with fear, and the women and children wailing and crying.

The mountain continued to labor for many days; when, at last, one night, when the sky was of inky blackness, a bright ray of light shot up from its peak, and in a few seconds the entire sky was illumined by a dazzling light of rosy hue. The assembled Indians with one accord cast their eyes to the peak of the mountain, when there slowly emerged therefrom the figure of an Indian. The figure was about ten feet in height, and straight as an arrow. It was clad in buckskin, richly embroidered with beads; its ears and nose were decorated with bead rings; the head was surmounted by the pinion of an eagle, and around its waist was a belt containing upwards of three million (according to Indian count) glass beads. For full ten minutes the figure stood gazing at the astonished and terrified Indians, when, fixing an arrow in his bow, he discharged it at a range of hills opposite him. A flash of light like the trail of a meteor followed the discharge, and in a moment the range, which was before barren, was covered with *pinons*, laden down with luscious pine-nuts. Another discharge of an arrow at the stream which rippled at the foot of the mountain, and the river was almost overflowing with fish. The figure then pointed its finger significantly at the large rock on which it was standing, and slowly disappeared into the mountain, which then ceased its shaking and rumbling; the light went out, and a solemn silence came over the scene.

The next morning, Salamahowich, a mighty warrior, who was then chief of the tribe, ascended the mountain, and stepping on the rock on which the figure had stood the night before, it suddenly gave way with him, and in a moment he found himself in the interior of the mountain. The description of the place in which he found himself, as given by the medicine-man, is beyond our powers; but he gave us to understand that the floor "all the same half-dollars," (meaning silver) and the roof "heap all same him," pointing to a cluster of icicles dependent from a porch, by which we suppose he meant it was covered with stalactites. While the chief was lost in admiration of the magnificence of his surroundings, the figure of the night before emerged from a recess in the cave, and bidding the chief to seat himself, he told him that he was the Savior and Guardian of the Shoshone tribe, born but the night before, and that the mountain was his mother. He commanded the chief to take word to the tribe, and to tell them that so long as they obeyed a certain code, which he laid down to the chief, but which is too long for repetition here, so long would he be their guardian and protector. Among other things, he demanded that a constant guard should be kept at the mouth of his cave; that no human being should be permitted to enter it; and that at a sound which he would strike on an immense boulder of pure silver, which stood near the mouth of the cave, signal fires should be built directing the tribe to hold a dance in his honor.

It is doubtful if any white man could find the locality of the mountain, or even if he would be permitted by the Indians to enter the region; so ambitious prospectors need not trouble themselves about it; but when fires which flash seven times seven times are seen on the mountains, it may be set down for certain that the big Indian is hitting his boulder, and then follows a grand fandango, which is religiously observed without regard to season or weather, oftentimes being held during a fierce snow-storm, or on nights when the thermometer is so low that the mercury tries to crowd itself out of the bottom of the instrument.

A Fandango.

I was one of a party who made a visit to one of the spring fandangos of the Piute tribe of Indians. The Indians were found encamped in a circle formed by piling up brush, and at the time of our arrival, dancing having not yet commenced, the children of the sagebrush were distributed within the circle in various picturesque groups. The camp seemed to be subdivided into smaller camps, in some of which games of cards were in progress; in others, the braves were sitting around a small sagebrush fire engaged in conversation, the light of the fire giving a subdued glow to the various-colored blankets and the painted faces of the Indians, and forming a picture such as I have seen painted of gipsy life. Other groups consisted of families, the women sitting or lying quietly on the ground, and the infants in their beds of rabbit-skins; and here and there a pair of tiny red feet could be seen peeping out from under the skins, catching the warmth of the sagebrush fire. On the outer edge of the circle a number of half-grown boys and girls were at play, running and jumping through a fire; and their glad shouts and frisky motions showed that they were happy in their rags, and felt not the lack of comfort and shelter which are indispensable to the children of the white man. The first dance being called, a number of bucks formed a circle around a small cedar which was set up in the center of the circle of brush, and commenced a slow, monotonous chant, placed shoulder to shoulder, and moved with regular step around the tree, keeping time to the chant with their feet. Gradually the circle became enlarged, squaws and children falling into it and taking up the refrain of the chant, till, at the time of the departure of the party—about nine o'clock P. M.—about fifty Indians were engaged in the dance. The dance, or fandango, as the Indians call it, is held in celebration of the approach of spring, being a sort of thanksgiving for the disappearance of the snow and cold, and the advent of mild weather. It is a solemn business for Mr. Indian, and he goes at it in dead earnest, not a smile or laugh disturbing his countenance during its progress. The feature of the evening was an Indian dressed in a harlequin custume, which some white man had worn at one of the masquerades given in town. The wearer felt himself a big Indian, and was an object of merriment to the other Indians and of awe to the children, who followed him around as though he were a whole circus in himself.

The inauguration of a fandango is occasionally foreshadowed by a migration of the tribe to some more desirable place, where the festivities can be held in comparative seclusion. I once witnessed the breaking up of a camp for this purpose. About six o'clock in the evening a great commotion was observable, bucks, squaws, and pappooses all being at work pulling down the wickiups and packing the horses with the household goods. Viewed from the opposite hill, the preparations for departure presented a picturesque sight. The ponies standing patiently to receive their burden of high-colored blankets, provisions, cooking utensils, and the miscellaneous traps that go to make up an Indian household; pappooses in all stages of raggedness tumbling about on the ground; squaws taking down the dirty and ragged odds and ends which serve for the covering of an Indian house; bucks riding furiously over the steep hill-side to get the horses together—all set off against the grayish background of the hills with the sinking sun casting a glow on the scene that made bright color look brighter, and dirty bits of cloth look clean. It was a pretty picture at a distance; a near approach would have destroyed the romance and picturesqueness, besides offending the nostrils and endangering the cleanliness of the spectator. About eight o'clock the cavalcade began to move, the braves and favorite squaws and children, who were mounted, taking the trail around the hill above the Clifton grade, and the blear-eyed old squaws, with burdens on their backs, taking the shorter cut over the mountain; and by the time it was fairly dark there was not an Indian left in the town or its immediate vicinity.

"Indian Al."

Indian Al is a California Digger, who was brought to this city when quite young, and educated with white children of his own age. During his boyhood he was taught to read and write, and was kept neatly dressed, and at one time gave promise of growing up an intelligent and respectable man. But when he reached man's estate the wolf cropped out; he threw off the restraints and clothing of civilization, encased himself in rags, allowed his hair to grow, procured a blanket, went to an Indian camp on the hill and fraternized with the Shoshones, becoming as one of them, and acquiring their tongue readily. He naturally gravitated to whisky, and a short time after his lapse from civilization became a recognized nuisance of the town. Shortly after the completion of the Central Pacific Railroad he removed to Battle Mountain, and since then has lived in the different camps along the line of that road between Reno and Elko. I saw him a few weeks ago at Carlin, when he told me that he had given up drinking and gambling, and stopped associating with the Indians; but his appearance contradicted his statements. Two days ago he put in an appearance at Austin. He is the biggest liar on the continent, and told some wonderful tales of his travels to both Indians and whites, even excelling Uncle John of the Sazerac—asserting that he had been all over Europe, to China, Japan, Australia, and the Sandwich Islands. The Shoshone squaws at once fell in love with him, by wholesale; they loved him for the lies he told, as Desdemona did Othello; and, clustering around him, would swallow the biggest of his yarns, with the utmost confidence in their truth. There is a Shoshone Indian in town from Belmont, who until Al's arrival was the admired of all admirers among the squaws. He is a handsome young fellow, and, tricked out in a red shirt and plug hat, has been strutting around with half the young Indian ladies of the vicinity at his heels. With these two gallants on the street at the same time, there could be but one result; and it soon came in the shape of a quarrel between them, during which Indian Al drew a huge knife on his rival. The former was arrested, and now occupies a cell in the City Jail. Here his education serves him in stead, and with the stub of a pencil he whiles away the dreary hours inscribing on the wall the words, "The course of true love never did run smooth." It is perhaps necessary to say that this is strictly true.

This Al got into an argument with a store-keeper the other day, during which something was said about keeping books.

"Do you keep books?" asked he.

"Yes," said the white man, "I keep my own books."

"It's a bad practice," returned the Indian; "more men have got broke in this country by keeping books than from any other cause. You should confine your operations to a cash basis."

The white brother weakened, and the argument closed.

Belmont Johnny, Al's rival, also soon came to grief. A few days ago, he went to the City Marshal, and related a tale of wrong and injury sufficient to move the stoutest heart. Johnny's particular affinity was a squaw named Topsey, a fat and rollicking Shoshone maiden; but another member of the Piute tribe succeeded in inaugurating himself into her affections and estranging them from Johnny, and on the wings of night fled with her to the fastnesses of Hot Creek, on the Battle Mountain road. Johnny's sorrow was genuine when he asked the Marshal to "send 'em paper, and heap bring 'em back," and tears came into his eyes as he depicted Topsey's ingratitude.

"Yesterday me give him fibe dollar, me give him pair shoe, and buy him silk dress."

"A *silk dress?*" asked the Marshal, "how much did you pay for the silk dress?"

"Me give three dollar," replied the sorrow-stricken red man.

The Marshal informed Johnny that the law was powerless to redress his wrongs, and that his only remedy for the injury wrought upon him was personal vengeance.

"All right," said Johnny, "you no put 'em jail-house, me catch 'em Topsey, maybe-so me catch 'em back silk dress."

The Courting Season

That "in the spring a young man's fancy lightly turns to thoughts of love," applies with particular force to the noble red man of the sagebrush. Both the Shoshone and Piute tribes of Indians have a regular courting or love-making season, which generally begins about the first of April and lasts until the spring fandango, at which wives are chosen, and such marriage ceremony performed as the Indians employ. Owing to the inclemency of the present spring, the fandango has been postponed, and the Indians have not yet commenced making love on the street corners, a thing not unfrequently seen in this town. No Indian—or even white man—would feel like courting in the open air with the thermometer below the freezing point, and the wind sending the snow rushing through the streets at the rate of sixty miles an hour. But, after all, this courting-season business seems like a pleasant custom, and it might even be adopted with profit by the whites. How much cheaper and more systematic it would be for Charles to call on Araminta, and open the conversation by saying: "My dear Miss Araminta, the courting season has opened, and I have come to ask if you will permit me to pay my devoirs to you during the said season," than for him to be going up to the house every night for six months, or a year, maybe, with his pockets full of gum-drops and peanuts, and sitting in a corner and looking foolish, and letting Araminta's baby sister lick the blacking off his boots, and her little brother borrow (and keep) his jacknife. And then, after all this trouble and expense, to have her tell him that she had formed a previous attachment, and never, really and truly, ever dreamed that his attentions meant anything more serious than friendship. But she could love him as a brother, and all that sort of thing. If custom had allowed Charles to state his case at the outset, he would have been saved all the expense for the gum-drops and peanuts, and the humiliation of having his suit rejected; and Araminta would have been saved the painful duty of saying those little, but difficult words, "No, sirree; not if I know myself."

An Elopement.

Owing to the excitement of the election and the occupation of our space by matters connected therewith, we have been unable until to-day to make mention of an elopement which took place last week.

Out of regard for the feelings of the families concerned, we refrain from mentioning names, which, however, are well known in this city. The couple had long loved; and, a short time since, the gentleman requested the hand of the lady in marriage, from her stern and cruel father, and was kicked down a long flight of steps for his presumption. Nothing daunted, however, by this cruel rebuff, the young man continued his attentions, and although frequently treated to showers of hot water by the maternal parent of his adored, and interviewed by the family dog to the extent of three pairs of pants, he still continued his attentions. The object of his affections viewed with heart-breaking sorrow the persecutions of the idol of her soul, but was powerless to prevent them, as she was kept confined in a cabin in a secluded part of the town, and kept from all communication with the unfortunate young man. Last week, however, the young man discovered the whereabouts of his beloved and managed to communicate with her, when she expressed a willingness to fly with him.

On the appointed night the lover was on hand. The night was pitchy dark, and a gentle rain pattering on the roof prevented the stern parent of the girl from hearing the stealthy footsteps of her lover. Approaching the cabin, he drew his trusty pocket-knife, and soon picked enough of the mud which filled the interstices of the logs of which the cabin is composed, to enable the prisoner to crawl through. As the last flicker of her dress passed through the "chink" she fell into his arms, and throwing her on his shoulder he flew to the hills.

When the old man awoke, next morning, the elopers had a wickiup of their own erected; and as the excited parent approached, with his bow and arrow cocked, and fire gleaming from his eye, the now husband threw his protecting arm around the waist of his bride, and defied the old duffer. The husband settled the matter, however, by the payment of three ponies, a deck of greasy cards, and a flannel shirt. A grand banquet of entrails was given at the slaughter-house, and as soon as the squaw gets over the honeymoon, she will be again ready to do washing by the day.

An Unhappy Medicine-Man.

The squaw over whom the medicine-man has been howling so much, to the annoyance of our citizens, has gone to her last account. Yesterday afternoon, observing that matters on the hill south of town bore a somewhat unusual appearance, we walked to a wickiup, where a large number of Indians had congregated. The wickiup consisted of a piece of drilling stretched over a few bent poles, and beneath this canopy was a ghastly sight. Stretched on the ground was the dead body of a squaw, her features almost unrecognizable as those of a human being, on account of being covered with dirt and clotted blood. In a circle around the corpse were seated about twenty Indians, who with grave and serious faces rocked to and fro and sang a monotonous chant. Within this circle were seated a number of squaws, who were crying and tearing their hair, while at the head of the corpse was seated the medicine-man, a gray-headed, miserable-looking old wretch. His arms were folded across his breast, and his body swayed to and fro in time to his continuous groaning. It is stated that when an Indian medicine-man fails to effect a cure, the Indians accuse him of having bewitched the patient; and immediately after the death of the patient they put the doctor to death, so that he shall not have an opportunity to bewitch others. Last night there was no fire or light of any kind in the Indian camp, and it was as still as the grave; and there can be no doubt that the red men were up to some deviltry. They probably buried the squaw and put the old medicine-man to death. Stoning to death is the method used in these cases, and in all probability the old fellow is mashed up as fine as sausage-meat by this time. He seemed to understand what was in store for him, and was as miserable and woebegone a specimen of humanity as can well be imagined. As to the Indian who beat the squaw to death, nothing will be done to him, as he is a brave, and the woman was his wife, which gave him a perfect right to kill her.

The REVEILLE sanctum was honored, this forenoon, by a visit from the chief justice of the Piute tribe of Indians—Judge John, as he calls himself. The Judge is the most intelligent Indian we have ever met, not even excepting Indian Al, and seems to be pretty well posted on matters and things. After informing us that the old men of his tribe prophesy that there will be severe storms throughout the whole of the present month, he proceeded to question us about the news. He asked us what was going on at Virginia, Carson, Eureka, Hamilton, Salt Lake, the Black Hills, Montana, and the United States, about the affairs of all of which he exhibited a knowledge remarkable for an Indian. He asked us our views of the coming Presidential election, and who we thought would be Grant's successor, and wound up by giving us his opinion of the Chinese question. Said he:

"Chinaman no good—he come here, heap work, no spend 'em money; but take 'em all money 'way over big water. Injun—my tribe—no like Chinaman; heap down on 'em. Too many Chinamen come San Francisco, Virginny—all United States; heap work for little money; whita man, whita woman, and Injun no got work. Bimebye heap kill 'em Chinaman; send 'em back home."

He explained that the Indian, unlike the Chinaman, spent his money in the stores for gloves and clothes and food, thus keeping it in the country; and he argued from this that while the Chinaman is an injury to the country, the Indian is a benefit. He stated that he is a second cousin of Naches, son of old Winnemucca, and that he has a brother who can read and write English well. Like all the Indians of the present day, Judge John has ever been a steadfast friend of the whites, and would rather win all the money in an Indian poker game than harm a hair of a white man's head.

An old Piute Indian departed for the happy hunting ground, via old age and general debility, from the camp back of the City Hall, last night. It is not the custom of the Piutes to bury their dead; and in this instance they merely carried the body a few rods from the camp and deposited it on the ground. The City Marshal, learning that the late Lo was lying exposed on the hillside, commanded Al to have it properly buried. Al made no objections to this order; but five other Indians standing by, whom he requested to assist in the funeral, positively refused to do so. Upon this, the officer threatened that unless they proceeded forthwith to bury the dead Indian, he would arrest them and have them fined four million dollars each. This threat had the desired effect, and the funeral commenced. They wrapped the body in a robe of rabbit-skins and tied it up with ropes, making a bundle the shape of a ball. This they dragged over the hill to an old shaft, into which they dumped it without ceremony. In reply to a question as to the cause of the Indian's death, a dusky maiden, who was an interested spectator of the funeral, replied: "Heap too dam old."

The Piutes and Shoshones of this vicinity have inaugurated a grand rabbit-drive in Reese River Valley, which will last five days. The valley is teeming with rabbits, and the method pursued by the Indians insures the slaughter of thousands. Their mode of procedure is nearly the same as that of the Irish soldier, who captured a prisoner by surrounding him.

The Indians select a piece of ground which they know to be the resort of their game, and, each man being armed with gun or bow and arrows, form a circle. Inside of this ring the women and children are placed, and the space is gradually contracted, the squaws and pappooses meanwhile beating the brush with sticks to start the rabbits. The bewildered little animals rush hither and thither, finding no escape from the wall of hunters, and being hemmed in on every side, and gradually driven into smaller space; until, when the supreme moment arrives, the Indians turn loose their guns and arrows on the confused and affrighted creatures, slaying large numbers of them at each discharge, and the women and children even killing many with their sticks. Captain Charley, a Piute, who is chief-engineer of this drive, says that after it is over there will be a joint fandango of the Piutes and Shoshones, at which his son, "Liar," will "make heap big talk." Charley's son was dubbed Elias by some white man; but the Indians cannot pronounce the word Elias, the nearest they can come to it being "Liar," and by that name is he called and known.

In a couple of weeks the Piute and Shoshone Indians of this section will assemble at Mammoth to gather the pine-nut harvest. A short time before the ripening of the nuts, which grow in great profusion on the hills in that vicinity, the Indians will meet to the number of more than a thousand. They go from Austin, Belmont, Stillwater, and other places within a circuit of 150 miles, and have a grand fandango, lasting upwards of a week; and when the nuts are ripe the squaws collect and roast them for winter use. When the harvest is over, the Indians return to the haunts of civilization, where they live comfortably through the winter on this pine-nut bread, with the addition of such kitchen refuse as they can get. Entrails roasted in the ashes, and cakes made of crickets and pine-nuts mixed together, form a royal feast for an Indian; and when seated in his wickiup, enjoying this savory mess, he doesn't care a continental about civil service reform, is perfectly indifferent whether gold goes up or down, and absolutely neutral on the great question as to the eternity of hell.

A Piute passed down Main Street yesterday, whose appearance excited the attention of the white beholders, the jealousy of his male companions, and the admiring glances of the Indian maidens who were sitting on the curbstones pursuing investigations in natural history in their hair. He was mounted on a sleek pony, and was attired in a flaming red flannel shirt, two pairs of new blue overalls, a stiff-brimmed Peruvian *sombrero*, and a yellow linen duster, whose ample folds spread gracefully over the back of the pony, almost hiding that animal from view. As he rode along, he seemed to be aware that he was the admired of all admirers, and carried himself with an air of conscious pride, occasionally bestowing a contemptuous glance on some less fortunate Indian whose clothes were held together by bits of hay rope, or vouchsafing a patronizing glance on the dusky maidens of his tribe. Grant would have been required to give about eleven horses, sixteen squaws, and a barrel of whisky to have changed places with that Indian. But Indian happiness is as short-lived as that of his white brother; and it is sad to think that this noble red man, so happy yesterday, may have struck an Indian poker game last night, and to-day he may be a total wreck, with nothing to cover his manly form but an old plug hat and a lariat.

As is well-known to those conversant with the Indian character, the Indians none of them know their ages. Before the advent of the whites in this country their computation of time did not extend beyond moons; though many of them now understand what a year is, and are able to compute time by years. Yesterday, an old Indian on Main Street was asked how old he was, and replied he did not know.

"Do you savvy what a year is?" he was then asked.

"Yosh," he replied, "*me* heap savvy; most Injun he only savvy moon."

"Why Injun no count how old by moon?" asked the red man's questioner.

"Him too goddam lazy count 'em," returned the brave.

It is difficult to judge of an Indian's age by his appearance. The exposed life they lead ages them fast, and an Indian at fifty looks as old as a white man does at eighty. This particularly applies to the women; a squaw at thirty is an old hag. A young squaw begins to lose her youthful looks in a couple of years after marriage, and grows old in appearance so rapidly that a person who had not seen her in the intervening two years would not recognize her as the same woman at the end of that time. Very few Indians live to an old age, and we are of the opinion that the average age to which they live is not over thirty years.

A couple of days ago, a squaw died out at Yankee Blade, and the Indians buried her and her infant together, without taking the trouble to make a corpse of the latter. It is the custom with the Piutes and Shoshones to consign the dead mother and living child—when the latter is too young to help itself—to a common tomb. In this instance they dug a hole, threw the woman into it, and laid the infant on her breast, covering them both over with brush. In explanation of this, one of the tribe said:

"Baby no good; no got milk; bimeby heap cry; die pooty soon anyhow."

It would be impossible to convince an Indian that he is doing wrong by thus abandoning a helpless infant to the coyotes and carrion birds; it was the custom of his fathers, and he can see no crime in it. A white man does not like to interfere, for to try and rear the child would be a hopeless task, and besides, the Indians would feel greatly aggrieved if any one meddled with this pleasant custom.

The Piutes have established a new settlement on Union Hill, at the head of Cedar Street. The houses are composed of pieces of house-lining discarded by the whites, old gunny-sacks, strips of blanket, and any remnants that the Indians could pick up around town. One aristocratic red man secured a piece of lining large enough to line the Boston Mill, and has erected a mansion of magnificent proportions. It is in this that the nightly festivities are held. A fire is kept burning throughout the night; and by the light of its flickering flame the noble sons of a fast-fading race probe the mysteries of Indian poker, tell of the heroic deeds of their fathers in scalping emigrants and defenseless stage-drivers, and roast the entrails cribbed from their white brother's slaughter-house. Here may be seen the stalwart brave stretched upon his gaudy blanket, smoking the cigarette of peace, and ruminating on the possible supply of cast-off grub on the morrow; while seated in the shadow is a gentle Hiawatha, mourning the loss of her last string of beads, and rocking to and fro, wearily singing the death-song of her tribe; while the pappooses are scattered around promiscuously.

A daughter of the forest, with a rabbit-skin robe wrapped closely around her noble form, was meditatively meandering along Main Street, this forenoon, and stepped on a slippery place on the sidewalk, and suddenly sat down with a bump that shook the planks. As soon as she had recovered from the shock she cast a glance of indignation at the spectators, and uttered an ejaculation which indicated that her knowledge of the English language had not been derived from a very refined source; and arranging her ruffled dignity and other clothes about her, she said to the most boisterous of the spectators, "You heap dam smart!" and marched off as though she didn't care if the world dropped down a hole in three minutes by the watch. A prominent citizen, who slings big words and is very precise in his conversation, remarked that people ought to put ashes on the sidewalks, as it was too bad to see a poor Indian female "prostituted" to the ground in that manner.

"There," said a prominent citizen on Main Street this morning, pointing to an Indian who was carrying a sack of pine-nuts, "there you see the bounty of Nature to her children, the wise provision which she makes for these untutored savages, who, living in a country to the eye barren of all that is necessary to sustain life, yet find on these sterile hills the means of subsistence in the nutritious pine-nut. The pine-nut," he continued, "grows only in countries possessing characteristics such as we find in Nevada; and just look at it, how, by a generous Nature, it is planted here and flourishes to ripeness for the benefit of the aboriginal inhabitants."

"Ye——s," remarked a bystander, "but if Nature wanted to be so powerful particular about furnishing grub for these Indians, what made her plant the red cusses in such a God-forsaken country as this in the first place?"

The other man said that the forces of Nature were so immutable, and cause and effect were so hidden in the deep recesses of mystery, that science had never been able to penetrate them, and he guessed he couldn't answer that question till he had consulted the authorities.

The Indian children, less fortunate than the white juveniles, are, except in a few isolated instances, unable to procure the luxury of a sled. They take great delight in coasting, but to them to even wish for a sled is to launch out in the direction of the unattainable. To make up for this deprivation they have invented a cheap and simple contrivance for coasting, which, though less comfortable and more dangerous than a sled, enables them to pursue the sport after a fashion. Their coasting apparatus consists simply of a barrel stave, and a piece of rope or stout cord passed and fastened through a hole in one end of the stave. They stand with the right foot on this stave, facing the string, which they hold in their hands, and by its means guide their craft; and giving themselves a start by pushing the left foot on the ground, go scooting down the steep track in the position taken by a boy skating on one skate. They get frequent falls and many bumps, but the little wretches are as tough as a pine knot, and are heedless of the mishaps which befall them. Necessity is as much the mother of invention to the redskin as she is to his white brother.

A short time ago, a couple of Piute Indians went to a store on Main Street and purchased the entire stock of playing cards contained therein. They took them to their camps, and having secretly marked each one, came back to the store, and putting on that look of misery which only an Indian knows how to assume, whined out that they were "heap broke," and offered to sell them back for one-fourth of what they had paid. The pasteboards were purchased on these terms, and were subsequently sold, a pack at a time, to the Shoshone Indians. The Piutes knew that the Shoshones made their purchases at this particular place; and the guileless Shoshone, unaware of the manipulation, bought and played poker with the wily Piute, without a suspicion that all was not—as Governor Bradley would say—"on the dead squar'." The result was, the Piutes won all the money the Shoshones possessed, and now there is weeping, and wailing, and gnashing of teeth, and sackcloth and ashes, in the camp of the Shoshone.

Belmont Johnny, and Topsey, his affinity, the principals in the Shoshone riot night before last, have buried the hatchet, shaken hands across the bloody chasm, and let the dead past bury its dead. In other words, having both got sober, they have made up the quarrel. They were walking Main street together last evening, Topsey all smiles, and Johnny with his head swollen to twice its natural size, and bruised and cut up so that he was hardly recognizable. Topsey, being interviewed, gave an account of the affray of the preceding night, as follows:

"Johnny heap dlink wiskakee; heap git mad cause me talk other Injin; heap blake my dless; me git mad. Me knock him down; heap kick him head; heap git eben, you bet."

She further stated that Johnny won ten dollars at poker that day, and had given her a pair of shoes as a peace-offering, and that they had made it up, and were again good friends. Where do the Indians get their whisky?

A game of marbles between a white boy and an Indian youth attracted quite a crowd in front of Horton & Sawtelle's, yesterday afternoon. The sympathy of the crowd was, of course, with the white boy; but, either through good luck or skill, the son of the forest got away with the baggage; and as the shades of evening closed over the scene, and the sun began to scoot behind the hill, the red boy pocketed the white boy's white alley. With a sigh that seemed to be drawn out of his boots, the last boy brushed the dirt from the knees of his Sunday pants, and went home and read in his Sunday-school book about the fate of the wicked little boy who played marbles on Sunday, who lost all his marbles, ripped the seat of his breeches, got the delights whaled out of him by a big boy, and got an additional dose from his dad as a punishment for letting the other boy lick him. Truly, the way of the transgressor is not soft.

Printers' rollers—the rollers with which type is inked on the press—are composed of glue and molasses. We don't know the exact ingredients of printers' ink, but it probably contains lamp-black, turpentine, epsom-salts, coal-tar, and assafœdita. The combination of the glue and molasses forms a composition which an Indian squaw will eat with as much delight as a white boy will muzzle a jar of preserves. After being used a certain length of time the rollers become impregnated with the ink, and the composition is torn from the stock on which it is fastened, and thrown away. Then is the opportunity of the gentle maidens of the sagebrush. They gather up the discarded material, and squat on the ground, and hold a roller-composition festival. It is the molasses in it that attracts them, and they deceive themselves into the belief that the stuff is a new kind of jujube-paste, a substance which it much resembles in appearance.

There was a close struggle between the wind and Mr. Indian, this afternoon, for the possession of the latter's blanket. The red man wrapped the blanket closely around his noble form, and the wind tore away at it like "all furiation"; but the son of the forest finally obtained the victory by sitting on it—the blanket, not the victory. Indians fear windy weather far more than snow or cold, as their wickiups protect them in a great measure from the two latter. But when a howling wind gets to rampaging and cavorting through the ragged edges of the flimsy wickiup, his house and home are likely to come rattling down on him in the winking of a cat's tail. Captain Tom, a representative specimen of the Piute race, sought shelter in the Reveille office during the gale of this afternoon, and, as he listened to the howling of the wind, remarked: "Him wind dam humbug; heap bustem wickiup."

Somebody dropped some quicksilver on the sidewalk on Main Street, to-day, and an Indian tried to pick it up. First he made a grab at it with his thumb and forefinger, and was astonished when he found he couldn't pick it up. He was determined to have that quicksilver, anyhow; so he unwound a handkerchief from his hat, and, spreading it on the ground, got a chip and scraped the quicksilver into it. A look of triumph shot from his eagle eye as he gathered up the four corners of the handkerchief; but it was replaced by one of horror and disgust when the metal ran through the fabric like water through a sieve. Looking at the metal, as it lay on the ground, in a puzzled sort of way for a moment, he launched a vicious kick at it, and uttering the ejaculation used by a keno-player when some other fellow makes keno, he turned on his heel and left the quicksilver for some other untutored son of the forest to experiment on.

Sam, the Indian who cleans the streets, has met with a severe bereavement in the loss of his oldest wife, who departed this life night before last, at her residence in the Indian camp on the hill back of the City Hall. Sam is grief-stricken over the loss of his helpmeet, and shed tears profusely while telling of it. Said he: "Him woman keep me heap long time; me so sorry she die; other wife too young; no got much sense; don't keep me so long as old woman." Although he has got a young and pretty wife to console him for his loss, and although the deceased sharer of his sorrows and bearer of his burdens was old and homely, Sam seems to feel very bad over her death, and to not entertain a very great affection for the living wife, who is the best-looking Piute squaw in that portion of the tribe resident here.

A squaw in a millinery store, purchasing a new "bunnit" to wear at the fandango, which shortly comes off at Stillwater, was what this reporter beheld last evening. She was as fastidious and as hard to please as a white woman is when engaged in a similar pastime, and tried on, and looked in the mirror to see how it became her, nearly every hat in the establishment. Having made her selection, she rolled it in her handkerchief, and putting it under her arm, marched out of the store, saying to herself in the Indian tongue: "I'd just like to see the shape of the copper-colored woman that can put on more style than I can at that fandango."

The sudden advent of cold weather caught Mr. Indian napping, he not having yet put his house in order, and exchanged his linen ulster for a beaver overcoat lined with sealskin. The old man and his wife and his son and his daughter, likewise his aunt and his mother-in-law, turned out of their wickiup early this morning, and the whole family might have been seen shivering over the bonfires built on Main Street of the rubbish swept out from the stores. Last week, the noble son of the forest elevated his nose and uttered an unseemly ejaculation when offered work; to-day, he goes around pleading for a chance to chop a little wood, saying: "Heap cold; me heap dam hungly."

Judge John is a venerable sage of the Piute tribe, whose face is familiar to the majority of the people of Austin. The Judge usually wears a dilapidated plug hat, but when he came into the REVEILLE office this morning his head was destitute of that adornment, its place being supplied by a dirty and tattered cloth.

"Where's your plug, John?" inquired our devil, addressing himself to the Indian and pointing at his head. And the red man made answer thus:

"Me flug him heap git old; maybeso heap pooty quick heap blake (break); me put him my wickiup so keep him for Sunday. Sunday heap my head put 'em on flug; heap put 'em on style—all same Jludge Logan."

The fine weather has encouraged the Indians to resume playing marbles, and numerous groups of them were to be seen about the streets today engaged in that absorbing sport. To an unaccustomed eye, it looks strange to see a lot of grown-up men, ranging in age from twenty to forty years, playing marbles with all the glee and interest of ten-year old white boys; but we are used to it in this country, and it excites no comment. In such a matter as play, the Indian is but a child, and it is a common thing for adult Indians and fathers of families to indulge in the sports of small white boys. Tops, marbles, and sleds are favorite pastimes with the Indians, and, next to food and whisky, are looked upon by them as the grandest products of the white man's civilization.

The provident Indian covers his hat with a dirty handkerchief to protect it from the snow. The improvident Indian hasn't got either hat or handkerchief. The provident Indian is the one that is successful at poker. When the red man gambles, he plays for all that's out. As "the boys" say, "he's blooded"; and when luck is against him, he plays off hat, coat, boots, horse, wife, everything. When he has had a run of bad luck, and the weather is as severe as that of to-day, he lays down behind a woodpile and takes his solemn oath that he will never touch another card as long as he lives; but soon recovers from his fit of despondency, and hunts a job to earn money with which to again woo the fickle goddess.

An aged squaw, who had evidently struck a bonanza of discarded clothes, strutted proudly up the center of Main Street this forenoon. Over her ragged dress she wore a tattered under-garment of the feminine persuasion, what edges were left of it being richly embroidered. We don't know the name of the article, but do know that it was not a gentleman's shirt. The head of the aboriginal female was decorated with a hat that once was new, garnished with feathers, flowers, and ribbons, all tattered and torn, and her feet were encased in a pair of miner's boots. Under her arm she carried a yellow cur, and as she strutted through the street she was the observed of all observers, and seemed conscious and proud of the attention her appearance attracted.

The horse trough on Main Street, just above the REVEILLE office, is where the Indians who live and have their being in and about Austin perform their ablutions. The washing is confined to their faces, hands, and hair; their bodies are never washed from the moment of birth until they are summoned to the happy hunting ground. Taking a bath would be considered by a Shoshone or Piute as an unwarrantable waste of water, which at least shows that they feel the touch of nature which makes a good many people kin; as now and again, during the course of the white man's career, he meets with instances where white men and women take a similar view to the Indian on the bath question.

Some people think it very funny to chaff a squaw, and sometimes, when the squaw talks back, they don't think it quite so funny. A case in point occurred in town the other day. A group of men were standing in front of a popular Main Street saloon, when a squaw leading a pappoose came along. One of the party hailed the squaw with—

"Hello, Sally, whose baby is that?"

The daughter of the forest stopped and eyed her questioner, and then, pointing her finger at him, said earnestly:

"Him your pappoose."

There was considerable laughing from the bystanders, but they were not laughing at the squaw.

Captain Tom entered our sanctum, this morning, and informed us that he "maybeso heap go Carson, see Governor Bradley; maybeso heap catchum beef," and requested us to furnish him with a paper. By virtue of the authority vested in us, we drew up a paper for the worthy Captain, commending him to the good will of all white men, who are therein directed to furnish Tom and his family with whatever cast-off clothes or victuals they may need. The document is adorned with eleven gilt and five red seals, and its imposing appearance will command the awe and respect of every Indian in the country. Thomas inclosed the document in the lining of his plug hat, fully satisfied that it was *carte blanche* to beg in any part of the civilized globe.

Human nature is the same the world over, and an Indian child takes as much pleasure in a doll as does a white one. We were amused this afternoon by observing a little Indian girl, apparently about three years old, who had found the head of a china doll, probably cast away by some white child, which she was fondling and nursing and talking to after the manner of ordinary doll-mothers. Frequently we see on the street little mites of Indian girls with miniature baskets, containing rag pappooses, on their backs, which answer the same purpose to them as the most expensive and elaborately-gotten-up doll does to a white child.

The sun has shone brightly to-day, and the daughters of the forest took advantage of the circumstance to squat on the street corners where its rays could strike them squarely, and get out their fine-tooth combs and sticks of cosmetic, and shine up their luxuriant locks and make it warm for insect life. At noon to-day, they could be seen scattered all over the north side of Main Street, and all busily engaged in some occupation. Some were playing cards, some making gowns, some spanking their pappooses, and others stringing beads. They seem to be a happy set, and the summit of bliss is reached by them when they have full stomachs and can find a streak of sunshine to bask in.

Everybody has heard of the costume of the Georgia major, which consisted of a collar and pair of spurs; but a young Indian appeared on Main Street to-day in a costume almost as scanty. It consisted of a jacket and a piece of buckskin string. The appearance of the young aborigine created a great deal of merriment among the people on the street, but we noticed that most of the ladies either turned up a side street or only looked at him from behind their pocket-handkerchiefs. The child was too young to appreciate the attention he attracted, but his father seemed proud that his offspring was so generally noticed by the white men.

On Saturday night last, a Piute, with disheveled hair, distended eyes, and a general look of wildness, rushed into Sower's store, and throwing down a dollar, excitedly exclaimed:

"Gimme deck cards and four bits candles!"

We knew by his excitement and eagerness to obtain the articles that a big poker game must be in progress on the hill, so we questioned him regarding it.

"Yes," he replied, "heap big poker game; me heap loser; play 'em all night—maybeso get even; hell! dam!" and grabbing the cards and candles he struck a bee-line for the camp on the hill.

A squaw sat down on the curb in front of the Post-Office, this forenoon, and unrolling a bundle of calico, commenced to manufacture a dress. In less than an hour it was finished; and putting it on over her old clothes, she pulled out a pin here, a peg there, and untied a string in another place, made one step, and, presto! the old clothes lay in the gutter. Gathering up the rags just shed, the noble daughter of the sagebrush cast one look of triumph on the spectators, and skipped gracefully off in the direction of the Indian camp, as proud as a Saratoga belle at the first ball of the season.

Captain Breckenridge, sub-chief of the Piutes, called on us in our sanctum yesterday, and requested that we would "put 'em in noo'paper that he was in town, come Stillwater four days." The reason he assigned for desiring this notice inserted was, that he wanted Naches, the chief, to know he was here; and some white man in Winnemucca would read the paper and tell it to Naches. Breckenridge told us all about his visit to San Francisco to see General McDowell, and said that city "too many people, heap, lots people," and he even hinted that there are more people in that city than there are in Austin.

We did not attend the grand ball given by the Piutes to the Shoshones in Crow Cañon last night; but Captain Steve informs us that it was a grand success, and that Pine-nut Jane was the belle throughout the early part of the evening; but that, unfortunately, she became involved in a game of Indian poker with Horned-toad Sally, in which she lost her gorgeous attire on a queen-full, and her place as belle was taken by the aforesaid Sally. Steve says everything passed off peaceably. "No dlinkum whisakee; no fightum."

No class of our population takes more kindly to the sport of coasting than the Indians; and during the time when the fun is at its height, the sled of the red man may be seen moving, with democratic familiarity, close to that of his white brother. The white man coasts noisily; the Indian quietly. The first goes with a shout; a "hi-hi," or a toot-horn; the latter never utters a sound until the end of the track is reached. He sits on his sled oblivious to all earthly things but the sport in which he is engaged, his face beaming with pleasure and excitement, but by no sound does he betray how thoroughly and entirely his soul is filled with the enjoyment of the moment.

Yesterday morning, while passing down Main Street, we observed a squaw seated on the sidewalk dandling her babe. The infant was not to exceed a week old, and all the covering on it consisted of a breech-clout; but, though the air was raw and sharp, it did not seem to suffer in the least from the cold, but crowed as merrily as if its father owned the big bonanza, and it was clad in purple and fine linen, and a patent India-rubber what-you-call-'em.

A resident of Austin has an Indian employed in chopping wood at his residence, and that the aforesaid is an aborigine who goes through the world with his eyes open is evidenced by what is as follows narrated:

Yesterday (Sunday) the Indian refused to chop any wood, and when his employer asked him the reason of his refusal, he replied:

"Heap no work Sunday; all same whita man, heap play poker."

Jim evidently recognizes Sunday as a day of rest in its full sense.

Not more than a dozen Indians are left in town, and the absence of the noble red men and their consorts creates a blank not easily filled. For washing, chopping wood, and various other menial services, the sons and daughters of the forest are able and reliable citizens, and those who depend on them to perform such services sadly deplore their absence; but the pine-nut crop must be gathered if every restaurant in town has to close its doors and if every woman has to die at the wash-tub and lose her piano practice.

Owing to the near approach of the Fourth of July, the Piutes are disinclined to leave Austin and go to Stillwater, as requested by a message from Breckenridge, their sub-chief. They say they are doing pretty well here, and that if they go to Stillwater, "maybeso heap hungry."

There was never a small white boy that looked forward to the Fourth of July with more joyous anticipation than does an Indian, and he would rather sacrifice his chances of salvation than miss the opportunity of taking a hand in the celebration of that day.

Belmont Johnny, a Shoshone Indian, hailed us on the street yesterday, and asked us if we knew how to "mark stamped cards." Of course we immediately denied the possession of any such wicked knowledge; but the guileless Indian thinks a newspaper editor knows everything. However, we asked Johnny the object of his question, and he explained that he wanted to get some white man to mark a deck of cards for him, and teach him to read them by the backs.

"And what then, Johnny?"

And in reply he said:

"Me heap break every Piute son of gun in Austin."

The Indian did not use the word "gun" as above quoted, but we substitute it for the word he really did say, as a figure of speech, as it were. Johnny speaks English plainly, and has acquired to its full extent the white man's facility of forcible expression.

The noble red man has found a new sphere of usefulness, and in defiance of the Civil Rights Bill has trenched upon a field hitherto given over exclusively to the colored man. We refer to the art of whitewashing, in the practice of which we to-day saw a stalwart brave engaged. He handled the brush with all the dexterity of his African prototype, and his admiring squaw, who sat on the ground watching him, remarked to a bystander:

"Maybeso bimebye, him heap paint, all same white man."

We can imagine no greater misery than to be a non-English-speaking Indian in such weather as the present. Put yourself in his place, and imagine yourself the inhabitant of a residence composed of old gunny-sacks and containing more holes than house, and then depict to yourself the affliction of being unable to curse the weather in a string of good, round, North American oaths. The Indian language contains no words capable of expressing a man's true inwardness under such circumstances.

Sacramento is excited over a red-headed squaw, who is looked upon there as a great curiosity. She would not be a curiosity in Reese River Valley, where young Indians with hair of all the shades that hair assumes can be seen at any time. Only the other day we saw a squaw sitting on the curbstone on Main Street, who had true blonde hair and a pull-back dress. In reply to a question as to the paternity of the half-breed, one of her companion squaws simply said: "Heap coalburner."

The rage with the white boys at present is kites, and of course the Indian boys follow suit, and imitate to the best of their crude ability. The kite is a new revelation to the Indian, but he takes to it naturally nevertheless. The kite used by the Indian boys is a clumsy affair at best—just a piece of paper tied to a string, and it will not fly; but the red urchins get lots of fun out of it and play with it by the hour, fondly hugging the delusion that they are flying a kite.

In front of the Cosmopolitan Saloon, yesterday afternoon, three stalwart Piutes were engaged in a game of Indian poker, the stakes in which were chewing-gum. Each Indian would bite off a piece from the wad of gum in his mouth and place it in the "pot," and the one holding the high hand would rake down the three pieces and put them in his mouth. The sons of the forest were as deeply absorbed in the game as if the stakes had been thousands.

The love-making season has opened among the Indians, and housekeepers find it almost impossible to secure their services for the various kinds of labor to which they are accustomed. A lady of this city, this morning, sent her little boy to find an Indian to chop some wood. After an absence of several hours the boy returned and laconically reported:

"Can't get one; all off huntin' squaws."

A picture of happiness, supreme and complete, is an Indian lad with two hats on his head, a man's boot on one foot, a woman's gaiter on the other, and a flag of truce fluttering in the wind from a breach in his rear entrenchments, as he skips along trying to fly a white boy's discarded kite, and both ignorant and unmindful of the philosophy of the tail.

Some squaws found a battered umbrella in the street this morning, and they thought it was a ready-made wickiup. A brave who sat smoking a cigarette on a goods box, watching the dusky maidens as they squatted under the umbrellageous shade, remarked to a white brother standing near:

"Injun squaw all same white squaw; heap scared sun freeze him face, no look pooty."

The snow was falling thick and fast, and a member of one of the first Piute families sat shivering under the shelter of an abandoned charcoal sack, which served him for a blanket. As the REVEILLE reporter passed him, Lo the poor Indian raised his noble head, and cocking his left eye up toward the obscured sky, remarked in piteous tones:

"Heap dam cold to-day."

An Indian came into our sanctum, to-day, to tell us about the eclipse. He said the Indian word for an eclipse of the sun is "annonguiyaipe," which signifies, literally, buried—"All same you dead and cold and covered up in the ground."

People who imagine that the Indian cannot be civilized and educated would acknowledge themselves mistaken were they to see an Indian youth knuckling down close to a china alley, and hear him cry "Fen kicks!" and "Knuckle down close, you son-of-a-cloudburst!"

Some white men tackled some Indians in a game of Indian poker to-day; but the son of the forest rung in a cold deck and cleaned up all the money on the blanket, and then the pale faces said he was a son of something else than the forest.

The Indians have evidently heard of Pleasanton's blue-glass cure. Yesterday afternoon, a sick Piute was sitting in the sun on Union street, clad only in a pair of blue overalls and a pair of blue-glass goggles.

Hans.

There is a barber shop in Austin conducted by Germans, and in their employment is a Chinaman whom they have dubbed "Hans." He is an observing Celestial, and, like all of his race, apt in learning American customs and phrases. The Chinese are notoriously imitative, and about the first thing American that they learn is to swear. Their native vocabulary has no words of such strong emphasis as the Nevada oath, and consequently the acquisition of a language containing words that enables a man to give a full expression to his true feelings, is one of the greatest boons the Mongolian has gained by the contact with our superior civilization. Hans is doubly fortunate in this respect; for, in addition to his knowledge of nearly all the leading American expletives, he has a fair store of the most elaborate German oaths and by-words, and can swear grammatically in the two languages, with dialectic variations. He is quite a philosopher in his way, and loud in denunciations of the leading vices and sins of his race. Among other things he abhors opium-smoking. The habit is a curse to any people, and contact with the Chinese has corrupted a large number of the young men and women of the Pacific Coast to the adoption of this terrible, degrading, mind, body, and soul-destroying evil. It is practiced almost universally by the Chinese, and is spreading among the whites to such an extent that stringent legislation and strong prohibitory laws have been found necessary to check its demoralization of our youth. Knowing the strong opinions entertained by Hans on this subject, and having myself seen its effects in the lack-luster eyes and wretched faces of those whites who were addicted to the habit, I one day questioned him as to the effects of the use of the drug on his countrymen. His reply was prompt, terse, and to the point. Said he:

"Chinaman smoke opium one year, he all same monkey, all same white man"; a comparison I did not appreciate, but which served to show that a frank answer is not always flattering.

Hans is also opposed to the female slavery practices of his countrymen. The Chinese who immigrate to America are seldom accompanied by their families. They do not come here to remain, and therefore have no home ties. The majority of the males are brought to this coast under a system of coolieism, which, although not actual slavery, is the next thing to it. But the women who come are absolute slaves, having a high value as chattels, varying with age, physical attractions, and condition. They are imported by the wealthy Chinamen of San Francisco—if not directly by the great "Six Companies," which control all the Chinese in America—and the purpose of their importation is the vilest that can be conceived. Hans is about the only Chinaman whom I ever heard denounce this infamous system. He says it is "too muchee bad; sell woman all same Melican man sell mule"; and he expresses a determination never to own one of his countrywomen by this method. Talking about matrimony, he said:

"Me get lich, me go Chiny, make love nicee tiptop Chiny girl; heap marry him, all same white man."

But when asked if he would bring his wife to this country, he replied:

"Not by dam sight. Some dam tiefee Chinaman stealee him and sell him."

Once, a Chinaman passing the shop where Hans is employed, and seeing him engaged in putting a shine on a customer's boots, derisively called him something which sounded like "Tu-na-ma-hing—highlowjackandthe-game," which Hans afterward explained was Chinese for bootblack. Hans immediately replied in good, solid English, "Go to blazes, you rat-eating scrub!" and in a tone that indicated the utmost contempt for everything wearing pig-tails, "Me no washwoman Chinaman."

Hong Sing claimed that Sam Hing owed him two hundred dollars; Sam Hing said he didn't, and both Celestials agreed to leave the matter to the arbitration of the heads of the different wash-house companies in town, who consulted together and pronounced a verdict that Hing must go down to the graveyard and solemnly cut off a rooster's head that he was not indebted to Sing in the above named amount, decreeing likewise that Hing should pay Sing $2.50 for taking the oath—a sort of notary's fee, as it were. In accordance with this verdict the parties litigant, in company with a number of other Chinamen, armed with knives, bludgeons, and six-shooters, repaired to the graveyard, where Hing decapitated the fowl over the grave of a departed countryman, and solemnly asseverated that he didn't owe Sing a dog-goned cent. Sing paid Hing the $2.50 for taking the oath, and then foolishness was about to commence; but the City Marshal, who was on the watch, stepped in and read the riot act, and disarmed the party, capturing a number of six-shooters, knives, and iron bars. Had it not been for the interference of the Marshal, there would have been bloodshed, and Hong Sing's bones would have been put in condition for shipment to the Flowery Kingdom. He remarked to the Marshal that "maybe so you no come, me no more washee."

Owing to the high license levied on banking games by the State laws, the Chinese of Austin no longer play their national game of "Tan," but have substituted therefor the good, old-fashioned, North American draw-poker. Each night, when the hour arrives for business, a Celestial stands on the single street of Chinatown, and, in a voice which can be heard throughout the quarter and the neighborhood surrounding, proclaims that the game is open to all comers. The proclamation is uttered in the Chinese language, and literally translated is as follows:

"Hear ye! Hear ye! The poker game of the Chinese quarter, in and for Lander County, State of Nevada, is now open; free for all, without regard to age, sex, or previous condition of servitude. Come one, come all—white, black, yellow, and copper-colored—and take a hand in the game of the barbarian."

When the crier has concluded, the Chinamen rush into the house where the game is played, and business commences. There is scarcely a night that white men may not be seen, side by side with Chinese, deep in the mysteries of poker; and, though the white players cannot translate the words of the proclamation, they know by the sound and by instinctive feeling that it is a solemn announcement of the opening of the game.

Out at the Chase Mine, New York Cañon, the miners have been greatly troubled by mountain rats. They have been a particular source of annoyance to the Chinese cook, and he had vowed by all the gods of the Flowery Kingdom to wreak a bitter vengeance on the first marauding rodent which should fall into his clutches. Last Saturday, while busily engaged in cutting meat for the morning's hash, he heard a rustling noise, and looking round, saw what he supposed to be a rat's head protruding through a crack in the floor. Seizing a carving-fork, and gliding stealthily up to the object, he plunged it into its body, and, with a yell of triumph, uplifted the impaled animal, exclaiming, "Me catchee dam lat!" The miners, hearing his cries, rushed into the kitchen; but paused on the threshold, for they smelt a smell. About this time, the Chinaman smelt something too, and exclaiming, "Hi yah, me smellee hell!" dropped the fork, and broke from the room. The animal which he had impaled was one of the genus known scientifically as *Mephitis Americana*, vulgarly termed a skunk.

A Chinaman with a terrapin attracted a crowd on one of the street corners, at noon yesterday, and various were the conjectures as to what kind of a bug it might be. One called it a mud-turtle, another an ostrich, and one man was even bold enough to pronounce it a whale. The Indians, who composed a portion of the crowd, were greatly puzzled over what was to them an entirely strange bird; and one noble red man, in reply to an inquiry as to his opinion of what it was, said, "Maybe-so him father tarantula; him mother horn-toad." The Chinaman stated that he had a dozen of them, for which he asked one dollar apiece; and when one of the crowd tried to cheapen the animal he said:

"Yesterday me sell 'em one dollar quartah; man keep saloon buy one, and woman like one put him in cage—all same bird. Me got too many; sell him one dollah—belly cheap."

All Chinatown was drunk last night, owing to the copious potations of rice brandy indulged in by the Chinamen at the dinner in honor of the opening of the new store of the Fat Chung Company. During the night the Chinamen got up a game something on the principle of "Simon says thumbs up," the penalty of losing being that the loser must take a drink of China brandy. White men were allowed to take part in the game, and one of them, as soon as he dropped on it that the loser had to take a drink, commenced "throwing off," and got "stuck" every time. His dodge was soon detected by the Chinamen, and before the white player had lost games enough to get up a respectable drunk, he was indignantly "barred out" of the game, and ignominiously "fired out" of the house.

A Celestial maiden named Sing Loy passed in her checks, in Chinatown, yesterday afternoon, from the effects of a dose of opium administered with suicidal intent. Jealousy was the cause which led the maiden to commit the rash act which terminated her earthly career and shut her off forever from breathing the rarefied atmosphere of this altitudinous region. She was the wife, or chattel, of "Doc," a Chinaman. The bereaved "Doc" is almost inconsolable over his loss, as the woman cost him $400 when she was new. Her remains were borne to the silent tomb in a job-wagon this forenoon, being followed to the grave by a solitary heathen, who, when asked the occasion of so light-waisted a funeral, replied:

"Chinawoman takee medicine, heap die, no Chinaman go funelal. Him sick, heap die, plenty Chinaman go funelal."

Yesterday being the last of the Chinese New Year, the heathen gave a grand jubilistic blow-out, and made night hideous with the notes of the one-stringed fiddle, the gong, the tom-tom, the Chinese bag-pipes, and other ear-splitting instruments of their native land. At midnight the entire population of Chinatown united in singing the Chinese national hymn, which sounded like the expiring howls of three thousand poisoned dogs, with variations by several hundred feline musicians. The music and the firing of bombs and crackers was kept up almost until daylight; and many a man who before was indifferent to the Chinese question, arose this morning from his restless couch and expressed a determination to sign a petition for the immediate abrogation of the Burlingame treaty.

The Chinese are firm believers in necromancy, fortune-telling, and kindred arts. The visions seen while under the influence of opium are by them interpreted into meanings. Several Chinamen in this city make a profession of fortune-telling. Their method is to take a smoke of opium, from the effects of which they have visions, from which they interpret whether certain sick persons will die or get well, or whether certain individuals will win or lose in gambling games in which they propose to engage. They have a small ivory figure to assist them in the interpretations, which represents a certain god who never sleeps, eats, or drinks, and never dies. If the seer's prognostications are verified, he is a smart fellow; if not, the blame is laid on the god, whom they charge with being bewitched, and he is thrown away and a new ivory god purchased in his stead.

A few nights ago, a Chinaman was coming up on the stage from Battle Mountain. He was thinly clad, having no warmer clothes than a regulation Chinese blouse and trowsers, and being destitute of blankets. The night was fearfully cold, and the Celestial suffered severely; but for a long time he bore the hardship with the meekness and patience so characteristic of his race. He tried to sleep, and snuggled down on the floor with his head under one seat and his feet under the other; but the pitching and rolling of the stage over the cut-up and frozen roads bumped him unmercifully, until at last even his Chinese stolidity gave way, and he rose from his uncomfortable position on the floor, and seating himself on the front seat, said to the other passengers:

"Hell dam! Thissee lodgee house no good."

Even the Indians have their grievances against the Chinese. Captain Thompson, the Piute oracle, came into the REVEILLE office this morning, and inquired if it was the intention of the whites to drive the Chinamen out of town. It was explained to him that the white people desired to get rid of the Celestials, but by peaceable means. This did not seem to suit Thompson, and he indignantly exclaimed:

"No good! Why no whita man heap kill dam Chinaman? Chinaman heap all same bad."

When asked in what particular the Asiatics were so bad, he said:

"Him Chinaman too dam schmart (smart)—all time heap cheat 'em Injin play poker."

The 21st instant is the Chinese festival of something or other, when they decorate the graves of their dead with roast pigs, cups of tea, rice, confections, slips of red paper, and other Chinese edibles. As in this country a license tax is affixed to almost everything, John got it into his collective head that he would be required to take out a license to feed his dead, and a delegation of him waited upon the City Marshal to inquire "how muchee licee." The officer gave them permission to hold their festival without money and without price, and on the date mentioned the graves will be decorated in accordance with Chinese custom. This will offer to the numerous tramps now in Austin a most magnificent opportunity for a moonlight picnic—if the coyotes don't get there ahead of them.

A Chinese merchant came into the REVEILLE office this morning to purchase some paper, and while waiting for the boy to bring the paper, he asked us if we had heard of the "big Chinaman fight in Virginny." On our replying in the affirmative, he heaved a deep sigh, and said:

"Him Chinaman allee same dam fool; him got littlee money; then him fight, and give allee him money to dam lawyer for makee talk; then him lawyer he too muchee talk, and Chinaman him bloke, and go washee for money for give him big-mouf lawyer."

This particular heathen don't seem to entertain a very high opinion of the legal fraternity.

A delegation of the Chinese residents waited on the City Marshal to-day, and preferred a request that he lock up the members of the Sazerac Lying Club in the City Jail until after the souls of the dead Chinamen had had a chance at the food they intended to pile on the graves of those departed Celestials to-day. The Marshal could find nothing in the city charter and ordinances authorizing such a proceeding, and the Chinamen concluded to stuff the pigs and chickens with nitro-glycerine and garlic.

Two Chinamen entered the telegraph office this morning, and inquired the cost of a telegram to Hongkong or Nagasaki, as they said that some cousins of theirs were passengers on the ill-fated steamer *Japan*. The operator informed them that the cost would be in the neighborhood of $100, when one of them exclaimed:

"Me no send 'em; hundled dollah too much for dead Chinaman!"

Contents.

www.ingramcontent.com/pod-product-compliance
Lightning Source LLC
LaVergne TN
LVHW050521100826
845148LV00002B/402

* 9 7 8 1 4 2 5 5 2 1 0 2 8 *